GETTING LIFE IN PERSPECTIVE
A SPIRITUAL ROMANCE NOVEL

ENDYMION: BOOK I.

A THING OF BEAUTY
IS A JOY FOR EVER:
ITS LOVELINESS IN-
CREASES; IT WILL
NEVER PASS INTO
NOTHINGNESS;
BUT STILL WILL
KEEP A BOWER QUIET FOR US,
AND A SLEEP FULL OF SWEET
DREAMS, & HEALTH, & QUIET
BREATHING   THEREFORE,
ON EVERY MORROW, ARE WE
WREATHING A FLOWERY BAND
TO BIND US TO THE EARTH,
SPITE OF DESPONDENCE, OF
THE INHUMAN DEARTH OF NO-
BLE NATURES, OF THE GLOOMY
DAYS, OF ALL THE UNHEALTHY
AND O'ER-DARKENED WAYS
MADE FOR OUR SEARCHING: YES,
IN SPITE OF ALL, SOME SHAPE
OF BEAUTY MOVES AWAY THE
PALL FROM OUR DARK SPIRITS.
SUCH THE SUN, THE MOON,
TREES OLD & YOUNG, SPROUT-
ING A SHADY BOON FOR SIMPLE
SHEEP; & SUCH ARE DAFFODILS

"...magical, intricate, enchanting ...a romantic adventure, touching and real. What masterful linking of the wild west and trains to Post-Modern Gay America and Macintosh computers! It's the best Gay fiction I've ever read!"

Thom Prentice
Austin community activist

"Johnson combines the gay past, the difficult present, and an author's driving need to forge a new life to create a story that makes fantasy psychologically real."

Marvin Shaw
A Viewer's Guide to Art

WHAT IS A GAY SPIRITUAL ROMANCE NOVEL?

While it entertains, a truly enjoyable novel also suggests appropriate attitudes toward important personal issues for the reader. A good novel makes ideas understandable by placing them in a fictionalized real-life context. In the 1990s, for gay men especially, such a context almost necessarily includes AIDS and its effects in gay culture. But the novel need not, for that reason, be a so-called "AIDS novel."

Partly because of the increasing median age of the population and partly because of the impact of AIDS, there has been an upsurge of interest among lesbians and gay men in matters of both romance and spirituality. The 1980s were difficult years. They concentrated people's attention on the issues that matter and that determine lasting happiness and satisfaction with life. The threat of sexually-transmitted disease dampened sexual adventure and encouraged romantic intimacy. The experience of so much dying all around raised deep spiritual questions about life and death and the place of individual consciousness in the scheme of things.

Romance is what powers life. We long to feel love. When we've found it, we long to deepen and enrich it. We continue to enjoy and relish the thought and the prospect of others in love. One way of enjoying our own love and the love of others is reading romance novels. And some of the most moving romances are those that recount lovable fantasy characters' discovery of high erotic arousal in the context of emotionally fulfilling intimacy.

Spirituality is what gives depth to life. We seek deep meaning in our experience. We feel wonder at the world around us. We sometimes feel complete and comfortable in the universe, buoyed up by luck, satisfied with what comes to us because our needs are simple and our souls open. One way of encouraging and cultivating such an attitude is reading spiritual books. And some of the most accessible spiritual books are novels that deal with characters' interior lives in the language of myth, religion, and metaphysics.

A truly good gay spiritual romance novel then tells an entertaining, erotically arousing and emotionally fulfilling tale about the interior growth of likeable gay characters, easy to identify with, whose life problems are like the reader's own and whose mythical and mystical discoveries educate the reader about the spiritual traditions that teach appropriate attitudes toward sex and love, life and death—toward the issues that matter.

A gay spiritual romance is about getting life in perspective.

"So much rings true to me... A simple love story of two young men finding each other through long and complicated adventures and mishaps—and discovering an ideal community—perhaps seems naive and even inappropriate in a world increasingly torn asunder. Not so! Their story can capture your heart and, even more, tap into your deepest wisdom and shine a light toward the world that *is* possible—for all of us."

> Ralph Walker
> The Loving Brotherhood.

"The narrator of this clever and fast-moving novel creates two characters who tell their story of gay life and relationships the way it might have been in turn of the century America. Weaving the spiritual messages of Edward Carpenter and Joseph Campbell into the plot adds a provocative and timely theme... a thoughtful book as well as simply great good fun."

> Michael Shernoff, MSW
> Chelsea Psychotherapy Associates, NYC

"...a gift, the accumulated wisdom of our fairy sages passed on to a new generation, a Horatio Alger story exploded into empathic gay celebration."

> Eric Gordon
> *Mark the Music*

"Toby Johnson's most recent work evokes a natural strength from the soul of this gay man. Truly a significant piece regarding our integrity and growth as illustrated through his marvelous characters and storyline. A great read."

> Michael Ganther
> Men's Movement facilitator

"*Getting Life in Perspective* interweaves the social structure of yesteryear and today giving one an eerie understanding of perhaps how little the fabric of society has changed in the last century. Toby's literary use of Ben and Tom as extentions of Rick's reality is a fascinating technique. Josh's character keeps haunting me over and over again... I'm proud to have participated in the creation of this delightful production. It's a gift to our culture."

> Tom Turbeville
> Graphic artist

GETTING LIFE IN PERSPECTIVE

A SPIRITUAL ROMANCE NOVEL

BY

TOBY JOHNSON

Lavender Press
South Norwalk, Connecticut
1991

Published as a trade paperback original
by Lavender Press, P.O. Box 998, South Norwalk, CT 06856

Distributed in the U.K. by Turnaround Distributors; in Australia by Stalione; in the
U.S. by Inland Book Company, Bookpeople, Golden-Lee Distributors, & the
Connolly Concern

First U.S. edition: April, 1991

ISBN 0-938743-17-1

In Memoriam

Joseph Campbell
(1904-1987)

Michael Stevens
(1942-1990)

With special thanks to

Lois C. Johnson
Kip Dollar
Eric Ganther
Paul Reed
Marvin Shaw
Tom Turbeville
and everybody at
Lambda Rising

And so, to grasp the full value of the mythological figures that have come down to us, we must understand that they are not only symptoms of the unconscious (as indeed are all human thoughts and acts) but also controlled and intended statements of certain spiritual principles, which have remained as constant throughout the course of human history as the form and nervous structures of the human physique itself. Briefly formulated, the universal doctrine teaches that all the visible structures of the world—all things and beings—are the effects of a ubiquitous power out of which they arise, which supports and fills them during the period of their manifestation, and back into which they must ultimately dissolve.

...The function of ritual and myth is to make possible, and then to facilitate, the jump—by analogy. Forms and conceptions that the mind and its senses can comprehend are presented and arranged in such a way as to suggest a truth or openness beyond. And then, the conditions for meditation having been provided, the individual is left alone. Myth is but the penultimate; the ultimate is openness—that void, or being, beyond the categories—into which the mind must plunge alone and be dissolved... Therefore, God and the gods are only convenient means... mere symbols to move and awaken the mind, and to call it past themselves.

...The Kingdom of God is within, yet without, also; God, however, is but the convenient means to wake the sleeping princess, the soul. Life is her sleep, death the awakening. The hero, the waker of his own soul, is himself but the convenient means of his own dissolution. God, the waker of the soul, is therewith his own immediate death.

Joseph Campbell
The Hero with a Thousand Faces

1

he house was empty when I arrived. I wandered through the stark and barren rooms, wondering if I'd made a mistake agreeing to take on this project.

There were at least twelve rooms, I counted: kitchen and breakfast nook, maid's quarters, and a large utility room tiled in black and white squares—all in a kind of low-roofed wing stretching out from one end. Then, in the house proper, two very large bedrooms with baths upstairs, and downstairs the dining room, living room, music room, master bedroom and bath, a spacious entrance hall, and finally the "big room." That's what Dave Lovejoy, the real estate agent who picked me up at the airport, called that grand room with white stucco walls, prismatic glass windows, Spanish red stone floor, heavy black wrought iron fixtures and Mexican blue ceramic tile framing a huge fireplace. I could see now why he used such a vague description. Of course, everything was terribly dusty and old, but calling that room a den would hardly have done it credit.

That first day, in mid-afternoon, the big room was flooded with light. Along one wall, six circular-arched windows looked out onto a steep ravine. Oak and pecan trees growing up from around the stream at the bottom formed a ceiling of faintly green budding leaves just below the level of the windows and allowed the early spring sun to pour in through the panes of beveled glass.

The house was cold that day. And those islands of light stretched out on the floor lured me to bask in their warmth. Not sure how to start getting moved in, I sat crosslegged on an old woolen blanket in a kind of depressed meditation for at least an hour. Later that night, I came into the big room to find moonlight illuminating those same islands. I was chilled by the sight and wondered for a moment if the house were haunted. The long rectangles of wan light looked like ghosts lying wearily on the cold stone floor. That image then seemed to me as lonesome and despondent as I was feeling.

You must understand, I didn't really believe in ghosts yet—or hope. And I hadn't learned the lessons that old house had to teach me.

Perhaps I should explain. About a month ago, after returning from a very upsetting visit with the specialist my doctor had sent me to see, I poured out my soul—all my fears and apprehensions, regrets and seemingly doomed hopes—to my friend and coworker, Elizabeth Steed. Elizabeth and I were the only upfront gay members on the editorial staff of the progressive consciousness publishing house in Boston that had occupied the center of my life for the last ten years. Over that time she and I had become close. Elizabeth, by chance, had begun working there only a month before me. Perhaps that—as well as our common identification—is what drew us together. I had a reputation around the company for being self-obsessed, demanding, perfectionistic, and something of a slave-driving bitch. My boss loved it, of course. Almost singlehandedly, I kept the company on schedule. But 'Lizabeth was one of the few other employees who got along with me. (She didn't take my bitching seriously.)

"Creutzfeldt-Jakob's Syndrome he called it," I'd explained to Elizabeth. "He said it can cause deterioration of the brain," I said dismayed. "I'm liable to turn spastic and then go insane."

"Well you know, my dad's a doctor, and I know doctors make mistakes, Rick" was the first thing she said to me.

"I know about the denial stuff, 'Lizabeth," I answered. "You don't need to encourage me in that."

"I didn't mean about the *diagnosis*," she hurried to reply, "but the *prognosis*. I mean, you need to relax, change your life, do things different. Reduce stress." She said the words with just the tone of voice that made them sound as trite as they'd become in the pop culture of the early 1990s.

"How am I going to reduce stress?"

"Move to the country."

"I can't do that," I answered proudly. "I'm a busy man. I've got obligations."

"None of 'em's worth your life, Rick. Look, I know relaxing and getting out from under the pressure helps things like this. Remember that book you edited last year by that doctor who teaches his patients to meditate?"

"Sure," I said. "But that was different... "

Two days later, Elizabeth came into the crowded little space in the front of the company's warehouse I euphemistically called my office.

"I've got an idea," she said. "Don't stop me till I finish. Okay?"

"Okay," I answered, thinking I'd humor her. What difference was it going to make, anyway? I wasn't expecting to like her idea. But I wasn't getting any work done. Though I had a manuscript on my desk, I'd been lost in grim thoughts about the future.

"The other day I suggested moving to the country. Well, my family has some land in Texas—"

"Land in Texas?" I interrupted with feigned shock and an attempt at a Texas accent.

"You promised you wouldn't interrupt," she scolded. "In the hill country, between San Antonio and Austin. It's quite beautiful."

"But Texas," I fussed.

"Hush. Now listen. My dad's got this land. There're a couple of houses on it. One's this great old Spanish-style mansion you'd just love. You know, red-tile roof, iron gates, cliff gardens, the works. Well, the place has been sitting empty for nearly ten years. Dad wants to get it ready for sale. Right now the real estate market is depressed. But they're expecting a recovery soon."

I'd met Elizabeth's father. Robert Steed was an old-time "family doctor," the kind Marcus Welby, M.D. might have been modeled after. He'd been, I knew, physician to Boston's blue bloods *and* to the inner-city's homeless. I had especially admired him because he'd championed the cause of AIDS prevention early on, calling for distribution of condoms to street hustlers and prostitutes and clean needles to junkies.

I wasn't surprised he'd invested in land. I'd supposed he must have been rich—he was a doctor after all. Though from Elizabeth I'd understood he lived simply, almost austerely, and gave away most of his earnings. (Elizabeth occasionally acknowledged her fears she'd be left penniless because her dad would have given everything to the poor.)

"Anyway, I saw my dad yesterday and he asked me if I'd like to go down and work on the place. He's hiring some laborers to clean out the barns and things, but he needs somebody to oversee them. He can't do that from Boston. And he wants somebody to replant the gardens and fix up the house."

"So you're suggesting I come visit you down there?" I decided to cut the story short. It sounded like a nice idea for a vacation, but I didn't need to hear all the details of the renovations.

"Visit me?"

"Yeah, aren't you and Marla going?" Marla was Elizabeth's lover, who worked in administration over at Harvard.

"Rick, I told my dad we just couldn't get away. I've got a stack of manuscripts and Marla's just started writing grant applications for next year."

"Oh?"

"But I promised him I'd see about getting somebody to do it. I was thinking about you."

"Me?"

She nodded.

"All by myself?"

"It'd be great. You could relax. And you could write that novel you've always talked about."

"What about money? What am I going to do without a job?"

"Dad said he'd pay your food and living expenses and throw in $500 a month. There's an old station wagon down there you can use. All you'd have to pay for is your trip down."

"But what about my job?"

"What about your life, Rick?"

I was skeptical that this project would save my life. But, on the other hand, what would I do if I remained in Boston? Just keep at the job till I dropped dead or turned into a vegetable? It just didn't seem fair. I was hardly more than forty years old, too young to be dying—though friends of mine, much younger than me, had died in the last decade, I reminded myself with a twinge of guilt.

Still, I thought I had escaped the pestilence, even thought I'd deserved to escape it. I'd been careful. Partly because of my influence, our company had published some of the very first books on AIDS and the precautions it enjoined. We published progressive political texts, scientific popularizations, and intelligent New Age and psychological self-help books. I'd been exposed to enough positive thinking that I expected it to have protected me, even if I'd become a little skeptical and professionally cynical. (All that stuff was work, after all.)

I wrestled with the decision about the future for almost a week. Then one night we had a heavy snowfall. I was already coming down with a cold and ached all over. The idea of trudging through the snow to get to the T, Boston's crowded, noisy and, in the winter, steamy subway, to go to work absolutely overwhelmed me. While I was watching the morning news during my breakfast of a piece of toast and a pot of strong coffee, I tuned in to Willard Scott's prattling about the sunny weather in Texas. The temperatures were in the 70s.

What the hell, I thought, go. At least, Texas will be an adventure. There was a time in my life, I reminded myself, when I thought adventure far preferable to security and stability. After I went back to my warm bed, I called Elizabeth and agreed to her offer.

Over the next week, as I prepared to leave, I began to get enthusiastic—about getting warm and, especially, about finally getting a chance to write.

One of my last projects at the company had been to read a manuscript of a gay science fiction romance called *Secret Matter* by a writer named Toby Johnson with whom, one might say, I felt a certain special connection. Unfortunately, the book wasn't right for our company. I wrote a gentle rejection letter and mentioned that I knew a guy named Joe Letendre was starting up a new small press and was looking for positive gay genre fiction. I suggested Johnson submit the manuscript to him. It seemed perfect for this Lavender Press. I liked that novel; it made me feel good. It made me feel romantic—something I didn't usually allow myself to feel. When I finished it, I wanted a sequel.

I wondered if I could write a novel myself with the same sweetness and innocence. I couldn't steal Toby Johnson's characters, of course, but maybe I could devise a similar story about a world in which what we currently call "gay love" is normal and in which the emotions of such an orientation could be freely and honestly expressed. I felt inspired. I couldn't write the sequel, but I could write a continuation of the message, I told myself.

So, feeling full of sweetness and light and optimistic about my upcoming adventure, I grabbed a bunch of books from my shelf and sent them down UPS. I knew I was going to have lots of time for reading: Jonathan Katz's books on gay American history and several other books that were current the last time I stopped in at Glad Day, the local lesbian and gay bookstore. I threw in Scott Meredith's *Writing to Sell* to assist me structure my novel and—to assist me structure my interior attitude—a couple of books I hoped might give me some sort of spiritual solace, including Mark Thompson's anthology, *Gay Spirit: Myth and Meaning*. I wanted to investigate this so-called "gay spirituality" that seemed to be coming into vogue, though I have to say I thought most of what I'd heard about in the media was just warmed over Christian Science. I didn't think much of religious stuff anyway, but I certainly thought it ought to be about more than putting off death.

I also threw in a couple of books by Joseph Campbell. I'd studied one of them back in college for a course in Jung and Literary Symbolism. A lot of the authors I worked with quoted Campbell. Some of them had known him personally. They all said good things about him. Recently, I'd watched the series of interviews by Bill Moyers with Campbell on PBS. I'd liked what Campbell had said about the real meaning of religion.

By the time I arrived in Texas, my inspiration had waned. My emotions were a roller coaster, up and down, as I tried desperately to resist the new reality of my life. I'd read some of the Campbell on the flight down and was pushing myself to delve into the other books, but I kept thinking about what was liable to happen to my brain.

I spent the first week making a small area of the house livable. I scrubbed the kitchen and bathrooms, dusted and washed windows, and dragged enough furniture out of a storage shed in back for my needs. In the mornings I went out and stammered in broken Spanish and pidgin English to instruct the two Mexican laborers who came around every day.

The second week I started puttering in the gardens, tearing out weeds and dead shrubs and planting seeds and small plants I found at a nearby nursery. It felt good to strip off my shirt and let the sun reach flesh that had grown pale through the New England winter. I wasn't sure Elizabeth was right about relaxation as a panacea. I knew that deep down in the cells of my body something really was going wrong. But still, I could feel a new strength developing in me. I slept more soundly and woke more refreshed each day. The anxieties about an impending, inexorable doom were fading in the simplicity of the physical work and the warmth of the spring sun.

Soon my Macintosh computer which I'd set up in a corner of the big room began to "call" me. I was feeling the assignment I'd given myself to justify this sojourn in the country.

It was a postcard from Elizabeth that got me going. She'd picked it up at the gift shop in the Gardner Museum. "A reminder of Boston," she wrote.

5

Indeed it was. That museum was a place I'd often visited (usually with tricks whom I felt an obligation to entertain but did not have quite enough interest in to have to talk to). I loved roaming through that collection of medieval art and reconstructed monastic cloisters, sometimes imagining monks entoning ancient chants, sometimes entertaining the fantasy that I'd once been incarnated as such a monk. Though I hadn't been religious since grammar school—and, in fact, generally thought badly of people who were—the atmosphere of the place inspired me with reverence. (I preferred to think of these feelings as historical sophistication.)

When I got the postcard—which I've chosen to use as a frontispiece for this book—I'd hoped my novel was going to be the "thing of beauty." I was going to discover it was something else. But you'll have to wait and see. Just as I did.

I've agreed with a comment by Edmund White, a writer I've admired and occasionally striven to emulate, that because of AIDS the gay novel now must always be in some ways elegiac. For hours at a time I sat in front of my computer struggling to compose words to celebrate—and mourn—a life that had passed. I was amazed at how difficult it was. I understood how the writers of the books I'd edited felt as they forced themselves to spit out words.

I formatted my disks. I set up the pages. I played with all the options in WhiteWrite, my recently purchased, state-of-the-art word processing program—all the while trying to remember what it was I wanted to elegize, what wonderful world of my youth I wanted to relive in my imagination and document for future generations.

It wasn't just AIDS in gay life that influenced what I'd write, it was everything about the modern world. *Everything* was changed. The past was gone. And, with the possible exception of the science fiction writer, every author necessarily elegizes some memory of the past he or she holds dear. Given the speed of change today, every description of the world is outdated by the time it's put on paper—or diskette or hard disk or whatever new storage medium has just replaced whatever we were using before. *Everything* we say is obsolete by the time we say it.

Maybe that's why the so-called "postmodern" novel is so introspective, reflexive and self-obsessed, nesting novels inside novels, almost compulsively observing and commenting on the writing process. The only truth we know is our own experience and—in a world of instant news, ever-recurring "revolutionary new ideas" and world-shattering paradigm shifts—we have to keep reassessing even that. So instead of content, we look for gimmicks, fresh complexities, clever shifts of perspective, twists of the medium (after all, "the medium *is* the message") to make our own novels different from all others.

So I sat in front of my Macintosh trying to conjure up a gimmick— occasionally wondering if I shouldn't be going into town today to buy another more updated model—and trying to recall why I'd want to elegize the world of my youth.

I'd discovered the gay counterculture while I was in college in the late 60s struggling desperately to understand why I felt so lonely and so different. At first the discovery seemed promising: finally I realized the nature of the love and loving I had been hankering for. I was a good student, a right-thinking person with the properly anti-authoritarian, leftish utopian, "make-love-not-war" mentality that I expected would soon be rewarded with just the right lover.

But I was never satisfied for long with any of the lovers who came along. And after I got out of school and into the "real world" and left my hippie politics behind, I guess I got cynical about love. It was the mid-70s and there were glitzy clubs and discos and the promise of uncomplicated hot sex to satisfy me. I don't know that I was any less lonely, but I had given up on hankering for love. I knew what I wanted and I knew how to get it.

Away from the office at least, I was a nice guy. My friends liked me. (I think!) Though I was having fewer and fewer friends. I'd certainly "lost my innocence"—which is to say, I was cashing in on the benefits of what the pundits were calling the "me generation." I'm not going to say the sex was wrong. That would be selling out to the enemy. But I wonder what all that did to my personality. Did it prepare me for growing older and needing to have other things satisfy me?

Were those years what I was supposed to elegize?

2

ne morning, after a gentle shower, I went out and sat on the tiered patio behind the house. Inspired by the freshness after that rainfall, I imagined this old mansion as it might have been in an earlier time. The red Spanish tile roofs glistened wet and dark from the rain and looked practically new. The white, faintly pink stucco exterior of the house almost glowed in the morning sun. It was easy to imagine the house brand new. I knew nothing about the history of the place, though I imagined it dated back to the late 1800s. There were no records around to document the past. All I had were imagined fantasies. I visualized the house full of people. A party of some sort. I could almost see them moving through the rooms. The characters that filled my imagination that day were not from the world of my youth, but from a much earlier era, a time before the onset of ever-accelerating progress, a time when the future seemed to look better and brighter. Of course, I told myself, they were no more real than the faint rainbow that hung in the distance where the rain showers were blowing by.

It seemed to me that in imagining that past I was devising for myself a kind of myth. I use that word in the technical way championed by C.G. Jung and Joseph Campbell and psychologists and religious anthropologists like Christine Downing, Robert Bly, Elaine Pagels and the rest—authors frequently quoted in manuscripts that had come across my desk back in Boston. In one of those manuscripts, I recalled, the German poet Rilke was quoted that the message of any true myth is always: "You must change your life." Myth, in this sense, is a dramatization of an idealized history that has significance for the present and conveys a message about the future. Myth comes from the same place as dream.

Well, a writer is a dreamer. Those characters I was imagining were not historical. The events they were living were not recorded in any books. They came forth only from vague impressions of the past I carried in my memory of high school history classes. And yet, in a way that neither real history nor the years of my own experience could match, I began to think these characters might hold out a message for me.

Instead of elegizing my youth, maybe I could mythologize my personal past into collective history.

I used to suggest to novelists suffering writer's block that they visualize their characters as real people sitting across the desk from them and ask them what was happening. "Let them tell the story," I advised.

That afternoon, after digging all morning in the rock gardens behind the house, I sat down at my desk and tried that with the young man I'd been imagining during my gardening chores. I was careful to fill in all the details of my image of him. Dressed in white homespun cotton—a fabric from an earlier, simpler age—he was slight, a little under 5' 10", but with a body solid from a childhood of work on the farm. He looked to be about eighteen. His hair was reddish-gold, his eyes vivid blue. As you might imagine, of course, he was an example of what I've looked for in an ideal lover, what I've sometimes thought of as "my type." His eyes were set wide; his face was heart-shaped; his expression clearly communicated openness, honesty, and simplicity. He was surprisingly pretty even to me, his creator. I decided he should have some slight flaws in his beauty to give him more reality: a crooked nose from a fistfight with his brother, freckles across his cheekbones, and an unruly shock of hair that wouldn't stay out of his face.

I laughed with pleasure at my conjuring job. If only he were real, I thought to myself, I'd have found the love of my life. If only I'd met somebody like him ten years ago… How different my life might be now!

"What are you laughing at?" my imaginary figment said to me. His tone sounded hurt.

I was surprised. For all that I'd believed in my technique for overcoming writer's block, I hadn't expected it to work so well. "At creating you," I answered.

He dropped his eyes and stared down at the desk. "Please don't laugh at me," he stammered. "I just can't bear it anymore."

"I wasn't laughing *at* you," I answered defensively. "I guess I was laughing at myself."

"Everybody's been laughing at me," he said with tears in his voice, "and calling me awful names. I'm afraid to go out of the house anymore."

"I'm sorry. What's happened?" I figured I'd play out this technique and see how far it could take me.

"It's all my brother's fault. I mean, if he hadn't told those guys about what happened at St. Athanasius'... " He looked up at me, his eyes almost pleading. "You believe that wasn't my fault either, don't you?"

For a moment I felt like God must have felt when He found Adam and Eve hiding in the bushes. My creation had already gotten out of my control. "Perhaps you could explain," I asked politely.

He looked at me with an expression of shock. "Are you really willing to hear my side of the story?"

"Of course. But first, perhaps we should introduce ourselves."

"Oh, sure. It's just, well, nobody's wanted to listen to me. I mean you're the first person... " he hesitated. His face clenched with pain. (His youthful upset tugged at my heart.) "But if I tell you, you'll hate me too."

"No I won't. I promise. Look, tell me your name."

He propped his elbow on the desk and held his chin with his hand and looked off into space. Every so often he'd glance at me out of the corner of his eye.

Finally he replied, "My name is Ben Mayfield."

"I'm Rick Carton," I answered.

"You remind me of somebody... " he said.

"I hope that's good." (He smiled.) "Now," I asked, "what happened that's got you so troubled?"

He looked off into space again. I wondered if my writer's block was showing up as his inability to continue his story. I thought for a moment that's kind of how it's been all my life: I could create marvelous fantasies of young men to fall in love with, but they never quite materialized. I felt sorry for myself, thinking that was never going to happen again.

But my moment of self-pity gave me an idea. I remembered what it was like to be eighteen. "Is this something sexual?" I asked.

Ben's face reddened with embarrassment. "Oh no. I mean, not me. I mean, well yes. But it wasn't my fault."

"Why don't you start the story a little earlier," I suggested. "Where did all this happen for instance?"

You have to remember I was living in this huge old house, twenty

9

some odd miles from the nearest city. The only people I saw were the Mexican yard men who didn't speak enough English to carry on a conversation. It's not altogether surprising my imagination would get a work out. I just don't want you to think I was going crazy out there, I mean, talking to hallucinations and all. I'd read enough of those Jungian manuscripts to know Ben was coming out of my own unconscious.

And I think I'd better tell you Ben's story myself instead of having him tell you, because his friend Tom showed up a little later with another side to the tale and if we all speak in the first person you're probably not going to be able to keep straight whose story is whose. Not that any of them is straight, of course, if you'll pardon a bad pun…

3

en described Saint Athanasius Seminary as a dark and foreboding building that "scared the heck out of him"—those were his exact words—the first time he saw it when he and a couple of other new seminarians were brought up from the train station in a rickety horse-drawn carriage. He'd been only fourteen then. Three years later, when he was driven away in that same rickety carriage, it was even darker and more foreboding. But by then it had become home.

From the time Ben was a little boy he'd wanted to be a priest. He loved getting dressed up on Sunday morning and climbing into the wagon with his Mom and Dad and three brothers to go in to Mass at the little parish church on the outskirts of Bloomington, Illinois. Because he was his Mom's favorite child, he usually got to ride on the buckboard with his parents while the other kids, two older and one younger, rode in back. His mother would hold out her missal for him to see. Though he couldn't understand them, he was fascinated with the Latin words. They seemed downright magical.

And at St. Gabriel's church, he watched the priest move mysterious about the altar, mumbling what he knew were those magic words from the missal. He thought the priest in his rich-colored vestments so impressive. Not quite thinking it in so many words, Ben knew there was something about himself that just didn't fit. He didn't belong in the normal world and so he believed he wanted to be like Fr. Moriarity: different from the rest of the parishioners, and respected because of it, able to wear red and green and gold flowing robes instead of dark and confining suits. He liked that the priest, unlike all the other men in the parish, was free to talk to everyone and be friends with everyone. Father Moriarity didn't have to spend all his time shepherding a wife and family. He had the opportunity to stay the whole day in church, conversing with St. Gabriel and the Blessed Mother Mary whose statues stood on either side of the altar and to say the Mass as an *alter Christus*. Ben would shudder to think of being like Christ whose nearly naked body hung from the cross at the center of the sanctuary.

Ben said he cried as a child to think of Jesus's terrible suffering on the cross. As an adolescent he said he longed to touch the body painted so lifelike. He wondered if the statue might actually be warm and pliable. As a priest on the altar he knew he'd be so close he could touch the feet of the body on the crucifix.

Ben's mother loved the prospect of her son as a priest. "Your prayers could free my soul from Purgatory," she told him. "But don't be just any priest. You don't want to be like Fr. Moriarity, just an ignorant priest in a farm parish. Ben, you should be a Jesuit. You might even go to Rome." And though he was only fourteen she wrote letters to the Bishop and to the Provincial of the Order and arranged for Ben to attend the minor seminary of the Society of Jesus in the neighboring state of Indiana.

During the winter before Ben was to leave, his mother got sick. "Consumption," the family doctor diagnosed it. "Bad time o' year for somethin' like this. Keep her warm and rested."

But in her zeal for Ben's vocation, and perhaps out of the holy hysteria that accompanied this disease that seemed so often to take saints and mystics, Mrs. Mayfield would kneel at the little altar to the Blessed Mother she and young Ben had constructed next to her bed and, between bouts of coughing, pray long into the night that Ben's aspirations to Holy Orders not be destroyed by temptations of the flesh.

In the spring of 1890 she died suddenly, not of tuberculosis but of the influenza that swept the country that season. After her death, just two months before Ben was to leave for seminary, his father turned bitterly against Ben. He blamed him for his wife's death and proclaimed his upcoming departure good riddance.

Seminary life wasn't exactly what Ben had envisioned. St. Athanasius' ran a dairy and huge farm that was more work than his father's. Prayers went on day and night, but he was seldom alone with the saints and angels or the Blessed Mother. There were always other seminarians around. And they were always dressed in black. No red and gold and green robes. Not yet anyway. And when he finally got to touch the statue of Christ, the painted flesh was cold and hard and unyielding. It offered no comfort to Ben's own warm skin.

Occasionally there'd be holidays when the seminarians would not have to work and pray all day. On hot summer days the priests would sometimes let them go down to the swimming hole in the creek behind the property. They were, of course, supposed to wear decent swimming suits that covered their bodies from mid-thigh to mid-bicep or the linen chemises they called "monastic underwear." But, after all, the seminary was in the middle of Indiana; most of the seminarians were farm-boys; and so, when Father Master wasn't along to oversee their play, some of the boys stripped down to shorts or even nothing at all.

Ben loved the solemnity of the place, the haunting chants and richly melodic hymns they sang long into the star-studded nights. But he also loved the chance to get away from the dark halls of the seminary and the onerous work of the farm. And when they had a chance to go swimming he loved to see the other seminarians play in the water of the swimming hole. He'd think of them all as disembodied souls finally in heaven, at play in the fields of the Lord. And that thought would take his mind off the burning, slightly sick, but gnawingly pleasurable sensation in his abdomen that seemed to arise whenever Father Master hadn't come along and the dress requirements were innocently violated.

One afternoon in the spring of his third year, when there was a meeting for priests of the Order from miles around, morning classes and afternoon work were dismissed and the seminarians were given what they called "free recreation" which meant they could do whatever they wanted so long as they didn't leave the property, go to their rooms in the dormitory, or "violate any laws of God or man," Father Master had joked when he sent them off for a day of play.

It was unseasonably warm, warm enough for the first time this year to dare the swimming hole, Ben thought. When he arrived he found several others had already had the same idea. He ducked into one of the wooden cubicles built for dressing rooms a few dozen yards from the creek and changed into the white chemise he usually wore for swimming. As he was coming out, he saw that one of the older seminarians, a third year scholastic named Brother Jeremy Bates, had climbed up on the diving board and was making an announcement.

"The Novicemaster asked me to come watch over you boys, make sure you don't get into any trouble down here." (Ben knew when a scholastic gave orders the younger boys obeyed. That training was part of learning the obedience that the Jesuits proclaimed their special virtue.)

"Today," Brother Jeremy continued, "I'm proclaiming a bare-bottoms day. All you guys, get those swim suits off."

Ben felt a rush of embarrassment. Even on the days when the Master wasn't around and he'd allowed himself to go bare-chested, he worn a pair of baggy trunks. He knew that sometimes the scholastics would do something like this, kind of as a hazing. But he didn't like it. In almost four years it had never happened to him before. He didn't like what Brother Jeremy was doing. He started to turn around and go change back into his clothes. Just then he heard his name.

"'Specially you guys in those silly chemises. You, Brother Ben," Jeremy Bates shouted, "you look like a girl. This ain't the middle ages anymore."

"Look, Brother, I don't have to obey an order like that from you. It's

12

a violation of religious modesty."

Bates deflected the argument. "What you got to hide under there? C'mon, let's see."

"Yeah, Ben. Be a sport," a classmate of Ben's shouted from the water. He'd already stripped naked. Ben turned to look toward him and felt that awful burning in his abdomen at the sight of the boy's pale but muscled physique.

Ben turned for support to one of his closest friends, a boy named Jack. Brother Jeremy seemed to anticipate Ben's reaction. "Hey, Ben, you got a 'particular friendship' with Jack there?" He used the ecclesiastical euphemism for an illicit sexual or emotional relationship between religious. "'Fraid we'll all see a little 'reaction' 'tween you two."

"C'mon, Ben," Jack said, obviously forced into siding against him.

"Let *him* take off his clothes then," Ben said defensively to Jack.

"Sure thing," Brother Jeremy answered from his perch on the diving platform. "I got nothing to hide."

Ben stood there, burning with embarrassment, humiliated now whatever he did. Struggling to maintain some dignity, he crossed his arms in front of him and stuck out his chin, waiting for Jeremy Bates to obey his own command.

"Maybe that was a bad idea," Ben said to me, as he went over his story. "As Jeremy started to strip, I couldn't take my eyes off him. I mean, for a long time, I'd sort of noticed him. He was pretty good looking. I didn't like him. He was a bully. But there was something about him that was just so, so, attractive.

"I watched as he, a little slowly, unbuttoned the tunic he had on, letting his chest show teasingly. It was like he was undressing just for me. And he didn't have anything on under it. Usually, you know, we wore shirt and pants or, during the summer, at least underwear. He slipped his arms out of the sleeves and let the tunic drop round his feet.

"You know, my heart's pounding just thinking about it," Ben said. "His body was just gorgeous. He was real blond and light-skinned, but had short dark hair across his chest and running down in a line to his navel and then down to his, uh, well, you know... "

I grinned at Ben's modesty. "I know," I answered. "His cock?" I asked that as much as a question as a completion of his unfinished sentence.

"Huge," he replied, smiling with a glint in his eye, that belied the naive innocence he'd been showing.

I noticed my own late twentieth century sophistication was showing through my nineteenth century creation. And with that, I wondered how I knew so much about Catholic religious life, I mean, to get this figment of my imagination to report such detail. I remembered being fascinated with religious life for a little while when I was a child; I think for Halloween one year my mother dressed me as a monk. But at least since I'd become an adult, I'd thought anybody who wanted to be a priest ought to have his head examined.

"You saw Audrey Hepburn in 'The Nun's Story,' didn't you? And Tom Tryon in 'The Cardinal'? And Sean Connery in 'The Name of the Rose'?" He started ticking off Catholic religious life movies I'd watched on late night TV, both as an answer to the question about my own familiarity with such things and, I suppose, to reassure me of the source of his existence in my own imagination.

"Okay, so what happened?"

"I'm being honest with you, aren't I? Well, I started to get an erection. And I didn't know what else to do, but run straight into the water. I did it in a way that splashed all over Brother Jeremy. So I saved face that way. And, once cold and wet, it was okay for me to pull off that silly linen chemise I was wearing."

"Is that what you were so embarrassed about, Ben?" I asked.

"Oh no, that was just the start."

4

here were very strict rules about the seminarians' behavior in the dormitory. Each had a private room, with nothing in it but a small desk with a single candle on it, a kneeler for praying before the picture of the Sacred Heart of Jesus hung on the wall, a chair, a low chest with two drawers, and a bed. At the threshold of the door was painted an inch-wide white line. Nobody, *nobody* was allowed to pass over that line except the occupant of the room or, in unusual circumstances, the Master of Students.

The seminarians spent very little time in their rooms. Other than for sleep, of course, they were there only to change clothes after work periods. During Lent, before going to sleep, they would take a small braided leather thong called a "discipline" from the bottom drawer of the chest and kneel before the Sacred Heart and, fixing their eyes on the picture, lash themselves across the bare shoulders or buttocks with the thong. There wasn't supposed to be anything enjoyable to do in that room.

After Compline, the series of songs and prayers that made up the final ritual of the day, the seminarians would go directly to their rooms. They were allowed to say absolutely nothing to anyone until after the next morning's opening ritual. This was called Grand Silence and it meant not only silence of words, but also of any communication or contact with another person.

The night of Ben's confrontation with Brother Jeremy at the swimming hole, Ben spent an extra fifteen minutes in meditation, giving thanks to the Blessed Mother for getting him through that humiliating experience without

14

anything worse happening. In fact, it had appeared to have all ended pleasantly. Once Ben was in the water and had also stripped off his chemise, Jeremy had tossed his tunic on the shore and jumped in. He played along with the others in a game of ball. And then, when everyone was tired and began to go in, he sought Ben out and apologized.

That event in itself had been slightly embarrassing as well. They were in shallow water and Jeremy stood so that he was out of water from the waist up. Ben stayed submerged, only his head and shoulders above water. He was afraid to look at the other boy's body so he locked his gaze on Jeremy's eyes. What was intended as an effort to avoid seeming sexually interested, then, ended up creating an eye to eye intensity that left Ben shaken for hours.

He thanked the Blessed Mother for his getting the apparently heartfelt apology from Brother Jeremy, but prayed that would be the last he'd have to deal with the older scholastic.

If there was a Blessed Mother answering prayers that night, she may have heard something in Ben's fervent pleas that made her look ahead into his future. She may have answered a prayer. But it wasn't the one he thought he was making.

As he had almost every night of his years with the Jesuit Fathers, he fell quickly to sleep. Rising time was early, almost an hour before dawn; and after a day of study, work, and prayer, sleep came easily—even on this night following the scene at the swimming hole. Ben was a sound sleeper and so, apparently slept through the sounds that should have awakened him to the realization something irregular was happening. He apparently did not hear the click of the latch of the door to his room being opened, nor the subsequent click of its being closed, nor the soft padding of stockinged feet across the room, nor even the creaking of the bedframe as the weight of another body was slowly lowered onto the edge of the bed.

What woke Ben was the pressure of a hand laid lightly across his mouth to hush him lest he make a noise and the sound of his name whispered in his ear. He was disoriented at first. It didn't make any sense. No one should be speaking during the Grand Silence. As he became conscious, he struggled to think if perhaps he were somewhere other than St. Athanasius'. He felt something warm slip inside his flannel pajamas and slide up his torso. A hand. He opened his eyes.

There was enough light from the moon suffusing through the window above the bed for Ben to make out the face that hovered over him. It was, of course, Brother Jeremy Bates. Ben suddenly startled and tried to sit up.

Jeremy's hand clamped harder across his mouth. "Hush. Don't make a sound or we'll get caught."

Ben nodded affirmatively, lay back, and the pressure was released. "What is it?" he asked innocently, still confused about what was happening. "Is something wrong?"

Jeremy kept one finger laid across Ben's lips to remind him to stay quiet. He leaned down to whisper in his ear. "You were the best-looking of

15

them all out there today." Jeremy's lips grazed Ben's cheek. Something warm and wet touched the lobe of his ear—Jeremy's tongue. A surge of pleasure and horror shot through Ben's body. He looked up helplessly into the eyes of the scholastic.

Though Brother Jeremy had hardly ever spoken to him directly before today, Ben had been aware of him almost since his arrival at St. Athanasius'. He'd been curious about some sort of cast in his eye, a certain way he smiled at him, half suppressed, when they passed each other in the halls or when they were both out working in the fields. Whatever that fascination, it had always caused Ben to feel something deep inside his body he could only barely identify. He'd never known whether it was pleasure or anxiety. This afternoon it was that amorphous feeling that had created his humiliation and then surged into sudden anger. It was that feeling now that caused him to tremble all over even as it spread out from the touch of Jeremy's hand on his belly.

"What do you want?"

"What you want... to touch you."

"Jeremy, what are you... ?" Ben raised his voice and Jeremy clamped his hand over his mouth again. Hard.

"Just keep quiet. If you make another sound and bring somebody in here I'll say it was all your doing and you'll be out of the Order so fast it'll make your head swim." Jeremy let his cheek rest on Ben's.

Ben was confused. Whatever was happening seemed an inexplicable mixture of tender affection and brutal anger. He knew this shouldn't be happening. This is what Father Master had warned about, but had never explained. Whatever this was in his body—and between him and Jeremy—it had always been talked about in perplexing circumlocutions. The only times Ben had felt such feelings were in dreams when he'd awake in the night humiliated by the wetness of his pajamas or in those desperate moments when he'd touch himself *down there* and feel guilty and afraid.

And now Jeremy's hand was moving. Down. To touch him down there. He was trembling with fear. And with longing.

"Just relax." Jeremy's hand closed around Ben's already hard penis and sent a shock of pleasure through Ben's whole body. No one had ever touched him there before.

Jeremy pressed his mouth against Ben's and forced his tongue through his teeth. Ben let out a muffled groan and told himself to try to relax. He couldn't fight this.

"Shut up," Jeremy whispered viciously in his ear and confused him once more with the emotional swing from tenderness to anger. He sat up and, very businesslike, began unbuttoning first Ben's pajamas and then his own tunic. Ben simply watched in fearful fascination. Jeremy stood up for a moment and pulled the tunic over his head, leaving himself naked in the moonlight. Ben remembered how electrified he'd been earlier in the day when he'd first seen Jeremy's body.

Jeremy then threw the covers away from Ben and tugged at his pajama

16

bottoms. Jeremy was only pulling the knot tighter and Ben had to stop him and then himself release the slipknot in the draw-string. In doing so he somehow knew he was giving his assent to this act he knew must not be allowed to happen. He did not want it to happen. And yet he could not stop his hands from releasing the knot and then, even, reaching up toward Jeremy. There was something about the flesh of the older boy's abdomen that Ben could not resist touching.

He whispered a prayer in his mind to Our Lady to protect him from whatever was happening. And then he closed his eyes and realized his hand was moving down the warm hardness of Jeremy's belly toward his penis. It was all seeming to happen just beyond his volition. And it was terrifying to him. And it was immensely gratifying. He knew somehow he'd been waiting for this for a long time. He knew he'd really known what this was about all along, but that knowledge had never quite been allowed to enter consciousness. And now it had.

Ben felt Jeremy's naked body press slowly down atop him. Jeremy squirmed so that their bodies touched closer and closer. Ben reached around with both arms and squeezed Jeremy tighter. He was still afraid, of course, but the touch and the warmth of the other's flesh against his were overwhelming. Indeed, the pleasure of it all was so new and so overpowering that Ben couldn't tell where to put his consciousness. Part of him wanted to retreat into the safety of his mind, to flee the strangely alluring sensations coming from the body. Another part wanted to rest comfortably in his chest and shoulders, to grasp the other to him and to feel himself grasped close: the touching of chest to chest satisfied an aching hunger in Ben. And yet another part—the part he had been taught to most fear and loathe—wanted to focus fiercely all his attention in the throbbing head of his penis where it pressed against Jeremy's tight belly and where he could feel Jeremy's penis pressing likewise against him.

In his mental confusion, Ben almost detachedly observed the muscles of his lower back and hips and thighs working quite independently of his consciousness as they rhythmically slid his penis alongside Jeremy's. Ben wondered how the body knew so easily what to do...

And then suddenly Jeremy's whole body shuddered and writhed in his arms. What's happening? he thought and tried to say something but found the ability to speak was lost to him as the sensations surged through his brain. He felt something in his own belly that felt like the floor was dropping out from under them. He clutched tighter to Jeremy, tighter still, trying to hold himself from losing whatever was about to be lost as the falling sensation began to sweep over him. It was like the last moment in those humiliating dreams, he realized, when whatever was happening in his body would wake him just in time to feel himself lose control and wet himself. But this time, he knew, he wanted it to go on, wanted it to go on and on...

Then suddenly Jeremy struggled to break away from him. He fought to push Ben's arms away and Ben's muscles struggled to pull himself closer, to let whatever uncontrollable reflex had started complete itself. "What are you doing?" Jeremy spat out in an angry whisper. "Let go of me."

Shocked and frightened, Ben let go. Jeremy pushed himself away with his arms and then stood up quickly and pulled his tunic over his head. Then he bent down over Ben. Ben thought gratefully for a moment he was going to kiss him.

"If you tell anybody, I'll deny everything. They'll believe me and you'll be thrown out."

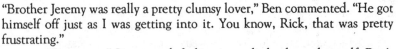

"Brother Jeremy was really a pretty clumsy lover," Ben commented. "He got himself off just as I was getting into it. You know, Rick, that was pretty frustrating."

"I guess so," I answered, feeling just a little cheated myself. Ben's description of his first sexual experience had been surprisingly detailed and I'd begun to get aroused listening to him. Sitting across the desk from him, I longed for him to be real. I wanted nothing more at that moment than to take him in my arms and show him what loving sex could actually be—and maybe, really, to show myself what my own sex could still be, to prove to myself it wasn't all gone for good...

But he was just a fantasy. No flesh to hold against my own. No warmth, except in memories.

"I lay awake for a long time that night. I felt so awful. There was dried semen all over my abdomen. I didn't dare wipe it off. I thought the Brother in the laundry room would recognize the stains or something. I felt so guilty. And so rejected. I didn't want to blame Jeremy. I think I was sort of falling in love with him. You know the way you do, even when you ought to know better. I was half crying. And half struggling not to give into the temptation to finish on my own what Jeremy had started.

"It's funny now to think about that. How important it seemed I stop myself from coming. What crazy ideas those old priests had instilled in us. I think Jeremy Bates might have made a wonderful lover. I mean, he was bright. He was beautiful. Probably he was really very kind and well-motivated, but, you know, in different circumstances."

"You mean that's all that happened between you and him?" I asked disappointed.

"Oh no. It got worse."

"Worse?"

"Well, maybe better in the long run. But I didn't know that then."

The next night, Ben explained, the same thing happened again. All day he'd felt a swirl of emotions: love, anger, guilt, shame. He went out of his way to try to pass Jeremy in the halls or going into chapel. But there were over two hundred seminarians in the place and, anyway, the scholastics were generally kept separate from the minor seminarians.

During dinner, while one of the Brothers read from a book about the life of some Jesuit saint—as they do in monasteries to distract you from enjoying your meal or maybe just to save time and get in more reading—Ben broke the rule about not looking up from your plate and happened to catch a glimpse of Jeremy far across the room looking back at him. Their eyes held for a moment. Ben hoped his own eyes held a question—he knew his mind held a million questions. Jeremy's eyes seemed almost to smile. And then, just as he did last night, just as the connection was about to happen equally between them, Jeremy looked away. Ben felt a sinking feeling in the pit of his stomach, but this time it wasn't impending orgasm, but fear and rejection.

That night, for the first time, he couldn't fall asleep easily. He lay awake wondering what Jeremy was doing. After a while he got up and stealthily moved the wooden chair from his desk to the door, lodging it under the knob to create a makeshift lock. But almost no sooner had he climbed back in bed and pulled the covers over himself than he decided he shouldn't do that. What if Father Master comes to the door? he asked himself. Though, of course, in four years that had never happened, so far as he knew, to any of the Brothers. But still, it seemed like a reasonable concern. And so he got up and removed the chair.

He then curled up in bed, facing the wall, and slipped into a few minutes of restless sleep from which he woke gratefully when he heard the faintest whisper of a sound as someone—he knew who!—touched the outside knob of the door. He didn't move at first. He was afraid of scaring his visitor away. He just listened carefully to each sound, identifying in mind how the sequence of clicks and squeaks and shuffles and thuds were Jeremy's movement through the door and across the tiny room to his bedside. He felt a hand touch his shoulder.

As he started to roll over, he wondered with a start if this might be a trap. What if it were one of the priests coming in to see if he would violate the Grand Silence!

But, no. Indeed, as expected, it was Jeremy who touched his shoulder and who now stood over him. Neither said a word. A long moment passed. And then, by way of giving the consent that had not been asked for the previous night, Ben threw the bedcovers aside. In the faint moonlight filtering into the room through the window above the head of the bed, Ben thought he saw Jeremy smile.

The scholastic undid the top few buttons of his tunic and then pulled it over his head, just as he had done previously. But now there was a certain teasing seductiveness to it. Ben waited till Jeremy stood over him, fully naked. And then he tugged at the knot in the waist of his pajamas and pushed the bottoms down to his knees. Quickly Jeremy joined into the act and undid Ben's top even as Ben was pulling his legs free.

They clutched at each other fiercely. Tonight there was no hesitation in Ben's mouth as he responded to Jeremy's kisses. Tonight there was no confusion in his mind as he let his thoughts go entirely and allowed his body to slip into its almost automatic rhythms. Tonight there was no miscalculation of timing as they both pumped against each other and ejaculated innocently on each other's belly almost simultaneously.

Still they didn't speak. There were no words of affection. But no words of threat. After coming, they fell into that post-coital torpor that is so familiar to the sexually experienced and that perhaps comprises the most healing and most satisfying moments of sex. They lay for a while with their limbs intertwined. Ben felt satisfied and relaxed. The strain of the day wondering what would come of that awful experience of the night before had dissipated. Ben felt himself loved. It surprised him that those were the words that came to mind. He hadn't realized that was the issue.

Then finally Jeremy kissed Ben a peck on the lips and began to extricate himself. "Aren't you cold?" he whispered as he got out of the bed and pulled the light summer blanket back up over Ben. A moment later, Jeremy was dressed and had slipped out the door.

As the silence of the house closed back around him, he thought to himself he ought to put his pajamas back on. He was just struggling to find them in the dark, when he realized he could hear a shuffling sound in the hall. Someone was out there. Jeremy coming back? Why? Maybe he'd left something by mistake.

The sounds got closer. It sounded like two sets of footsteps. And then there was a light under the door. Someone with a lantern.

The door opened abruptly. He'd have expected one of the priests to knock. But there had been no knock. No ritual of calling out Our Lady's name in announcement of a visitor at the door. No pause for the answering "Deo Gratias." The door simply flew open.

And there in the bright light of a kerosene flame was the face of the Master of Students. Behind him in the shadows, his face downcast, stood Jeremy. The priest said nothing. He made a gesture which Ben somehow understood meant "come with me." Shaking, he got slowly out of the bed, his eyes locked on the priest's. Suddenly a wave of repugnance crossed the Master's face and he looked away abruptly from Ben, forcing him to realize he was still naked.

The priest kept his face turned away till Ben had found the pajamas and put them on. He moved reluctantly toward the door. The priest looked at him again. And again looked repulsed and annoyed. He made a gesture toward the closet that Ben understood meant, "Put on your tunic." He did as he knew he was instructed and then, still barefoot, followed the priest down the hall.

The Master managed to communicate by stern look and angry gesture that he expected Jeremy to walk ahead of him and Ben to follow behind. He obviously could not bear the thought of the two of them any closer to one another than he could help. He marched them down the hall, down to the next floor, past his office, and to the chapel.

He gestured to Jeremy to kneel in the first row of pews. And then led Ben back to the back of the long, narrow, and high arched room and pointed for him to kneel in the last row. Then, with a bit of high drama, he held the kerosene lantern up to his face so that Ben could see the full measure of his disapproval, then held the lantern in Ben's face so that he was momentarily blinded by the light. Then the Master blew out the flame.

The room went absolutely dark. Ben could hear the solid footsteps of the priest as he walked back to the doorway which opened into the chapel about midway down the ranks of pews. He heard him close the door firmly. And then he heard a sound he'd never heard before throughout his years at St. Athanasius'. The priest locked the chapel door.

"I was too scared to do anything but kneel there. I mean I kept thinking about going up to talk to Jeremy. Or wishing he'd come back to me. But I think both of us were so afraid that somehow Father Master would know. Or, I guess, that Jesus and Mary would know.

"Oh, it was so awful. The chapel had stained glass windows so no moonlight came in at all. The only light was from the red candle in the sanctuary that was supposed to proclaim that Jesus was present in the tabernacle, a prisoner, a willing victim, suffering under the appearances of the bread of the Eucharist to save sinners from the fires of hell. And I could only think all night how now I was a sinner. And how if something were to happen, if I were to die tonight, I'd be cast into hell for all eternity—and all because of this urge in my penis that Jeremy started."

"Jeremy never said anything to you?" I asked. "It was all his fault, wasn't it?"

"Who knows? Maybe it was the Blessed Mother's fault. I don't know," he said, sounding a little exasperated with me.

"You know I'm not Catholic," I explained.

"You're doing a surprisingly good job of fantasizing Catholic religious life."

"Am I? I don't think I can trust you as a judge." I tried to make a joke of this whole thing. "But, you know, I did always like those movies, like you mentioned. Maybe I was a monk in a previous incarnation… "

"Do you believe in that?"

"I can believe in a lot of things without having to decide whether I think they're real or not. If I've learned anything from all my editing New Age books, it's that all these religious ideas are metaphors. Believing in one of them means enjoying the particular metaphor, not necessarily taking it seriously."

"I was under the impression you were having a problem believing in life," Ben answered, "and that that's why I'm here."

"Oh, really. Well, then, I believe in you." I paused, then added, mainly to myself, "Don't I?"

"Do you?" He smiled wryly.

"Anyway," I continued, "I always thought there was something neat about religious life—I mean if you leave out the religious mumbo-jumbo—all those men, or women, living together. Seemed like a homosexual's dream."

"Not this one."

"Oh? So what happened?"

"I fell asleep after a while. In the morning, everybody came into chapel for Prime and Lauds just like every other day. I'm sure they were curious what Brother Jeremy and I were doing in there already. And both of us with our hair mussed up, looking like we'd just got out of bed.

"Then while the rest of them went down to do the housework and prepare for breakfast, the Master called us into his office."

"Together?"

"One at a time. I never got to speak to Jeremy again. I don't know what happened to him."

"You mean they threw him out?"

"Both of us, I think. The Master gave me this terrible sermon about how wicked I was and how my soul was lost forever. He never asked me to explain. He'd talked to Jeremy first. I guess I thought maybe Jeremy put all the blame on me, like he threatened to. Anyway, by noon, they had me on a train going back home.

"And that priest made me watch while he wrote a letter to my father explaining why I was sent away. It described how I was caught in a mortal sin of perversion. I thought maybe he was going to give it to me to deliver and I knew I was going to destroy it. But it wasn't like that. He waved it in front of my face and then put it in an envelope and stamped it. And told me he would have the Brother that took me to the train station take it directly to the post office."

"Good Lord."

"Well, yes. But I didn't know that at the time... Look," Ben interrupted himself, "we've been at this a long time. Aren't you hungry or something. Why don't we take this up tomorrow?"

"You'll promise to come back," I asked, feeling a little bereft that this beautiful young boy was about to leave me.

"I'm at your disposal," he answered, smiling. I almost thought he'd lean over the desk and kiss me. But, of course, he didn't. And maybe couldn't.

He was right. I was hungry and thirsty. And actually a little horny, I realized. I quickly went through the saving and shut down routine and switched off the Macintosh. I was already starting to wonder what there was in the kitchen to eat for dinner.

22

5

irst thing the next morning while coffee was brewing, I rumaged through a storage closet under the stairs to check out a vague memory. I'd been right: stuck back in a corner was a low bookcase containing a set of the Encyclopedia Britannica. It was nearly thirty years old, but I knew it'd have information that would help me construct the world my new friend, Ben Mayfield, lived in.

I carried them into the house and set them up next to my desk. While I munched on an English muffin and drank my morning coffee, I skimmed through the encyclopedia entries for Roman Catholicism, Monasticism, U.S. History. After a while I looked up from the books and, to my surprise, found Ben sitting across the desk watching me.

"Find anything interesting?"

"I was trying to get a little background information on you. But you know, I don't exactly know when you lived."

"Well, let's decide then," he answered matter-of-factly.

"Don't you know?"

"Sure, for myself. But I want to make certain we're dealing with issues that are important to you." I think I must have looked dismayed. "Look, if I'd lived through the Civil War and Reconstruction and my life was about learning to live peaceably with darkies, I wouldn't have much wisdom to convey to you, would I? I mean, you're not particularly racist. Right?"

"I guess not. But I'm not Catholic. Monasteries aren't important to me."

"Don't be so sure. You brought all this stuff about spirituality to read. Besides, I thought you said you used to be a monk in a previous incarnation."

"Well, maybe that was just a metaphor... "

Ben burst out laughing. "What do you think *I* am?"

I wanted to tell him he was the lover I'd been hunting for all my life, my *raison d'etre*, the fulfillment of a thousand nights of disappointing liaisons and lonely fantasies. But I knew he'd think that melodramatic. I did.

"So tell me about your life. What *are* your issues?" he pressed me.

"Are you playing psychiatrist with me?"

He grinned at me out of the corner of his eye. "I bet I was born before Herr Doktor Freud." He feigned a German accent. "C'mon now. You're resisting."

"I guess *that*'s one of my issues," I conceded.

"And?"

"Well, when I was younger I was a hippie, lived for a while in a commune, and hitchhiked around the country looking for an adventure that never quite happened... "

"You came out, didn't you? That was certainly an adventure."

"I guess you're right. Gay liberation was a sort of culmination of the hippie movement and the counterculture. But all homosexuals come out, don't they?"

"Oh?" he answered smartass.

"Lately I haven't been so sure that was such a good thing... Anyway, I ended up in Boston, got a job with a publishing company. I made pretty good money, but have been feeling the economic crunch lately. I worry sometimes I've "sold out" my counterculture values. My days as a hippie taught me to live simply. I liked the job, though I never felt I was being creative enough, you know, on my own. I worked my way up to Senior Editor. But then I got sick and came down here to rest. And now I'm supposed to be writing a novel."

"I thought you said you never did anything monastic. What could be more monastic than living in poverty and making copies of manuscripts?" he laughed again.

"You seem to be enjoying this all more than me," I retorted, hurt by his slightly skewed humor.

"Moi?" he replied in totally anachronistic 1980s gay humor.

"This is serious. I mean, we're talking abut my life."

"I think *that* must also be one of your issues. Your seriousness and, shall we say, *self-importance.*" He seemed to delight in that last word as though he'd really gotten one up on me.

"Well, okay. But this *is* serious. I mean, my life is at stake."

"Is there something you haven't told me?"

"I thought you'd know," I answered. "But, anyway, we haven't done anything that would, uh, require I tell you about my health concerns."

"You mean make love?" he said tenderly.

"I wish you could. I'd love to fuck with you," I retorted a little crudely. I didn't want to get to feeling maudlin, and he'd touched a nerve...

"We'll get to that later. At any rate, you were saying that one of your issues is dying—alone and too young."

"Did I say that? I said I wanted to fuck you."

"Now, Rick, you sound like Brother Jeremy," he scolded coyly.

"Is that a proposition?"

"That's a reminder it's time to get back to the story." He pointed at the pile of encyclopedia volumes on the desk. "You lived through the 1980s, a time you thought was too complex. You wanted to fantasize a simpler time. Well, how about the 1890s—a little numerical transposition there! Let's say I was born in 1876, just at the start of America's second century. I was seventeen when I got thrown out of the seminary and went home on the same train that was carrying that letter to my father exposing me as a pervert."

Ben's father never said a word to him about the letter. But then he barely said a word to him about anything after he got home. Even after almost four years, the household still seemed in mourning for Mrs. Mayfield. The wreath was gone from the front door, but there seemed to be invisible black crepe draped throughout the house. Ben's two older brothers had left home, and though they lived in town nearby they hardly ever came to visit the family farm. And there wasn't much left of the farm.

Mr. Mayfield had continued to work hard, but times weren't good. Crop prices kept falling. There wasn't enough money coming in to pay regularly on the mortgage. Fortunately the farm had been in the family for generations and the place was paid for. And even though the land had to be put up as collateral for loans to keep the business of the farm running, the president of the bank was Mr. Mayfield's cousin. There was no real danger of the family losing the house, but that was because the land could be sold off in parcels to the railroad which—fortunately or unfortunately—owned a large right of way that bordered on the southern end of the farm. Of course those sales were often at a loss because land values were falling along with the price of grain as the nation fought about shifting from a gold to a silver standard for its currency.

Ben came home to find himself blamed both for his mother's death and for the failure of the farm. Neither of these events, of course, did he have much to do with: his mother died in the influenza plague along with some fifty thousand other Americans; and the failure of the farm, while partly the consequence of the older Mayfield boys abandoning the family business, was more a result of the corruption and bad management policies in the Republican administration of Benjamin Harrison. But, as Ben observed, homosexuals are often blamed for disease and economic hard times, if only just because they're easy and sometimes willing bearers of opprobrium.

He found a job at the soda fountain in Pickney's Drug Store. It wasn't a great job and it required him to walk sometimes as far as five miles a day to and from the farm if nobody driving by picked him up in their wagon. And that meant he wasn't around to help much with the farm chores. He got hell for that. But the fact was both he and his father were glad not to have to see much of each other. It was his younger brother, Jeff, on whom the burden fell hardest. He was still in school, had to go to class daily, had homework, and was struggling to develop a social life with the few girls in the class. And he had to do most of the farm chores, either early in the morning or late at night.

Ben tried to help Jeff, but he almost always got a cold shoulder. Though he never said so in so many words, it was apparent Jeff had read, or at least heard about, the letter from the Master of St. Athanasius' Seminary. Whenever Ben helped with feeding the chickens or milking the cows or most any other daily chore, Jeff would complain that Ben had done something wrong and he himself would have to spend even more time repairing the damage.

"If you'd just show me how you want it done, I'll do it that way," Ben shouted at him one morning as Jeff complained about the way he milked the cows. "Dammit, don't you realize you're just making it harder on yourself."

"'Dammit'? Did I hear 'dammit' coming from those lily-white lips of Brother Benjamin?" Jeff said the religious appellation in a whiny, affected voice. "Or maybe those lips aren't so pure, after all?" He spat. "Look, you could get away with all that stuff when Mama was around. She'd protect you. If you can only get one bucket out of 'em, that's fine with me." He held up the two buckets he'd collected, as though it were evidence of Ben's failure. "I'm not going to make excuses for you. And Mama's not here anymore. No thanks to you!"

"Please, Jeff, don't talk like that. I didn't cause Mama's death. Why do you want to hate me so much? I don't hate you." Ben reached out.

"I don't want you lovin' on me," Jeff pulled back as though Ben's hand were a burning torch.

"Oh God, Jeff, please, please… " Ben pleaded as his brother threw down the milk buckets he was carrying and strode off down the road toward school.

That afternoon Joe Heatherson, Jeff's best friend, came into Pickney's with Beth Ann Blanchard. The four-room school house was around the corner from the Drug Store and a lot of kids congregated there before going home to whatever chores their place in their families demanded. Ben got along well with the kids. They respected him because he was a couple of years older; most of them knew he'd been in seminary while he was away those years and, even though he decided not to continue with the priesthood, they tended to look up to him.

Joe sat Beth Ann down at one of the tables and then came up to the counter. He climbed up on the foot-rest and leaned over as though he wanted to say something to Ben privately. Ben leaned forward himself.

"How about a nice little 'ol cherry phosphate for me and my *girl* friend over there," he said in a breathy affected voice. And then he smiled and batted his eyes.

Oh my God, Ben thought. He started trembling all over. He wasn't sure what this little act meant. But it came so close on the heels of this morning's run-in with Jeff that the implication was obvious.

"Yes, sir. Two cherry phosphates." He retreated into officiousness. "That'll be fifteen cents. I'll bring them to the table."

"You do that, honey," Joe answered suggestively.

While Ben was preparing Joe's order, the rest of the school kids began to pour into the store. As usual, that brought old Mr. Pickney around from the drug counter to the soda fountain to help out in the rush. This was his busiest time of day and he wasn't going to let any sales go. (That, in fact, is why he hired Ben: to assist him during the busy times of day, lunch and afterschool.)

The kids tended to crowd together around the little tables. While Ben was setting up the two phosphates to carry out, he looked up and saw that now there were six kids at Joe's table and they were all huddled toward the center whispering. One of the boys looked up and saw Ben watching them; he in turn said something to Joe who turned around and shouted, almost angrily, "What's takin' so long with my phosphates?"

Mr. Pickney glanced over from the banana split he was just starting to make, "Let's not get behind, Ben? Okay?" His tone was polite, but there was an edge of command underlying the friendly suggestion that only worsened Ben's nervousness as he obedientlyplaced the two glasses on Joe's table and hurried back behind the counter.

The next thirty minutes or so were strained. Ben kept working as fast as he could. He managed to stay back away from the customers letting Mr. Pickney take the orders so he was only having to fill them, putting together various ice cream, fruit, and soda concoctions till the kids had their fill and began to slip out for home. Jeff Mayfield came by for a minute. He didn't say a word to Ben—but that wasn't unusual. He spoke to one of the girls Ben had seen him with a couple of times before, then he whispered something to Joe, and then left.

There'd been a touch more whispering back and forth between the tables than usual, a tension in the atmosphere that seemed to drive the girls home more rapidly than the boys. Ben kept telling himself he ought to make up an excuse to leave early and just get out of there. But he kept delaying saying anything to Mr. Pickney, fearing he'd endanger his job if he left now.

He was washing out glasses and putting them on a rack to dry. Mr. Pickney came by and patted him paternally on the shoulder, saying, "Well, look's like we got through another day."

Ben was just about to ask if he could take off a little early, when there was a commotion at one of the tables. Both Ben and Mr. Pickney looked up. A couple of the boys were shouting playfully at Joe, urging him on to what Ben feared was exactly the reason for his needing to get out of there. One of the boys was jostling Joe's arm and suddenly the glass of Coca-cola he was drinking from tipped over, pouring its contents into Joe's lap.

Serves him right, Ben thought.

"Hey, we need some service over here," another of the boys shouted.

"Ben, you go clean up that mess those boys are making," Mr. Pickney instructed quite innocently.

Ben was frightened, but what else could he do? He reminded himself to be brave. *Sticks 'n stones...* He took a deep breath and went out to see what had to be done to take care of Joe Heatherson and his friends.

As Ben approached the table, towel in hand, Joe swiveled his chair around and slouched down as if offering his lap for Ben to dry. The Coke had, of course, spilled right onto his fly. A little of it was puddled on the table and a little more on the floor. Practically ignoring Joe, Ben wiped off the table.

Almost angrily, as if blaming him for the accident, Joe snapped, "Here wipe this off my clean pants. I don't want 'em stained."

Ben proffered Joe the towel. One of the six or seven boys standing now in a circle watching shouted playfully, "He don't wanna touch that. You do it. You're the... " He didn't finish the sentence, but Ben knew he hadn't been

27

about to say "waiter."

"C'mon, c'mon. It's gonna stain if you don't wipe it up."

For a moment, Ben noticed how vulnerable Joe looked. He imagined reaching down with the towel, grabbing Joe's testicles, and squeezing till he begged for mercy. But that isn't what happened.

When he reached down with the towel to sop up the Coke that had soaked into the pants, he felt Joe's penis hard under the thick twill fabric. Ben flinched and jerked his hand away.

"What's the matter?" Joe said. "Never felt one of those before?" The boys howled.

Ben quickly bent over and wiped up the spilled Coke from the floor. Suddenly one of the boys kicked one of his legs out from under him as another pushed down hard on his shoulder. He fell to the floor in a kneeling position, his face only a few inches from Joe's crotch.

"Brother's praying... " somebody teased.

"Yeah, praying for this," Joe pointed crudely at his lap. "Don't you want to suck my pud," he taunted, suddenly explicit for the first time.

A couple of the other boys joined in the chorus, "Suck my pud. Suck my pud."

"Hey, what's going on over there?" Ben heard Mr. Pickney call out. But he could think of nothing else to do but run. With a sudden burst of motion that took his taunters by surprise, he jumped up, threw the wet towel in Joe's face, and ran out the front door.

He was practically exhausted when he got home; he'd run most of the way. But at least all the anger and fear had been driven out of him by the exertion. He went straight to his room in the attic and lay on the bed, sobbing softly till he fell asleep. Sometime later he woke to the sound of Jeff or his father clunking around below. He heard doors open and close. But nobody came up to his room and he never went down.

The next morning when he showed up for work, a little before the lunch rush in order to wash lettuce for the sandwiches most patrons were going to order, Mr. Pickney took him back into the little office where he kept the safe. "Look, I know that was pretty cruel, what those damn boys did yesterday. And I'm not sayin' it was your fault. I know better than that. But look, Ben, after you left, Joe Heatherson told me what that was all about. Now I told him he could take his business elsewhere. I don't want his kind around here. You been a good employee, Ben. But I gotta let you go. What if this rumor gets beyond the school kids? And it's bound to."

"But, Mr. Pickney, what if it isn't true? I mean, you haven't even asked me."

"Young man," Pickney said indignantly, no longer the understanding paternal old man, "in this kind of accusation, the seriousness is so grave, it doesn't matter whether it's true or not."

"My God, Mr. Pickney, sir... " Ben stammered. "This is America. People are innocent till proved guilty."

"Don't you use the Constitution to hide sin. America is a Christian, God-fearing country. And Americans don't talk about things like this." Then he relented, "Look, kid, I'm sorry. But I just can't keep you on here. It'd scare customers away. And these days with money the way it is and all, I just can't afford that. Besides, I just hired Beth Ann Blanchard to take over the soda fountain. Her family's hurtin' for cash. It's coming up the end of the school year and she needs a summer job."

So that's what this was all about, Ben realized. Joe Heatherson was getting his girlfriend a job. And I can't show my face in this whole goddamn town anymore. All of a sudden the weight of it all bore down on him. And he started to cry.

Just then the bell over the front door to the store tinkled and Beth Ann called out, "Mr. Pickney, Mr. Pickney. I'm here."

"I got turned down for a job once," I said to Ben, almost as if I needed to justify myself in the face of his terrible fortune. "I'd applied for a position as a food stamp eligibility worker. They called me back for a second interview, but then didn't give me the job. It might have been because my hair was so long then, but I always thought it was cause they realized I was gay."

"Yeah," Ben answered softly.

Just then we were interrupted by a pounding on the back door and a voice calling in a heavy Mexican accent, "Senor Rick, Senor Rick, por favor."

"Undocumented aliens?" Ben said with a gleam in his eye.

"One of the laborers Mr. Steed hired to help with the heavy yard work. And," I added self-righteously, "I don't think its any of my business *or* yours whether they're documented or not."

"I only meant to observe that it isn't any easier for them. Finding a job, I mean."

I felt duly castigated.

6

he workers had come up to tell me they'd finished with the yard and needed another job to do. In my hesitating Castilian and their broken Tex-Mex we discussed the next project: cleaning out the barns. I followed them down to the complex of smaller cottages, barns, and sheds that must have once been a working ranch. They'd done a wonderful job so far, I commended them. The yard was no longer overgrown with brush nor the trees hanging dreary with parasitic moss. My spirits were buoyed. The place was being transformed.

After returning to the house, I decided to call Elizabeth's father to report on the progress. After a surprisingly long delay, the phone was answered.

"May I speak with Dr. Steed?" I asked.

"He's not available. This is his daughter. Can I help you?" answered a faint voice on the other end.

"Hi, 'Lizabeth. It's Rick. What are you doing at your father's in the middle of the day."

"Oh, Rick. It's good to talk to you. I guess I'd have called you soon anyway. Something awful's happened. Daddy's been accused of spreading AIDS. He's being sued for ten million dollars. And the story's all over this morning's paper."

"I don't understand. What's this all about?"

"Oh, Rick, I'm so scared. Daddy's practically having a nervous breakdown." She sounded nearly hysterical.

"Elizabeth, calm down and tell me what happened. It'll help you feel better to talk."

"Maybe you're right. Let me take a deep breath here." I could hear her put the phone down for a moment, then she returned. "Does the name Georgie White mean anything to you?"

"Sure. He's the computer genius playboy, isn't he?" In the last few years the name of George White—Georgie as the gossip columnists always called him—had become renown and notorious in Boston. The son of a blacksheep member of an old Boston Brahmin family, he'd recently outshone his disapproving relatives by making millions in computer software development. "WhiteWrite" and "WhiteHot 1, 2, 3" had become the standards for business application wordprocessing and spreadsheet programs. I was running a Mac version of WhiteWrite myself.

"Well, he's got AIDS."

"He's not gay, is he? I thought he was a notorious womanizer."

"Right. And probably a cocaine user, don't you think?"

"I guess it goes with the territory," I answered. "Successful yuppie, works hard, plays hard."

"And shoots coke, right?"

"What's that got to do with your dad?"

"It hit the papers last week that White's been diagnosed with AIDS. He passed out at some big socialite's party. The scandal sheets just loved it. Well, so all of a sudden this family that's blackballed him for years is now terribly concerned about his health—and his reputation. They insist he couldn't have got it through sex or drugs… "

"But that's crazy. I mean, that's how you get it. And he was famous for doing both."

"You and I may think so, but not the Whites of Boston. Suddenly Georgie White's the *cause célèbre* of the whole yuppie and Boston blue-blood Establishment. And you've forgotten the one other way to get it… "

"Neonatally?"

"No, Rick," she sounded exasperated with me. "Transfusion."

"Not since blood's been screened."

"Well, a year or so ago Georgie White came to see my father for bleeding hemorrhoids. Daddy referred him to a specialist but White insisted he stay on the case. Georgie wanted the proctologist to perform surgery right away. But the proctologist balked at the rush. He told Georgie to go home, rest for a week or two, and eat liver to build up his blood cell count. Apparently he was weak and was going to need more red cells before they could operate. He didn't want to wait, so Daddy signed the order for a transfusion instead."

"Was that kosher?"

"Oh, I don't know. It sounds a little unprofessional to me. But you know how rich people are. Georgie White wanted it done and he wanted it done now. And Daddy went along with it. In retrospect, I think it's obvious White was so weak because of the AIDS, but he wouldn't sign for an HIV test—claimed he'd already taken one and it was negative. Anyway, White's attorneys are suing the proctologist and Daddy for giving him AIDS in that transfusion."

"But that's nonsense."

"But the papers love it. Daddy'd stirred up a lot of shit last year when he attacked the health department for going to court to stop that AIDS program from giving out clean needles."

"But the story doesn't even make sense. Blood is tested for HIV."

"Yeah *and* the right-wing conspiracy nuts are just looking for ways to threaten the public with any AIDS scare they can. AIDS hysteria sells papers. There hasn't been any in a while. So now Daddy's their chance. Oh, Rick, it's so unfair."

"I'm sorry" was all I could think to say.

"Hey, did you call for a reason?" she asked.

"I was just checking in about the renovation around here. Phase One is complete." I said that as though there were some sort of master plan we were following.

"That's great," she replied. "You know, maybe we're gonna have to rush the sale of the ranch. This suit is liable to take all the money Daddy's got. I mean, he'll probably win, but even so the attorney's fees are going to wipe him out. He doesn't save money. Almost everything is tied up in that property."

I realized to my surprise that Elizabeth's suggestion of selling this property suddenly upset me. I hadn't known I was getting attached.

"How is your dad? You said he was having a nervous breakdown?"

"Not really, I guess. A doctor friend gave him some Xanax and he's sleeping now. But I'm worried about him. That's why I'm here instead of at work. What if he needs medical care? He's getting to be an old man." She changed the subject. "Speaking of medical care, how are you?"

"You think of me as a medical case?" I teased. "Actually, I'm doing great. I feel better than I have in years." Until I said that I hadn't realized how really true it was.

"Have you seen a doctor down there?"

31

"Well, no," I admitted. "But I'm eating really well and getting lots of sun and working in the garden. Just like you ordered, Ma'am."

I could hear her laugh momentarily. Then hesitantly she said, "I thought you were, you know, dying."

"Not yet," I answered.

"How's your writing coming?" She let the subject drop.

"Great. I've got a good start." I found I didn't want to tell her about my "visitations" from Ben Mayfield.

"Look, Rick, I gotta go. Keep up the good work. I'll give you a call in a day or so to let you know what's happening."

"Bye now," I said.

"It's good to hear your voice," I heard her say as I placed the receiver in its cradle. I was moved by the wispiness of her voice. It was almost as though Elizabeth and I had agreed to never really acknowledge the depth of our feelings for one another but they just slipped out now and then anyway.

I went back to my desk and tried to get started writing. I tried to conjure up Ben's image, but nothing was coming to me. After a while I got up and went out to work in the garden, feeling almost as bad now about the progress we'd been making with the ranch as I'd felt proud earlier. The sooner we finished, the sooner I'd have to make a decision about going back to Boston, and the sooner—maybe—I'd lose my magical connection with the spirit of Ben.

7

s Ben walked home angry, confused, and downcast from the humiliating meeting with Mr. Pickney, two of Jeff's classmates, perhaps playing hooky, came riding by on horseback. Seeing Ben trudging down the road, the boys slowed their pace till their horses were walking along almost beside him. They talked loudly back and forth about how terrible it was for Jeff that first his mother died in the influenza epidemic and then his father had to sell off the farm, and now "this." They never acknowledged Ben's presence. And he was too ashamed to say anything back. Soon they galloped off, perhaps disappointed that they hadn't got a reaction out of him.

But the reaction was burning deep down inside him. He wasn't going to take any more of this, he decided. It was all too unfair. He'd never done anything wrong. It had all been Jeremy Bates's doing. For a moment he wondered wistfully what was happening to Jeremy. Just then he heard a train whistle blow and he knew what he was going to do.

Not long ago he'd read a newspaper at Pickney's about the labor unrest in Chicago. He knew from the article that there were a lot of bad feelings going on between workers and bosses, but he also knew there was work there. If the workers were on strike, then somebody had to be replacing them in the factories. Ben was too naive to appreciate that in the eyes of unionized labor in Chicago scabs might be almost as hated and reviled as homosexuals.

He went home, slipped upstairs without speaking to his father who he saw was sitting at the kitchen table apparently staring mindlessly off into space, and packed a couple of changes of clothes into a knapsack. He'd kept some of the money he'd made at Mr. Pickney's—especially tips that the older customers occasionally left him. It wasn't much, but it was something. He had a handful of greenback dollars which he carefully folded and slipped into his sock. He hoped this would be a safe place. The loose change he stuck in his pocket. He quickly wrote a note saying something to the effect that the family wouldn't have to be burdened with his presence anymore. He stuck it in the frame of the discolored mirror above his dresser and then tossed his knapsack out the window into some bushes.

As he came down the stairs, he saw his father look up at him and then look away quickly. He wasn't even going to ask why Ben was not at work. Maybe he knew... Maybe everybody in town knew...

The knapsack had fallen into a thorny old rosebush and Ben pricked up his hand and forearm in the process of retrieving it. Then he ran as fast as he could toward where the railroad tracks ran by the farm, on their way he hoped, to the big city of Chicago.

Ben huddled behind the embankment alongside the railroad track. He hoped the cars would not yet have built up speed at this point. He'd never tried to jump a freight before. There's always a first time for everything. And he knew he had to get out of town.

It was a couple of hours before a train came by. As it approached, Ben recognized it as a passenger train. Not the thing to jump. Obviously a conductor was going to expect him to be carrying a ticket. He gave thanks for the days he'd spent as a kid out here along the track with his brothers—in the old days when they all got along—waiting to ambush the train with rocks and sticks and good-natured waves to the passengers or crew as the big machines rolled by in their restless journeys to distant and exciting places. Ben kind of wished he were on that train, riding along first class, watching the countryside speed by leisurely. His years in the monastery though had taught him poverty and so he thought about Jesus who had nowhere to lay his head and about the rich man Dives and the beggar Lazarus. He thought those rich men in their first class cars with plush leather seats were like Dives and he proudly identified himself with Lazarus who was finally taken into the bosom of Abraham.

He recalled that it was just this train he'd taken four years ago on his way to St. Athanasius'. That had been his first train trip anywhere and he remembered the details well. He remembered they'd stopped at a siding somewhere up the track to let a freight train pass them by. A conductor who'd happened to be standing near Ben's seat as they waited had explained how, since the local passenger trains stopped more frequently, they occasionally had to let the freights go by them. The recollection made Ben worry that the freight train he was hoping to catch, and that he thought would be coming along pretty soon now, might not be stopping in town and so might be going too fast for him to jump.

Ben whiled away the afternoon singing hymns to himself, praying to Jesus and Mary that the awful thing that had happened to him at St. Athanasius' not follow him any further. He prayed that he was doing God's will in running away like this. It was toward the end of such a heartfelt prayer that he heard the sound of a train whistle and realized the locomotive had indeed stopped in town to pick up grain and was going to be lumbering by in only a few minutes. His heart started to race. He told himself he was making the right decision. He thought again about Dives and Lazarus and about Jesus and St. Francis of Assisi and all the monks who'd wandered across Europe in the early Middle Ages preaching the message of love and trust in God's Providence. And as the locomotive approached and then passed, Ben began to say the St. Francis prayer as he started running to match the train's speed. He grabbed hold of a handle near the end of a box car which had the door open and pulled himself up onto the train.

The sudden jerk of his arm and the rush of wind exhilarated him. He laughed half out of fright as he clung to the side of the moving boxcar and edged his way toward the opening.

Ben was surprised to find a couple of other men already huddled inside the car. "C'mon kid, get in here. The brakey's liable to see you and we'll all get ditched," one of the men snarled, as Ben hung back at the door to the car, the wind blowing hard against him but his fear of the hobos keeping him out. The man who had spoken looked weathered and beaten-down. His gruff voice and crazy eyes looking out through a full head of gray hair and gray beard startled Ben.

"Sorry," he said sheepishly as he swung himself into the relative security of the bouncing car.

"Hey, step right in," announced the other man, this one younger but little less weathered. "What's a pretty-faced rube like you doin' out here on the road?" He chuckled a little ominously, Ben thought.

"I'm going to Chicago to find work."

"Goin' to Chi, huh? Done heard things is pretty hot up there. Bulls breakin' heads. Me? I'm goin' to Cincie. Got a dame up there."

"That's a ghost story if I ever heard one," said the older man.

"Aw, you just jealous..."

"What do you mean?" Ben asked, still standing up and holding onto the inside of the door.

"C'mere. Sit down 'fore you fall out," the old man laughed. "It means he's lyin' through his teeth," he answered as Ben let himself sit down across the car from the two men. "You get away from the openin'. Don't wanna get seen by nobody." Ben obeyed and the man continued. "What dame you think's gonna want a stiff like 'im?" The old man batted his eyes. "He's lucky if he can jocker a young cat like you."

"Hey, who you callin' a jocker? Ain't me!"

Ben was a little frightened by this talk, though he presumed it was just talk. A few times he'd listened to some tramps out back of Mr. Pickney's whom the old man had felt sorry for and given a couple of sandwiches. They'd carried on like this. Didn't seem to mean anything beyond "chewin' the rag." Ben wondered how much of their slang he was going to understand. He did think, however, he'd already figured out what "jocker" meant and he didn't like it.

"This train *is* going to Chicago, isn't it?"

"Yep," said the old man, "and I was tryin' to get some doss, 'fore time for me to change trains. So you two can shut yo' traps a while. We got a long night ahead of us." He rolled over so he was facing away from Ben.

"It'll be late 'fore we get in. You get some shut-eye, too. And, look, I ain't gonna bother ya—not like the old 'bo said." He apparently had noticed the look of fear in Ben's eyes. "I ain't like that, you hear. Least most o' the time anyway. You'll see."

Ben tried to stay half-awake, just in case, but the rolling and rocking of the car had a soporific effect. And the wind by the door made the car pretty cold. Ben pulled a sweater out of the knapsack. He realized he needed to be careful not to let the knapsack get free from his grasp. Who could he trust?

He awoke with a start. The train wasn't moving. He was dazed for a minute. Maybe we're in Chicago. As his eyes adjusted, he saw the two hobos crouching at the door, murmuring to one another.

He scrambled over to them on all fours and, trying to see what they were looking at, asked innocently, "Is something going on?"

"We 'bout to get timbered," the old man said.

"What's that mean?"

"Look," said the younger of the two, as he pointed out at the landscape.

For a moment Ben couldn't make out what he was seeing. There just wasn't any landscape outside the car. It was as though the blackness of the night had swallowed up the countryside. Then with a little effort he could see glints of light, maybe even fires, way down below. "What's that? Where are we?"

"Look, kid, the train's stopped on a trestle. That's water down below."

All of a sudden Ben heard several thuds and an anguished shout. "The shacks 're timberin' every 'bo on the train."

"What do you mean?" Ben asked, not understanding the words, but catching a frightening implication from the man's tone.

"The railroad don't always like us takin' 'vantage of their horspitality. To teach a few lessons, they pull up the train where you can't get off and then make their way down the line checkin' each boxcar and takin' their clubs to any easy rider, I mean, to any hobos they find."

"You mean they're coming after us?" Ben felt sick to his stomach. "Can't we get away?"

"Sometimes the beatin' ain't so bad. Tho' I been in cars where a couple o' men got killed. Gotta watch your head. Keep your arms up, ya hear?"

"Oh God, no. Can't we jump?"

35

"How're ya at swimmin'? The river's a hundred feet or more below. Ya might make it."

"Or ya might not," the old guy spoke up. "Me? I been beat 'nough times in my life. I'm goin for it." He stood up, looked out the door, glanced back, right into Ben's eyes and maybe he smiled, and then was gone. After a surprisingly long time, Ben heard a loud splash below.

"Think he made it?" the remaining hobo asked, his voice shaking.

All of a sudden there were loud shouts from a boxcar just a couple ahead of the one they huddled in.

Ben didn't know what to do. There didn't seem to be any alternative. For a moment, he thought perhaps he could simply climb out of the cars and walk down to the trainmen and turn himself in, perhaps offer to pay what money he had toward his passage. But then he realized how foolish that plan sounded. He probably wouldn't even get a chance to explain. And if he were outside the cars, he might end up pushed into the water far below anyway.

He took a deep breath. Started to say a "Hail Mary." And just as a beam of light from a lantern caught him in the eye from down the track a short way, he hurled himself out into space. He fell for what seemed an impossibly long time, all the way worrying he was going to hit rocky bank and not water. He prayed there really was water in that gully below. In that odd way that the mind sometimes does when faced with terror, Ben tried to remember whether it'd been a dry or wet year so far. He just kept falling and falling.

"Weren't you afraid of dying?" I asked.

"How do you know I didn't die?" Ben asked me, looking more serious than I expected. "I'm a ghost, ain't I?"

"Are you?" For the first time it occurred to me that Ben *really* was more than a fabrication of my novel-writing exercise.

"Are you?" he retorted, "I mean, afraid of dying?"

8

I slept fitfully most of that night haunted by fears of decay and death. I kept hearing a song unreeling in my mind. Just before I left Boston, a good friend of mine had given me a tape of the original cast recording of *Les Misérables*. He assured me the musical version of Victor Hugo's novel about the French Revolution would appeal to my populist, revolutionary sentiments. The show's rousing march did indeed. But that was not the song that had begun to play over and over in my brain.

36

That was the sad plaint of the tragic Fantine who, in the song "I Dreamed a Dream," sang of how the realities of her life had killed her dreams of love and happiness. I identified with her. This rotten turn of luck—my karma? I thought cynically—had certainly killed my dreams. It seemed my life had become a hell from which I was able to escape only by fantasizing characters who'd lived a simpler life, before such horrors as the bomb or the deterioration of the ozone layer or cancer or viruses.

The specialist had told me the peculiar disease he'd determined I had—with that awful German six syllable name—had until recently been thought to be genetic. It manifested in a variety of ways, but usually as deterioration of the neurons in the base of the brain. (I'd gone to see the doctor originally because I was experiencing transient tingling and numbness in my fingers.) Now, he said, it was believed to be caused by a slow virus, perhaps even a retrovirus like HIV.

There was a part of me that was immensely grateful I didn't have AIDS, though yet another part of me felt immensely guilty and excluded from my community. I'd already seen too many friends die of AIDS. I didn't like that kind of death. But I also didn't like that I was going to die alone of some strange ailment no one had ever heard of.

The specialist had hinted that I might be one of the first to show signs of a new epidemic disease. If, in fact, this turned out to be viral like HIV, he suggested, it could be contagious through intimate contact. Though he didn't explain, I'd known what that implied for my sex life.

I held out for myself the possibility it would strike me like that marvelous malady that killed Bette Davis in *Dark Victory*. Remember? No symptoms till an hour before death, then she went painlessly blind, having just enough time to say good-bye to her Beloved.

The truth was I was more likely to end up a spastic vegetable. I'd already decided I was going to kill myself responsibly before that happened. I didn't exactly mind being dead. I'd had so many friends die, I'd come to understand that death can be blessed relief. But how was I going to know when to choose to go? I couldn't count on an indicator as sure as Bette's.

Around three a.m., a heavy rainstorm blew in. I got up to close the windows. For reasons that made more sense in the night than they do in the daylight retelling, I didn't turn on any lights, but went from room to room in the dark. The sheer white curtains hanging in most of the rooms danced and fluttered in the dark, reminding me of ghostly apparitions. Outside, the darkness hid all signs of the green budding of spring. The trees beat against the windows looking like dead and gnarled skeletons reaching for me. I wondered if ghosts really do become attached to particular houses. Was Ben Mayfield a ghost in this house? And if he were killed in that fall somewhere in Illinois how did his soul ever get to this place? And why?

In my nighttime consciousness, perhaps slightly fevered, it seemed to me I wouldn't mind haunting this house—especially if Ben were here with me. Maybe that's what it would take, I thought, for me to satisfy my longing for him.

I sat down on the low steps between the entrance hall and living room. It's hard to describe the peculiar mixture of fear and desire I was feeling, of dread and pleasure. There was something immensely beautiful about the dark house, the moist breeze blowing through cool and fresh carrying the smell of wet grass, and the silence. Of course, in fact, the night was full of the noise of the pounding rain and whistling wind. But what I heard was the silence, the absence of human voices and artificial sounds. I felt as lonely as I ever had in my life yet strangely satisfied. At the same time I felt as happy as I'd ever been: the night air soothed my soul with its hint of new spring life. I thought I could sit there forever.

In the morning I slept late, then sat in a hot bath and carefully felt my body all over, searching out the trains of lymph nodes, checking for discolorations or lesions on my skin, feeling my pulse, trying to sense my blood pressure from the gentle pounding of the vein in my wrist against my fingertip. To my surprise, what I found were signs not of impending death, but of improving health. In the Texas sun, my skin was darkening. With the garden work and exercise, my muscles were tightening. My pulse was nearly down to sixty beats per minute, in sync with the passing of the seconds.

Later I wandered through the garden, noticing that seeds I'd planted were beginning to sprout. In a few weeks, the gardens would likely be in flower. The trees were budding bright green. How different they looked from last night. The rain had cleaned the dust from the leaves and sent the signal for nature to awake. There'd been enough rain so that where the creek in the ravine below the house was dammed up to create a small lagoon the water was pouring over the spillway in a rushing stream.

I spent a while watering behind the house where the terraced plots were sheltered by the overhanging eaves of the red tile roof, checked on the laborers who, I saw, were nearly halfway through clearing out the barn area, then prepared lunch for them and myself, and sat down at my desk to work.

As I turned back to review my work from the day before, I expected Ben to appear to me. I was anxious to know what happened when he plunged from that trestle into the cold river below. But when I looked up, it wasn't Ben sitting there across from me.

"Ben Mayfield asked me to talk to you," said the vision. I was a little hurt. And confused. The young man looked to be in his mid-twenties, a little older than Ben. His hair was dark, his color pallid. You could tell he had a man's body, and not a boy's. A tuft of dark hair showed at his neck, even above the tight starched high collar he wore. The shadow of his beard was heavy and coarse hair curled on the backs of his hands. He was a handsome man. But not my type.

"Who are you?" I asked.

"My name's Tom Milam. I'm a friend of Ben's." He said "friend" in a tone that made me instantly jealous. "We're in Texas, aren't we?" he added, looking to his left so he could see out the window. Something about his profile, the aquiline nose and strong chin, seemed familiar to me.

"Where's Ben? What happened to him? I mean, what happened to him when he jumped from the railroad trestle? Is he alright?"

"We're both dead, Mr. Carton. Don't you know that? We lived and died long before you were even born—in a simpler time." His directness took me aback.

"Well, yes, but... "

"There's more to this story. And now it's my turn to tell you about it."

9

t offended Tom Milam that his mother insisted he take a job as a sales clerk at Strinke & Millburn's Drygoods Store on Alamo Plaza in downtown San Antonio. It just didn't seem to him like a manly thing to do.

"Times are hard. And getting harder," his mother answered. "You could do a lot worse than work for Mr. Strinke and Mr. Millburn."

"But, Mama, I don't want to be a drygoods clerk all my life. I want to make something of myself," he'd demurred.

"Money isn't everything. Look what all that did to me," she sighed.

"I'm not talking about money." What he was really talking about was love. But even he hadn't figured that out yet. "I want my life to be an adventure."

"Stability, Tom. You need some stability. Look what's happening in Washington. The country's falling apart the way Harrison's running things. You can't afford to not protect yourself. Security. That's what counts."

Tom's mother came from money. Her family was one of the most respectable in town. Milam was an old Texas name. But Jenny Milam had been a little too interested in adventure herself. And twenty years ago she'd gotten pregnant, unmarried. They couldn't take away her name. She was still a Milam. But the family disowned her. She was lucky she could go to work for Mr. Strinke.

Tom never knew who his father was. Jenny Milam always told him he was better off not knowing. Tom guessed the man must have already been married and that's why he couldn't have saved Jenny from ignominy. In Tom's darkest moods, he suspected his mother had been a high class prostitute and the gentleman had passed through without ever knowing the consequences of their momentary dalliance. Texas in the middle years of the 19th Century had still been frontier country. The Milams may have been rich and their blood may have run blue by the time Jenny was disinherited, but they'd once been cowboys and wranglers. A certain kind of sexual license went with that frontier identity.

39

One thing that argued against those fears was that occasionally his mother would suddenly come into money. She'd always say she'd just been lucky at the gin rummy game she played with friends on Friday nights. But there seemed to be more money than that story could explain. Tom always suspected that his father was giving her something toward their support—perhaps out of a sense of responsibility, perhaps out of guilt, perhaps out of fear of exposure.

As he got older these sudden windfalls came less frequently. He was having to take over supporting the two of them himself. He was twenty years old when his mother told him Mr. Millburn had offered to give him a job at Strinke & Millburn's, in the same department she'd worked in for years. She'd had to quit recently. Arthritis, attributed to a fall from a horse when she was just a girl, was gradually crippling her. Someplace deep in his mind Tom guessed it wasn't arthritis as much as shame that was sucking the life out of her and turning her prematurely into a decrepit old woman.

Jenny Milam got to spending her days in bed. After a while it seemed as if she couldn't tell the difference between the present reality and her dreams of the past. Sometimes Tom would come home from work to find her talking on and on about the great party they were going to throw that night. She'd regale him with stories of her life as a girl. She used to talk about the family's horse ranch up in the hill country: the high society parties, the wonderful emerald green silk dress she wore with the hoop skirt, the big house all lit up with candles, people coming in by horse and buggy from as far away as Austin and Bandera. They'd stay the whole weekend and the house would ring with laughter and partying long into the night.

Now all that was gone.

Jenny promised Tom it was all going to be different someday. She told him wistfully that the family would forgive and forget and that he'd be remembered in some Milam's will, that maybe he'd even inherit the horsefarm. "I'll have to talk to Pater about that," she'd always say. (Her father had died several years ago, Tom knew from reading the newspapers, but he never mentioned that fact to Jenny.) "That's where I had my fall, you know," she'd say in her delicate, genteel country voice. Tom never knew whether she meant the fall from the horse that was supposed to have resulted in her crippling or the indiscretion at one of those weekend parties that was to have resulted in her fall from grace and in his birth into the Milam family—unwanted.

Tom had inherited her shame, he realized. Not because of his illegitimacy exactly. That had bothered him, but he wasn't the only bastard child in this erstwhile frontier town. But there was something, he knew, that he always felt ashamed of. He wasn't sure what it was. He had a difficult time putting words to the feelings. He just knew there was something he had to keep secret. Years before, when he was in school, he'd struggled to explain these feelings to Johnny Kincade, the boy who'd become his best friend and stayed his best—maybe his only—friend until Johnny's family moved up to Chicago a few years ago. Johnny had somehow understood. There was something they shared, something that neither could explain or say aloud.

40

Whatever it was, it had something to do with Tom's fear of being identified as a ribbon clerk in a drygoods store. That was woman's work. And though he didn't find the cattle business, for instance, especially appealing, he knew, it was man's work.

He'd been doing the kinds of odd jobs around town that teenagers could get easily. Once he reached his twenties, he had to settle on something more permanent. When his mother insisted on the job under Mr. Millburn, she promised him that at least it would be secure. She'd been right about that. Even when he'd made bad mistakes during the five years he'd worked at Strinke & Millburn's, he was always forgiven. Tom sometimes wondered if his father was somehow behind the job. That would help explain things. He tried to recognize his features in the men in the age group appropriate to his father, but with no success. The fact was he took after his mother. He had the Milam coloration and facial characteristics. He'd have been hard pressed to determine just what features he might have inherited from his father. His mother always told him it didn't make any difference, that his curiosity was only likely to cause him trouble.

Tom's life was running smoothly, if not adventurously. He resented the routine, but accepted it as a necessary part of life. Besides, he had to keep working to support himself and his mother and put away a little nest egg for the creation of his own family—whenever that was going to be. Tom kept waiting, wondering how a man ever chose a wife, fearing that his own fatherless upbringing had confused his familial instincts. He assumed it would just happen to him one day. He hoped fervently that he'd have his chance for adventure first. And he secretly thought of the money he was putting away not as a nest egg for a family but as a passport to a different life.

Recently there hadn't been much money going into savings. Jenny's arthritis had become much worse. In the five years since she'd quit work, she had become practically bedridden. Partly out of his secret guilt and consequent sense of being responsible for everything that went wrong in his world and partly out of genuine horror at his mother's almost constant pain, Tom began seeking out non-conventional arthritis cures. There were many. They were costly. And they were dangerous.

One winter evening Tom came home from work to find Jenny paralyzed on the right side of her body. She'd apparently had a stroke, Tom feared, as a result of the injections of "miracle metals" the latest quack he'd found had been giving her. He rushed to the doctor's home, which proved to be a room in a nearby boardinghouse, to demand help. The doctor refused to make a house-call after dark, he said he had a cold and couldn't go out in the chill air, but he assured Tom this was just a passing side-effect of the medication, that it showed the regimen of metals was working, and he promised to show up at Jenny's bedside first thing in the morning.

Tom stayed home in the morning to be there when the doctor arrived. But he never arrived. Just before noon, Tom went to the office to find that the little room in back of a drug store had been cleared out. The druggist said the "doctor" had apparently moved during the night. He went directly to the man's room in the boardinghouse and found the same thing. He had left in the night.

Tom rushed back to his mother who was now unconscious and breathing laboriously. Weeping, he gathered up her small body in his arms and carried her to a clinic a few blocks from their house in downtown San Antonio. She was dead by the time he arrived.

Everyone at work was supportive. Robert Jeffries, a young man about his own age, offered to fill in for him so he could take some time off to recover. For weeks several of the ladies in his department took turns bringing him fried chicken or roast beef or stew for his dinner. Mr. Strinke himself had come to Jenny's sad little funeral (none of the Milams—or any of their blue blood friends showed up); afterwards, he'd taken Tom aside and offered to send his personal attorney around to help with Jenny's affairs. Tom was grateful for the help. He was surprised how grief-stricken he was. He hadn't realized how dependent he'd been on his mother or how guilty he was going to feel for having found the quack treatment that killed her.

He made it through the winter. The attorney Mr. Strinke referred him to handled Jenny's will; there wasn't much to it. Tom was surprised to find she'd had a small portfolio of stocks and bonds. The attorney assured him they were good investments—many of them in the booming railroad industry. In fact, the attorney convinced him to put some of the cash he'd been saving into those same stocks, promising it would increase their yield and put the money to good use, allowing Tom to share in the good fortune of the Eastern millionaires whose wealth and profligacy were the talk of the day. Tom wondered how his mother had ever had the sense to make such investments and began scrutinizing local stockbrokers in search of features that might identify one of them as his long-lost father.

That was the winter of 1892. On February 20th, the Reading Railroad collapsed, carrying with it the nation's economy, and making a good portion of Tom's stock certificates worthless. The panic was one of the worst the country had ever seen. Railroad construction came to a halt; workers went on strike. The cattle industry in Texas was hit by the troubles in the railroads. Freight trains were needed to get beef to market in the great urban centers of the country. Prices on all sorts of goods began to rise as trail drives and wagon caravans and other alternative means of transportation had to be used. At the same time, local cattle prices fell. Ranchers couldn't get their investments back and, in turn, couldn't pay back their bank loans. There was a run on the banks across the country. Currency became scarce. Business fell off.

One rainy Friday afternoon, Mr. Millburn asked Tom to follow him up to Mr. Strinke's office. "We need to talk with you about some matters."

Tom was feeling optimistic that day. For all that business was bad, he felt secure in his job—as his mother always told him he should. And he was finally throwing off the burden of guilt for her death. He thought perhaps Mr. Strinke was going to offer, out of kindness, to make up for some of the losses he'd incurred because he'd taken that attorney's advice. Tom always thought of his employers as honorable men.

Mr. Strinke was sitting behind his desk, smoking a cigar. As Tom entered the room, Strinke generously proffered the box.

"Thank you, sir. I've never developed a taste for those," he replied politely.

"Nonsense. Make a man of you." But he closed the cigar box and tucked it back in the top right-hand drawer of his desk. Charles Millburn walked around and stood to Mr. Strinke's right. He was not offered a cigar.

"What can I do for you, sir?" Tom broke the silence that seemed to be dragging on a little too long for comfort.

"Well, son, you know how bad business has been lately. Things just aren't good these days. I've got to make some hard decisions."

Uh-oh, Tom thought.

"I want to talk to you about Bob Jeffries," Strinke continued. Jeffries, of course, was the other male working in Tom's department. He was slightly Tom's junior at the store and not quite as good a worker. But everybody liked him. Tom didn't want to get involved in something that might cost Bob his job.

"He's a very good employee, sir."

"And a married man. You know, don't you, that he's got three children to support?"

"I didn't realize his family had gotten so big," Tom laughed amiably. "I've met Bob's wife, Sarah. 'Guess I can see why the family's growing."

"Well, now, Tom, I'm glad you understand about that. It makes this easier."

"What's that, sir?"

"You know, we just can't afford to keep on so many employees, especially now that sales are so far down. It's not a matter, you understand, of clearing out dead wood. If I could do that I'd do it happily. I've got to be trimming back the green as well... " He fell silent.

"I'm not certain I understand your meaning, sir."

"Now, Tom," Millburn spoke up. "This company's been good to you for a long time—out of deference to your mother. God rest her soul," he said piously. "Even when you stopped coming to work last winter and Jeffries had to fill in for you... "

"Bob offered to work for me a little while after mama's death," Tom answered defensively. The conversation had suddenly taken an unexpected direction.

"All the more reason for you to feel indebted to him," Strinke spoke up.

"Are you saying you're letting me go?"

Millburn continued. "We can only keep one of you in that department. Times are hard. It's certainly going to be easier for you, a single man"—he said those words as though they were an indictment—"than for a family man like Jeffries. Men with families, like myself, don't have the freedoms. Why, you're young and strong and... "

"But what about the promises you made my mother?" Tom interrupted. His voice sounded strained. "She said this job would be secure. Always."

"Look, son, your mother's gone," Strinke spoke up. "Whatever debts we had to her are all acquited now. She kept her end of the bargain. We expect you to do the same."

"Bargain? What do you mean?"

"He means this company took her in when she was on hard times," Millburn replied sternly. "She understood that. Now the company's on hard times."

"Maybe I could change to a different department," Tom changed the subject lest he offend against some secret arrangements with his mother. "I'd be happy to take another job. You know, I always wanted to work at something, you know, more manly than clerk. Maybe I could be a driver. I get along good with horses."

"Well, then, here's your opportunity to get a job you'll really like. We knew you weren't entirely happy with the position you've been in."

"You mean, I can transfer?" The bad news seemed to have a silver lining.

"I'm sure you can find a teamster job," Millburn answered.

"With the company?"

"I'm sorry, Tom," Mr. Strinke took control of the interview again. "There just isn't any room right now. We're having to let people go who've been part of the family for a long time. We just have to do it in the least hurtful way. And that means that the young and strong and the, well, unmarried have to go first. You understand?"

"Sure I understand," Tom shot back. "But what am I going to do?"

"Now I know your mother left you a tidy sum. And we've paid you well. I hope you've put some money away."

"That lawyer you sent me to got me to invest it all. There's practically nothing left."

"Well, I'm certainly sorry about that," Strinke replied. "But at least you'll have learned a lesson."

"Look, Tom, this isn't getting us anywhere. And there are other employees to speak to today. You're not alone, you understand. And this is all very hard on Mr. Strinke," Millburn said, ending the interview by walking toward the door and opening it for Tom. "You can stay on till the end of the week. And there'll be a small severance allowance in your next check. Thank you. Now you should get back to the floor."

"Thank you," Tom answered automatically as he left.

Millburn closed the door behind him. For a moment Tom leaned against the doorframe to steady himself. He suddenly felt faint. Through the door he heard Millburn say something he could not make out. Then he thought he heard Strinke reply, "Looks like Jenny kept her promise. Good girl."

Anger began to surge up in him. Something was going on behind his back. It had been going on all his life. He felt betrayed by his mother. He thought for a moment about going back into that office and telling those two sons of bitches what he really thought of them and their damned company. Then it dawned on him. He was free. He was finally free. Whatever hold his mother had had on him was gone. He'd been right this morning when he thought he was finally getting over her death. Now he was going to get over her secret.

Maybe I can find out about my own, he said to himself, half-expectant that soon he'd understand what it was he'd been longing for all his life.

Tom finished out the day and overcame his urge to skip work the rest of the week. He knew he was going to need the money. By the time he left the store, he was feeling excited about the future. Money was going to be a problem. But at last he could seek the adventure he'd been wanting.

One of the first things he did was to fish out the last letter he'd gotten from Johnny Kincade. It had been almost six months since he'd heard from his old friend. But maybe he could find him. After all, Johnny was the only person he knew outside San Antonio. And he was the only person who'd ever seemed to really understand Tom.

The envelope was postmarked Chicago. The letter had a return address. He quickly wrote Johnny a note, saying he was coming to Chicago and inviting Johnny to join him in the adventure. He walked out to drop the letter in the mail and then, while he was out, strolled over to the train station. There were still some passenger trains running despite the strikes. Maybe he could be in Chicago by next week.

❧

"Where's Ben?" I asked once Tom broke off the recounting of his story. "You still haven't told me what happened to him." I liked Tom, but I wasn't smitten with him the way I was with Ben.

"Don't worry," Tom Milam answered me. "He'll be back. But there's more to this story. It's important you hear it all."

10

 ell, I did worry. Not about Ben or Tom. For all that I wanted to recover my fantasy red-head, all-American boy, I knew both of these young characters were creations of my own mind. I doubted I'd lose the ability to conjure up Ben Mayfield again. I'd certainly been able to recall sexual fantasies in the past. But I was worrying about myself and the completion of my novel.

Around dinner time, Dave Lovejoy, the real estate agent, called to say he'd talked with Dr. Steed's attorney. The man had called from Boston to inform him of Dr. Steed's legal difficulties and to urge him to press forward with the sale of the property. The money would be needed for legal expenses, he said, or, perhaps, for settlement of the suit. Lovejoy was calling to ask me if the place were ready for showing.

I assured him it looked very good and that he was welcome to show the house to prospective buyers whenever he liked. I did ask him to call me first so I could straighten up a little. He agreed. (The truth was that on some of these warm spring days, especially when the laborers weren't around, I didn't bother to dress. It seemed like a good exercise for me in getting back in touch with my body. Since the diagnosis I hadn't felt like letting my consciousness reside in my body very much of the time. But I didn't want the real estate agent and his client to come upon me unawares.)

It wasn't the possible exposure of my exhibitionist tendencies that worried me, it was the fear of where I'd go if the property were sold. I just didn't want to go back to Boston and the life I'd been leading. It had come close to killing me. I felt the death sentence perhaps on hold out here in the countryside. Besides, I wanted to finish my novel.

And, just between you and me, I have to admit I was beginning to believe that Ben Mayfield and Tom Milam really were ghostly residents of this house and not *just* figments of my imagination. I didn't want to lose them. Certainly not before I heard the rest of the story *or* learned the lessons Ben had promised me.

Later that night I was a little intoxicated. I'd drunk more of the blush wine I had with dinner than I probably should have allowed myself. In a slight euphoric stupor and with a scheme in mind, I called Elizabeth to try to convince her how wonderful life was here. I thought maybe if she and Marla and her dad would move down here we could stay on the property forever. At the time that seemed like a good idea.

Elizabeth wasn't home. I left a message on her answering machine inviting her to join me in never-never land. After I hung up, I felt a little silly and wished I could undo the message.

❧

The next morning Tom started right in on the story. He didn't flirt with me the way Ben did. I was probably thankful for that. I didn't think I could keep up with him if he did. I mean, flirting takes a certain amount of realistic interest from both sides. It was easy to flirt with Ben. Not with Tom.

He skipped the last days in San Antonio. "Nothing interesting happened at all. I was much too concerned about leaving," Tom explained. "I took care of practical matters, got together as much cash as I could. There was really nobody close enough to me to say good-bye to. I wished I'd hear from Johnny Kincade, but I knew there wasn't time for my letter to reach him and for him to answer. What I was really hoping is that if he knew I were coming—

if he weren't going to be at the address of that letter—he'd arrange for somebody there to know how to direct me to him."

Tom Milam boarded a train for Chicago on Saturday about mid-morning. He felt some tension in the station. There were a couple of pickets passing out leaflets about the oppression of labor. Tom agreed with their sentiments. But he had to get out of town. He worried that something might happen to stop his departure. He'd heard rumors of trains being sabotaged up north. He wasn't sure he believed them. But he certainly felt relieved when the locomotive blew its whistle and the car he was in started to move.

In Dallas the train took on more passengers. One of them, a handsome but weathered man probably ten years Tom's senior with a great mane of blond hair and a carefully manicured goatee, walked up and down the aisle several times before settling into the seat next to Tom. Each time he'd walked by he'd glanced at Tom out of the corner of his eye. It slightly unnerved Tom, though he didn't think the man looked dangerous. In fact, though he'd have had a hard time explaining what it was, he thought there was something appealing about the fellow. His choosing the seat next to Tom was, at least, going to allow Tom to satisfy his curiosity.

After the man fiddled a while with the worn old carpetbag he carried, apparently making certain he had his ticket and whatever other papers he was carrying, he let out a deep breath, leaned back into his seat, then turned to Tom. "Name's Eli Hauptmann," he said. There was an edge of foreign accent in his voice that, to Tom, made him seem both more intriguing and more sinister.

"I'm Tom Milam."

"I'm going all the way to Chicago. You?"

"Me too," Tom answered

"You must be from there," Hauptmann said. "You certainly don't look like a cowboy."

"Nope. From San Antone," Tom answered, not sure whether he'd been complimented or insulted.

"Well, well. You'll like Chicago, I suspect. Ever been to a big city?"

"Never been out of San Antonio," he said jauntily. "Born 'n raised in Texas."

"Ah, I hear the accent now. Sounds manly."

Tom liked hearing that. That, of course, had been one of the things he'd worried about throughout his five years as a clerk at Strinke & Millburn's. Chicago's going to be a fine place, he told himself. I'll make it big. He didn't know how to respond to Hauptmann's comment and remained silent.

The man smiled, looked away, then looked back and smiled again. Still Tom said nothing and Hauptmann let out another deep sigh and relaxed into his seat. He had had a book in one hand ever since he'd rummaged through the carpetbag. Now he opened the book and began to read.

Tom felt slightly ill-at-ease. He wasn't sure whether he'd snubbed the man or been snubbed. He realized he didn't know how people acted on trains.

47

He looked around, trying to avoid being too obvious. Some people were chatting amiably with their seatmates—of course, they could be friends traveling together, he thought to himself. Others sat side by side in stony silence. He relaxed into his seat, letting out a sigh and then laughing to himself that he'd inadvertently mimicked Eli Hauptmann's behavior. He looked out the window at the passing countryside.

The rhythmic clacking of the train's wheels and the monotonous passage of plains land out the window lulled Tom into sleep. The next thing he remembered was Mr. Hauptmann tugging at his sleeve with one hand and extending a bottle of soda toward him with the other. Tom looked up to see a vendor with a push cart standing in the aisle counting change into one of those coin dispensers he wore at his waist. "I bought you a creme soda," Hauptmann announced. "You must be thirsty. It's hot as tarnation in here."

As he came to, Tom realized that indeed his throat was parched and he'd been sweating profusely. "Thank you, sir. Don't mind if I do." He reached into his pocket to search for change. "How much do I owe you?"

"Not a thing. Accept it as a *bon voyage* for a young adventurer."

"Huh? Sorry. I don't speak German."

"French," Hauptmann corrected. "That was French for 'good journey'."

"Well, thank you very much. Mighty kind o' you." Tom realized he was inadvertently accentuating his Texas drawl.

"I've been reading here about young adventurers," the man held up the book he was reading. It looked as though it were hand-made. The book was worn and Tom couldn't make out the title on the spine.

"Listen to this." He read from the book:

"The friendly and flowing savage, who is he?
Is he waiting for civilization, or past it and mastering it?

Is he some Southwesterner rais'd out-doors? is he Kanadian?
Is he from the Mississippi country? Iowa, Oregon, California?
The mountains? prairie-life, bush-life? or sailor from the sea?
Wherever he goes men and women accept and desire him,
They desire he should like them, touch them, speak to them, stay with
    them.

Behavior lawless as snow-flakes, words simple as grass, uncomb'd
    head, laughter, and naïvetè,
Slow-stepping feet, common features, common modes and emanations,
They descend in new forms from the tips of his fingers,
They are wafted with the odor of his body or breath, they fly out of the
    glance of his eyes."

"Pretty," Tom replied. "Tho' can't say I understood it. Sounds sorta like poetry, but I couldn't catch the rhyme."

"You're right. It is a kind of poetry, a new verse form. And there isn't any rhyme exactly."

"Oh?"

"This is probably what poetry will all sound like in the future. This book's going to be very influential. Already is."

"How come you know about such things?" Tom asked ingenuously as he drank the soda Mr. Hauptmann had bought him.

"I am a professor of comparative literature."

"Do you write poetry yourself?"

"Well, I've published a few monographs on the French impressionists. Do you know Baudelaire?"

Tom didn't know what a monograph was much less whatever the fancy French name the man had just said. "Was that who you were reading?"

"Oh, no. Not at all." He laughed in a friendly way that made Tom realize the man was being very careful not to sound condescending. He laughed almost as though he were sharing a joke with Tom about Baudelaire.

"Walt Whitman." He held up the book. "*Leaves of Grass.*"

"Name sounds familiar," Tom answered truthfully, but also a little pretentiously. The name did sound familiar, but he realized he thought it belonged to a chocolate manufacturer.

"He's a contemporary, you know. He only died two years ago. Maybe about this same time of year, in fact. This is an early edition. A prize possession of mine." He held out the book, open to the title page. "See, it's signed by the author." There was an inscription written in a fluent, but difficult penmanship. Tom thought he could make out: "To Charles, strong worker and mighty lover. Your comrade, Walt."

As Hauptmann closed the book and let it settle back in his lap, with one finger still inserted to hold his place, Tom asked, "Are you Charles?"

"Oh no. Sometimes when I'm reading these words, I wish I were. No. I never knew Whitman. But a few years ago, when I'd first come to America, in fact, I met this man Charles. He'd known Whitman many years before and had been given this volume. He was ill and said he was afraid he'd die and his children would find this book among his possessions, and so he gave it to me."

"If it's so precious, why would he have been afraid of his children finding it?"

"Well, my young man, *that* is a good question. I think you'll have to learn more about my Mr. Whitman here to understand. Perhaps you'll allow me to teach you... " Then quickly he seemed to interrupt himself. "This book was banned at one time. You see, Whitman was very aware of how the human body expresses the divinity of God—yes, I think that's a good way to say it," Hauptmann added this last as an aside to himself. "He used words that shocked certain people. They said it was obscene. He spoke, you know, in the idiom of the common man. He was a great advocate of democracy."

"What kind of words?" Tom asked. He felt a funny queasy feeling in his stomach.

"Oh, oh, words like, like 'balls' and 'sweat' ...words the working class man might use about the parts of his own body. And he spoke about things most people are too shy to mention."

Tom felt slightly embarrassed for Mr. Hauptmann. He hadn't meant to make him say anything quite so obscene. "Oh! I see what you mean."

"Let me show you," Hauptmann said, paging quickly through the book. He seemed enthusiastic and at the same time shamed. "Perhaps you could read this yourself." He held out the page. From where Hauptmann pointed with his finger, Tom read silently:

> Strong shoulders, manly beard, scapula, hind-shoulders, and the ample side round of the chest,
> Upper-arm, armpit, elbow-socket, lower-arm, arm-sinews, arm-bones,
> Wrist and wrist-joints, hand, palm, knuckles, thumb, forefinger, finger-joints, finger-nails,
> broad breast-front, curling hair of the breast, breast-bone, breast-side,
> Ribs, belly, backbone, joints of the backbone,
> Hips, hip-sockets, hip-strength, inward and outward round, man-balls, man-root,
> Strong set of thighs, well carrying the trunk above...

"I see," Tom said as he handed back the book. Hauptmann turned a few pages and returned the book, again pointing:

> The young man that flushes and flushes, and the young woman that flushes and flushes,
> The young man that wakes deep at night, the hot hand seeking to repress what would master him,
> The mystic amorous night, the strange half-welcome pangs, visions, sweats,
> The pulse pounding through palms and trembling encircling fingers, the young man all color'd, red, ashamed, angry...

"You said this was about 'divinity'?" Tom asked.

"Yes, yes. Whitman always wrote about God, about how God lives in each person. Very much like in the Upanishads." He paged through the book some more. "Here, this is a beautiful passage:"

> I hear and behold God in every object, yet understand God not in the least,
> Nor do I understand who there can be more wonderful than myself.
> Why should I wish to see God better than this day?
> I see something of God each hour of the twenty-four, and each moment then,

In the faces of men and women I see God, and in my own face in the
    glass,
I find letters from God dropt in the street, and every one is sign'd by
    God's name,
And I leave them where they are, for I know that wheresoe'er I go,
Others will punctually come for ever and ever.

❦

"You probably use words like cock and balls all day long, don't you?" Tom
Milam said to me. "And you don't feel even slightly embarrassed."

"I probably wouldn't have used such words or talked about such things
in front of my mother," I joked. "But, sure, those don't have the same taboo
value they used to. I mean, one of the big changes in recent decades has been
what you could call the democratization of the language. Even the educated,
upper classes have taken to using the language of the common people.

"You know," I went on practically lecturing him. "That's especially
true among gay people. It's maybe part of the leftist, Marxist bent gay culture
picked up in the 60s. It's certainly also part of the fact that gay people are
déclassé and so can move between and mingle the styles of different classes.
Walt Whitman probably had a lot to do with starting that."

"Gay culture?" Tom looked at me skeptically out of the corner of his
eye.

"Well, isn't that what you and this Mr. Eli Hauptmann were talking
about?" I challenged.

Tom laughed uproariously. "That's certainly easier to see with
hindsight. I didn't quite know what he was talking about. How in the world was
a Texas boy supposed to know what the Upanishads were? I was pretty well
educated. My mother saw to that. But, my God, Vivekananda had only come
to Chicago the previous July!"

"Now you're even out of my league. What are you talking about?"

Tom laughed again. For the first time I was beginning to relax with
him. He really was a nice fellow. I'd gotten to like his smile.

"Eli went on and on about Whitman's mysticism and what he'd
known about 'Hindoos' and the Self. It was all very beautiful and kind of
hypnotizing. It was also all mixed up with this sexual innuendo that kept me
pretty frightened—and at the same time, pretty fascinated. At that time in my
life, I don't think I'd have had the patience to sit through a lecture on Eastern
mystical influences on American poetry. But there was something about the
way Eli was talking, the way he'd occasionally reach out and touch my hand
or grab my arm, that made me think he knew something I, well, *needed* to know."

"And was there?" I asked facetiously, trying to suggest a little sexual
innuendo of my own.

51

Tom looked me straight in the eye. "He told me things *you* need to know, Rick Carton."

"Mind if I take off my jacket?" Tom asked. It was late afternoon and the hot sun was pouring through the train's windows. "It's like a hothouse in here."

"Of course not," Eli mopped his brow with a big red handkerchief. "That's a good idea." He stepped out into the aisle to allow Tom room to stand up. While Tom removed the wool jacket he'd been wearing, Eli perched on the armrest of the seats opposite and watched attentively. "Why don't you take off the tie and open your collar?" he suggested as he began to undo his own highbutton collar.

About that time the conductor entered the car. "Dinner is being served in the Dining Car," he announced. "Dinner is being served." The conductor continued down the aisle repeating his message in a kind of sing-song.

"Almost like a mantra," Eli commented after the conductor had passed.

"A what?"

"Never mind," Eli laughed. "Now that I've gotten you to disrobe, young man, let me suggest you put your jacket back on and join me in the dining car."

"Oh, I'm not hungry," Tom answered.

"Nonsense. You must be hungry. If it's a little, er, pecuniary embarrassment you're experiencing, well, let me treat you. I certainly can afford it."

"Well, thank you very much," Tom answered, relieved. "I don't know if I should expect that of you. But the fact is I really am starving."

"My pleasure," Eli commented as they both replaced their ties. In a moment they started down the aisle toward the dining car. "You appear to have a good physique, Tom," Eli commented when they reached the door and he stepped back to allow Tom to precede him.

"Huh?"

"I mean, you must keep up your strength. Eat hardy." His blue eyes sparkled. He seemed to be smiling at a personal joke.

Eli insisted on purchasing a bottle of wine with dinner. And with the food and the alcohol, whatever tensions Tom had been feeling disappeared altogether. He was thoroughly pleased at having found himself such a wonderful benefactor. After dinner they sat together in the club car and sipped brandy while Tom told Eli about the scandal surrounding his birth, his upbringing in Texas, his hopes for adventure, and his plans to meet his friend Johnny Kincade.

Eli asked tentatively about Tom's plans to marry and raise a family.

"I guess I will. I mean, everybody does, don't they? But I'm not ready for that yet. I want to have my adventure first. I envy you, you know, a man of the world. You've had adventures, haven't you?"

Eli smiled as if in affirmation.

"I want to be like you."

Eli Hauptmann had reserved a sleeping berth in the Pullman car for the night. Tom was, of course, planning simply to sleep in his seat in the coach. After their third glass of brandy, Eli excused himself saying he wouldn't manage to find the Pullman car if he didn't get started now.

"I hope I'll see you in the morning. I'll buy you coffee," Tom added sheepishly.

"I will relish the expectation till morning," Eli answered standing up. He sounded a bit formal, perhaps due to the amount of alcohol they'd consumed. "I must tell you about my friend Karl Heinrich Ulrichs." Then rocking forward tipsily he added, almost under his breath, "It's too bad we must wait for the morrow... " Then, "Ah, but parting is such sweet sorrow... "

"What's that?" Tom asked nervously.

"It's Shakespeare, isn't it?" They both laughed.

In the morning Tom was awake long before Eli came looking for him. The coach had gotten pretty noisy once the sun came up. By fortunate coincidence, the vendor, pushing a large steel urn on a cart, came through hawking coffee and rolls at almost the same time Eli entered the car from the other direction.

Savoring the hot fragrant liquid that promised to end the pounding in his head, Tom said, "You were going to tell me about some friend of yours?"

"Let's let that wait," Eli answered. "It's awfully early in the morning for, er, such a discussion."

They both fell into silence. Tom had earlier found a newspaper on one of the seats. He offered a section to Eli and the two of them read for a while. They passed the day with few words, occasionally commenting on the sights or joking amicably about other passengers walking up and down the aisles. Tom was surprised how comfortable he felt with Eli and with the silence. I guess I've made a friend, he thought happily.

In the late afternoon, the vendor came through with sandwiches. Agreeing they'd both had enough food at dinner the night before to last the rest of the trip, each bought himself a light supper. After that, Eli got to talking again about his academic studies. He talked about French poets Tom had never heard of and British and American writers whose names were vaguely familiar but whom Tom had certainly never read.

The train was scheduled to arrive in Chicago late that night. As it began to get dark, Eli invited Tom to join him for a final drink in the club car. They sat together, Eli occasionally speaking, but by now obviously talked out, watching the lights of the passing countryside.

At one point the train rumbled clackety-clack over a high trestle. At Eli's urgent suggestion, they rushed to the back of the car and stood in the opening between coaches and looked down into the depths below. The wind blew at their hair, chilling them pleasurably. High above, the stars burned bright in the country sky. Far away at the bottom of the deep valley flowed a mighty river. Faint glimmers of light reflected off its moving surface.

"Glorious," Eli commented. "Just glorious."

"What are the fires down there?" Tom asked, noticing bright spots of red-orange light along what must have been the bank of the river. They seemed almost to mimic the stars overhead.

"Probably a hobo jungle," Eli answered as he tugged at Tom's sleeve to get him to follow him back into the car after the train had reached the end of the trestle.

"An interesting phenomenon," Eli continued once they'd resumed their seats in the club car. "Walt Whitman glorified such wanderers." He paged through the little book he was carrying in his pocket. "Here:

> As I lay my head in your lap, camerado,
> The confession I made I resume, what I said to you and the open air
>   I resume,
> I know I am restless and make others so,
> I know my words are weapons full of danger, full of death,
> For I confront peace, security, and all the settled laws, to unsettle
>   them,
> I am more resolute because all have denied me than I could ever have
>   been had all accepted me,
> I heed not and have never heeded either experience, cautions,
>   majorities, or ridicule,
> And the threat of what is call'd hell is little or nothing to me,
> And the lure of what is call'd heaven is little or nothing to me;
> Dear camerado! I confess I have urged you onward with me, and still
>   urge you, without the least idea what is our destination,
> Or whether we shall be victorious, or utterly quell'd and defeated."

"That sounds a little sad," Tom replied, also feeling it sounded a little romantic, but not quite sure how to say that.

"The lives of many of these men are sad. Though some are glorious also. Many of them are nomadic agricultural workers who migrate from one job to another as the seasons change what crops need harvesting. Apples in the Northwest in the fall; wheat in the spring in the Midwest; maybe cotton in the South?"

"I think the cotton gets picked by darkies," Tom observed.

"Most of the tramps and hobos, I think, are white men. Some of them are down on their luck. There's a serious depression happening in your country right now. That certainly increases the number of men out looking for jobs... "

"I know," Tom answered succinctly.

"Many of the tramps are drunks and petty thieves. At least that's what most people think. Like the gypsies back in my country. Whitman certainly

54

portrayed their existence as romantic and manly and spiritual... "

It occurred to Tom that Eli used that word "manly" a lot.

" ...perhaps part of a tradition that goes all the way back to the wandering monks of the early Middle Ages. The Church never approved of that and made the monks vow to stay in one place. But that didn't stop them being wanderers. You know, Jesus was a wanderer... " Eli said wistfully.

"I guess you and I are too."

"Men like that don't have families," Eli continued. "They exist outside the social norms. In a sense, they live like the animals, children of innocence, I mean, in touch with nature, close to the seasons, paying attention to the heavens."

"They must watch the sky more than men and women who live with a roof over their heads," Tom agreed.

"They must learn to accept things as they are instead of as they wish they could be, to take life the way it is instead of the way the rule books say it's supposed to be. I certainly think that would suggest a different sort of morality. Who's to say that getting married to a woman and raising children by her is the right way to live? Especially if one doesn't feel the urge in his blood to do so." Eli seemed to be talking to himself as much as to Tom.

"Living as a wanderer, dependent on Providence, teaches them mortality and death," Eli pronounced solemnly. "No pretense for them that having children and possessions and houses and jobs gives any protection from the grave. No wonder they are hated by the established proprietors, householders and the fathers of families who do not wish to be reminded that all existence is transitory, that life is constantly wilting, and that merciless, icy death fills the cosmos all around... "

"Sounds like something I read in Herman Hesse," I interrupted Tom's narrative.

"He was German too."

"Swiss, I thought."

"Born in Germany," Tom answered, "but moved permanently to Switzerland as an adult. He was living in Switzerland when he wrote *Narcissus and Goldmund*."

"So you recognize the source of that quote," I said, victorious.

"Well, of course. So what? It's still profoundly true."

"That's an anachronism. I mean, in 1894 Eli Hauptmann couldn't have been quoting something Herman Hesse wrote in the 1930s."

"That kind of literal, linear thinking, Rick, is what gets you in trouble. That's what makes you so afraid of death. Life starts at one point and ends at another and then it's all over. Boom," he said, "and you're dead."

"And you're suggesting otherwise?"

"Each life is an experiment by God in creating a universe—if I may

55

cite Hesse again. You are that universe. Eternity is in the moment. Heaven isn't waiting for you to die. You're either in it right now, or you're not and never going to be."

"I see you learned your Upanishads," I answered cynically.

"What have you learned?"

"From you?" I leaned back in my chair and glared at him. "That I've got a pretty vivid imagination."

"You mean to create me?"

"Sure."

"And what am I?"

I laughed. "At times I've thought maybe you're a ghost in this house. I don't really know how ghosts live. Maybe you spend the summers in heaven when it's hot as hell down here in Texas. I don't know. Maybe this is heaven for you."

He looked at me intently. "Maybe this is heaven for you," he repeated my words exactly.

11

hat evening Elizabeth returned my call. She said she'd certainly be interested in coming down. She'd never seen the place. She only knew it as an investment her Dad had made when Texas was supposed to be booming. She joked about me calling the place "never-never land."

"I've got a pretty vivid imagination," I replied tersely. I didn't want her sending the men in white coats out here to protect me from myself.

Her father was doing better, she explained. His mood had changed from despair to anger. He'd made the headlines that morning accusing George White of using IV drugs and declaring that if White had just followed his advice about keeping his works clean he'd never have gotten ill. White's attorney answered by threatening to add breach of confidence to the suit.

She asked me what I was going to do after I finished the work here. I told her truthfully I didn't know. Then kidded with her again about her joining me on the estate. "We could be like king and queen of the manor."

"You," she said irreverently, "can be queen. Marla and I have got jobs here, obligations we can't get out of."

"Oh, 'Lizabeth, all existence is transitory, remember? Life's too short to worry about obligations. Do they really matter to you?"

"Your life may be too short. I'm planning to live to be a hundred and ten," she said and then caught herself. "Oh, Rick, I'm sorry. I didn't mean... "

I hadn't really noticed the implications of her comment. I was realizing how much like Tom Milam—or maybe Eli Hauptmann—I'd just sounded.

Tom declined Eli's offer to stay with him in Chicago, explaining he was going to stay with his friend Johnny Kincade. But, as the train was pulling into the station, Tom took Eli's address and promised he'd contact him once he was settled. He did want to see Eli Hauptmann again, though he didn't want to get any more indebted to him. He liked Eli and thought the visiting Swiss—he'd learned he was from Switzerland, not Germany after all—an important resource for his education. He knew he wanted to improve himself and this world-traveled scholar seemed an excellent role-model.

In fact, it was practically the middle of the night when the train arrived and so, once Eli had made his farewells, Tom checked his valise at the station and found a cheap hotel for the night. In the morning he'd go find Johnny.

The hotel proved scary. All night long he heard sounds of people grunting and groaning and shouting and slamming doors. He'd never experienced anything like that in San Antonio. He finally fell asleep and slept well into the morning. He was awakened by the housekeeper who told him he had only twenty minutes to get out or he'd have to pay for another night. He'd wanted to take a bath. He usually bathed at least once a week and the night on the train of sleeping in his clothes had left him feeling grimy. But apparently there was no time for that.

The desk clerk reluctantly gave Tom directions to find the address he had written out on a small piece of paper. Tom was surprised at how rude the people seemed. Very unlike Texas. Maybe this is what they mean by "the big city," he thought.

He got lost a couple of times but finally found what seemed to be the location he was seeking. It was a partially burned out tenement building. There were no apartments above the first floor. The piece of paper he held in his hand indicated Johnny lived in No. 6.

Tom knocked on the door of one of the first floor apartments. Soon the door was opened by a middle-aged black woman who explained in a heavy accent Tom had difficulty understanding that the upstairs had burned about two months previous. There was suspicion of arson. She said there'd been no trouble in the building for years. Then about six months ago a young man moved in—"'bout yo' age," she said with a hint of accusation. That started all the trouble.

"Some peoples say he no good. Me? I ain't got no 'pinion 'bout such matters. None o' my business." He was always bringing people around, she said, and some of the neighbors disapproved of the likes of them. Some of his friends looked practically like children. "Maybe dey burn'd dis place out to get rid o' him."

Her story didn't sound like it described Johnny. Tom knew him as a kind and friendly soul. He didn't understand why the neighbors would have treated him so. But, the lady assured him, "dat was 'im in No. 6. I knows cause I'd watch 'im come down dose stairs dere," she pointed. "He sit on da front steps and read. One day I come out 'n asked what you always readin'? 'Walt Whitman,' is what he say. Now I never heard of no Walt Whitman, sos I ask'd him who dat was. He read to me from the book. Fancy words. Didn't sound like no po'try I's ever heared befo'e. Dat's how comes I 'member da name. Walt Whitman. Sound like yo' friend?"

The coincidence was shocking. Tom left before it occurred to him to ask the most relevant question of all: in the fire that was supposed to have burned him out of his apartment and apparently destroyed most of the building was Johnny killed?

Where was he going to turn now? How was he going to find Johnny... If he were alive?

Tom carefully tucked Johnny's now useless address into his billfold and extracted the other address he'd stored there. He was a little afraid of pursuing that. What might he be getting himself into? He wanted to find Johnny.

He looked around and noticed a produce stand at the corner. Johnny probably bought his food from there. Maybe the grocer would know? He headed that direction, understandably a little afraid of identifying himself as a friend of the neighborhood villain.

12

s Tom was starting to tell me what happened, I heard a pounding on the back door and the familiar call: "Señor Rick!" The men had accidentally cut an electric line and I had to spend the rest of the morning helping them fix it.

In the late afternoon I went back to my desk. Instead of Tom waiting for me, Ben was there.

"I'm sure glad to see you," I greeted him. "You two sure know how to keep me in suspense."

"Gotta keep 'em wonderin'," he replied. "You learned that way back in that creative writing course you took sophomore year, didn't you?"

"You two seem to know more about my life than I do."

Ben laughed.

"I was worried about you," I said.

"That's sweet."

"Look, Ben, Tom reminded me of something I guess is obvious, I mean, that both of you would have died by now."

"Yep." He grinned at me.

"Well, then, I wonder… I mean… can you tell me about dying?"

Ben smiled broadly. "Ah, you want in on the secret?"

"I'm worried about it."

"I know," he answered solicitously, reaching out toward me. "But there's not much to tell. You know it all already, don't you? At least the part I could describe?"

"What do you mean?" I pressed.

"Remember, Rick, all that stuff about afterlife is really about how to live well now. Heaven is here and now. There may be something else, but unless you find it here and now, you certainly won't find it then."

"Okay, but is there 'something else'?"

"You're not going to let this go, are you?" He mockingly scolded me for my spiritual desperation. "Well, then, when you die, first there's the Clear Light. If you choose it, you know, you immediately go right into Godhood. But they say no one ever does; because they're always dragging their opinions and expectations along with them, people think 'Oh, this couldn't be it.' So you end up in that tunnel with the light at the far end and all your memories strung out along it."

"And then?" I knew I was about to get the answer I wanted. I was feeling curiously thrilled.

Ben laughed at me again, gently. "That's as much as I can tell you. It wouldn't make any sense. I mean, if you get to the light at the end of the tunnel there's no you left."

I must have looked heartbroken.

"Let me suggest a reference," he continued. "Look in the chapter called 'From Psychology to Metaphysics' in *The Hero with a Thousand Faces*. It's in that box of books in your closet."

"How do you know about that book?" I asked, thinking again I'd caught an anachronism.

"'Cause I'm inside your head," he laughed. "Now let's get back to the story."

"Well," I asked, "what happened to you?"

From a time when he was about ten years old and he and his friends played around an old rock quarry on the edge of town which filled with water every spring, Ben knew the only safe way to perform a dive into waters of unknown depth was to clutch your knees and pull yourself into a tight ball and keep your head up so whatever part of you hit the water or the bottom first wasn't your head or back. A cannonball the kids had called it.

He fell through the dark for a long time. He reassured himself the rains had come early this year. The water in the river was bound to be high—*if* he managed to hit the water. Peeking out above his knees, he could see stars shining brightly in the sky around him and spots of red-orange fire flickering below him. He wondered for a moment if he'd somehow missed the instant of death and was falling into hell. He searched his conscience for some mortal sin that would have barred him forever from God's presence. He thought of Jeremy Bates, of course, and about his hate for Joe Heatherson and his brother Jeff and the way he abandoned his father without even so much as a good-bye. But these had not been sins. If anything, they had been impulses—"actual graces" in theological jargon—sent by God to impel him to whatever fate had been planned for him. Then suddenly, without warning, the world turned icy cold.

Once he plunged into the swift-surging water, Ben began to roll as his momentum carried him deeper and deeper. Fighting the urge to panic, he kept his arms and legs tucked into the cannonball. The impact had knocked the air out of his lungs, but he wasn't suffocating yet, he knew, though he wondered how deep he could go before he struck bottom or was so far below the surface he couldn't make it up before his lungs gave out. He wondered if he might simply freeze solid, he was so cold. An image passed through his mind of being washed ashore somewhere down the river frozen into his cannonball. It almost made him laugh.

And then he realized he wasn't falling anymore. The laughter surged through him, turning into joy as he realized he'd survived the fall and providing him with the energy to kick out and begin to swim upwards. His heart was pounding and his chest was burning. Just then his head popped up through the surface of the water and he began to gulp in the night-air. He laughed and laughed as he let the water carry him downstream.

Once he'd caught his breath, he began to swim. He could see the lights of the fires along the bank and aimed in their direction. At the last he had to fight the current to reach the bank, but finally he was ashore and standing on solid ground, still laughing and sputtering river water, he climbed up toward where the encampments were. Only as he reached the edge of the firelight did it occur to him to wonder who'd be camping out here in this ravine beneath the railroad trestle. But at this point, what difference did it make? All he could think about was the warmth of those fires and the chill that even now was causing him to shiver uncontrollably.

As he stumbled toward the fire, Ben said, he fully understood that poem by Robert Service "The Cremation of Sam McGee."

"Now I know that's an anachronism," I interrupted his story. "That poem was about the Alaska Goldrush of the 1890s. I don't think it could have been written the poem yet."

"Don't blame me. You're the one dreaming this up. Better check your dates."

"Anyway," I summarized, "you didn't die."

"Right," he grinned and pointed his finger at me in a gesture that somehow seemed so affectionate it made my heart melt.

"I thought you were here to teach me a lesson about dying."

"The story about Sam McGee is about dying, isn't it? About finally getting oneself out of a painful situation."

"Is that the message you've got for me? Suicide?" I said that last word hesitantly, reverently.

"Not yet. We've got a job for you," he said happily. "Well, you find out about Sam McGee—and check out those books in the closet. But, anyway, I was so-o-o cold."

"Yo, lad," a voice called out. "Come warm your bones. You look a-mighty wet there."

"Train dicks throw you off?" another voice asked.

Shivering so bad he couldn't stop his teeth from chattering, Ben tried to answer, "I jumped first."

"Get up close here by the fire," the first man said. As Ben obeyed, he could see a circle of about five or six men lying or crouching around the blazing fire which was set in a shallow, rock-ringed pit. On one of the rocks set a soot-blackened coffee pot.

"Coffee... " he managed to spit out.

"And maybe some soup left," another man offered, getting up to look into a pot that had been left sitting cockeyed by the edge of the fire.

"Get his clothes off," a gruff voice commanded.

"I know what you want," somebody else teased. His voice sounded young.

"Look, kid, you'll warm up faster if ya don't have to dry the clothes on your body first," the gruff voice answered.

"Well, c'mon, c'mon," the man who had spoken first said to Ben. "Get over here by the fire before you freeze your balls off."

"Ah," somebody else said, "Josh'd love that. Add 'em to his collection."

"You shut your trap," the gruff-voiced man scolded.

As the first man poured coffee into a tin can and handed it gingerly to Ben, warning him it was hot, Ben managed to take a look around the circle. A couple of the men looked like the guys he'd met earlier in the boxcar he'd just escaped: hair and beard long and unkempt, clothes grimy, faces weathered. A couple of the others looked like farmers: hair trimmed, faces shaved—though perhaps in need of another shave soon, clothes rugged but recently washed. One of the men looked like what Ben imagined the legendary Paul Bunyan to have been: a huge man with bushy beard and hair pulled back into a braid; he wore a red plaid flannel shirt and had a knit cap pulled down over his forehead.

As Ben sipped at the coffee, letting its acrid taste and steaming heat warm his throat and insides, he noticed two other men. One looked like a school-teacher; he was wearing a white shirt and tie. He even had the wire-framed spectacles to complete the costume. Though the shirt collar was dirty and the tie crumpled, it was obvious the man struggled to keep some kind of dignity. Next to him was a boy, younger even than Ben. Perhaps father and son, Ben surmised at first. Though later as he watched them sleep curled together in the same bed-roll he wondered.

The Paul Bunyan character announced, "Look, I said for you to take those wet clothes off." Ben could feel an accusation of disobedience from a man who wasn't often disobeyed. From one look at his bulk Ben could understand why.

"He's right, you know," the school-teacher said. "You'll get warm much faster."

"Yeah," echoed the boy.

"Can I have a blanket?" Ben asked timidly as he stood up and began to unbutton his shirt. He noticed thankfully that his knapsack was still strapped to his shoulders.

"Don't play cute around here, kid," Paul Bunyan grumbled. "You ain't in no lady's finishin' school. And you ain't got no jocker to stake claim on you..."

Ben didn't know what that meant, but there was the word "jocker" again. When he'd heard it from one of the tramps on the train it had scared him. It scared him even more now.

"...yet," the mountain man added ominously.

Ben was careful to slip his socks off without revealing the small rolls of bills he had. He knew they wouldn't be his long if he did.

"Look, everybody," said the school-teacher, "we ought to introduce ourselves to this young man. He looks scared enough..."

"He looks like a wet rabbit," Paul Bunyan interrupted. "But, maybe a cute one—a little white bunny." He said the last words in a mock mincing accent.

"Josh, leave him alone a minute. He's just a kid." The man who'd spoken first, who apparently exercised some sort of authority in this circle, continued, "Four-Eyes is right. Let's make him welcome. Kid," he addressed Ben, "I'm called Jack The Hack, that's Four-Eyes over there..."

"Jeffery Singleton," the bespectacled man corrected the slang appellation. "This is Henry, Henry Peterson," he indicated the youngster.

"Fauntleroy," Jack The Hack explained the boy's slang name.

"Hey, call me Roy," the boy said spritely. "I ain't Henry anymore."

"Am not," Jeffrey Singleton corrected the grammar.

"I guess you've sort of met Josh," Jack continued.

"Joshua Anderson," the big man said. "M' monikey's Josh B' Gosh From Oshkosh. I used to work in Milwaukee," he explained. "In a fletchin' brewery," he laughed good-naturedly.

For a moment Ben didn't feel afraid of him anymore. "Like the overalls," he answered as friendly as he could. "Gosh, you were right about gettin' those clothes off, Josh. The fire feels really good."

"And you look good enough ta me ta eat right up," Josh replied. "Hey, Jack, maybe you better put 'im on the spit. Looks a little underdone to me. I got a mighty hunger a'comin'."

Ben's anxiety surged again. He felt so vulnerable standing there naked. He looked down at his body. His red-head's coloration always kept him from tanning and he hadn't been in the sun in a long time anyway. He felt he looked so pale, almost sickly, especially chilled as he was. His penis and scrotum were drawn up tight, looking boyish and underdeveloped. He looked so thin—'specially compared to a man of Josh's girth.

"He ain't as bad as he sounds, boy," Jack The Hack spoke again. He continued around the circle introducing the men by outlandish, usually rhyming monikers. Ben couldn't remember them all. "And what's your name?"

"Ben, Ben Mayfield."

"We gotta give you a monikey," Jack said.

"Hey, Ben," Josh commanded, "turn around."

"Huh?"

"Turn around. I wanta see your backside. Check out the hams."

Ben started to shiver again. He didn't like Josh's treating him like a piece of meat. He knew logically this was all a joke. But somehow he had to suspect there might be something real to the cannibalistic talk.

"Do as he says," Jack instructed.

"Well, mighty fine. Migh-ty fine!" Josh assessed.

"I got a monikey for ya. Pretty-Butt,"

"Pretty-Butt Ben," one of others in the circle echoed.

Jeffrey Singleton objected. "Don't start him off like that. He'll never survive."

"You just wish you could have 'im instead of little dick Fauntleroy," Josh quarrelled.

"Who you callin' little dick?" the boy shouted. "I'll show you somethin'."

"Henry, shut up."

"Don't call me Henry."

"Hey, Pretty-Butt, you warm yet?" Josh asked. Then getting up and lumbering around the circle, he handed Ben a blanket. "Look, I got me an extra here. You're welcome to it. Least for tonight."

The kindness of Josh's gesture, plus the softening tone of his voice, confused Ben. But he was glad to take the blanket to wrap himself in.

"You sleep over here, next to Roy," Singleton said. He looked defiantly at Josh.

"Just so long as he don't run off with m' blanket in the middle of the night. We got lots o' time to, you know, make friends." Josh giggled mockingly.

"There's some soup left here, Ben," Singleton offered. "You must be hungry."

63

"Oh, gosh, I guess so," Ben answered. He realized he was famished. But it took him a minute or two of looking pensively into the pot of soup Singleton had handed him to conclude this was beef soup and not human flesh he'd been offered. He didn't mind roughing it—though he barely understood yet what that meant—but he wasn't going to turn cannibalistic.

"You mean you thought that's what all the innuendo was about?" I joked with Ben.

"At first, yeah. 'Member I was pretty innocent."

"Yeah, I was innocent once myself."

I couldn't help thinking with a touch of irony of Eli Hauptmann's Hesse-like reference to the homeless wanderers as the children of innocence. What would Hauptmann have made of Joshua Anderson?

Maybe he would have preferred to be made by Josh.

Maybe that's innocence?

"Now *you* look pensive," Ben interrupted my thought.

"I was wondering if being innocent means being tightly self-controlled and disciplined or being totally spontaneous and instinctual."

"Why do you think it's either/or," Ben asked and then, as usual, disappeared leaving me with an—at least profound-*sounding*—riddle, like a Zen Buddhist *koan*.

13

n the morning Ben woke, sore from sleeping on hard ground, to see the hobo camp stretched out all through the steep-walled river valley. Dominating the whole scene was the railroad trestle, rising up above the river like some huge machine, mathematically structured, square and exact, contrasting with the free-flowing natural shapes of trees and rocks and the sinuous curve of the river which had cut the valley and demanded the construction of the trestle in the first place. A delicate mist rose up from the river in pale whiffs of translucence. The air was fresh and cold. Scattered through the valley were little encampments, most centered around a smoking fire. There was a sharp tang in the air from the smoldering embers. It was still early, the sun lit the sky above, but had not yet risen high enough for its rays to penetrate to the bottom of the valley. Most of the men were still sleeping, though a few were already awake to stoke the fires, gather wood, and prepare whatever would pass for coffee.

A few men were bathing in the river. Ben shivered to think how cold the water must be. He pulled the blanket Josh had loaned him tighter around his shoulders and felt for the clothes he stripped off the night before. They were still wet he discovered, as of course were the extra things he had in the knapsack he'd used as a slightly soggy pillow. He wondered what he was going to do this morning. He couldn't spend the day wrapped in a blanket. He reconciled himself to putting on the damp dungarees and chambray shirt he was wearing when he jumped from the train. They'd certainly dry in a while, he told himself, trying to avoid remembering times in the past when he'd had to wear wet clothes and had usually developed rashes between his legs and under his arms where the fabric chafed. He reminded himself he was going to have to accept certain hardships as a fact of his new life.

"'Mornin', Ben," he heard a voice say behind him as he was struggling to get his legs into the jeans. "You're up early. You can help me gather wood." It was Roy. "Here, wanna swallow?" he held out a bunged-up tin cup. "I got some coffee from the guys at the camp over there," he said pointing. "We'll get some brewin' over here in a minute."

Ben gratefully accepted the cup. It *was* coffee, though very weak and not as hot as he'd hoped for. He'd have liked milk and sugar in it, but those were luxuries he probably wasn't going to see for a while. "Thanks." He jumped up as he pulled his shirt on and buttoned it, shivering.

"You'll warm up faster if you move around some," Roy advised. "And I need some help." He grinned.

"Sure, show me what to do."

"Well, you can see these guys have cleaned out this whole area. But up there," he pointed to the woods that grew down the sides of the valley, "you can still find some sticks and stuff. Josh's got an ax. After while we can use that to maybe get some big logs for burnin'."

Roy had dumped a small bundle of sticks next to the fire. "Want to throw these on?" Ben asked helpfully.

"Let's get some more first. Don't want ta burn up all the kindlin' yet."

Ben followed as Roy led the way up the steep hillside. The worst part of this trek was the squishy feeling of his wet socks in his wet shoes. The wad of cash in one of them made him limp.

As they gathered armfuls of sticks and broken tree limbs, Ben tried to make conversation. "How'd you end up out here?"

"Me and Mr. Jeffery, well, got in trouble. He was the schoolteacher. I kinda took a likin' to him. And my ma found out and told the minister and things just got worse."

"You mean cause you liked your teacher?"

"Uh, you don't get my drift, do ya? I mean, it wasn't so much cause I liked him as that he liked me." Roy was obviously being evasive. "My pa had got himself killed a couple o' years ago doin' the hay bailin'. It was just ma and me. She moved us into town; she got a job mendin' clothes for the laundry. She told me I oughta make friends with Mr. Jeffery so I'd get, you know, a man's influence.

"But then when I did, she didn't like the influence he was havin', I guess. Anyway, she waled the tar out o' me and the sheriff went for Mr. Jeffery—that's him wit' me, you know—Four-Eyes... "

"I know."

"We beat it out o' town fore they could lynch Mr. Jeff or somethin'. We heard there was goin' to be a meetin' at the church. Jeff come an' got me and we jumped a freight. Like most everybody else down there." He pointed down into the valley. Ben noticed the sun was just beginning to illumine the first of the encampments high up the valley. It surprised him how peaceful and beautiful everything seemed. He'd begun to forget about his wet shoes and his worries about rashes. Roy had been right. The exertion of climbing had warmed him up.

"Me too," Ben answered. "But I still don't understand... "

"You just too innocent," young Roy scolded laughing. "Ya mean I gotta spell it out? One night I was over at Mr. Jeffery's doin' my homework and it was cold and I sorta crawled up in his lap in front o' the fire. And pretty soon, well, I guess I got carried away... Shucks, I just liked playin' wit' him. No harm in that."

All of a sudden it hit Ben what Roy was talking about: the same innocent affection that had been his own downfall. But Roy seemed like just a boy...

"Look, we better git down there wit' this wood or Josh'll wake up and won't find no coffee and be pissed. He can be mighty mean."

"You been campin' here long?" Ben changed the subject.

"About a week or two now. Ya lose track o' the time. Mr. Jeffery heard 'bout some work pickin' fruit—maybe cherries or plums or somethin' south o' here—in a couple o' weeks. We just hangin' out here till then. These guys ain't so bad."

"How about Josh? He scared me last night."

"Yeah, he can be pretty scary. But he's not so bad. I don't think. The first couple o' days we were here—we'd met up with a hobo on the train who told us 'bout this here jungle—well, it seemed like Josh was tryin' to take me away from Mr. Jeffery. Said he could use a wife to fix 'im his coffee and... you know... I got real scared. But Mr. Jeffery stood up to 'im and Josh backed down. Said he'd never stole what wasn't his to start wit'.

"But, Ben, look here. I'd be careful if I was you. I mean, you ain't got nobody watchin' out for you yet. You need a jocker of your own."

There was that word again.

A while later, Jack the Hack was pouring coffee into a tin can for Ben. "I traded a couple of pints o' moonshine whiskey for a pound of coffee," he whispered conspiratorially. "Figured I needed to wake up in the mornin's more than I needed to put myself to sleep at night. My belly was achin' a lot from the moonshine. Maybe it was bad stuff," he cackled, "maybe I got the better end o' the deal. Coffee sure is damn good."

"Damn good," Ben concurred, hoping to please his benefactor. The coffee didn't taste all that good, but it was hot and sweet and he was hungry. He was grateful Jack had thought to include sugar in the deal.

"...and it satisfies my friend Josh here," Jack continued, pouring another cup for the big mountain man. Ben wondered if Jack was simply intimidated by Josh's size and strength or if he was buying himself protection or if he just liked the man. "Josh sure is a good man ta have on yo' side in case o' trouble," Jack continued to Ben almost as if Josh were not sitting across the fire from him listening. "You could do a lot worse in findin' a friend."

"Yeah, Jack 'n me been buddies for years. Met 'im first time I was out on the road. He showed me the tricks o' the trade."

Jack whispered to Ben, "Josh is a little simple. Maybe got hit on the head when he was a baby." Then he continued loud enough for Josh to hear also, "Got a temper, but he can be real sweet too."

"Yeah," answered Josh lazily, "maybe just like this here little Pretty-Butt."

Ben felt a wave of fear pass through him. "Hey," he retorted. "Don't call me that. Please. My name is Ben."

"Okay, Benjy you are."

He was surprised how easily Josh backed down from that. Maybe the man wasn't all that bad after all. In fact, maybe he'd be a good friend to have, Ben thought, scheming just a bit now how he could best assure his own survival in what seemed like a threatening situation.

By helping Roy with the wood-gathering and thus providing the circle with fire, Ben had earned a right to share in the food. As it happened, one of the men produced a hatful of fresh eggs he'd stolen the previous day from a chicken farm near the railroad tracks. Another added a loaf of bread he'd been given as a handout by an old woman who'd sympathized with his plight. Jeffery Singleton still had some of the apples he'd brought with him when he and Roy fled. All together there was enough for everyone in the circle, including Ben, to have an almost filling meal.

Even as they were finishing breakfast, conversation turned to plans for dinner. Several of the men talked about hunting rabbits in the woods. Another said he'd be going into a nearby town to see what he could beg or steal. Ben was amazed that with as many men as there were out here it would be possible at all to live by scrounging. Jack pointed out a ragged tent down the valley aways. "The Church Auxiliary comes out here on Sunday and Wednesday mornings and sets up a soup line. 'Course you gotta sit and listen to the preacher tell you what damned souls ya are for being out here 'stead o' workin'. I'd sure be workin' if there were any jobs to be had."

"Not me," spoke up the man who'd produced the eggs. Ben couldn't remember his moniker. "I'm out for the adventure. Don't want no job, no responsibilities."

"Now, Panama, what kind of a way to live is that?" chided Jeffrey Singleton, reminding Ben that the adventurer's name was Panama Pat. (It annoyed him momentarily that most of these men had alliterative appellations that suggested their place of origin or perhaps their preferred destiny, not denigrating nicknames like the one Josh proposed for him. Only then did it occur to him that he had to choose his own moniker.)

"Sure that's the way to live. Right out here in God's country, like the lilies o' the field. Trust in the Lord, I always say."

"Pass the bread, I always say," answered Jack.

"I mean it," insisted Panama. "What's life for if it ain't for the enjoyment of creation. Those people who lock themselves up in them 'spensive houses, dolled up in fancy clothes, they're the ones missin' out... "

"I'd like to be back in a house myself," little Roy said plaintively.

"It'll be okay, Henry. We'll find us a place soon." Mr. Singleton patted Roy on the back. Ben could hear guilt in his voice as he reassured the boy. "I don't know about this God business of yours, Panama. It was the preacher that got us thrown out of our nice warm house... "

"I ain't talkin' 'bout no preachers," Panama rebutted angrily. "They just as bad as the rest. I bet none of them ever lived like Jesus—'the Son of Man hath no place to lay his head'." He was kind of ranting. He pulled a small Bible out of his jacket pocket and started reading seemingly at random. Ben was put off by that, but he had been moved by the hobo's spiritual sentiments. It hadn't really occurred to him before that this strange adventure he'd been thrown into might be as much a continuation of the spiritual life he'd been taught to value as his four years in the seminary. Maybe Panama Pat was right. Maybe life as a hobo was closer to the life Jesus lived than life as a Jesuit priest in some secure Church job. Still... Memories of how he thought he was going to live his life flooded his mind. It wasn't supposed to be like this.

The banter went on. Sometimes the men talked about serious issues, sometimes about gossip; sometimes they told jokes, sometimes stories about how to survive in this city or that; sometimes they seemed like wise philosophers, sometimes like drunks and criminals.

Ben noticed Josh had said very little. He probably didn't think too much, Ben imagined. What few comments Josh made, usually about simple survival issues, had softened Ben's impression of him. Maybe Jack was right. Maybe Josh would be a good man to have as a friend. He certainly knew more about this kind of life than Ben did. And Ben wasn't really interested in any of the other men in the circle. He felt a sort of kinship with Roy and Jeffrey Singleton, but he was reluctant to admit it and afraid of getting mixed up with the wrong crowd if he seemed too friendly with them. He liked Jack The Hack, but realized he was just an old drunk who might be somber now but probably wouldn't be for long. Panama Pat was appealing in a spiritual way, but Ben didn't want to get involved with anybody toting a Bible. His face reddened with memory of the Biblical passages the Master at St. Athanasius' had hurled at him before finally casting him out as a damned sinner.

"I been thinkin' 'bout headin' on to Chi," he heard Josh reply to somebody's comment about leaving of the hobo jungle. It brought him out of his reverie back into the real world in which he needed to get on with his journey. He didn't want to become a hobo himself. He was still thinking about that job in Chicago he was expecting to find. Ben screwed up his courage, wondered if he were making a terrible mistake, and then bravely added that he too was "headin up to Chi."

14

he first thing is you gotta be choosy," Josh told Ben. "You was lucky last time. You coulda been killed dead jumpin' outta that train. Next time you will be. So. You gotta figger out what trains are gonna have dicks on 'em. The railroad's can't put those damn bulls on every train so's you need to pick 'em right.

"My rule is this: short train's easier to stop, it'll fit on a trestle like that," he pointed back at the great scaffolding they'd just climbed as the first stage of their journey north to Chicago, "and it takes 'em less screws to patrol it. So maybe you avoid them kinds of trains. Look for the long ones. Make sense?"

"Sure," Ben agreed. He was glad to get some practical advice about this unconventional—but by now necessary—mode of transportation.

"'You gotta stay clear o' baggage cars. You get in a blind-baggage and you might as well be turnin' yo'self in."

"What's that?"

"Car wit' no door out of it from the front. A trap."

"Oh," Ben had replied. He was still so inexperienced some of Josh's tips were meaningless.

Josh explained how to pace the train when it was moving slow and which handles to grab onto and which to avoid. "You grab that damn bar on a boxcar 'n the door's liable to roll shut and cut yo' fingers off," he pointed out as they watched a train rumble by. "Now you see'd there weren't nobody up in the cab but the engineer. That's a mighty good sign. 'Cause when they're gonna timber the po' blokes ridin' the rails, they usually start in at both ends o' the train. Got it?"

"Makes sense."

"You ready?"

"Now?"

"What better time 'n right now," Josh said as he started a slow lope alongside the moving train. Josh's legs were longer than Ben's and it took a major effort on the young man's part to keep up with his mentor. But by carefully mimicking Josh's technique, in a moment he was on board and standing next to the big man. From the open door of the boxcar they waved as if in a farewell to the hobo jungle in the ravine now left behind them.

In a couple of hours the train was making its way by neighborhoods in the distance with neat little white houses surrounded by white picket fences. As they got a little closer in to the city the neat white houses gave way to dingy tenements alongside the tracks. "Gotta git out 'fore the train goes into the yard, 'cause there all kinds of bulls just awaitin' in there to timber yo' ass. Hear?"

"Got it, Josh," Ben had replied over and over as he tried to assimilate all this new knowledge. He was grateful to Josh. By this time the anxiety he'd been feeling had abated. He was still afraid, of course, of the big man's strength. He'd come to think of Josh as a little like his dad's prize bull. The animal was docile most of the time, but when you were in his pen you had to keep an eye on him lest he suddenly turn on you. If he did, there'd be no soft-talking him then. The only thing you could do was run. Ben was most afraid of what might happen if Josh got to drinking. He suspected that's what had been responsible for his frightening demeanor the first night.

After they jumped off the train, rolling through gravel that scratched Ben's hands and face, Ben got Josh to explain where they were in relation to the city of Chicago. Then he thanked Josh and said he'd be on his way.

"No you don't," Josh said affectionately. "I cain't let my new friend go roamin' off in no town like this here Chi. Too many things to hurt ya. Stick wit' me. Least till ya git yo' bearin's."

"I'm really thankful for all your help, Josh. But, you know, now I'm here I gotta go find work and a place to live."

"Well, where ya gonna go?"

Ben was momentarily dumbfounded by the practicality of the question.

"See, see. You stick wit' me. Couple o' days more. We'll find you a good kip-house or maybe a song 'n dance o' your own." Josh grabbed Ben by the neck in what was obviously intended as a gesture of affection, but smacked too much of a gesture of dominance for Ben to handle it easily.

"What's a kip-house?" he shrugged his shoulders and pulled away.

"See, see. The kid still needs m' help." Josh laughed heartily, "A kip's a lodgin' house and a song 'n dance is yo' ticket for scoff."

Ben was a little bewildered. His quizzical look brought further explanation from Josh that if he was going to be a successful hobo he had to develop a line, either a convincing begging story that would bring tears to the eyes of any rube he tried it on or a con that would get him some fast cash.

"I don't really want to be a successful hobo."

"You be a gay-cat then for all I care."

"What's that?"

"Ya begs when ya begs and works when ya works. But ya stay free and loose, ready to git back on the turf when ya had enough o' respectability."

"Okay, so you'll show me how to be one of these 'gay-cats.' But then I got to get settled here in Chicago."

"We'll see. We'll just see." Josh guffawed in a way that scared Ben again. What if he couldn't manage to get away from this man?

At the same time, Josh's suggestion made sense. Not that Ben wanted to become one of these "gay-cats," whatever that was, but that he could still use Josh's assistance. After all, Ben was just an innocent farmboy. His only experience of the world beyond a farming town was in a seminary. Neither of those seemed like preparation for a city like Chicago.

Chicago. Chicago. Chi. Every time he said it to himself he felt a rush of excitement. He really was in the big city now.

That had all been in daylight. Now it was dark. He was following Josh deeper and deeper into the low-life center of the city. He was getting frightened and, for that very reason, more and more dependent on Josh. Josh seemed to know exactly where he was going, but hadn't bothered to tell Ben.

After a while they arrived at a boarded-up warehouse. "The way in's 'round here," Josh pointed out as he slipped into a narrow crack between brick buildings alongside the warehouse. There was just barely enough room for him to pass through. In a couple of feet the opening widened and then soon they came upon a break in the brick wall where a window had once been. Josh picked Ben up in a single swift motion and deposited him on the inside of the wall and then clambered through the opening himself.

There was little light. Ben could barely see. He had to follow Josh who seemed to know the way by heart. There were crates and what looked like piles of brick strewn around randomly on the floor. Josh led Ben through easily. As they rounded a broken wall they came upon a fire blazing in what must have been an open courtyard or a wagon depot behind the warehouse. A circle of five or six men were gathered around the fire swapping stories.

As Josh entered the orangey light, with Ben a foot or two behind, one of the shadowy figures raised his head, noticed Josh, and shouted a greeting, "Josh B'Gosh, c'mon sit yo'self down. Take a *big-g-g* load off them feet o' yours."

Everybody laughed good-naturedly.

"This here's Ben."

Ben made a slight bow in acknowledgment of the introduction.

"What's his monikey?" somebody asked.

"Don't got one. New to the road," Josh answered as he sat down in the circle and beckoned to Ben to sit next to him. "I been thinkin' maybe Benjy Pretty-Butt'd be a good 'un for 'im."

"Hey, I didn't know you was into jockerin' boys."

"Ain't never said I was. Just said my friend Benjy here got a nice lookin' bee-hind and I thinks he deserves the recognition. Besides, the rest o' you keep away." Josh said the last menacingly.

Ben felt frightened by the nickname Josh suggested. It reactivated all his fears. But then he recognized what seemed to be a workable strategy. As long as these men thought he belonged to Josh, nobody was going to bother him. He just wasn't sure what all the innuendo was about. He understood there was a sexual tone to it that suggested what he intuitively guessed the Father Master had meant by "the sin of Sodom." Though that knowledge didn't exactly explain things to him. In seminary that sin was too unspeakable to

71

explain, so he'd never understood what it was supposed to be. All he knew was that young boys sometimes got treated like women by certain kinds of… well, perverted men. He knew he didn't want that to happen to him. But he didn't really understand what it would be like if it did. He knew it had also to do with what happened between him and Jeremy Bates that night that now seemed so long ago. He wasn't sure that he didn't want that to happen again. But what had that to do with being treated like a woman?

Most of all he was confused because he'd imagined perverts to be rare and maybe living only in Canaan or Philistia. He didn't think they had much to do with hobos and tramps—men who might be out of work and down on their luck, but were still Americans and still Christians… It all just confused him and made him feel that much more dependent on Josh. And that seemed like a double-bind to him, though he would have had a hard time explaining what he meant.

"Hey, m' monikey's Ben Blest," he suddenly exclaimed. He'd been thinking about what kind of nickname to take. Nothing had sounded right to him till just now when he felt a wave of fear and threat pass over him and then dissipate. He'd said the name with as much of a hobo accent as he could muster. "Yeah, I been real blest. I mean, finding Josh here. He done took me under his wing and showed me the ropes. Yeah, God bless."

Ben thought maybe the sound of a little religious fervor would keep the other guys away from him. At least, that's what *he*'d felt earlier when Panama Pat had started in on his Biblical jag.

Josh just smiled and then scruffed Ben on the head much as he might have a stray dog that had followed him. "We just come from down south. Been runnin' from the screws all day. We're mighty hungry. You blokes got some grub?" He winked at Ben.

With that song and dance Josh got them a share in the thick beef and carrot stew that was cooking on the side of the fire—and the offer of a swig from a gallon crock of moonshine whiskey.

Ben passed on the whiskey, then when Josh whispered to him that it made him look sissy, he took the jug and held the spout to his mouth. He let a little of the burning, bitter alcohol slip through his lips, but then passed the jug. He didn't like how it tasted at all. And he didn't like how Josh was drinking it with gusto.

"You didn't understand about gay sex at all?" I asked incredulously.

"Rick, you have got to remember this was 1890's. There were no sex education classes in school. There were no sex books in the library. The only way to know about sex was from your parents or from, you know, dirty talk with other kids. But none of them knew what they were talking about. My dad had sorta explained the birds and bees stuff, but not the rest."

"Yeah, but weren't you sexual yourself? Couldn't you guess?"

"If you mean had I discovered ejaculation on my own, I guess the answer is yes. But I didn't connect that with sex. I didn't really connect what I'd done with Brother Jeremy as sex. You know, you people today live in a very different world. It doesn't seem to me any human beings ever had quite so much knowledge and freedom about sexuality."

"What about the French court or Renaissance Italy?" I objected as though I really knew something about the sex lives of the rich and famous in the times of Marie Antoinette or Lucretia Borgia.

"Maybe certain aristocrats all through history have been sexually liberated. But even so they probably didn't have the words for it."

"Speaking of words," I changed the subject. "What did Josh mean by 'gay-cat'?"

"Exactly what he said: a tramp who went to work now and then, especially when he didn't have the nerve to beg or steal."

"Anything to do with our word 'gay' today?"

"*Your* word, you mean," Ben distanced himself from my world. "I don't know. Nobody seems to know where that word gay came from. In that hobo world it seemed to suggest youth and timidity, maybe a lack of macho."

"I'm surprised how much homosexuality you seem to be alluding to."

"Look who I'm talking to," he laughed as if to attribute the homosexual interpretation all to me. I was reminded momentarily of that story—is it Woody Allen who tells it?—about the man who gave sexual meanings for all the Rorschach ink blots, then when his psychiatrist suggested that perhaps he was sex-obsessed, the patient replied, "Who me? You're the one with all the dirty pictures." Maybe all our sexual liberation, seemingly so hard won through the 1960s and 70s, was really just a matter of having the words for what human beings have always done. They just didn't talk about it—and interpret it—in the same way.

"Is it really so surprising? Weren't there a lot of homosexuals among the beats and the hippies?"

"Were there?" I thought about my own excursions into hippie life. That's where I'd first seen openly gay people.

"Sure. In every counterculture. Homosexuals—male and female— are bound to show up disproportionately in socially ostracized groups and idealistic movements. You saw the same thing I did."

"You think there was a parallel between your experiences as a tramp and mine as a hippie?"

Ben looked at me with a cockeyed, half-smiling expression. He tapped at his temple with his right index finger. "Bright, huh? Real bright. You're basing my story on your life, aren't you? Well, why else do you think we're talking about this stuff?"

I was embarrassed by Ben's affectionately cynical candor and changed the subject. "So did Josh get drunk?"

"Oh, Rick, that was the start of pure hell."

Later that night after the fire had burned down a little and the men had gotten drunk and sleepy, Josh suggested to Ben that they bed down behind a pile of crates a dozen yards or so from the circle. "'Case it rains tonight, we'll be dry," Josh pointed up at the sky. He was right, it was cloudy.

For the first time in his life Ben saw a night sky lit from underneath by the lights of a large city. For a moment it frightened him. His image of hell, conveyed through Catholic training not at all unlike that the young James Joyce would be experiencing at about the same time and writing about in a few years, had included fire-lit skies.

"Just lights from the city," Josh explained. "Hardly ever gets dark 'round here. You just a country boy. Wait'll ya see—" He laughed drunkenly.

Josh had his two blankets in a roll he carried slung from his waist over one shoulder. He undid the roll and spread the blankets out.

"This for me?" Ben asked.

"One for the ground and one for cover. You just climb in here wit' me. We'll stay nice 'n warm."

Ben would have preferred rolling up in a blanket of his own, but he was trying to humor Josh. Earlier the mountain man had got into a shouting match with one of the other hobos. It had scared Ben and convinced him he needed to keep things as peaceful as possible.

Josh lay down on the blanket and then pulled the other over him. He lay looking up at the arched ceiling for a moment, waiting for Ben to get under the cover with him. About the time Ben did so, Josh complained, "It's hot, ain't it. And this here floor's mighty hard." He sat up and carefully unbuttoned the red plaid flannel shirt he wore. As he pulled it off, Ben was repulsed by the man's strong odor. "Make a pillow outta this," Josh said as he rolled the shirt up and lay it at the head of the blanket.

Ben closed his eyes. After a moment, Josh punched him on the arm. "How come you don't make yourself a pillow, Benjy?"

"Ben, call me Ben, please Josh. Look, I'll use my knapsack."

Josh was silent a while and then said gruffly, "Take off your shirt, Benjy."

Ben recognized the tone of voice from his first encounter with Josh. All of a sudden he began to question his reassessment of the man's character.

"Take off your dungarees."

"What are you talkin' 'bout, Josh?" Ben pretended even more ignorance than in fact he was suffering from. "You was gonna protect me?"

"I won't hurt ya, Benjy Pretty-Butt. I just wanna touch you. Won't hurt ya none at all. Promise."

"I don't know, Josh."

"I ain't been with no lady in a long time. Promise I'll just run my hand over your butt and 'magine you some gorgeous girl. You don't havta do nothin' but lie there. I won't hurt ya none."

Ben lay stiff, almost paralyzed.

"C'mon, Benjy, ya gotta show me a little thanks for all the help I been givin' ya." Josh sounded now like a little boy begging for a chance to play with a puppy. "Just a touch, just a touch."

"You'll go to sleep then?"

"Sure, I'll sleep just like a baby." His voice was soft and harmless. He's just an overgrown child, Ben told himself. I've managed to keep him under control all day. Maybe I can still.

"Well, Josh, you promise... "

"Look, damn it. I said I promised I wouldn't hurt you, you little son of a bitch." The anger that Ben had been afraid of was suddenly rising.

"Okay, okay. Calm down, Josh. Just calm down."

"You'll let me touch... " Again he sounded like a child.

"Just for a minute," Ben agreed. He pushed his dungarees down to his knees and rolled over on his stomach. That allowed Josh the chance to touch his backside, but seemed to keep him protected otherwise.

Josh's hand was hard and calloused. Ben's muscles tightened everywhere that hand contacted him. At the same time there was something soothing about the warmth of the strong, muscular hand caressing his buttocks. He was confused about what to feel. "You like that, Josh?" he asked tentatively. "You can think about making love with a lady?"

Josh's fingers strayed between Ben's legs, lightly touching his testicles. The sensation sent a wave of pleasure—and terror—through Ben. "What're you doin'?"

"Thinkin' about the last lady I fucked, Ben," Josh answered languorously. "She wasn't near pretty as you... " He was silent for a while as he continued to lightly caress Ben's buttocks, his fingers occasionally searching between the cheeks. Each time Ben would tighten up and shift a little to communicate his displeasure. He didn't understand at all what Josh was doing. Whatever was going on wasn't sex. He knew that. This was dirty, that's all. People don't touch each other's, uh, uh...

Josh rolled closer so his big bulk was pressed against Ben's side. He pushed Ben's shirt up to increase the skin contact. Ben heard Josh murmur under his breath, "I told ya to take off the fuckin' shirt."

Ben wasn't sure he was supposed to hear that. He didn't want to have heard it and pretended not to. He was becoming less and less conscious of what Josh was doing and more and more aware of his fear—fear of Josh and maybe fear of his own enjoyment of the touch.

"Lemme fuck you, Benjy," Josh said softly, slowly. Ben wasn't sure what that meant. It was a forbidden word, he knew. He knew it was something men did to women. But he didn't understand—at least in his conscious mind— what that was. He knew it had something to do with what Jeremy Bates had done to him.

He'd gotten in terrible trouble for letting Jeremy do that to him...

with him. But there was nobody here to scold him or throw him out.

"What do you mean, Josh?"

"Lemme fuck you. Please?" Josh nibbled on the top of Ben's ear, sending shivers down his back. He tried to turn his head away, but Josh's tongue followed.

"I said please." Josh's voice took on the edge of hardness Ben had been trying to prevent.

"What is it you want to do, Josh. You said you just wanted to touch me and think about doing somethin' else."

"You goddamned son of a bitch. You think you can play wit' me. You tease me all day long, struttin' around lookin', lookin' as pretty as ya please." His voice was angry.

All of a sudden Ben felt Josh's full weight press down on him. He could feel something hard like a stick pushed between his legs. Josh's erect penis, he realized. The man pushed himself up with one hand and apparently was maneuvering his sex organ with the other. Ben could feel the head of the hard penis against his anus. He felt a burning sensation as the weight against the penis increased and the hardness pushed into him.

For the first time it dawned on him clearly what Josh had in mind. And it terrified him. "No, Josh. Don't. You can't do that. It's not right."

"Shut up, you bastard. Open your legs or I'll hurt you more," Josh answered his objections through clenched teeth. "I'm gonna fuck yo' ass."

Ben squirmed. He managed to get Josh's penis away from his anus. Josh pulled back and then hit him on the side of the head with the back of his hand.

The force, and Josh's shift in position, allowed Ben to roll out from under the man's bulk. He grabbed at his knapsack and swung it as hard as he could. It struck Josh squarely in the face.

"My eye," he screamed and started whimpering.

"What happened?" Ben said. He hadn't meant to hurt Josh.

"Somethin' sharp hit my eye," Josh whimpered again. "

"Sharp?" Ben questioned, feeling the front of the knapsack even as he struggled with his clothes. The knapsack had a heavy metal buckle right in the middle of the front flap. The prong extended beyond the edge of the buckle. Ben could feel it in the dark. "Maybe the point hit your eye… "

Josh raged, "You goddamn bastard."

In the momentary pause, Ben managed to pull his dungarees up to his waist. He looked down to make sure he was wearing his shoes. At that moment, Josh jumped to his feet, still bellowing. Ben turned and started to run.

As he darted past the circle of men around the fire, some of them apparently still awake and talking, he heard cat-calls and whistles. "Wha'sa matter, Josh. Yo boy don't wanna git jockered?

Ben could hear the sound of Josh's bare, or maybe stockinged, feet running after him. And he could hear Josh howling. "You blinded me, you bitch. I'll get yo' ass for this."

He ran faster and faster, trying to figure out the path through the crates and piles of debris. It was so dark up here away from the fire. How was he going to get out? He stopped and crouched, hiding behind a dark mass of something. Peeking around he thought he could see Josh as a dark shadow moving through more darkness. He couldn't be sure. He began to fear that at any moment the big man might suddenly loom over him and literally beat him to death—or worse. He thought of the pain that shot through him when Josh tried to push his penis into him. Ben trembled all over. The sexuality of it all confused him totally. The good feelings were all mixed with guilt and violence.

"I'll find you, you bugger. I'll find you. You'll regret the day you tried to jigger Josh B'Gosh." He shouted it almost ceremoniously, like a vow. And that made Ben even more frightened. He knew he could get out of this warehouse. It was just a matter of waiting for Josh to go back toward the fire. But what if Josh kept hunting for him all over Chicago. How could he know? Maybe he couldn't stay in Chicago.

Ben prayed that the buckle of the knapsack had only grazed Josh's face and that in a day or two he'd forget the incident. And forget being humiliated in front of the other hobos; Ben imagined Josh must be feeling stung by that as well. But Ben also realized that in the dark, the sharp point could have actually slashed Josh's open eye. And then he wouldn't be likely to forget the incident any time soon at all.

Ben heard a commotion as some of the others came up toward where he was. They found Josh and started joking with him, laughing and making fun of him, then they led him back to the fire to see if his eye was really hurt.

"Damn queer kid," he heard Josh's voice fading as he was taken back to the back of the building. "Wait'll I get my hands on 'im... "

Ben took the opportunity and scurried in the direction Josh had been going. Indeed, the break in the wall was there. He scrambled up over the wall and down the narrow passageway and out into the street.

15

 he city of Chicago was a dream—and a nightmare. Ben slept in a large wooden crate he found about five blocks from the warehouse. The crate stank of urine, but it offered shelter and a place to hide till daylight came and he could get his bearings.

He woke to the clip-clop of horses and the clanging of trolley bells. He was careful to peek through a crack in the crate before crawling out. He didn't want to find Josh or one of his cronies prowling the street. Of course, he couldn't be sure he'd recognize any of the men who'd been around that fire last night. So he had to wait till the block was pretty deserted. Fortunately, he was on a side street with only occasional traffic and after a while he spied no one walking nearby and crawled out from under the crate and hurried down to the main thoroughfare from where he could hear the clanging bells.

"State Street" read a sign on a pole at the intersection. The street was bustling with traffic, both on foot and in carriages and streetcars. For the first time he saw horseless carriages running on rails down the middle of the street. Electricity, he told himself amazed. It'd be easy to get lost in the crowd. He wasn't sure which way to go. Did it matter? Letting whim decide for him he turned to the left, noticing a sweet shop that direction in the middle of the block on the other side.

Earlier, while still in the crate, he'd pulled his small wad of cash out of his sock and peeled off a couple of bills and stuck them in his pocket. He wasn't sure how long the cash was going to last him. He needed to find a job, but first he needed to find something to eat. He stood peering into the window of the shop letting his mouth water at the thought of the dark chocolate brownies and the crisp apple squares and the slices of spice cake heaped high with sugar frosting. The door swung open and a gentleman dressed richly in a dark gray frock coat with a creamy-white silk ascot at his neck stepped out, looked up and down the street—noticing Ben with disdain—and then walked on. Through the open door wafted the smells of coffee and hot cocoa.

Ben opened the door and stepped in. A little bell at the top of the door tinkled to announce him. He stood for a moment transfixed by the smells and sights. The whole place sparkled with cut-glass crystal and polished brass. Ben had never before in his life seen anything so beautiful.

A woman with her long blond hair tied into a severe bun on the back of her head was standing at the shiny brass coffee urn with her back to Ben. She was humming to herself as she polished the urn with a white cotton cloth. After a brief inspection of the shine, she turned to wait on her newest customer. "And what can I do for… " Suddenly her exaggerated smile disappeared. "Get outta here, boy."

"Please, Ma'am, can't I get a cup of coffee and a sweet roll?" Ben begged politely, only then realizing that with his knapsack, dirty clothes, and unkempt hair he looked like a street urchin.

"We don't want the likes of you round here. We don't give hand-outs."

Ben pulled his hand of his pocket and held up the dollar bill he'd been clutching. "I wasn't asking for a hand-out."

The lady looked around the shop as though making sure there were no respectable customers to observe her breach of etiquette in talking with the urchin. Her face was still stern, but she beckoned to Ben, "Here boy, you come back here." She showed him into a small space just off the kitchen where the garbage cans were kept. "Now, what do you want?"

Ben didn't exactly like the accommodations, but he was hungry. "Coffee and a roll."

"What kind of roll?" she snapped.

"What?"

"What kind of roll? Apple, boysenberry, cherry, date," she announced the flavors almost as though they were a list of indictments being brought against Ben by a magistrate.

"Apple, I guess."

"Well, why didn't you say so, boy?" She bustled off, leaving him alone with the garbage. Ben realized he had to do something to change his appearance or he'd never get anywhere in Chicago.

A moment later the woman returned with a roll and a cup of coffee, just as he requested. Each was on its own saucer. She handed the two saucers to him and then stood waiting. She wasn't actually tapping her foot, but Ben could feel the same message. He wasn't sure what to do with the saucers. There was nowhere to set them except in the open garbage cans. He stood nonplussed for a moment, then saw that the woman had her hand extended, obviously demanding the bill he'd held up earlier. "Well... " she said.

Ben crouched down and placed the saucers on the floor and then handed her the money, "Thank you, it looks very good," he said as politely as possible.

"Hrumpf." The lady threw back her head and went back to her counter.

Ben's humiliation passed as he sipped the flavorful hot liquid. It was much stronger and richer than any of the coffee he'd been given during his brief sojourn with the tramps. And the roll was fresh and sweet and delightfully flaky. Just perfect.

As he sat on the floor eating his breakfast, he noticed the corner of a newspaper sticking up out of one of the garbage cans. He carefully extracted it and sat back down to read while he finished the coffee. In the classified section in the back he found an advertisement for a lodging house, "near downtown, twenty-five cents a night, 200 Esmeralda St." There were also ads for jobs. He tore the page out of the paper, folded it and stuck it in his pocket.

He drank down the last of the coffee and decided he would go find lodging and a bath. Then he'd find a job.

He walked back to the front of the shop. The lady was waiting on a well-dressed woman wearing a great wide-brimmed straw hat with silk flowers piled atop it. Ben set his dishes on the counter and waited, trying to remain as inconspicuous as possible. After the woman in the hat took her wax-paper bag of goodies and stepped out the front door, the saleslady turned to him and snapped again, "Yes?"

"My change, please?"

"Change?" the lady looked him quizzically.

"I gave you a dollar."

"Look, boy, don't ever come back in here. You don't belong."

Ben stood his ground. A dollar was enough money for four nights lodging. He wasn't going to waste it on one cup of coffee.

"Please, just give me my change."

79

"What do you think this is?" the lady said, even as she went to the shiny brass register and extracted several coins. She turned and tossed them at him, so that he had to scramble to the floor to pick up the quarters.

Ben was going to ask her for directions to Esmeralda Street, but decided against it. "Thank you," he said politely, wishing by his tone that he could communicate to her that he was not what she thought he was, that in spite of his appearance, he was a moral person with high expectations and ambitions. But such was not possible, he realized. He started to remind her of the old chestnut about judging a book by its cover, but then simply turned and walked out of the shop.

Well, at least the food was good he told himself.

Once back on the street, he remembered he was in Chicago. He said the name to himself over and over again as he strolled, letting excitement speed his step. All the buildings were so big. The windows full of beautiful clothes and beautiful furniture. Everything your heart could ask for. On every corner stood a tall gas street lamp that he knew at night must light up the streets with a warm golden glow. Strung from pole to pole were wires that he guessed might sometimes carry power to illuminate the street with electric lights. (Last night Josh had managed to reach that warehouse without ever actually walking down one of the lit streets. That fact reminded Ben that beneath all the glamour was a whole other world.) He remembered last night thinking that the clouds overhead, lit by those streetlights, had looked to him like the skies of hell. How different it all seemed today!

After a couple of blocks, he saw a policeman directing traffic and asked for directions to Esmeralda Street. Without seeming to ever look at him, the policeman pointed back the way he'd just come. "Ten, maybe twelve blocks." Jauntily he turned back, crossing the street so he wouldn't pass in front of the sweet shop.

There was no vacancy at 200 Esmeralda, but the proprietor was nice. He joked with Ben about his needing a bath. Ben agreed. He suggested he try another lodging house a couple of blocks down the street. He said he was pretty sure they had a room available. His brother ran that place.

Indeed, there was a room. With one meal a day, the price came to three dollars a week. Ben could afford that for a couple of weeks. And he agreed immediately. But he was going to need clothes and other basic items. He'd need to find a job soon. He asked the proprietor about work. "Jobs hard to come by these days. 'Specially round here. Railroads all on strike. Men with families needin' to work. Not much place for young whipper-snappers like you. Ya might look in the classified ads in the paper."

A bath was an extra nickel. Ben realized he was lucky to find a lodging house with a bath available. The public baths were not far and were actually cheaper. But Ben didn't exactly like the idea of taking a bath in public. (He wondered if the women bathed in the same room with the men. Surely not, he told himself and then got frightened by the idea that there were just all those men together!)

The extra set of clothes in his knapsack had dried wrinkled from the plunge into the river. They smelled musty, but they were clean. Besides, there was a bottle of bay rum in the bathroom. Ben soaked in the hot sudsy water till it cooled off, luxuriating in the cleanliness and in the independence he was experiencing. He doused himself generously with the bay rum and then donned the clean clothes. Before he let the water out of the tub, he rinsed the clothes he'd been wearing since he fled from home. Then he went back to his small room, lay down on the soft mattress of the bed, and fell asleep.

In the afternoon, he searched for a job. There'd been several in the want ads that had sounded promising, but when he applied, he found the jobs were already taken or required training he didn't have or, most often, were being held for family men.

It was a couple of days, during which he became more and more worried about his future survival, before he found a job in a print shop. The printer mainly did menus for restaurants and receipt books for small businesses. He needed somebody to deliver the jobs when they were done. It wasn't a good job, Ben got paid a nickel for every delivery he made and didn't get anything if there was nothing to deliver—and sometimes the deliveries required long hikes. But if the distance was too far, the printer would pay his fare on the horse-drawn—or on a few streets electric—street-cars. And he promised that if Ben worked out on the job, he'd consider training him to use the press.

But one of those first days while he was out looking for work something did happen that was going to affect his future much more than finding a job.

Ben had just come from a grocery store, where he'd been told that, in spite of the fact there'd been an ad in the paper, no one was needed. He was feeling despondent and singled out because, he assumed, he wasn't a "family man." He wondered if he should tell future employers that he was fresh out of the seminary. Maybe that would impress Catholics. But maybe then they'd want references from Father Master, he worried. He sat down on a bench in a small park built around a fountain to let himself wallow in his feelings of despair and guilt for having failed at priesthood and now, maybe, failing at life.

He happened to look up at just the right time and in just the right direction to see that staring right at him was a handsome dark-haired man who was also sitting at one of the benches facing the bubbling fountain. Ben started to smile, but the man looked away quickly. For a moment Ben had felt almost as normal as back home in the Bloomingon where he'd grown up. Back there if anybody looked at you, it was always with a smile and a "Good day to ya." He'd already discovered the big city wasn't like that. After all the rejections he'd heard asking for work and all the rude behavior he'd seen in the bustle of the city, that mean lady at the sweetshop now seemed almost affable. Ben laughed to himself at that thought, even as his despondency worsened and the laugh felt as much like a tear.

He glanced back at the dark man on the other bench. He was dressed in a fashionable dark wool suit, though its cut looked a little unusual to Ben.

81

It took him a moment to recognize it as a Western style. He remembered hearing back home that so-called Western styles might become popular as Texans and Arizonans and Californians were moving back east now that the frontier had been settled. Well, Ben thought if that's the Western style, it looks pretty good. At least on him.

He noticed the man's broad shoulders and thin waist beneath the yellow-flowered vest he was wearing under his open jacket. The tight-fitting vest made his torso look long. Ben felt funny as he realized he was noticing these things about the stranger over there. He wasn't sure what those feelings were. He looked back down at the concrete of the sidewalk, not wanting to seem rude by staring. Perhaps he'd think Ben was assessing him as a foreigner or something. Little would he know how much like a foreigner Ben felt.

Strangely, Ben found his eyes wanting—almost of their own accord—to glance back at the man over there. He wondered if perhaps there were something familiar about him. Maybe he recognized him from somewhere. Was that possible? How could it be?

He looked up again. And again saw that the man was looking over at him with a blank, almost anxious stare. Ben held his gaze for just a moment, hoping a memory might surface of how he'd known him before or else looking for a glimmer of a smile in the man's eyes. But then the gaze lasted too long and Ben felt himself embarrassed and frightened, not recognized or welcomed. He looked down again and wondered what was happening. All of a sudden he felt threatened. He jumped up and turned and walked away from the park and the bubbling fountain and the benches as fast as he could without seeming to run.

He got a few blocks away and then realized he'd gotten himself lost. He'd been very careful to stick to streets he knew so he could get back to the boarding-house. And now, in his moment of anxiety, he'd taken a wrong turn. He cursed himself for being so impulsive... and for being so stupid and jumping to conclusions. That man had looked perfectly harmless. In fact, he looked, well, very nice. Maybe he would have become a friend. Ben knew he needed friends. He explained his fear to himself as his worry that Josh the mountain man might suddenly appear on some street corner and come after him and, perhaps, literally tear him to pieces. He felt guilty for having hurt Josh. He hoped he really hadn't put out his eye. And he felt guilty for that strange incident between Josh's blankets. He imagined the feeling of Josh's strong hand on his buttocks and between his legs. He blushed and tried to stop the memory.

Ben felt even more embarrassed as he realized he was standing on a street corner with people passing him by. They must wonder what I'm doing. In part to create some justification for himself, he exaggeratedly looked up and down both streets that came together at the corner, then finally stopped a passerby and asked directions back to Esmeralda Street.

But after getting the information and starting to walk in that direction, he decided there was still time to seek work. By now he was going into most every shop he passed along the busy street. He passed a soda fountain and then stopped and went back. He'd worked in a soda fountain before.

There was no job available. But as he came out of the shop and turned to continue in the direction he'd been going, he saw coming toward him the dark-haired man from the park. His heart started to pound. He wanted to go up to the man and introduce himself. Maybe the other man could explain how he looked familiar—and now he certainly did look familiar. Ben was sure he'd known this man before. Maybe they were from the same town.

Ben was walking slowly, staring right into the man's eyes. The man was coming toward him, holding the eye contact. He looked worried and serious. There was no trace of a smile on his face at all. Ben tried to imagine what he'd look like smiling. They drew closer and closer. Ben slowed even more. And then the man looked away, just at the last moment and passed him by. There was no chance to speak now. Ben felt both relieved and bereft.

16

The sky's been hazy lately. The rest of the country seems to be having a heat wave and drought. Surprisingly, Texas is cool and occasionally rainy. I'm getting to like this place more and more. Elizabeth, you wouldn't believe the wildflowers. Do come visit.

Rick

That was the postcard I sent Elizabeth. It was true. The time I was spending with Ben Mayfield and Tom Milam—my imaginary friends?—made up for the social life I might have been missing in Boston. The last couple of years, though, my social life had fallen apart anyway. Friends had died; others moved away; I wasn't very good company. Maybe I was stressed out all the time then. And now I wasn't.

The other day I came in from my gardening, wearing only an old pair of faded red gym shorts. I came in through the front door, an entrance I didn't usually use. As I stepped up the short flight of stairs into the living room, I was surprised by the sight of another man in the house. I thought perhaps Dave Lovejoy had reneged on his promise to call me before bringing anyone out. But I was surprised to see that this intruder was also wearing only shorts. Not your typical real estate investor. But that was okay. He looked good: healthy tan, nice muscular body.

It took me a moment to recognize the faded red of the shorts and then to realize the door of the coat closet had blown open revealing the full length mirror on its backside—and that was me.

I walked up to the mirror and consciously examined my reflection for the first time in a long time. (Do you realize how you can shave and comb your hair every morning without ever quite seeing your own face?) The lines around my eyes and furrows in my brow had smoothed out. My hair, usually kept stylishly short, had gotten long and formed soft dark curls around my face. My eyes seemed almost to glow from within. The tan? I stepped back and took in my full physique. My chest had developed and my waist thinned. There were faint ripples down the middle of my torso. (I thought for a moment of Ben's description of the stranger in the Western-cut suit who'd cruised him in the park.)

For all that I was as old as I'd ever been, I realized, I was also in as good a shape as well. "Country life is doin' good by you," I said aloud to my reflection. He laughed back with me.

"Funny," I went on, "a couple of weeks ago you thought you were dying."

"You still are," I nodded gravely, forcing my reflection to acknowledge the truth to me. "But maybe not as fast."

When the doctor first presented me with that awful prognosis back in Boston, I'd wished he hadn't left the death date so open. I just wanted to get it over with. The fact that I might live for a year or five years or ten years under the burden of that diagnosis didn't seem particularly hopeful. Life hadn't looked very sweet to me then.

Now I realized I was looking forward to each day, to spending time with my imaginary friends in that 1890s world of theirs, so untouched by the tragedies that faced the brave new world of the 1990s, to working in my garden and helping the laborers reconstruct the old barn. Now I realized I wanted to live—at least to see if the red and blue and purple primroses with the deep yellow throats I planted would survive the Texas summer, perhaps to see myself come to terms with death.

Speaking of which, let me mention that I followed up on Ben's reference to *The Hero with a Thousand Faces*. Somewhat to my surprise, when I looked in the chapter he suggested, I discovered, that—apparently back in college—I'd highlighted a couple of passages with a yellow marker. I've placed them as the epigraph for this book. If you go back and read them you'll see they seem to summarize the "truth" not only about death, but about the nature of reality itself.

Moved by those words and feeling that perhaps these pages held important spiritual truth for me, I started rereading Campbell's book. It was heavy reading; it was going to take me several weeks to get through it, especially since Ben's reminder of that box in the closet had got me to reading the other books I'd brought with me. In the eclectic Jungian and comparative-religions approach I found in Campbell, I began to find hints at the answers to the important questions of life—that the religion of my upbringing had failed to address and, consequently, turned me against religion. In the revisionist gay history I read in Thompson's *Gay Spirit: Myth and Meaning*, I discovered a connection to a rich spiritual past—that my experience of gay life in the bars around Boston's Copley Square had never taught me about. These ideas were to influence most everything I learned that summer and everything I wrote. Later when I sat down to write and conjured up my inspiration, I found it was Tom Milam who came to visit.

Eli Hauptmann had graciously assented to Tom's request for assistance. "It is the least I can do for a brother in need of assistance," he said when Tom showed up at his door and explained his plight.

"I still want to find Johnny... I mean, he's all the family I've got in the world."

"I hope you will allow me to become part of that family too. And perhaps I can assist you in finding your friend. I am not a native to your country, you know, but I have been traveling all over America. I may not fully understand how your legal and social institutions work, but, Tom, I think I understand how certain—shall we say—underground networks operate. Perhaps within such a network we might be able to find your Johnny Kincade. Come, sit down, tell me more about him."

Tom explained about his feelings for Johnny, about their correspondence, about the special connection he felt with him though couldn't put words to, about the strange story the old black woman had told of Johnny's ostracism from the neighborhood. "The grocer played dumb. Sounded like he might've been involved in the arson. He insisted Johnny wasn't home at the time and that nobody was killed in the fire. He said the neighbors just didn't like what was going on and tried to make their point dramatically. They didn't mean to burn down the building."

"Perhaps a burning cross that got out of control?"

"But Johnny ain't a nigger, Eli. How come the Klan would have been after him, if that's what you mean?"

"There are other types of people, Tom, that narrow minds don't like. It seems to me that your friend may have been just such a type."

"What do you mean?"

Eli offered Tom a glass of sherry. "You look like you can use some help relaxing."

The interruption to pour the sherry allowed preparation of a small plate of hors d'oeuvres the likes of which Tom had never seen before in his life: canned pâté de foie gras, exotic cheeses, little triangles of dried toast, figs from Greece. "My friend in Zurich sends me a package now and then, to remind me of home," Eli explained, "maybe to remind me to hurry home. Ah, but I like America," he said wistfully. "So young and strong and innocent."

After the lunch that Eli referred to as "a small repast," Tom was given a tour of the man's townhouse. Tom assumed the style must be European. Everything seemed to him rather breakable. The furniture had spindly legs, the lamps were all cut glass—it was all so formal. "I'm quite proud of the delightful antiques I've found. Not that it was so costly. Indeed, I'll probably have to leave it all behind when I return home. More expensive to ship than it's all worth. Perhaps, if you're still in Chicago when I leave... " He let that offer trail off without committing himself.

The apartment was small, a parlor and study downstairs next to the kitchen and two bedrooms up. It had indoor plumbing which is something Tom had seen in San Antonio, but never lived with. It was lit not with kerosene lamps, but with gas lights that protruded from sconces on the walls or else hung down in delicate brass fixtures from the ceilings. "I must apologize for the accommodations. The guest bed has only a straw mattress. But, of course, you're welcome to join me on the feather bed in my room if you'd like."

"Thank you very much," Tom answered politely. "I've slept on straw mattresses most of my life."

"Well, yes, I see... "

"Oh, no offense. I just don't want to be no trouble, you understand?"

"I understand, Tom, of course. You're no trouble, no trouble at all."

Back down in the parlor, Eli inquired more about the emotional relationship between Tom and his friend Johnny. He seemed to be asking about something that Tom couldn't quite understand. Finally, Eli inquired more directly. "Did you two boys ever, uh, touch each other?"

"Touch?" Tom felt a wave of anxiety. He knew he could answer that, sure, they'd palled around together and, of course, they'd touched each other, giving one another a hand-up a tree or onto horseback. But he knew from Eli's tone that that wasn't what he meant. He was silent for a while, then hung his head in embarrassment and replied to the question.

"We were just kids, you know. I mean, sometimes we played around, did things we weren't supposed to." He stammered. "Sometimes we'd go skinny-dippin' down at this pond and... and... "

"Perhaps you touched one another's penis?" Eli suggested helpfully, obviously more at ease than Tom with the words.

Tom blushed. "Well, usually just our own. But, yeah, I guess so. I mean with each other."

"Did you perhaps put your mouth to Johnny's penis or vice-versa? Or perhaps place your penis into Johnny's rectum?" Tom thought Eli sounded like a doctor; somehow that helped him to think about the meaning of the questions.

"Do people do that?" Tom sounded shocked.

Eli smiled. "I assure you."

Tom struggled to answer. Finally he managed to say, "I don't know. Maybe so. I mean, I can't exactly remember what we did. We were so scared of anybody finding out. Does that make sense?"

"Yes, it does. Now let me ask you another question. Do you or did you love Johnny?"

"I thought that's something only husbands and wives said."

"Mothers and fathers certainly say it to their children."

"I don't mean like that. I mean, you know, like you just said."
Eli laughed. "It is difficult to talk about these matters, isn't it?"
Tom nodded.
"Have you ever heard the term 'urning'?"
Tom shook his head.
"Intermediate sex?"
Again Tom shook his head.
"Perhaps 'invert' then? Well, of course, I'm not surprised. The first word has been used by my friend Heinrich Ulrichs and the second by an English writer Edward Carpenter. You should know about these men."
"Will you tell me?"
Eli smiled.

"He didn't ask you about 'homosexual'," I asked, "the obvious word?" Now Tom laughed at me. "It wasn't so obvious. That word had only just been coined in Germany in 1869 by Karl Maria Kertbeny. You should know that."
"I guess maybe I do," I replied, but then continued. "You mean there wasn't any such word as 'homosexual' until just over a hundred years ago? How did the Bible and the Church manage to condemn us if there was no word?"
"Now, Rick, that's a good question. You'd have to ask a theologian about how you can condemn something you can't even name. But haven't you been told you ought to read that book by John Boswell, that Yale classics scholar, *Christianity, Social Tolerance, and Homosexuality?*"
"Yeah, but I never have," I admitted. "I read a couple of reviews that said he proved the Bible and the Church Father never really meant homosexuality, at least as we know it today, and that all that condemnation stuff didn't start till the time of the Bubonic Plague when the Church was pushing repopulation. Is that right?"
Tom looked at me quizzically. "Rick," he said condescendingly, "if *you* haven't read the book, how do you expect *me* to know what it's about?"
"Oh yeah, I guess not. Well, so what else did Eli tell you?" Then I grinned and added salaciously, "Or show you?"

The next morning Tom lay in the warm, soft comfort of the feather mattress. When Eli awoke and crept out of bed to avoid waking him, Tom, who was already awake and already fretting, pretended to be asleep so he'd have a chance to be by himself to think through what had happened.
"Eli certainly never forced himself on me or anything," Tom said to himself. "But if he hadn't started talking about... that stuff, I'd never have

agreed to anything like that. Besides, I really didn't do anything myself. I just let him."

For all that he felt dirty and guilty this morning, when he remembered what had happened last night he felt his body responding just as it had before—and he liked that. And when he thought about everything Eli had said, he knew it made more sense than anything he'd ever been told before by anybody about sex.

He remembered how the wine Eli had served him with dinner had loosened him up a little. He'd become more talkative. But he never got drunk. He knew that.

He remembered how gently Eli had suggested that to really understand his own feelings and his own sexual desires, he'd have to experiment with them. That had seemed like such a sensible argument. It was certainly true about other things: from riding horses to eating new foods to learning to sing. If he never tried anything how was he going to know what he liked?

He remembered how surprised he'd been when they came upstairs to Eli's room and Eli had turned back the soft comforter and then took his clothes off and invited Tom to do so as well. He had been perceiving Eli Hauptmann as an old man, a professor, a Swiss comparative literature scholar, maybe even a doctor. He hadn't thought about his body at all. And so it was a surprise when Eli proved to have a well-developed muscular physique. (Later that day Eli would show him the little yard behind the house where he did his daily calisthenics and a routine of stretching and breathing exercises he called by the exotic name "yoga.")

He remembered how Eli had carefully and gently allowed him to touch his body, to feel what another man felt like, to feel his erect penis with his hand, to feel Eli's hand on his. They lay together gently holding one another while Tom's trembling subsided. He remembered how humiliated he'd felt when he finally got up the nerve to acknowledge, "I've never been with a woman." "Nor I," Eli had responded, "and it certainly makes you no less a man."

He remembered how Eli had coaxed him to relax and enjoy the sensations in his body and then how Eli had taken him in his mouth and produced the most marvelous sensations. And he remembered how thankful he was that Eli never seemed to expect him to reciprocate. Though now, this morning, in his welter of guilt he wished Eli had forced him to. This morning he wondered what it would have been like. "And," he told himself, "I might as well hang for a pound as for a penny."

After a while his recollections were interrupted by Eli's arrival with a tray carrying a cup of coffee, a roll, and a single red rose in a crystal bud vase. He'd been afraid he would be too embarrassed to face the man. But instead he discovered that when Eli, now dressed in a flowing robe of royal purple silk, bent over and kissed him lightly on the cheek, he was genuinely happy to see him.

As he stirred a little sugar into his coffee, Eli went to the armoire and took out another robe. "Perhaps you'd like to put this on before you come down." It was brilliant emerald green.

17

om tied the robe around himself and then looked in the mirror. The robe was beautiful. He brushed his hair down with the palms of his hands. I look like a king, he told himself. But he felt silly. It just didn't seem right. Maybe it was okay for Eli Hauptmann—he looked handsome in the purple robe because he was European and cultured and educated. But I'm a Texan. The robe was almost the same color as a bolt of fabric he'd once sold a lady who'd come into Strinke's to get material for a wedding present for her daughter. Perhaps it was also the color of the dress his mother had said was her favorite when she was a young woman. These memories brought back the fears Tom had felt of not seeming manly enough.

He took one more quick look in the mirror. And then took the robe off and put back on the clothes he'd been wearing. He didn't allow himself to look at his own body in the mirror till he was fully clothed. He paced back and forth for a few minutes until he heard Eli's soft footsteps on the stairs. Abruptly he pulled open the door.

"*Guten morgen*," Eli beamed. "Again."

"Yeah, good morning to you too. Look, Eli… Dr. Hauptmann… "

"Oh, Tom, you must be upset. I'm sorry."

"It's just, well, I need some time to think. You understand?"

"Would you like to come down to the yard while I do my exercises? We don't have to talk, you know."

"Well, sure." Tom followed him down. Eli explained briefly that he was going to do his calisthenics and yoga and Tom was welcome to join in or watch or just sit in the sun. Eli took off his purple silk robe to reveal tight-fitting trousers that reached only to mid-thigh. "The latest thing on the Mediterranean," he joked and then got down to his exercises, leaving Tom in silence sitting on a small canvas-covered chair.

After a little while Tom got anxious and declared that he needed to get out and walk some. "I'll be back. I promise. I'm leaving my bag here, you know."

Eli was in the middle of holding a deep breath while he pinched one nostril with his finger. He glanced at Tom and nodded affirmatively.

Fortunately Eli Hauptmann's townhouse was in a neighborhood not far from downtown and the train station. Tom had managed to locate the address easily enough yesterday and he believed he had a good enough geographical sense to find his way back. He set out walking, more for the exercise and release of tension than to get anywhere. Where was there to go? Of course, he was a tourist in a new city and wanted to get a chance to see what Chicago looked like. He'd heard there'd been a World's Fair the previous summer and thought perhaps he could find the fairgrounds.

Eli had told him about the "underground network" of these people he called "urnings." Am I an urning? he thought to himself dismayed. Eli had suggested he might find Johnny Kincade through such a network. But the conversation had never moved toward the practical implications. He didn't know how to find another urning to ask if that man knew where Johnny might be. And did he really want to find Johnny now? What if Johnny is one of these strange men who want to do things with one another that men aren't supposed to do? What if Johnny wears purple or emerald green silk bathrobes and eats canned gooseliver on triangular pieces of dried toast and sips on sweet sherry? What if Johnny puts his…

Tom tried to calm his thoughts, to tell himself that what happened last night wasn't really so frightening, that it was just part of life in the bigger world outside little San Antone. Eli had told him about how these urnings liked to move to certain cities: Berlin, Paris, New York, San Francisco. He'd suggested life in one of those cities would be far more comfortable than in a small town. He'd said in those big cities the urnings had a better chance of meeting one another and developing relationships—just like men and women.

Tom walked down the street noticing couples. He observed how men and women walked sometimes with their arms entwined, how ladies looked so delicate and needed to be protected by strong men. Tom imagined himself being strong for a lady who would bear sons and daughters for him. He liked the idea of being a strong man for her, but he wasn't sure he'd want to do with her any of the things Eli had talked about urnings doing with one another. Do people really do such things?

Of course they do, he scolded himself for seeming so naïve. I know what sex is about. I know it feels good to excite my penis. I'm not so stupid. I used to see men buying prostitutes or going with those painted up ladies in the saloons and dance halls. I knew what my mother was warning me about. It's just, it's just…

It's just I never wanted to do any of that. All I've wanted for years was to take care of my mother—his eyes filled with tears as the irrevocable truth of her death resounded in his mind—and to be friends with Johnny Kincade.

Tom tried to catch the eye of women as he walked. He'd seen men do that and wanted to try it too. He watched the way certain men walked, with a kind of swagger. He tried to mimic that walk, but felt so silly and unnatural he was sure everybody would be noticing his pretense.

After a while he stopped thinking of these things. He happened to come right up on Lake Michigan. He was surprised. It looked like what he figured an ocean would look like. He couldn't see the other shore. He'd been down to the Texas Gulf Coast once with his mother; she said she had never seen the sea and would not rest in peace till she did. That had been ten years ago; seeing the Gulf did not precipitate her death. But all during that long trek by mule-drawn coach and for weeks after, Tom had worried that now that she'd seen the sea his mother was going to die and leave him alone. He felt that same sense of dread and loneliness now as he looked out at Lake Michigan. He thought his life was changing. He was never again going to be the naïve and innocent kid who'd held his mother's hand as she daintily tiptoed down the beach to where the waves splashed on the sand.

He stood looking out at the lake for a long time. There were street vendors along the shore selling fried fish which he assumed came right from the lake. Tom bought himself a plate of fish and some fried potatoes—men's food, he thought to himself.

He felt better after eating. In fact, he began to feel hopeful. He walked through the big city streets enjoying the start of a new life as a Chicagoan. Or maybe a San Franciscan? He thought about the possibility of continuing his journey. Now that Johnny wasn't here—*if* he wasn't here—Tom had nothing to hold him in Chicago. He didn't think he wanted to go to San Francisco because Eli said there were these urnings there. But it had given him an idea. He knew there was gold in the hills above San Francisco. It's been forty years since the Gold Rush, but there's still bound to be gold running in the rivers there like honey flowing from a beehive. All for the taking. That'd be manly work.

But first he had to make sure Johnny wasn't still here. He couldn't leave yet.

By late afternoon, Tom was tired of walking. He knew he had to go back to Eli's soon, but he wasn't quite ready. He was enjoying his independence a little too much. And he was afraid of what might happen if he went back.

He sat down in a little park and watched pigeons playing on the ground around a fountain. He fell asleep for a few minutes he thought. At least he suddenly found himself sitting on that bench feeling kind of disoriented and dizzy. He looked up and right across from him he saw Johnny Kincade sitting on another of the benches around the fountain. He thought for a moment he must be dreaming so he didn't jump up and run over. He just sat quietly and reminded himself to think this through. Could that be Johnny?

As he looked closer, it occurred to him that the boy didn't look right. He was too young for one thing. Johnny was Tom's own age. He'd be twenty-five now. He should not still look like an innocent freckled adolescent. The afternoon sun was dazzling and obscured Tom's vision. He stared harder trying to recognize the features of a face he hadn't seen in many years, trying to guess how those features would have changed.

The boy looked up and saw Tom staring. Tom hoped Johnny would recognize him. He held the gaze for a moment and then embarrassedly looked away. There didn't seem to be any recognition on the other's part. But then he looked up and saw that the boy was now staring at him. Maybe he's thinking he recognizes me, Tom thought.

Then suddenly the boy jumped up and bolted out of the park, leaving

Tom as confused as ever. What if that was Johnny and he's ashamed to speak to me because of what happened with his apartment and because maybe he's become… an urning! Tom had to struggle to say that word even to himself.

But it'd be okay with me, he thought and surprised himself. He realized then that it would be okay, that it might even be more than okay. Maybe that's what both of them had wanted all along.

But he's gone. The boy had disappeared into a crowd. Tom stood up and started walking, hoping he'd get a chance to see the boy closer up, maybe even to get a chance to speak to him. That's what I've got to do—ask him if he's my friend Johnny Kincade. All he can say is no. And he might say yes.

Tom walked round and round the neighborhood. Then: there he was, the boy was coming out of a soda fountain halfway down the block. Here's my chance to see him up close, Tom thought excitedly, nervously.

They were walking toward each other. Tom was trying to study everything about him, the way he moved, the color of his hair, hoping to recognize him. Strangely, after looking at this boy so long, he now wasn't sure anymore what Johnny looked like. And the boy was looking right back at him, but with a questioning gaze that didn't seem to show any recognition.

Tom got closer and closer. All of a sudden he realized that something wasn't right about the boy's face. Something was different enough to assure him that that wasn't Johnny Kincade. And then he realized that that gaze the boy was giving him was just like the eye he'd tried to give to women he passed on the street earlier. He realized the boy was looking at him the way Eli Hauptmann had looked at him on the train, looking at him… like… like an urning.

He turned his gaze to the ground and walked on by as fast as he could. At that moment he made up his mind to tell Eli Hauptmann that what happened last night must never, never happen again.

18

 have some news for you, son," Eli said as he let Tom into the apartment. Tom recognized from the appellation that Eli too recognized some barrier had arisen between them. He was glad of that and at the same time felt sad for this man who'd been such a generous benefactor.

"While you were out I visited a friend of mine who—how do you say it?—keeps his ear to the grapevine. He told me he'd heard about the incident of a young man being burned out of his place. He thought it was probably your friend. He said he'd understood that the young man stayed for a while with a mutual friend of ours and then left for California. Do you remember I was telling you about San Francisco?"

"I remember, of course," Tom snapped. He was surprised at his emotions. "What about this mutual friend?"

"He lives very far from here on a farm—almost a day's journey. It happened that the comrade of my friend was planning to go out there this weekend to visit. I asked him to inquire for us about your Johnny Kincade. Tom, I'm very sorry it's not more specific. But frankly, I think we're quite lucky to have discovered this much. Chicago is a big city. Many injustices go on here—especially to our, er, my sort of person. It's quite a coincidence... I mean, if it really proves to be your Johnny that my friend knew about."

"So you think he may have gone to San Francisco."

"Perhaps. We must wait and see."

"I don't know if I can wait around. I mean, Dr. Hauptmann, I'm grateful to you and all. It's just, well... "

"Yes, Tom, these things can be very disturbing... "

"...oh, I didn't mean about Johnny."

"Neither did I. Self-knowledge," he continued, "is very difficult. We don't always like what we find. That is probably why Socrates considered it the basis of wisdom."

"Eli, who is Socrates?"

"Come in, my boy." They were still standing just inside the front door of the townhouse. "We can discuss the Greeks over dinner."

"Look, I don't want to impose on you."

"Tom, you're not imposing. Indeed, perhaps it is I who was imposing on you—last night, I mean. It would have been difficult for you to refuse my... er... Well, anyway, Tom, I promise it will not happen again. I only want to assist you. I did not mean to let my own feelings get in the way of that."

Tom was surprised at how tongue-tied Eli seemed to be this evening. He had usually been quite glib. Tom realized his unusual behavior and apparent rejection today had hurt Eli.

"I'm sorry too, Eli," he said and reached out to grasp the older man's arm. "Not that it happened. I mean, that it's all so confusing to me."

Eli moved a step closer and then both spontaneously fell into a warm embrace in the other's arms. But that was all the expression of affection that was going to happen between them, at least tonight.

"But you'll stay through the weekend, of course. You must find out about Johnny Kincade."

Over dinner—a light white fish topped with *beurre noir* and capers, baby carrots (which Eli had been given by the man he'd visited earlier), and egg noodles, served with a dry French Chenin Blanc—Tom described how he'd mistaken the young man in the park for Johnny.

"It's too bad you didn't speak to him."

"Why? I'm sure that wasn't Johnny."

"Yes, but obviously something about him appealed to you. And apparently he was not averse to your attention. You know, Tom, as hard as this may sound, the fact is you may not find your Johnny Kincade and—and this is even harder—if you do find him, you may discover you don't… well, that he is a different person now."

"I don't understand. Johnny was my friend."

"People change, Tom. You're going to change just from having come to Chicago, perhaps from having met and talked with me on the train. You said it's been some years since you've actually seen Johnny. He's changed a lot in that time… "

"Things like that don't change."

Eli smiled kindly. He reached across the small round table at which they were eating, overlooking the garden. He touched Tom's hand gently. "There is a certain of amount of—shall I say?—biology about people's appeal and attraction to other people. I don't mean to say that you and Johnny would not be friends. But… "

"Biology? You mean… 'sex,' don't you?" Tom objected. He had a hard time bringing himself to say that word. It was a word people didn't use in polite society.

Eli looked down at the table, stung by Tom's reaction. "I think I mean affection, but certainly affection has a biological, sexual substrate to it."

"I don't understand the words you use." Tom shot back almost angrily.

"Forgive me. We are so used to speaking about these matters… delicately." He paused. "I did not mean to upset you."

"I'm not upset," Tom snapped. "I just don't want you to be suggesting… well, what I thought you were suggesting."

"That you may not feel that special connection with Johnny?"

"That my friendship with Johnny is only what you called biological."

After coffee, Tom offered to wash the dishes. Eli puttered about the kitchen putting things away and straightening up. They hadn't said much to each other in a while.

"Perhaps you were right, Eli."

"Oh? What was that about?" Eli replied tentatively.

"That I should have spoken to that fellow I saw in the park today. I can't get him out of my mind."

"You're still wondering if that might have been your friend?"

"I suppose so. But, no, I know he wasn't. I just kinda think maybe I need to make some new friends, I mean, here in Chicago."

Eli grinned, perhaps suppressing an inadvertent chuckle.

"By all means you should make friends, Tom."

"Maybe I can find that soda fountain he came out of. Maybe he works there."

"Yes, perhaps. Well, Tom, would you join me in the parlor for a sip of brandy."

"Thank you, Eli. That sounds real good." Tom was smiling as he dried his hands on a towel hanging by the sink. "There were a lot of shops around there," he said more to himself than to Eli who had stepped into the next room to pour two small snifters of Napoleon brandy. "I should go look for a job. I'll bet that fellow works around there."

Later, in spite of the two glasses of brandy he'd consumed, Tom had a difficult time getting to sleep. It wasn't the narrow straw mattress that interfered with his slumbers, but his excitement about finding work in this city that was his newly chosen home and his expectation he might see that young fellow again and might make himself a new friend.

19

en Mayfield was also enjoying life in his newly chosen home. After a week on the job at the printer's, he was earning enough money to assure himself a room in the lodging house and the job was giving him something to do with his time. The only thing about it which bothered him was that he was working in the downtown area. Somewhere nearby, he knew, was that warehouse where Josh had tried to assault him. Perhaps the mountain man himself was still living back in there, sitting in the circle at night around that fire, getting drunk. Perhaps his eye still hurt from the blow from the buckle of Ben's knapsack. Worse, perhaps the blow had actually blinded him in that eye. No doubt he'd be imagining all sorts of ways of getting revenge.

Ben was particularly afraid of running into Josh because his delivering completed printing jobs kept him on the street. He'd managed to prove he could be useful inside the shop and so had chores to do all day long, but he couldn't get out of making the deliveries.

On Monday of his second week at work, just before lunchtime he was given a large package of specially printed receipt forms to deliver to an address on State Street. When he found the location he was surprised to discover it was the sweetshop he'd gone into that first morning in Chicago. He entered warily, wondering if that same lady would be working behind the counter. She was. Ben's heart skipped a beat. But he mustered his courage and stepped right up to the counter.

"Good morning," he said politely. "Here are the receipt forms you ordered."

The lady looked up at him and smiled warmly. "Thank you, son. Here I'll take them." She stepped around the counter and then saw that Ben had his arms full. "Well, perhaps you can bring them back here for me. That's quite a bundle." She laughed. "Here, bring them back here." She was gesturing toward the kitchen.

Ben felt eerie. Barely more than a week ago he was sitting in that same kitchen on the floor beside the garbage cans wondering what would ever happen to him. Ben was glad he was wearing a clean white shirt this morning and had his hair combed.

"Well, you arrived just in time," the lady said. "I was about to use up the last book of receipts. And just in time for a hot cookie." She cocked her head and looked at him oddly.

Uh-oh, he thought.

"You're new, aren't you. I didn't think I recognized you."

Ben blushed. "Been on the job 'bout a week, Ma'am."

"Well, well, such a nice-looking young man. You deserve a reward for getting here before lunch when all my customers show up, and me on my last receipt pad. You go sit down. I'll bring up a cup of cocoa and a cookie fresh out of the oven."

Following her instructions, Ben went back into the front of the shop and took a seat at one of the small tables near the window. A moment later the lady brought him a plate with a couple of cinnamon sugar cookies and a mug of hot cocoa. Ben recognized the shop's trademark printed on the mug. It was the same kind of cup he'd drank the coffee from before. "Thank you very much."

He sat at the table munching on the cookies and sipping the cocoa and thinking how superficial and unfair the world is. He was the same person he was last week. The only thing that had changed about him was the cleanliness of his clothes. Now he had a job and could afford to come in here (though it was overpriced, he knew, and he wouldn't choose such a shop on his own). Now the lady was nice to him. Last week when he really needed help she was rude. It was all turned around backward.

He was just finishing the last cookie when he happened to look up and saw a tramp amble out of the alleyway a couple of shops down on the other side of the street. The tramp had turned the other direction, so Ben couldn't see his face. But the man was big, had dark hair, and was wearing a red flannel shirt. Josh B'Gosh. Maybe.

Ben tried to calm himself with the thought that lots of tramps look like that. And this man walked with a limp that he didn't recall Josh having. Nonetheless it all seemed too close.

Suddenly he felt it was a mistake coming into this place, especially accepting the saleslady's hospitality. He should have made his delivery and gotten out of there as fast as possible. He felt like he was being warned for having been smug and thinking himself better than the lady because she'd been taken in by superficials. He wondered if he ought to just leave Chicago altogether.

Heading back to the print shop, Ben walked through the little park with the fountain. Since the park was so close to work, he often made a point of coming this way. He enjoyed walking through the pigeons. He remembered he was going to bring some seedcorn down here one day and feed them. He'd seen other people doing that and it looked like fun. Today though he told himself that he needed to forget about such things and get out of town before he got himself killed.

Turning the corner and walking away from the park, he passed the soda fountain. He thought about going in. It was lunchtime after all. But he'd just eaten those cookies. He'd wait and maybe get a sandwich later. He glanced in and noticed that sitting at the counter was that dark-haired man he'd seen in the park last week who'd acted so strangely.

He must work around here, Ben said to himself.

20

om was elated to learn that Lewis, who lived on the farm south of Chicago, had sent word that the young fellow who'd stayed with him a while had, indeed, been named John Kincade. However, after a few weeks on the farm Kincade had gotten anxious to meet some new people and Lewis didn't know where he'd had gone. Eli's friend, who'd visited Lewis's farm for the weekend and who'd come by late Sunday afternoon to deliver a basket of vegetables from Lewis and to report on the news, had looked at Eli knowingly when he explained why Kincade had left. Eli had just nodded.

"Where *might* he have gone?" Tom broke into the report.

"Who knows. Lewis said he told him about the Clear Light Colony near Denver. The fellow had seemed more interested in getting to California, Lewis said. He thought maybe he was looking for gold or maybe somebody who'd already found gold. Anyway, this Kincade fellow didn't like living on the farm, was always complaining there wasn't enough excitement."

"Sound right?" asked Eli.

"I don't know," Tom answered. "When I knew Johnny he was a small town kid who thought the greatest thing in the world to do was goin' swimmin' in the creek or climbin' up a tree."

"It sounds like he's grown up a bit. Lewis seemed to think the Barbary Coast was more his style these days."

Now Tom remembered that conversation while sitting at the soda fountain, thinking maybe he'd continue on with his journey in search of his old friend. He hadn't found a job in the week he'd supposedly been looking. But then he hadn't really been looking that hard. He'd spent a lot of the time just walking up and down the street half-hoping he'd see that red-haired kid whom he'd mistaken for Johnny. He never had, but thinking he might take off for California soon, he'd come back to the soda fountain one last time. (Of course, he'd discovered last week that the boy did not work at the soda fountain.)

He was worrying about what to do. He went over and over the conversations—real and in his mind—he'd had with Eli. He still had some money, at least enough for a train ticket to San Francisco. His benefactor had reminded him that it might be foolish to go chasing after Kincade, especially after what they'd learned about him.

"That he likes excitement?" Tom scoffed.

"No, I don't mean that," Eli answered defensively. "I mean Lewis had offered him, well, love and a place to settle down. He hadn't wanted that. I think, Tom, that if you find him and offer him love, he's not going to want to settle down with you either."

"I'm not planning to offer him *that* kind of love and I'm not Lewis."

Eli smiled and muttered under his breath, "You should see Lewis... "

"What was that?"

"You're right, Tom. You're not Lewis. But I'm just warning you that if this boy's gone looking for excitement on the Barbary Coast... well, he just may be very different from what you remember. And, frankly, you seem so confused. A week ago you weren't so... "

"I'm just feeling unsettled, Eli."

"I can appreciate that. What about that young man you hoped to make friends with? Did something happen?"

"Something?" Tom objected. "No, no I never found him. I guess I got myself worked up over nothing. He was just a kid I saw on the street and mistook for somebody else."

"I'm sorry, Tom," Eli answered and they both fell silent a while.

Finally Tom spoke, "What is the Barbary Coast?"

Eli explained that the Gold Rush in San Francisco had brought a lot of men out to California, most of them leaving their wives and families at home. Some of them, of course, had never had wives; maybe they were as interested in going where there were a lot of single men as they were in finding gold. At any rate, he explained, a whole industry of dance halls and brothels and such places developed to exploit the Forty-Niner's occasional windfalls of wealth.

"Brothels?"

"Tom, you can't tell me you're that innocent?" Eli rejoined.

Tom also asked Eli about that place Lewis had supposedly suggested Johnny go to near Denver, the Clear Light Colony.

Eli explained that a friend of his named Montgomery Hightower had bought some land in a small mountain town for a retreat and center for intellectual study of issues important to urnings. It was a beautiful place, he explained, high in the foothills overlooking the Denver plain. The town had the appropriate name Perspective, Colorado. "In fact, I first came to the U.S. at Monty's invitation. We met in England. I was studying at Oxford and had heard about Edward Carpenter... "

"You've mentioned that name."

"Carpenter has a farm in Derbyshire. Lovely place. Called Millthorpe. He has a stream of visitors coming to see him—and each other, of course," Eli laughed at something Tom didn't understand. "Edward was very interested in the issues we've talked about, especially the spiritual implications of certain people being of what he called 'the intermediate sex'."

"This Carpenter guy is... uh, I mean, himself?"

"You mean, is he one of us, an urning? Oh yes, most definitely. Likes the working class blokes. Rather like Walt Whitman. At any rate, Monty Hightower lived on the farm at Derbyshire for a couple of years. Then he came back to America and wanted to create something similar here. Somehow he came across property in Colorado. It was very inexpensive. Apparently the old man who lived there had no family left and practically gave it to Monty. That's the Clear Light Colony. You know, Tom, you should visit there yourself."

The thought that Johnny Kincade might be there made it seem appealing to Tom as he sipped at the strawberry phosphate he'd ordered from the soda fountain. He cursed his fate. He was feeling despondent today. It had seemed like his time in Chicago had been an emotional roller-coaster. He'd vacillated from feeling elated to feeling almost suicidal. For a while the hope of finding that young man who'd reminded him of Johnny had staved off the realization that he had no direction in his life and that he wasn't at all sure he wanted to be where he was. But he never found him—and what would he do with him if he did? He needed a friend, he knew. Maybe that fellow would have been a friend. Maybe not. Right now his only friend was Eli and he wasn't altogether sure what he thought about that.

Oh, he liked Eli Hauptmann very much. The man had been immensely generous. He didn't think he could ever repay him—which is one of the things that bothered him. He also didn't think he should be around Eli so much. After all, he told himself, if I spend so much time with these urning people, I'm liable to get suckered in and end up like them.

But aren't I already? another voice challenged and started again the round of worries and denials that had been plaguing him.

He pulled himself out of his cogitation and looked around the soda fountain. The other patrons all seemed so happy with life. He wondered why it seemed so difficult for him. He drank down the rest of the soda and told himself to get back to his job search. Even if he did decide to follow Johnny to San Francisco, he needed to keep himself busy. And maybe he'd find a good job in the meantime. Though the truth was there wasn't anything available. The job market was as tight here as it had become back home in San Antonio. The railroad strike and the company's financial problems had made Chicago a hotbed of strife. And in the middle of all that there just weren't any jobs.

As Tom stood up from the stool at the counter, he glanced out the window. He noticed the back of the head of a passerby—that bright red hair that had reminded him of Johnny.

Maybe if I'd ever found that fellow... Tom thought.

On the other hand, he accused himself, maybe what I'm feeling is a symptom of a perversion I don't want to fall into. Maybe I ought to stop looking for red-haired young men!

21

en got off work late. His boss, the printer, asked him to stay to help finish a job that was already overdue. Ben was reluctant because it would mean missing dinner at the lodging-house; there was an absolute rule that residents had to appear in the dining room on time or forfeit their meal for the night. But the printer let him understand such extra work was necessary if he wanted to keep his job and, as a bonus, he offered to tip him a little cash to cover a nicer dinner than he'd have gotten at the lodging-house.

It was because he had the extra money in his pocket and was walking around looking at restaurants and cafes that he happened to be on Michigan Avenue just when striking railroad workers marched up toward a rally along the lake shore. Ben was dawdling along not paying much attention when suddenly he found himself engulfed in the demonstration. A string of men with torches led the march. Behind them came a large banner bearing the words JUSTICE FOR WORKERS. And behind the banner marched a crowd of men, some waving sticks, some carrying signs, still others bearing more blazing torches. About the time the crowd overtook Ben, they began singing some sort of anthem Ben.

It terrified him momentarily when he looked up and saw himself surrounded by men brandishing sticks and torches. For just a moment he thought they'd come for him. The singing relieved his anxieties and he let himself get swept up in the spirit of the march. He didn't think of himself as an oppressed worker, but during his sojourn among the tramps he'd seen what economic oppression could do to people. Ben knew that some of those men now living as hobos had once been farmers and factory workers who'd had the bad fortune of losing their job to protect some rich man's investments.

And so it was easy for him to push his hunger aside and to join in with the crowd. He still couldn't understand the words of the song they were singing, but he could understand their emotions. They were feelings not far from his own—a longing for justice, for job security, for happiness, for the promise of a future... for love.

Even as he thought that last word, he had to wonder if these other men felt love was a priority or if that were solely his concern. He knew, of course, that as human beings these men all needed to have a family and friends who cared about them. But he wondered if loving and being loved itself were so important. Among the crowd he saw a number of women, wives of the workers, he assumed, though realized they may have been workers too. Somehow it all seemed so much easier for other people to find love, he thought. He wondered why it seemed so difficult for him.

Ben understood the need for higher wages, for economic justice. He could shout those demands honestly enough. But there was something else going on for him. As he joined in the shouted slogans and allowed his feelings to surge with the crowds, he knew he wanted to demand something else, some other right to common human decency that he had no words or even thoughts for. He didn't know what it would feel like to be oppressed as a worker, but he remembered how oppressed he'd felt in the seminary, at least there at the end, when his side of the story was ignored and when the deep feelings that Jeremy had stirred were denied. Those memories powered his shouts for justice and fair play.

"Aren't you ever going to meet Tom?" I interrupted Ben's stirring account of the noble workers' march.

"What makes you think we're going to meet?" Ben razzed me.

"Well, I know perfectly well what those feelings of yours were and I would know what you needed to do about them?"

"Oh, you would?"

"I've been in all kinds of marches. Back in the sixties I marched for civil rights and against Viet Nam. In the seventies I marched for gay rights. In the eighties I marched for AIDS funding. I think all the while I knew what my personal agenda was. I was looking for a boyfriend—at least for after the march."

"That's all you wanted?"

"Okay, okay. I guess I was a little flippant about that."

"I'll say... "

"What I meant was that all those marches—whatever they're for—are about people calling for change and improvement in their lives; they see injustice and they want to do something about it. I think gay people are especially apt to see injustice because we live so close to it—my god, I mean, we even do it to ourselves. So there've probably always been a lot of gay people involved in radical movements."

"Yes," Ben said, "I'm listening."

"I think the first time I ever really realized there were other people like me, I mean other people who were gay as a class of people, not just as something they did in bed, was when I was at a poetry reading about the horrors of war. I really wasn't listening to the poetry. I was noticing these two long-haired hippie guys sitting on a sofa across from me. They were holding hands. It was so beautiful. Like a revelation. I didn't know what gay people looked like back then, but all of a sudden I knew I wasn't alone in that room... "

"So you weren't always so aware yourself, Mr. Sophisticate," Ben said. "You were making fun of me for being innocent and naïve."

"I was young," I countered plaintively.

"We were all young," he answered.

When Tom got home from his aimless wandering, he found Eli sitting in the living room dressed like a mountain climber instead of a professor. "I was waiting for you. There's a labor march downtown. I think we should go, if only to show our support."

"I'm not a union member," Tom answered.

"Neither am I, young man, neither am I," Eli answered somewhat indignantly. "But we can't ignore the plight of the common man. Besides, I thought you told me you'd been fired from your job for no reason. I think you have a grievance against the economic system just like those striking railroad workers."

"I suppose so."

"Tom, I certainly won't force you, but let me appeal to your humanity… "

"Well, Eli, maybe you're right. Let me change into something more rugged. I see you're dressed for trouble."

"You never know."

Tom and Eli joined the marchers at the very start of their route. They stood around in the milling crowd for a while. "Reminds me of that novel by Victor Hugo about the French Revolution," Eli shouted over the crowd. "The people rising up for their rights." Then he added, whispering in Tom's ear, "Strapping fellows, eh? Walt Whitman's type." Tom didn't reply, but he too was looking around at the crowd. Finally they heard whistles blowing and then with a great cheer the crowd began to move.

It was somewhere along Michigan Avenue as they were coming up to the rally that Tom saw a familiar face in the crowd. "Eli," he shouted over the din, "I think I see that young man I was looking for."

"Well, what are you waiting for then. Take courage, my son. Don't waste another moment." From the sound of Eli's voice it was obvious he'd really gotten into the swing of the march.

Tom too felt enlivened. There was a camaraderie in the crowd that promised to make it easy for strangers to speak to one another. Keeping his eye on the shock of bright red-gold hair he'd recognized in the light of a nearby torch, Tom pushed his way through the crowd.

"Hello," he shouted, reaching out his hand. "I think I've seen you before."

The red-haired young man looked at him quizzically. It took him a moment to respond. A moment that cut into Tom like a knife. What if this fellow doesn't recognize me? I'll feel like such a fool.

"Sure, you were in the soda fountain this afternoon."

"That *was* you." Tom exclaimed happily.

"Huh?"

"We first, uh, met in the park."

"Yeah, by the fountains with the pigeons."

Tom felt a surge of elation. "My name's Tom Milam."

"I'm Ben Mayfield. You don't sound like you're from around here."

"Texas."

"I'm from Illinois, down state. You work for the railroad?"

"Nope. I just came down here with a friend." He pointed at Eli.

"Can't see who you're pointing at."

"Don't matter." Tom answered and then found himself at a loss for words. He looked right into Ben's eyes and felt that same intense gaze returned. But then it lasted too long and they both looked down.

"Shucks," Tom said, sounding so Texan it embarrassed him, "sure am glad to meet ya here. That first day I thought I recognized you as this friend from downtown."

Ben laughed. They were both having to shout over the noise and to huddle together against the pressure of the crowd carrying them along. "I thought maybe you thought I was somebody you knew. I was trying to figure out who you were." All of a sudden a big man carrying a sign declaring DEATH TO THE BOSSES broke right between them and the crowd surged through behind him. Tom reached out and Ben grabbed his hand.

Once when a traveling science show came through San Antonio, Tom got cajoled by Johnny Kincaid into volunteering to be a guinea pig. The lecturer demonstrated electrical charge by vigorously rubbing a glass rod with a piece of cat fur. When the man touched Tom's hand with it, his hair stood on end. Then he got him to touch the live pole of a battery and Tom was practically thrown across the room. The touch of Ben's hand felt almost like that jolt of electricity, but this time it pushed him closer not further away. The crowd was starting to sing again and in the spirit of the song, as so many others were doing, Tom threw his arm over Ben's shoulder and they strode along together singing.

The march had reached the rally point and had stopped moving. Tom had already lost sight of Eli and figured he'd make it back home on his own. So he had no reluctance to step back out of the crowd when Ben suggested it.

They stood among some trees at the edge of the throng and talked casually, almost as though they were old friends, commenting on characters they noticed around them. In doing so, they managed to communicate quite a bit of information to one another. Tom learned Ben was living in a lodging-house not far away, somewhere on Esmeralda Street, and working for a printer near that soda fountain where he'd stopped for a strawberry phosphate. (He didn't admit to Ben that he'd actually been there a couple of times looking for him.) He also learned that Ben was really worried about some man who held a grudge against him and had threatened him. Ben said he was thinking about getting out of Chicago.

Tom rejoined that he too was thinking about leaving, going to California, maybe to work the goldfields. Ben agreed that sounded like a good plan. They actually began talking as though this were something they might do together.

"Let's talk about this some more," they both said simultaneously and laughed at the coincidence.

Then, abruptly, further conversation was drowned out by the sound of whistles and the roar of the crowd. Tom looked around to see what was happening. Armed guards were surging through the crowd with billy clubs breaking up the demonstration. Railroad police sent by the bosses, Tom thought. He learned later that they were actually the national militia sent in to quell the rioting by command of President Harrison himself.

Tom clutched at Ben's arm and they began running together. At first they thought they were running away from the crowd and would soon be out of the whole melee. But as they turned a corner they were suddenly back right in the middle of things and there were two militiamen brandishing clubs coming right at them. They had to let go of each other or risk having an arm broken. Both ran as hard as they could to get away. As it was, Tom barely avoided a blow of the club. He was sure he could hear the whirr of the wood through the air as it passed right by his ear.

He stopped running for a moment and looked around for Ben. He was nowhere to be seen. Tom called out Ben's name, but there was so much noise there was no way he could be heard for more than a few feet. All of a sudden he was alone. Again.

At least now Tom knew Ben worked at the print shop. He could find him this time.

22

en explained to me that he just didn't know how he let himself get separated from Tom. He'd thought that in the midst of that crazy crowd he'd found a friend, that he'd made the magical connection with somebody he'd been longing for. In fact, he admitted to me that while he stood there talking with Tom, he was offering thanks to the Blessed Mother for answering his heartfelt prayer for someone to love and to love him. Then, just as surprisingly as he had appeared, he was gone. The fleeing crowd and trampling militiamen had driven them asunder.

But that was not all. To make matters worse, as Ben wandered through the night calling out Tom's name, out of the darkness suddenly came the stumbling hulk of Josh B'Gosh from Oshkosh. He was obviously very drunk and could barely stand up straight. He grabbed at Ben's arm. "I'm gonna jocker ya to death, ya little bastard. Just you wait. You put out my eye and you gonna pay."

Indeed, Ben could see that Josh's right eye was swollen and festering.

"It wasn't my fault. Look, I'm sorry."

"Your ass'll be sorry, that's for sure," Josh guffawed.

"Leave me alone. Just leave me alone, please." Ben pulled away and started to run. Josh was too intoxicated to pursue.

"I been followin' you. I know where you work. I know you work at that print shop."

As Ben ran, he felt his blood go cold.

23

n the late afternoon of the next day, a little before most shops closed down, Tom went over to the print shop where he now knew Ben worked. He was feeling joyful about having made a friend. When he'd come home last night he'd felt whatever barrier had arisen between him and Eli was now gone. They'd had a delightful evening as Eli recounted the history of the labor movement in Britain and the U.S. and Tom excitedly described his meeting Ben. Tom had gone on to develop his plans for finding work and getting a place to live in Chicago—perhaps Ben would want to rent a small house with him. Eli cautioned Tom about moving too fast but was encouraging and quite happy for him.

From across the street Tom watched the printer come up from the back of the shop and pull down a shade over the window in the front door. That must mean closing time.

After a few more minutes, the printer himself came out through the door. Alone. He stopped, then went back in. (Tom's heart was beating hard.) And then he came back out and locked the door behind him. No Ben. For a few seconds Tom stood paralyzed, then realized he had to find out where Ben was. He quickly crossed the street and, hastening his step, caught up with the printer by the end of the block.

"S'cuse me, sir. I was waiting for your assistant, Ben Mayfield."

"You mean the deliveryboy?"

"He didn't come out of the shop with you…?"

"Funny thing. He seemed to be working out so well. Don't know. Help is so hard to find these days. Say, you need a job?"

"No sir, no… well, yes, in fact. But I was askin' 'bout Ben."

"Oh, the hell with him. I found a note stuck in the door this morning saying something had happened and he'd have to quit. The note was real polite. But, damn it, that's no way to resign a position. I had a stack of jobs for him to deliver. And then he goes and treats me dirty like that. Maybe he was put out 'cause I asked him to work overtime yesterday. These damn labor unions are making people think they can get away with murder."

Tom was trembling. The printer kept walking at a steady clip. Tom had to push himself to keep up. "Did the note say anything about where Ben might be?"

"Damn fool said he was going to California. Said he had to leave. Sure, guess he heard some drunk talking about making a fortune in gold. Take it from me, that is not the way to make a living. What kind of world would we have if everybody walked off their job every time they heard about some fool get-rich-quick scheme... "

"Did he say when he was leaving?" Tom persevered in spite of the printer's ranting.

"Look, mister, did you say you wanted that job? I won't hire you regular cause you're a friend of that Ben's. But I got a lot of work to get done tomorrow. I'll give you a chance."

"Thank you, sir. Really. But I'm trying to find Ben."

"Well, that's your problem. To hell with it. But, look, if you want to make some money, you come by the shop in the morning... "

"Do you know where he lives?"

"Where who lives?"

"Ben, Ben Mayfield."

"What's into you? How come you're so interested in this Ben? Ha!" the printer laughed scornfully, "I bet he owes you money. To hell with you too." He picked up his step, obviously intending to leave Tom behind. "Why don't you try the train station?" he shouted back, "or the freight yard... "

Tom was crushed. He remembered Eli warning him about moving too fast. What if it was his show of interest last night that scared Ben off?

Downcast, he turned and trudged back in the direction of the print shop. As he neared the now closed and shuttered doorway, he was accosted by a weather-beaten tramp, "Hey, Buddy, gimme a nickel."

Tom ignored him. The best thing to do in situations like this is to just keep walking, he told himself. If you even let them see you're looking they're liable to put the bite on you.

"I said gimme me a nickel," the tramp said, turning to follow Tom.

"Look, I ain't got a job and I'm broke myself. I just can't help you." He glanced up at the big man as he kept moving. He felt an odd mixture of intimidation, pity, fear, and disgust. The tramp was huge. Tom realized he could probably beat him to death with only a couple of blows and take all the money he could get. But he sounded half-witted or maybe just crazy from living on the road and drinking too much booze. His right eye was festered; pus oozed down his cheek.

"You lookin' for that bastard Ben too?"

Tom didn't understand what the tramp had said. If he'd heard him, it just didn't make sense. "Huh?" He stopped walking and turned to face him.

"Bet you wanna jocker his pretty butt too," the tramp spit out.

Tom's repulsion increased dramatically. "What are you saying?" he

106

half-shouted.

"I heard you askin' 'bout that kid. Hey, whaddya find out?"

"What kid?"

"Ben. Ben the bastard that put m' eye out," he barked.

"What do you know about Ben?"

"I know I want 'im. Want 'is pretty butt all fo' my very own... "

"Shut up."

"Then I'll wring 'is neck till 'is eyes pop out. Like he did ta me."

"He's gone to California. Left town where you'll never find him."

"Oh, I'll find 'im. Josh here's nev'r gonna give up lookin'. Not if it takes me all the way ta Cali-for-nee-ai... "

"You're drunk."

"You would be too if you was hurtin' like me. Look what 'e done ta m' eye."

"It ain't Ben's fault," Tom answered defensively for his friend, suddenly realizing that the threats of this tramp might be the cause of Ben's flight and not his own display of personal interest. "You should see a doctor."

"Gimme a buck for the doc then. How's I gonna get a doctor ta help the likes o' me. You tell me. You tell me that," he started shouting.

Tom was frightened. But at the same time, he felt relieved. He wasn't sure of all the implications of this new discovery, but suddenly he knew *he* wasn't at fault for Ben's disappearance. He could ill afford it, but he reached into his pocket and found a wadded up bill and pushed it into the tramp's hand. "Show the doctor this," he said. "Or go to a hospital. Don't waste it on booze. And don't blame Ben." He said all this as he backed away from the man. Then he turned and started walking away as fast as he could.

"I'll jocker both yo' butts. I'll show you." Tom heard the tramp raving on as he hurried down the street.

A couple of blocks away it occurred to him that the printer had had a good idea. He stopped and asked directions of a policeman and then headed toward the train station.

Later, back at Eli Hauptmann's, as he was packing the few clothes he'd brought as well as a few hand-me-downs Eli had added to his meager collection, Tom explained to Eli what he'd learned and what he thought he ought to do.

"I really appreciate all the help you've been. I could never repay you... " Eli held up his hand palm outward as if to say there was no need to be concerned. "I'm just not makin' it here. I can't find a job. There're labor riots and crazy people. I came to Chicago 'cause I thought I had a friend here. And now he's gone to California. And now the one friend I thought I'd made here has also gone to California... "

"I can see why you'd feel that way."

"The railroads are practically shut down by the strike. But there's a train leaving tomorrow morning. I bought myself a ticket. Ben might be on it. There was no train leaving today, so maybe... "

107

"Could he have left on a freight train? You said he'd hopped a train on his way up here." Tom smiled at the way the words "hopped a train" sounded in Eli's refined, carefully spoken English. He realized he'd really come to like and admire this man. He hoped this would not be the last time he would see him.

"Maybe. The man at the ticket window was reluctant to give me information about freight schedules. Though after I bought a ticket, he seemed a little less concerned that I was going to try to hitch a free ride myself. He told me all the trains were laying over in Denver. Nothing going straight through and nothing leaving there before tomorrow. Whatever Ben does, I think, I can be in Denver 'bout the same time."

"And if you don't find him?"

"Well, then I take your first advice, Eli, and go on to San Francisco. Maybe I'll meet the right kind of people out there. Maybe even strike gold. Maybe get rich and go back to Texas." For the first time in a long time he thought about the Milam family legacy and about proving himself worthy. He grinned. His adventurous spirit was alive again after a hard week in Chicago.

24

om walked up and down the aisle the length of the train at least four times hoping to find Ben. Finally, despairing of success in that endeavor, he sat down and drifted off into a half-dreamy sleep. He kept jolting awake every time the train stopped, thinking he'd arrived in California and both Johnny Kincade and Ben Mayfield were waiting for him on the platform with their arms full of gold nuggets the size of hens' eggs.

He tried to make some sense of the experiences of the last two weeks. But so much had happened so fast he didn't know how to assimilate it: the strangely-veiled conversations with Eli Hauptmann on the way up from Texas; the discovery that Johnny had become a different person and been driven out of his home; the revelation of what Eli had really been talking about, the night in Eli's arms and the terrible round of self-recriminations afterwards; the quest for the mysterious red-haired boy and the so-coincidental finding of Ben Mayfield and the unleashing of feelings Tom had kept so well controlled. Were those feelings the same things Eli had talked about? It certainly seemed that way. But... but...

Finally the train arrived in Denver. Because there was no Pullman car—the Pullman porters had respected the picket lines—the train would have an overnight stop. Tom was glad of that. That would allow time for his search through the station and trainyard for Ben. Though now that he was actually here, he realized he didn't know how to go about such a search at all. As it turned out he wasn't going to have to search. As he was getting down from the coach, he heard a scuffle coming from down the train a ways. Several porters and conductors were standing around at the door to one of the cars. Assuming there was some sort of labor dispute and feeling a connection with the workers' grievances as a result of participating in the march and rally two nights ago in Chicago, he went down to watch.

As he approached what he could see by the sign was a baggage car, he heard several pained cries and then saw that a body was being passed down from the porters in the car to those standing around on the platform. He could see it seemed to be just a boy, his face was bloodied...

And the recognition hit him... Ben!

He dropped his bag and ran up toward the porters who were now hoisting the boy on their shoulders—almost like a casket being carried in procession. "Wait!" Tom shouted. "What are you doing with him?"

A conductor who'd just jumped down from the baggage car clasped Tom's shoulder. "It's alright, sir. A stowaway. Hiding behind some crates. Cheats people like yourself, you know. Good paying passengers shouldn't have to put up with this kind of crap, if you'll excuse my expression."

"What'll they do with him?" Tom had the good sense to get some information before volunteering that he knew the young man.

"Well, it looks like he owes us the price of passage from Chicago to Denver. My guess is they'll throw him in jail till he pays up. Sometimes," the conductor winked as he included Tom in what was apparently supposed to be a secret, "they just beat 'em bloody and toss 'em back behind the platform. Dunno what 'appens to 'em after that. Maybe the dogs take care of 'em."

"If I paid for his ticket, would you let him go?"

"Now why would a nice gentleman like yourself wanna go wastin' 'is money on trash like that?"

"Would you let him go?"

"If he's got a ticket, I guess I don't see why not."

"Look, how much do I owe you?" Tom hastily pulled out the small wad of bills that was all that was left of his savings.

"Well, now, let me see... "

Tom interrupted, seeing that the porters were carrying Ben further back into the bowels of the station. "Stop those men before they hurt him anymore."

"Hey, boys, put 'im down. This 'gentleman's' gonna pay his passage." He snickered. "Now, as I was sayin' there's a slight charge for buyin' the ticket on the train stead o' at the station. And then there's a fee for buyin' it at this end. And, it seems to me we got a tax here in Colorado... "

Ben smiled in acknowledgement. He wasn't too badly hurt. His face was bruised up some and he'd probably have a knot on his head for a few days.

"Thank God I found you," Tom exclaimed as he daubed away the blood on Ben's face with his kerchief which he'd wet at the fountain in the waiting room. He'd helped Ben to one of the benches.

"The porter hit me upside the head with a piece of pipe, it looked like. I was crouching down behind a steamer trunk—I couldn't get out of the baggage car when we stopped. I 'member Josh warned me 'bout that," Ben said the last words kind of dreamily to himself. He was perhaps still a little delirious.

"Why didn't you buy a ticket?"

"I had to leave in a hurry. I mean there was this guy threatening to, uh, uh… "

"I know," Tom interrupted. "I saw him outside the print shop when I went to find you after work."

"He was there? Thank God I got away. But, see, I never got paid for my work last week. Just a couple of dollars and some change to buy my dinner."

"Well, I paid your way this far now. That's how come you're not dead or in jail."

"Gosh. Thank you. I promise I'll get you back the money."

"That's okay. Though, look, we ain't got much money left between us. And I don't see how we're gonna get to California."

"That's where you're going too?" Ben asked seeming surprised.

"I thought we talked about that. Ain't that why you're goin' west?"

"Guess so. I just didn't realize… "

Didn't realize I was following you, Tom finished Ben's sentence in his mind. What have I done? What if…?

"Well, I got us enough to buy dinner," Ben said. "And I sure am hungry. How 'bout you?"

Over a thick steak and baked potato and carrots at a saloon down the street from the train station, Tom finally got up the nerve to make a suggestion. "Look, Ben, I, I don't know how to say this."

"Go on, I'm listening."

"Well, I mean, here we are. I got a ticket the rest of the way to 'Frisco, but I see you're dead broke."

Ben grinned, "Yeah, 'specially after this meal… "

"I could cash in my ticket. That'd give us some money for a couple of days. We could work here a while. Make enough cash to get us the rest o' the way in a couple of weeks or something."

"We could hop a freight," Ben suggested.

"After all the bad luck you've had?"

"I guess so. Well, then, sure. Sounds great." Ben blushed and looked down at the table. "You sure you'd do this for me. I mean, how come?"

Tom felt his heart racing. What was he going to say? He wasn't sure himself how come he was doing it.

"I guess I'm plumb tired o' travelin' alone. And, guess, you know, Ben, I sorta like you."

Ben smiled a glowing smile that must've hurt the swollen tissue of his brow and cheeks. "I sorta like you, too."

After eating they both felt better. Tom's anxieties were allayed for the time being. Ben's wounds weren't hurting nearly as much. And they were both laughing. The couple of beers they drank with the steak certainly helped.

"Well, you said you ran into ol' Josh B'Gosh from Oshkosh."

"Who?"

"That tramp. That's his hobo name, his 'monikey' as they call it. The man you said was waiting for me at the print shop."

"Yeah. He looked pretty bad, pretty mean, and pretty drunk."

"He had *me* pretty scared."

"I can imagine. Well, he'll be no harm to you now. Like I told him, you're gone for good."

"Like you told him?" Ben inquired hesitantly. "What did you tell him?"

"Oh, I think I said you'd gone to California."

"Oh, Tom." Ben's voice was trembling.

"Look," Tom hastened to comfort Ben—and to defend himself. "Even if he hops the next freight to 'Frisco, if we stay here he'll be long gone."

"I guess so. I'm just worrying about nothing."

Tom decided not to mention that because of the strike the next freight train was probably going to get laid over in Denver. He figured they'd get a room for the night and hopefully by morning Josh would've continued on on another train. If there was another train...

25

 made a ribald remark to Tom that I was glad they finally made it to bed. I was getting tired of the suspense. "You sure had a rough time of finding sex in those days."

"I thought you thought everything was wonderful in the 'good ol' days'," he answered snidely.

"Well, I didn't realize being gay was such a burden."

"You think it isn't such a burden now?"

"Oh, sure, with AIDS and the backlash and all that. But it seems like we're so much more sophisticated about things today. I mean it sure wouldn't have taken me as long to get Ben in bed... "

"Oh yeah?"

"Oh yeah. I mean, I understand there were logistical problems and all that. But why all this fretting over...?"

"So you've never fretted?" he scolded me playfully. "But anyway so you think that's what happened?"

"Well, wasn't it?

Tom asked at the saloon where they'd eaten about an inexpensive place to stay for the night. The bartender said there were cabins out back as cheap as any they were likely to find elsewhere.

"Absolute rock bottom price on a room with a single cot."

"There're two of us. Shouldn't we have two beds?"

"Haven't got nothing else. It'll cost ya more elsewhere. Look, I don't care how many guys you put in there. Besides, there ain't no heat. It's gonna get cold tonight. You can keep each other warm."

Tom looked at Ben, somewhat embarrassed.

"Fine with me. Let's save the money. I'd rather eat. Hey, how about a bath?"

"'Nother nickel. And let's see, three cents for the towel."

"Okay, that sounds good," Tom agreed. He was glad Ben made the decision. And he was glad Ben suggested the bath. He knew that would feel good.

"Bathroom's back that way," the bartender pointed. "There oughta be a lady back there. You can arrange with her if there'll be anything else you're needin'," the bartender winked. "Say, you know, you can both get a girl for the price of one."

Tom blushed. Ben giggled nervously.

The bed turned out to be actually more than a cot. It was wide enough for both of them to lie on their backs at the same time so long as they didn't mind their shoulders touching. At first, each of them seemed to make an effort to avoid even that contact. They lay side by side and talked for a while—mostly about favorite memories from the past and dreams for the future. Neither of them mentioned marrying and raising a family as one of those dreams.

Finally, nervously, Tom announced it seemed like it was time to get to sleep. He rolled over on his side facing away from Ben.

"Good night."

"Good night." Tom could feel the warmth of Ben's back lightly touching him near the small of his own back. The warmth felt good. It reminded him just a little of the warmth he'd felt from Eli Hauptmann's body. As he let his consciousness focus on that warmth and his memory slip back to that night with Eli, his penis began to grow hard. He tried to fight the reflex. He didn't want the feelings he was feeling to be sexual like that. But fighting didn't do much good.

After a while Ben whispered, "Tom, hey, you still awake?"

At first Tom started not to answer. He was afraid of what might happen if he did. He was afraid of what he might *want* to happen if he did. But answer he had to. "Yeah."

"I'm cold. Mind if I squeeze up against you? You feel so warm."

"Guess not." He felt funny all over. His heart was pounding. He was both hot and cold at the same time.

Tom kept his eyes tightly shut, but listened to every sound as Ben sort of shook the blanket and then rolled over. The bed creaked with each movement. Ben carefully pressed himself up against Tom's back, curling his legs up so they fit into the crook of Tom's knees. Except for Ben's left arm that remained between them they fit up against each other perfectly.

After a moment, Ben reached his right arm around Tom's chest and lay his hand over his heart, gently ruffling and then smoothing the thick hair that grew there. "You're kind," Ben whispered. "And so warm. This is much better. Is it okay?" he asked.

"Sure," Tom answered. He was aware that he could feel a hint of pressure against the back of his thighs where Ben's penis pushed against him. He too was full. Somehow that reassured him. And wondering what it suggested that the two of them could lie there together so intimately, so trusting, so open and vulnerable with one another, Tom slipped into sleep.

"You mean that's *all* that happened?" I objected.

Tom answered, "That was really quite a lot, don't you think?"

"Maybe for you guys... "

"Rick, don't you know anything about courtship?"

"Certainly. I think I've courted enough men in my life."

"Where is he then?"

"Huh?"

"You said you'd courted men. Doesn't that mean you have a spouse? I don't think we've met. Is he here?"

"Now you know better than that."

"Perhaps you've been widowed?" he said sympathetically. "I know how hard that can be."

I had to think about that for a moment. The truth was I guess I had been widowed—now more times than I wanted to imagine. But, of course, those relationships had all been over long before the widowing. A lot of the widowings I probably didn't even know about.

"Now don't you go making fun of me. After all, I'm your creator."

"What a dismal world it would be if we couldn't have a little fun with our creator," Tom answered playfully. "I'm sure your creator would appreciate your having a little more fun with him than you do."

"It looks to me sometimes like my creator is more interested in torturing me than having fun."

"Oh?"

"Well, you were the one mentioning being widowed."

Tom shook his head. It occurred to me that perhaps he felt sorry for me.

I too wondered where my spouse was. What ever happened to all my dreams of finding Mr. Right and moving to the cottage with the white picket fence and the eternally setting sun? Had I gotten cynical?

I let my own head drop. And then I nodded gravely to myself. What did I know about courtship?

26

en awoke very early in the morning to find that sometime in the night Tom had rolled over and was now facing him. The bed sagged in the middle so they'd been pushed together naturally by their own weight.

Tom was still sleeping. Ben propped himself up on one elbow and studied the face of this man who was suddenly so close and so intimate. There was just enough hint of first light coming in through a transom window over the door for Ben to see. He thought Tom manly and handsome, dark and rugged in the way he'd always wanted to be. He thought Tom looked like what the heroes in adventure stories are supposed to look like. He thought he looked like a prince. He thought he looked like the ideal husband for an ideal woman.

Ben imagined for a moment that he was such a woman. He didn't feel himself all that manly anyway. He'd certainly never admit such a thing out loud, but here in the privacy of his thoughts in this dingy little room miles from where anybody knew or cared who he was, he felt it was alright to imagine he'd been born a girl instead of a boy. Thinking about how deeply moved he was by this man lying here with him he wished that that had been so, so that they could really bind their lives together.

He felt such a pang of dearness. He slipped the arm he'd been propping himself up on under Tom's shoulder, very gently so not to wake his sleeping prince. He nuzzled his face into Tom's neck, feeling the bristle of his beard. For the first time in a long time he felt safe. And in that safety he slipped back into sleep.

A little while later Ben was awakened by Tom's shifting positions. He startled into alertness realizing something was wrong. Between them, where their torsos touched, Ben could feel something slightly sticky, slightly crusty. He was terribly afraid that in his sleep he'd dreamed and in the dream become sexually aroused and committed this involuntary pollution. Embarrassed, he rolled over on his back, almost slipping out of the narrow bed. He lay staring up at the ceiling through half-closed eyes and remembered how Father Master had warned the seminarians that while this type of involuntary biological process could not be avoided entirely, it usually represented some spiritual laxness or failure to avoid a near occasion of sin; and above all, the priest had reiterated, it must never, never be given in to or relished.

Ben searched his conscience and the faint recollection of his morning dream. He could not remember having such a dream. Usually when this sexual reflex happened, he awoke immediately and had to struggle to prevent himself from enjoying the spontaneous ejaculation. But he could not remember any of that happening this morning.

Perhaps Tom... He was obviously a strong and virile man. And if he had not been with a woman in some time...

Ben remembered how the bartender had suggested hiring a woman to Tom. Maybe he had dreamed that such had really happened. Ben felt guilty that his presence had probably prevented Tom from accepting the bartender's suggestion. Maybe it was his fault after all.

He found himself obsessing again over the moral instruction the Master had given. For the first time he allowed himself to question the veracity of that. What sense could it make that God would send something so pleasurable and then demand that we prevent ourselves from feeling it? He thought about the time he was with Brother Jeremy. The Master had been wrong about that. Perhaps he was wrong about this too. Perhaps he—and all those other priests—had been wrong about a lot of things...

Ben looked over at Tom and saw that his eyes were fluttering. "Are you awake?" he whispered.

"Just barely," Tom answered.

Ben thought Tom's voice betrayed a hint of covert feeling. Maybe he's angry at me for not being a woman? Or maybe he's discovered what happened and knows it was me? Maybe he thinks I committed that pollution on purpose and... and polluted him with my sin?

Tom suddenly announced, "Well, rise and shine." He jumped out of bed and stood up, facing away from Ben.

Ben thought he could see Tom brushing the dried semen from his belly with the back of his hand. And he imagined again that whole series of projected reactions.

Pulling on his trousers, Tom said jauntily, "Let's find some coffee." He smiled warmly, though perhaps also showing a hint of embarrassment. "You game?"

"Sure." Ben jumped out of bed and dressed quickly. He avoided looking toward Tom lest Tom recognize feelings he knew weren't supposed to be there.

In doing so, of course, Ben failed to see that out of the corner of his eye Tom was watching him self-consciously.

115

27

he saloon was locked up tight. But down the street, right at the edge of the railroad yard, an old dining car had been rolled off the tracks and had been converted into a cafe. Tom checked his bag and Ben's knapsack back at the station and they headed down toward the diner. Tom could smell the coffee brewing from a block away.

Ben seemed awfully quiet this morning. Tom worried that Ben had correctly interpreted the tell-tale signs of his wet-dream. But he didn't want to broach the subject. Maybe it'd be best for all concerned to just forget about such things. Tom didn't even want to let himself remember the dream. He was sure the dream had been about Ben—or maybe Johnny Kincade. But either way, it needed to be forgotten.

They strolled down to the diner. The air was crystal clear. Great billowy clouds framed the horizon, rising up above majestic mountains.

"Hey, you ever seen a sight like that before?" Tom asked hoping to cheer Ben up and get their camaraderie back on track.

"Can't say as I have. It's truly magnificent."

The city of Denver was bigger than either of them expected. All around there were brick buildings; buggies rolled down the street. Even early in the morning the hubbub of a city was starting.

Over coffee, Tom suggested that perhaps they'd sleep better tonight if they found a bigger room. "Besides, we'll have jobs by then, won't we?" He said the last words more as a question calling for confirmation than as a statement of fact.

"I hope so," Ben answered. "I liked sleeping next to you though. You were real warm."

"Yeah, really cold night. Surprising it's not colder this morning," Tom answered, happy to let the cold explain away the night.

They asked the cook behind the counter if he knew of any work they could get. He was noncommittal, but did point them toward the industrial part of town.

It took several tries, but by lunchtime, they'd found temporary work cleaning out an old warehouse. There were already about five men working. It was hard work, but it paid pretty well. And it would allow Tom and Ben to work together, calming their private fears of another separation.

As he worked carrying boxes out to a wagon to be discarded and as he shoveled mounds of debris into crates for somebody else to cart off, Tom began to feel positive about his adventure again. He and Ben had managed to find work; after they got off they'd find themselves a room; that monster who had threatened Ben was left behind; the confusion about Johnny Kincade's disappearance that had beset Tom had faded; now there was just the present... and the future. Together, he was sure, they'd make it to California. And with each other's support, they'd find a gold mine. One day they'd marry great ladies who'd cook and take care of them and they'd live together in a big mansion on a hill overlooking San Francisco. Or maybe they'd go back to Texas and buy a ranch. Then they'd never have to remember the rough times ever again.

After their third day on the job, they were heading home to the lodging house they'd found not far from that diner by the railroad yard. Ben was laughing and cracking jokes. Tom was tired but enjoying Ben's little performance. Maybe they were both so tired they were a little punchy.

As they turned a corner to take a short-cut they'd discovered through an alley, they nearly ran right into the massive bulk of Josh B'Gosh. He was standing with a couple of other hobos, one of whom, rather ingenuously, asked Ben for a dime.

"Well, well. I thought youse guys was in Cali-for-nee, waitin' for me. Here I been just bidin' my time wit' m' buddies here. And I never knows you was in town." He sounded less drunk to Tom than before. Which meant he might be more dangerous.

Josh reached out and cuffed Ben on the ear, "Benjy, my boy. Good to see you. I've been keeping somethin' special just fo' you." With his other hand he clasped his crotch.

"Uh, how's your eye?" Ben asked, though the answer was obvious. Josh's right eye was covered with a black patch.

"Wanna see for yourself, huh?" he punched Ben lightly on the chest.

"Huh?" Josh started to turn up the patch.

"No," shouted Ben abruptly. "I just hoped you weren't hurt. I didn't mean to hurt you, Josh. I really didn't."

"Look how sincere he sounds," Josh said to his friends. He turned back to Ben. "Well, thanks to your friend here, maybe I weren't hurt so bad." He turned to Tom. "I took your advice. The doc gave me the patch and put on some salve that stopped the hurtin'. 'Course I can't see outta it," his voice turned steely again, "but it don't pain me none."

"I'm happy to hear that," Tom said.

"Well, you just be. You just be real happy. Cause I'm so-o-o thankful to you that I'm gonna let you boys pass right by here *this* time. You 'member ol' Josh got somethin' waitin' for you, but as a sign of my grat-tee-tood, I'm letting you pass right on by. But now I knows you're here, I'll be keepin' m' good eye out for ya."

Ben grabbed Tom by the back of his jacket, "C'mon," he shouted and started running.

A few blocks down the street both of them were out of breath. Ben stopped running. "We gotta get outta town. Now, Tom. I can't stand it."

"Ben, look, I don't think he's as dangerous as you think. I mean, that was his chance and he didn't do nothin'."

117

"He's playing with us, Tom. Like a cat playing with a mouse. But if we're around here when he's mad... well, I just don't want to be. I want to get out of here now. And I want you to come with me. But if you don't want to, I'll go by myself."

"Look, Ben, please don't run off without me. But right now, let's get home and have dinner and then talk about what to do. We can't make a decision when we're upset."

"But he'll find out where we live."

"How?"

"I don't know. He's got spies all around town. I don't know."

"Oh, Ben, come off it. He's just a hobo. Maybe pretty big and pretty stupid and pretty violent. But he can't... "

"Yes, he can, Tom. He can find us in the night and he can... he can ram himself up inside me and... and... "

"Oh, boy, calm down. Calm down. Don't talk that way."

Ben was practically blubbering. Tom guided him carefully down the street. He did his best to make sure they weren't being observed. But, of course, Denver was a big city and there were lots of people on the street. How could you tell if one of them was a spy for Josh? On the other hand, Tom thought, why would you think *any* of them would be?

After dinner—lamb chops, mashed potatoes, corn on the cob, and apple pie—Ben seemed to feel better. But he was still insistent they should speed up their plans to leave Denver.

"But we haven't made enough money yet," Tom objected. "Let's just work another week. How're we going to afford the tickets otherwise?"

"We'll hop a train."

"Sure. Just look where that got you last time."

"Okay. So I chose the wrong train and the wrong car. Look, I know how to do this. I can show you. Especially if we're together we'll be safe."

"I don't like this idea one bit."

"Look, if we wait around here he's liable to find us. So far he's just threatened. But, Tom, I'm scared. I just can't help it. And if we stay till we have just enough money for two tickets to San Francisco, we won't have any left when we get there. Right now we've got some spending money. If we hopped a freight in the morning, we can be rid of the threat of Josh and have some cash too."

Tom repeated himself. He didn't like this idea. But he realized he felt protective of Ben. Even if there was no real threat from Josh—and Tom was convinced that was the case—Ben's distress was a problem to be resolved all by itself.

The room they were staying in had two single beds. Sometime during the middle of the night Tom was awakened by Ben's insistent shaking. "Come here. Look."

Tom roused himself and followed Ben to the window. And mimicking Ben, he crouched low and peered up over the sill. There seemed to be several tramps lounging on the front stoop of a building across the street. Tom could see the red-orange tip of a cigarette occasionally erupt into brightness.

"He knows where we are, Tom," Ben whispered urgently.

"How do you know that's Josh over there?" Tom complained, feeling annoyed that his sleep had been interrupted for something so silly.

"Look, the guy in the middle. Isn't he big? Like Josh?"

"I dunno, Ben." There did seem to be a very big man in the group over there. Or maybe it was just a guy standing on a box or something. It could be Josh. But it probably wasn't. "It's the middle of the night. You're just imagining things."

"Tom, please. Let's get away from here."

"Go back to sleep," Tom said irritably turning away and climbing back into bed. It was cold out from under the covers.

After a while Ben did likewise. Tom lay awake for a long time unable to sleep. What if Ben was right? What if that was Josh? And what if Josh really was as dangerous as Ben believed? After all, Ben had half-blinded him. If he was unstable and potentially violent to begin with, something like that could have pushed him over the edge. Maybe he was playing with them now. But what if he finally turned on them?

Tom thought for a while that the two of them together could certainly beat him. He was big, but he wasn't invulnerable. But neither of them were particularly practiced fighters, he told himself. And even if they managed to fight him off, he might maim or even kill one of them in the process.

Tom was less concerned about the potential for sexual assault partly because that threat had never come close to home for him and partly because he wasn't altogether able to conceive just what it was about. At the same time, he understood that something pretty traumatic had happened to make Ben so skittish.

That's really what worried him the most: Ben's terror.

After what seemed like a very long time, Tom heard Ben whisper his name from his bed across the room. "You awake?"

"Yeah, guess so."

"I just wanted to make sure you were still there. I was afraid you'd left."

"You musta been dreamin'. I'm here, Ben. I promise I'll be here."

In the morning Tom awoke to find Ben stuffing what few clothes he had into the knapsack he'd managed to carry all this way. "Whatcha doin'?"

"I didn't sleep hardly any last night. Look, Tom, I just gotta go. If you don't want to come, that's okay. You don't owe me anything. In fact, I guess, I'm the one owes you. Maybe we can meet in 'Frisco when you get there."

Tom rolled on his side and propped himself on an elbow. "I thought we were gonna be partners."

"Yeah, well… "

"C'mon, Ben, just wait a couple days more."

"Tom, I heard him out there last night. He was calling out this name he made up for me, 'Benjy.' I know it was him. I know he's gonna do something awful."

"I bet you were just dreamin'. C'mere, boy," Tom reached out his hand.

Ben stood looking helpless across the room. His eyes were red, perhaps from crying. "It's not just cause you won't believe me. You treat me like a child," he blurted out, then picked up his knapsack and, in a flash, was out the door.

28

en ran down the stairs of the lodging-house. Darting through the kitchen, he grabbed a loaf of bread and an apple from the table and then left by the back door. He felt terrible about leaving Tom. But he also felt he owed it to Tom to release him both from the threat from the angered mountain man and from the unseemly feelings for him he knew were growing inside him. Besides, Tom wouldn't believe him. How could they ever be friends or partners?

He sneaked around the side of the house and then hunkered down so he could peer through some bushes at those men across the street. A couple of them were still there. This morning there was no big man in the middle. But that didn't mean he wasn't there last night. And it didn't mean that hadn't been Josh.

Ben's lack of sleep and that terrifying experience in the night—was Tom right that it had been a dream?—of hearing Josh calling out to him, serenading him from below the window with that awful nickname, "Benjy Pretty-Butt," left Ben confused and almost hysterical. He kept remembering lying on the hard floor of that warehouse in Chicago and feeling Josh caressing him and then trying to force himself into him. Somehow, in the night, those memories got all mixed up with his memories of sleeping with Tom in the little cabin behind the saloon.

In the way that fear and hysteria can do, Ben had begun to imagine that Tom too wanted to jocker him, to punish him for not being the woman that Tom really needed, maybe even to hand him over to Josh so that Josh could abuse him like that and then gouge out his eyes and leave him bleeding in an alley.

The fact was Ben had been through terrible trauma in the past two weeks. He'd been teased by his brother's friends at the soda fountain, fired from his job, driven from home, forced to jump from a bridge hundreds of feet in the air, been nearly raped, beaten by trainmen, and was now being tormented by this crazy tramp. In the middle of all that he thought he'd found a friend, somebody to love. But how could he be sure? Acknowledging the deep feelings of this friendship were forcing him to admit to desires he'd been taught to believe were mortally sinful and deserving of eternal punishment in the fires of hell.

So perhaps it's not surprising he was confused and hysterical as he peered out from behind the bush beside the lodging-house. Perhaps it's not surprising that when he heard his name being called from the front steps of the house (after all, he saw the men across the street point this way and jeer), he imagined he was hearing his tormentor Josh—and not Tom, the man who loved him.

He fled to the back of the house and out into an alley and down toward the trainyard. He'd been watching the railroad every morning when he and Tom went to work. He was sure now there was a train pulling out of the yard going west. This morning he could be on it. And be carried away to freedom and peace.

29

hen Ben slammed the door shut behind him, Tom rolled onto his back, let out a deep breath, and thought to himself, "Good riddance." The kid had suddenly turned crazy. Besides for Tom too the closeness had proved upsetting. Especially since that first night in Denver when he'd unintentionally allowed himself to treat Ben as Eli had treated him, as an object of sexual desire, he'd felt ashamed and afraid of his feelings. He let himself think the boy was better off without him.

But as he stared up at the ceiling, he realized how alone he felt and how much more alone he was going to feel later. He had searched up and down the streets of Chicago to find Ben and now, just when they were starting to develop an understanding between them, he was letting him go. No, that wasn't right.

Tom jumped out of bed and, not taking time to pull on his pants, grabbed a towel and wrapped it round his waist. He ran down the stairs, glanced quickly into the dining room in hopes he'd find Ben calmly sipping a cup of coffee, and then not seeing him, rushed to the front door. He threw open the door and called. "Ben... Ben... " He stepped far enough out onto the porch to look up and down the street a little ways. He couldn't see him. He noticed the tramps across the street were pointing at him, making comments he didn't bother to understand. "Apparently they've never seen a man in a towel before," he said to himself sarcastically. He made a rude gesture at them and then closed the door and ran back upstairs.

As he dressed quickly and stuffed his belongings into his little valise, he reassured himself that he hadn't seen Josh over there with those men. There hadn't been time for Ben to actually be accosted or pursued by him. Pushing himself as fast as he could, he listened for train whistles. He too remembered watching a train leaving from the depot westward in the early morning. He didn't know how much time he had. Nor did he know how he was even going to begin looking for Ben. All he knew was he'd come this far, he wasn't going to let this chance escape him. The fact is I love Ben, he told himself, at least as much as I'd loved Johnny Kincade.

It startled him to realize how easily he'd said those words to himself: "I love Ben."

30

en made it to the far end of the trainyard about the time he heard the whistle sound. He hoped that meant the train was pulling out. He'd run as fast as he could, taking as indirect a way as possible in case he was being followed. Several times he thought he'd seen Josh waiting for him at the end of a shadowy alley or behind the corner of a building. But he'd made it. As he rested on a fallen tree trunk a little ways from the tracks, he began to wonder if this whole thing had been imaginary.

He was just about to decide to go back to Tom and apologize for acting like a fool when he heard the whistle again and looked down the track to see the locomotive swing around a group of abandoned boxcars and head down the track toward him. At the same time he saw running along the track a figure he recognized immediately as Tom. He felt a sudden surge of affection and love.

Ben started to run back toward Tom. As they neared, Ben gestured to Tom to get back into the trees and undergrowth away from the track so the trainmen wouldn't see them and suspect they might be hitching a free ride. Ben didn't want to get caught again. As he thought that, he looked down the track to observe this was a long, long train coming. He remembered Josh had told him those might be the safest.

"I was just about to give up and come back," he said as he reached Tom and they threw their arms around one another and, losing their balance, fell together into the high grass. "I didn't want to leave you."

"And I didn't want you to leave without me," Tom answered, pulling Ben tight and laughing as they rolled into the grass.

The train came lumbering by, slowly beginning to pick up speed.

"What are we gonna do?" Ben asked.

"What a time to ask!" Tom exclaimed laughing, obviously happy he'd arrived just in time.

They looked at each other and then almost simultaneously shouted over the roar of the wheels on the track, "Let's go."

Ben took just a moment to point out to Tom what grasp to reach for as the cars sped by, then he started running alongside the train with Tom following. In a moment Ben had grabbed the rung of a ladder and pulled himself up and swung into an open boxcar. Tom tossed Ben his valise and then, panting and almost out of breath, grabbed hold of the same rung of the ladder and pulled himself up. Ben was laughing joyfully. He reached out to help Tom maneuver the short distance to the opening. They stood together watching as the trees rushed by.

"Not so hard, was it?" Ben asked.

Tom let out his breath in a great sigh and clutched at his heart. "Well," he breathed deeply again. "I was almost out of breath. But, hey, we made it."

"Now the next trick is staying hidden, just in case," Ben pointed out the obvious. He was looking back into the car to see if there were crates or something to hide behind when Tom called to him.

"Hey, look at this."

As the train continued around the broad sweeping turn it was making as it left Denver, they suddenly came upon an open field dotted with tents and little wooden lean-tos. Around the field fires burned, sending up columns of smoke. "A hobo jungle," Ben explained. "This is like the one where I met the first tramps."

"Where you met that guy Josh?" Tom asked

"Oh my God no," Ben shouted, pointing down into the hobo jungle near the tracks.

Standing there by a fire, casually sipping coffee from a tin-can, was Josh B'Gosh. He looked up just as Ben pointed. A look of recognition spread across his face, then humor, then anger. He dropped the can right where he stood and ran back toward one of the tents nearby, apparently to grab the bed-roll he usually kept slung over one shoulder.

The train kept passing by. Ben had to lean out of the car and hold on tight to the door to keep Josh in sight. He watched the big man lumber back toward the train, then start to run alongside it. Ben said a silent prayer that the train would be moving too fast by now. Then he saw Josh reach up and grab a handhold and yank himself up onto a flatcar near the far end of the train.

Ben started to tremble. "Oh God, he's on the train with us."

"We're okay still," Tom reassured him. "Look, he's a long way back there. How's he gonna hurt us?"

"Yeah, but if he can get up on top of the cars he can come right up here." He looked around the car, "And this'd be the perfect place for him. I mean, how could we get away?"

Ben peered out. The track was straightening out now and as the cars lined up with one another, he was losing the view of that flat-car Josh was on. But as the cars clicked into line, Ben was sure he could see Josh jumping from that car onto the flat bed of the car in front of it. "Tom, I'm scared. We gotta get outta here."

"I agree with you. Whatever I thought before, Ben, I see that guy could be dangerous now. I saw the expression of hate on his face as we went by. But, look, we can't just jump off. He'd follow us. We gotta calm down and make a plan. Okay?"

"Okay?"

A little bit later they'd developed what they hoped would be a good escape. Tom discovered he could get the door open on the other side of the train. Josh probably wouldn't be expecting them to get out on that side and so wouldn't be paying as much attention in that direction. As the train had made more gentle curves, winding its way alongside the mountains—actually heading north out of Denver till it reached Wyoming where it would swing west again—they'd seen that, indeed, Josh had managed to climb up on top of the boxcars—from where, Tom offered the opinion, it was too high to jump to the ground, at least while the train was moving. If they could get off on the far side, just before he reached the car they were in, at least, he'd have to climb down from the roof before he could leap. And that would give them some time—especially if he didn't see them jump off. Maybe they could hide. The train was moving fast. It'd carry him pretty far up the track before he could get off to pursue them.

"But it's gonna be rough jumping off with it going at this speed," Tom added.

"Yeah, but what choice do we have?"

"Stand and fight?"

"I dunno. He's mighty strong." Ben thought for a moment. "Let's try your plan. I think we can make it. Just try to jump out as far as you can so you don't land in the gravel alongside the track. Maybe roll yourself up in a ball." He couldn't help but remember how successful that strategy had been for him before. And he couldn't help remembering how right Tom had been about his bad luck with hopping trains.

Partly to keep track of Josh's progress and partly to distract Josh from noticing their escape from the opposite side of the train, Tom kept peering out the wide-open door of the car. (The side they were actually going to jump out they'd slid open only a crack, lest Josh notice the open door as the train snaked from left to right as it maneuvered along a narrow creek bed near the base of the mountains.)

They were both getting more and more nervous as Josh got closer. He was only a couple of cars away now. Tom looked toward the front of the train to see what kind of terrain they'd be jumping off into. To his surprise and amazement, he saw a wooden sign by the track up ahead, apparently bearing the name of the upcoming town where perhaps local passenger trains might stop—this freight obviously wasn't going to because it wasn't slowing down a whit. "Hey, this is perfect," Tom shouted.

He looked up and saw Josh leer down at him vengefully from the top of the car one behind them. As planned, he pulled the door closed, then turned and patted Ben on the back, the sign it was time to jump.

Ben went first. He took a short running start and threw himself out of the car as far as he could. He landed, rolling, in a thicket of lush green brush. Tom followed right behind. They almost rolled into each other as they hit the ground and scrambled under cover.

Ben peered up through the thick bushes as the train rumbled by. He couldn't be sure, but he thought he saw Josh crouching on the roof of the car as the train carried him out of sight. Catching their breath, the two young men ran away from the track and uphill as fast as they could just in case Josh had gotten down on the other side of the train.

Even after the last car of the train had disappeared around a curve up ahead and the rhythmic clacking of the wheels had faded away in the distance, they kept down in the greenery. Finally, Ben announced, "The coast is clear," and they both stood up, shook hands congratulatorily, and clambered down the hill and across the track. "What now?" Ben asked.

Tom pointed up the track. "Look," he said. "This is a miracle."

"Huh?" Ben wasn't sure he'd heard right. He realized his ears were ringing from the silence now that the roar of the train was gone.

Tom pointed again. Ben saw that he wasn't pointing the direction, but at the painted sign by the right-of-way.

"Perspective," it read.

"What does that mean?" Ben asked.

Tom just laughed gleefully.

"Oh, come on," I said scornfully to Ben. "You can't be serious. You expect me to believe a coincidence like that?"

"It's your novel."

"Yeah, that's the problem. You want me to write that your life had that many fortunate coincidences?"

"Now, Rick, wasn't that the commitment you made back when you called yourself a hippie and "cast your fate to the wind": that you could trust the process, go with the flow, that "today was the first day of the rest of your life..." "

I started to object that he was talking in clichés. But I kept my mouth shut, remembering that I once believed in those very clichés.

"...that when you hitched a ride on the highway you were, at least potentially, starting a grand new adventure? Didn't you *always* take a transfer when you got on a bus whether you needed one or not—on principle—to remind yourself to be open to some marvelous possibility changing your destination? Didn't you believe that life was ultimately benign, that things'd work out?"

"You're right that I used to believe such things."

"Is your life any better now that you've stopped believing?" Ben asked pointedly.

"But we were talking about the plot of my novel, not about my real life," I objected.

"Yeah, what happened to your real life anyway? You ought to be thinking about that. But I thought we were talking about my life."

"Well, I know, but... "

"Look, we'll have to talk about coincidence later on, Rick," chimed in Tom's voice from out of the ether. "I don't think you're ready for that part of the lesson yet. But, you know, take it or leave it. What are you gonna do with your characters up there in the mountains if you don't want to tell the story our way?"

"Yeah," echoed Ben.

"Okay, okay," I answered. "So tell me, what happened next?"

31

 talked with Elizabeth last night. She said her dad was being ripped apart in the Boston papers.

"I just don't understand. Why would they do this? He's been a great humanitarian. Two years ago one of the TV stations gave him an award for civic leadership for starting that medical clinic for the homeless. Now they're treating him like some kind of criminal."

"Your father violated one of the major rules of high society, Elizabeth. He turned his back on money and prestige," I explained sagely. "Everybody might admire him for the good work he's done, but I bet they also hate him, if only 'cause he shows them up for the selfish louts they are."

"But he's never said anything bad about anybody... "

"Anybody who gives away a fortune has to make all the other rich people nervous. What if it caught on? Or worse, what if some politician held your dad up as an example... "

"They practically all have," she interrupted.

"And that's precisely the problem, isn't it? Isn't the next step for one of those politicians to say something like: 'Well, if Robert Steed can give all his money away then so can the Cabots and the Lodges—and the Whites."

"So they make Georgie White a hero and Dad a villain just to protect their pocketbooks?"

"At least. At least," I replied cynically. "It's more than money though, it's the whole class structure. You're just not supposed to turn your back on your own class."

"He didn't. I mean, he stayed a society doctor even when he was volunteering in the clinic for the homeless."

"That's how come Georgie White was a patient of his, right?"

"Sure."

"Well, maybe he should've closed his practice and left town. At least then the blue bloods wouldn't have had to be confronted."

"Oh, Rick, you are so cynical. It's not fair to talk about the rich like that. I mean, honey, I'm one of 'em too, you know."

I feigned innocence. "*You* were the one just now complaining about the press coverage." I changed the subject. "Look, any news on the law suit? I mean your dad's certainly going to win if this gets to court."

"Well, the lawyers told dad he ought to settle and not take it to court. They said he'd be much safer if he just quietly paid off Georgie White and agreed to shut up about the whole thing. But, Rick, that'll cost us everything we've got... "

Including the ranch, I understood the implication.

"I think the lawyers just want their pound of flesh."

"You're mixing metaphors," I corrected her playfully. "I don't get it. What do they mean safer? It seems to me your dad's going to come out smelling like a lily and White'll look like a shit."

"I think *that's* mixing metaphors, Rick." We both chortled.

"But dad made a serious tactical error," Elizabeth continued. "Last week a bunch of reporters cornered him outside that new AIDS clinic he's helping set up. They started badgering him. And he got on his soapbox and, well, he fingered Johnny Donatello... "

"Who's that?"

"Well, he's supposed to be an upstanding citizen, great spokesman for the Italian-American community and all that. But he's a major investor in White's software cartel *and* his grandfather was the biggest mafia king-pin of all time. Daddy got up before all those reporters and accused White and Donatello of running a cocaine operation and said that's how Georgie got infected."

"Oh," I said, understanding.

"Yeah. What if Donatello goes after Daddy. I mean he's not going to file suit like a White. He's going to... "

I could hear tears starting in Elizabeth's voice. "Well, come to Texas," I said cheerily. "We can all hide out in this house."

She struggled to laugh through her tears. "We'll see, Rick. We may have to go to the North Pole or the Falkland Islands or someplace. I'm not sure the ranch is gonna be there when the lawyers are finished with us."

"I understand," I acknowledged the gloomy reality.

This morning Dave Lovejoy called to say he was bringing out a prospective buyer, a man named Hubert Dorsey. "He's a developer," Lovejoy said (I could imagine dollar signs flashing in his eyes even as he said the words). "Got an idea to turn the place into a country club with condos all along the stream down there below the house. It'd be great. Very exclusive, you know."

"I know about exclusiveness," I replied sullenly. At least at that moment I didn't like Dave Lovejoy very much.

I really didn't want this Dorsey guy to like the place. But, of course, I owed it to Elizabeth and Dr. Steed to help them sell the property if that would get them out of the jam they were in. So, halfheartedly, I spent the morning straightening up. I didn't think I could make the house look like the clubhouse of an exclusive country club, but I could at least make it look clean. In the afternoon I finally got back to the Macintosh while I waited for Lovejoy and Dorsey to show up.

The steep mountain valley was filled with morning mist through which occasional beams of sunlight burned like spotlights. The trees that reached high up into the sky toward the light were mostly thickly needled conifers and the ground below them was carpeted in a thick layer of fallen needles. Ferns burst through the carpet and deep green lichens clung to the face of rocks. Here and there where the light filtered down into open meadows delicate flowers erupted out of the ground in myriad bright hues. The air smelled sweet and rich, a mingling of the musty aroma of the leafmeal on the forest floor rotting slowly into fertile soil and the stinging scent of pine sap and the sweet fragrance of wild flowers.

"It's beautiful, isn't it?" Ben observed.

They climbed up away from the tracks just in case Josh had leapt from the train and was lurking somewhere up ahead. They soon came upon a deeply rutted road cut through the forest roughly parallel to the railroad. "This is bound to take us into Perspective," Tom suggested. "Keep your eyes out for Josh, but let's take the road."

After only a relatively short distance they came to a clearing and a small wooden train depot. Apparently this was the stop announced by that sign they'd seen from the train. Maybe they could get directions. Tom hunted through his pockets for a piece of paper. Ben observed that he checked the information on it and then went through the front door into the building. Ben followed timidly.

There was no one inside. It was just a small room with a bench in the center of it and a placard behind glass that must have once proclaimed the railroad schedule. It was now faded beyond legibility. "Hello-o-o," Tom called out.

"'m out 'ere," came a muffled answer.

"This way," Ben pointed leading the way through another door out onto the platform behind the depot. There was an old man sitting on another bench whittling away at what looked like a wood-carving of a rooster.

"Ya missed the freight," he declared.

"I see," Tom answered. "Perhaps you can help us with directions. I'm looking for Mr. Montgomery Hightower. Know him?"

"How's that?"

Tom repeated his question, a little louder.

"Sure I know Professor Hightower. Usually they send a wagon down to pick up visitors. Didn't you write you was comin'? How'd ya git here anyway?" The old man looked around as though perhaps there were a train standing at the platform he'd neglected to notice. "Passenger train's not due in 'ere till afternoon. Nothin's on time these days. Damn unions!"

Ignoring the questions and the opinions, Tom asked, "How can we get to Professor Hightower's place?"

"It's up above town. Ya gotta git up the mountain. Say, you two on horseback or somethin'?"

"Guess, we'll walk," Ben answered.

"Pretty good climb. Maybe somebody'll give you a ride—if they come by. Not many people come by, you know."

"It does seem like we're a long way from anywhere," Ben answered.

"Well now, hardly," the old man objected. "Perspective's just up the road a ways." He stood and looked up as though he might be able to see over the building. "Well, cain't see from 'ere. But up there a way," he pointed up. "Top o' the ridge. Guess that's why they call the town Perspective."

"You live up there?" Ben inquired politely.

"Yup, I do. Work the ticket window 'ere at the depot most days. Not much business. Mainly the only visitors come to Perspective these days are friends of the Professor's. Ain't been many around lately. Say, you boys friends of his?"

"Friends of a friend," Tom answered. "Well, thanks for your help. Let me get the directions clear. We go up the road toward the ridge, then what?" He was trying to keep the old gentleman's attention on the directions.

"Then you git to Perspective. There's a Genr'l Store up there and the First Baptist Church." The old man chuckled to himself. "Saloon's in back o' the Store, ya hear. You can git directions there lessen you're teetotalers, o' course. Then you can go to the church and ask the preacher. Everybody knows the Professor. But I guess you better steer clear of Colonel Dodson or any o' his men, least if you're goin' to the Professor's."

"How would we know?" Ben inquired curiously.

"Beats me. But take my advice. If you ask any o' 'em, they liable to give you wrong directions. Bad blood 'tween those two up there on the mountain."

"Well, thank you, sir," Tom answered. "And thanks for the advice."

Ben saw that Tom had already gone back through the depot heading out to the road. He hated to just leave the old man like that. He probably liked having somebody to talk to. He must get lonely out here.

"You walkin'?" The old man didn't seem to want to let the conversation end.

"Guess so," Ben answered.

"Whaddya say? Didn't hear ya," the old man shouted.

"C'mon, Ben. We ain't got all day," Tom called and, waving a farewell to the old man, Ben hurried along.

As the two young men trudged up the road the conversation ranged from curiosity about what the old man meant by "bad blood" between Professor Hightower and this Colonel Dodson to Tom's recounting of the story Eli had told him about the Clear Light Colony here—"or at least, up there," Tom said pointing up toward the top of the ridge quite a long way up.

After only a short ways, Tom noticed that Ben was limping slightly. "You hurt your leg when we jumped off the train back there?"

"Not just my leg," Ben answered, his voice stressed, "I sure skinned up my hands." He held up both palms to show Tom the scratch marks. "I put out my hands to stop myself from rolling and must've grabbed a tree trunk or something."

"That looks like it hurts. Wish we could wash it," Tom answered solicitously. "But how come you're limping."

"Guess that's from the beatin' I got the other day. You know, my ribs hurt and my butt's sore and there's still this lump on the side o' my head." Ben held his hand to the back of his skull. "And seems like I hit the ground back there pretty hard."

"Oh, Ben, I'm sorry. I didn't realize. How stupid of me... Look, maybe I could, well, carry you."

Ben laughed. "That's mighty sweet of you. But pretty unrealistic. I'll make it." He looked up into the dark green shadows above and the bright swath of blue sky high overhead. "I just wish it wasn't so far."

"Well, we'll take it slow. We can rest every few minutes," Tom concluded.

Ben really wasn't listening. Tom's unrealistic offer to carry him had touched him deeply. He felt a pang of affection and reached out and patted Tom on the back. "Thanks," he said. He was almost fighting back tears. That seemed like the nicest thing anybody had said to him in such a long time.

Tom stopped. It took Ben a moment to realize that. He turned around and looked at Tom quizzically. "Somethin' the matter?" He felt a sudden surge of fear. Maybe he'd offended him.

Tom looked back at Ben steadily, almost sternly. Then smiled. He dropped the little valise he'd been carrying this whole way and opened his arms. "I like you, Ben."

Ben stepped forward into Tom's embrace. "Me too," he answered. They held each other a moment longer than either of them felt proper. And then held longer. Ben could feel the warmth of Tom's body radiating through his clothes. Somehow it seemed to soothe the aching in his ribs.

Finally Tom giggled, sounding a little silly. "I can't think of any place I'd rather be right now than here with you."

"I wish you were up there," Ben gestured with his head toward the top of the ridge. "With me," he added just to make sure Tom understood his humor.

"I guess we've got the rest of our lives."

"To get to the top of the ridge?" Ben teased. "I'm getting hungry."

"Me too."

"Hey, you know, I picked up an apple and a loaf of bread at the boarding-house." He scrambled to get his knapsack off.

The loaf had been crushed in the rolling leap from the train, but it still tasted delicious. The apple had not survived as well. It was almost applesauce. But the two shared it joyfully nonetheless.

As they sat by the side of the road on a thick cushion of leafmeal, Tom started talking casually about his childhood and a time he'd once gone climbing in the hills north of San Antonio. Ben rejoined with a story about swimming in the rock quarry.

The food and the friendly, intimate conversation lifted their spirits. Neither—but especially Ben—had slept well the night before and out here in the cool, clean air, safe with one another, they drifted off side by side into a couple of hours of dreamy sleep, before starting the climb again.

By mid-afternoon when they limped up to the General Store in downtown Perspective—they were both limping by now—they'd even begun to tell each other about their sexual and emotional growth. Tom had recounted his attachment to Johnny Kincade and Ben his nightmare experience with Jeremy Bates. While they both carefully avoided too clearly describing the specific physical acts they were alluding to, lest they reveal too much and scare off the other, they were certainly opening up to each other.

"Let's finish this discussion after we get directions," Tom interrupted Ben's story of his dismissal from Mr. Pickney's Drug Store and Soda Fountain as they rounded a bend in the road and discovered the old barn-like building bearing the sign "Perspective, Colo. General Store" and next to it a faded white church building, complete with short steeple, bearing a sign "First Baptist." Beyond these they could see a sawmill and a couple of ramshackle houses.

"Can we eat something and rest a while," Ben said plaintively.

"Well, of course."

Standing in front of the store, they could certainly tell why this tiny settlement had been christened as it was. To the south and east opened the high plateau on which Denver was situated. To the north and west snow-covered peaks gleamed in the sun. Far below in the valley—up one wall of which they'd just climbed—they could see a river running back into the mountains. The sky was a more brilliant blue, the air crisper, the horizons wider than either of them had ever experienced before.

"Quite a perspective," Tom observed as he led the way into the store.

Ben and Tom were both surprised that when they opened the door a bell chimed loudly. Their entry had caused bright light to fill the dusty air in the room in what seemed almost like a tunnel right to the back. When they closed the door the room went dark. They stood still a moment to allow their eyes to adjust to the darkness inside. They could just make out three rugged-looking men at the grocery counter near the front of the store. Each had his arms full of crates of supplies. Behind them was an Indian squaw, sporting long braided hair decorated with brightly colored beads and wearing a long raw-hide skirt. She seemed to be counting out payment to a young man standing behind a shiny polished brass cash register. It was the register which had chimed when

Tom and Ben walked in.

The three men and the squaw, perhaps blinded momentarily by the bright light, turned toward the door.

"Hey, you two, get out of the way," one of the men shouted.

"Who are those guys, anyway?" another of the men asked. "Cain't see 'em in the damn shadows."

"Whatcha doin' 'round here?" the first man asked angrily as he swaggered toward them, forcing Ben and Tom to step aside for him to pass.

"Looking for Professor Hightower," Ben answered innocently.

"Come to admire the view," Tom interrupted as he stepped in front of Ben, reached for the door, and then politely held it open for the three men. "Beautiful day for a hike."

"Hightower, eh? Shoulda known. Well, you jes' watch yo'selves 'round here," the last of the men said, exiting and swinging the crate he was carrying up onto one shoulder, preparing to load it onto the wagon standing outside.

Not sure why they were being treated so rudely, but remembering the warning from the old man at the depot about bad blood between Hightower and this Colonel Dodson, Tom was certain he didn't want any more mention of Hightower's name. He was careful to continue to hold the door for the Indian squaw. She trailed out last, clutching a raw-hide purse to her breast. Her eyes held Tom's. Her face looked hardened and weather-beaten, but her features were delicate. Just as she passed Tom, she seemed to smile knowingly and then drop her gaze to the ground. Tom thought he heard her make a kind of clucking sound. He closed the door behind her. And the room was again swallowed in dusty gloom.

"Hullo," called out the young man behind the counter. "C'mon in. M' name's Henry. Welcome to Perspective."

"What was that all about?" Tom asked, half-rhetorically.

"That was Hummingbird, doin' the shoppin' for the Colonel's men," the young man Henry answered. "But, hey, you don't wanna know more."

"Was that a real Indian?" Ben asked.

"They say the Colonel took her for a slave when he fightin' in the Injun Wars," Henry answered. "Guess you gotta wonder if she weren't a fine-lookin' Injun maiden once. Now she do the cleanin' and cookin' for him."

Changing the subject, Henry inquired as to their health and cheerfully sat them down, then brought out three mugs of home-brewed beer and offered to fix them each a roast beef sandwich. Tom confirmed he had money to pay and they agreed on a very reasonable price. (Tom seemed concerned, perhaps rightly, about being gouged up here in the mountains.)

Bringing out the sandwiches, Henry pulled up a chair and sat down behind the third mug of beer. "Where you guys comin' from and where you headin'?"

Tom explained they were looking for the Clear Light Colony and Mr. Montgomery Hightower. Henry answered that they still had a ways to go. He pointed out how the road continued on through town and then forked in two. If they stayed to the left, it'd lead them up to Professor Hightower's place. If they went to the right, however, they'd end up in Colonel Dodson's. Henry didn't think they'd want to do that.

"What's the story with this Colonel Dodson?" Ben asked.

Henry explained how Colonel Charles Dodson owned most of the land surrounding the town of Perspective. He'd come here about ten years before and started buying up the mountain. "I guess just because he wants to own a mountain," Henry answered Ben's question about his motivation. Colonel Dodson was not exactly a bad sort, Henry opined, but lately it seemed he'd gotten into a feud with the one other land owner around. That was Professor Hightower.

"How come there's a town here at all?" Ben asked

"Got started back when the miners hit the Comstock Lode over in Nevada. That proved there was treasure on the eastern side of the mountains and brought prospectors all over out here lookin' for silver. Lot of people still live up in these mountains. I know it seems pretty far from civilization. But you should see how much farther you can git if you go up into the mountains. The Colonel's bought up the mountain, but he don't bother the people already living on the land. Some people try mining up here, some have got goats and sheep. It's a mighty nice place to live. Sure got a good view."

"So what's the feud with Hightower about?"

I was interrupted by the sound of an automobile coming down the road. That must be Dave Lovejoy, I told myself. I asked Ben to excuse me and I saved the file I was working on. I pulled a polo shirt over my head, noticing it was really the wrong color for the faded red shorts I was wearing. But I wasn't trying to impress Lovejoy—or his client. I did check in a mirror to make sure my hair was presentable before going out to greet them as they pulled around the circular drive in front of the house and stopped right by the front door.

As Hubert Dorsey got out of the car on the passenger side, I wished I'd taken a little more time to dress myself. Maybe I did want to impress this man. He was tall, strikingly handsome, with sandy colored hair and dark blue-green eyes. He took one look at me. And I took one look at him.

I was sure he was gay.

Did that change things? I wondered.

32

enry offered to let Ben and Tom stay the night out back of the store. "It'll take you past nightfall to get out there on foot," he said. But then he recommended that they camp out along the way. He told them about a wonderful spot. He "rented" them a couple of bed rolls, a grill rack, and a few other camping items if they'd promise to return all the things to him or leave them with Professor Hightower. ("Cain't hardly git outta town wit'out me seeing you no how," he laughed.) In return for his assistance, of course, Tom left Henry a little tip and purchased the makings for dinner: thick beef steaks, potatoes for baking in the fire, a loaf of bread, and a couple more bottles of the homebrew.

"It's gonna be a beautiful night. Moon's still practically full," Henry added as he bade farewell to the two young adventurers.

They hiked a couple of miles down the road till they reached the spot Henry'd recommended. A small stream poured out of a break in a cliff wall about twenty feet above the road and cascaded down through a rocky gully. Just to the left of the road was a small pool that had been cut into the rock by the force of the plunging water. The road detoured down the hill a little ways and then crossed over a rickety bridge with planks set so a wagon or buggy could pass over it—cautiously.

"Now where's the hot springs?" Tom asked, reminding Ben of what Henry had described as the most attractive feature of the spot—and which had decided Tom on taking his suggestion they camp out overnight.

"He said it was below the bridge. You want me to look?"

"Let's get a fire going before it gets dark. Then we can explore a little."

An hour later, the steaks were grilling over the fire. Tom and Ben were sitting far enough away to avoid the smoke but close enough to feel the warmth. After bathing in the hot springs and then splashing around in the icy cold water of the pool, they were both naked under the blankets they had wrapped around themselves.

Tom opened one of the bottles of beer and, offering to share it with Ben, screwed up all his courage and asked the question of the day. "I better tell you what I know about this Clear Light Colony we're going to. Ben, does the word 'urning' mean anything to you?"

"I don't think so. Have something to do with this Hightower fellow?"

"Yes," Tom hesitated. "And I think it has something to do with us."

"You mean you and me?"

"Yep."

"I bet I know what's about to happen," I interrupted gleefully.

Tom smiled at me. "I think you'd be right."

"Sure was an idyllic setting. Almost too idyllic, I mean, who's gonna believe this?"

"Would it make it any more believable if I told you the hot springs was only tepid and there were ants all over the place?"

"Well, maybe," I answered. "Look, Tom, can I, you know, watch? I mean I got myself all worked up this afternoon showing that guy Hu Dorsey around. I, uh… " I was writing into the evening, having lost most of the afternoon to the realtor's visit. (Dorsey and I never said anything, you know, open to one another. Dave Lovejoy was almost always walking along between us. But I certainly felt some vibes coming from him. I wondered when I was going to have to tell him I'd, well, made a vow of celibacy.)

"Of course, you can watch," Ben said, suddenly popping into reality next to Tom. (He was already undressed.) This was the first time I'd managed to get both of them to appear at the same time. I must admit it took a little straining of my imaginary faculties to do so.

Ben's hand rested lightly on Tom's on his knee. They were sitting tailor-fashion, half-facing one another. "I guess I didn't know the word," he replied to Tom's protracted summary of his lesson from Eli Hauptmann. They'd finished their dinner during the telling. "But I guess I knew what the feelings were. Maybe I didn't exactly explain the whole story about what happened with Brother Jeremy. You know?"

Tom laughed softly. "And I didn't exactly explain the whole story about Johnny Kincade. But those things don't matter anymore, Ben. Do they?"

Ben looked longingly into Tom's eyes. He shook his head in negation. And as he did so, he straightened and elongated his back and leaned forward slightly so that his face came closer to Tom's. "Is it okay?" he whispered.

Tom looked slightly quizzical. "What okay?"

Ben didn't answer, but just very lightly touched his lips to Tom's cheek.

Tom turned his face, almost as if accidentally, and his lips touched Ben's. Then without allowing their lips to separate, they each managed to wriggle up a little closer. The blanket, caught under Tom's knee, slid off his shoulder, leaving his chest half-exposed. Ben reached across and gently stroked Tom's chest with his hand, running his palm through the dark hair.

"I think it's more than okay," Tom said, though his voice was muffled as he spoke because his mouth was pressed against Ben's face. Perhaps under

Tom's guidance—it was hard to be sure who was leading and who was following—they both rose up on their knees so that the blankets fell away. They pressed their bodies together, cheek to cheek, chest to chest, belly to belly, groin to groin, thigh to thigh.

Tom's body was thicker, more developed. His shoulders were broad. The muscles of his chest stood out from his sleek torso. Along his sides, his ribs formed shadowed ridges in the flickering fire-light that accentuated his tight smooth stomach. His body was covered with fine hair that grew dark and thick across his chest and around his groin.

Ben's body was much finer and more delicate. His light skin was pulled taut across his skeleton showing his musculature with less bulk but more definition. His long stomach was rippled like a washboard. He was only slightly shorter than Tom, but his height was in his torso not his legs, so their bodies fit nicely together. Ben's flesh was smooth and hairless.

A thrill ran through them both. Their touch was vital, almost electric. If before, alone under the starry heavens, lit by the stark cool light of the moon ascending from the horizon, they'd been cold in the dark forest night, they were cold no longer. Their bodies flushed with each other's warmth.

Tom, perhaps slightly more experienced at this than Ben, let his mouth open so that their kiss deepened. At first Ben seemed surprised, unable to imagine what to do in response. But quickly he followed and quickly began to share Tom's breath as they drank each other in and breathed each other out.

Their penises had grown hot and pulsing with energy now where they pressed against one another's abdomen. At first each seemed afraid of seeking that touch with the other—there was a lot of conditioning and fear to break through in this act of lovemaking. But then Tom reached down and clasped Ben in his hand and squeezed gently, stroking, sending waves of pleasure through Ben's brain that slowly washed away the anxieties and fears and repressions.

Ben too then took Tom in *his* hand and felt the other's manliness. And, perhaps for the first time, he realized he didn't feel ashamed or afraid anymore of his own manliness.

They embraced again then with both arms. They pressed and ground their loins together discovering they could achieve complementary rhythms so that their pleasure and their affection and their awe at one another's presence pumped back and forth between them, so that it rose and grew stronger, overwhelming them with love and relief for years of pent-up wondering and waiting.

Tom pulled away and the surging tide of emotion and sexual pleasure subsided momentarily. Grinning at Ben, he shook out one of the blankets and spread it out so they had a place to lie. And then, pushing Ben down on his back he crawled over him and brought his face down to Ben's groin and took him in his mouth as he remembered Eli had done to him.

It took Ben a moment to catch on to what was happening. He seemed almost overcome by the discovery of that totally new sensation pouring up through his body. Then he shifted himself slightly and took Tom, hanging above him, in his own mouth and his pleasure seemed to fill him from all directions. They ate hungrily of each other's flesh, giving themselves to the other even as they struggled to consume more deeply for themselves. It was such a wonderful act of giving and taking, Ben later said he realized. He'd never been taught anything like that before about the act of lovemaking. Indeed, he'd always been told it was selfish. And yet as he held Tom's pleasure in his mouth and then later when he pulled away and licked at Tom's scrotum and into the fold of his thigh, he couldn't imagine anything more selfless or giving than this act of sharing ecstasy.

Later, this time at Ben's initiation, they shifted again so they were lying side by side, their mouths together, their penises sliding smoothly, rhythmically next to one another against their abdomens.

Ben pulled his face away and looked deep into Tom's gaze. The reflection from the fire occasionally glinted in their pupils so that light seemed to radiate between them from their eyes. Suddenly they were both, almost simultaneously, overcome by their feelings and by their arousal. And they were lost in their love as they came together in the peak of their touching.

"Wow," I said as I reached for the towel by my bed. "That was some sex."

"We loved each other," Ben answered.

"And we'd been waiting so long," Tom added.

"Well, thanks, guys, for letting me share that with you."

A little later I drifted off to sleep wondering if I'd missed something because my sex life had been so easy for me. Of course, at the time, I'd been forgetting how fraught with difficulties my first experiences had been. But later all that had changed. But it had also lost the magic.

But now it had become difficult again. I wondered if that would make it any better. So far it hadn't. And I couldn't quite conceive how it ever would again. Except perhaps in fantasy.

33

he next morning when I sat down to write, I struggled to relive that sexual fantasy of Tom and Ben's first lovemaking. After all, I'd have to struggle now to capture it in words that my computer could store away in its very prosaic memory.

As I pictured the scene again, I had a realization. To check it out, I got up, stripped off my T-shirt and stood in front of that full length mirror in the entrance hall. Indeed, it seemed to be true. Tom Milam was almost a replica of me, but idealized, the physical self I guess I'd wanted to be, but hadn't been. "Well," I said to myself, "It's not surprising. Ben is a perfect example of your ideal type; it's appropriate that Tom would be a perfect idealization of your own type. What's curious is that you hardly noticed it before!"

Throughout most of my life, as part of developing what the psychologists would call my personal self-concept, I'd struggled to see what I looked like to other people. At least at one time I sought out men who I thought looked like me in an effort to reassure myself I was at least attractive enough to attract myself. It had never seemed to work. My perceptions were always troubled by my own self-doubts and anxious judgments.

Funny, now my fantasy seemed to have solved that. It wasn't just that I thought I was looking better. Something about the way I perceived myself had changed. Now I felt oddly elated having the particular body that is mine.

Hmm, I thought, maybe my sex life is improving.

Speaking of sex life and fantasies, Hu Dorsey called me in the morning to thank me for "having been so helpful." He gave me his "private number," as he called it, and invited me to "call him sometime."

As Tom and Ben cuddled together sandwiched between the blankets, they stared up at the night sky. It was truly incredible. They were high in the mountains, as close as you could get on earth to the stars, and their light burned down in myriad points of brilliance. Tom noticed he could make out lights further down the road. A blazing fire in a hearth or perhaps the steady light of kerosene lamps suffused a warm glow through the windows of what appeared to be a long, low rambling house perched at the end of the valley right on the edge of the mountain ridge that comprised the town of Perspective, Colorado. "That must be our destination," he whispered to Ben. They both fell asleep imagining what they were going to find there.

When Ben thought about utopian colonies, as Tom had said Professor Hauptmann characterized the Clear Light Colony, because of his seminary background, he naturally thought of St. Ignatius Loyola and the early Jesuits. They had been Spanish soldiers and the paintings of them hanging on the walls of St. Athanasius' had shown them against the backdrop of old Spanish villages. Ben drifted off into a dream of buildings with red tile roofs and walls of white, faintly pink stucco.

"I think we shouldn't show up too early," Tom said in the morning, "give 'em time to wake up before visitors arrive."

"I agree," Ben answered, rolled over into Tom's arms, and closed his eyes ready to go back to sleep. The spot where they'd camped was shadowed by the mountain on the other side of the valley so sunrise came late. Though they'd placed their bedroll atop a mound of thick soft grasses, it had still made for uncomfortable sleeping. Neither was too anxious to wake fully.

After drifting in and out of lazy morning sleep, they cuddled again and made easy love, then bathed in the warm pool of the hot springs. Ben playfully pushed Tom off balance so he fell into the cold swift current of the waterfall. They laughed and laughed and Tom, in turn, coaxed Ben near enough the frigid pool so he could throw him in as well. By mid-morning the sun had risen above the facing peak and its piercing warm rays dried them.

"Let's go see who this Montgomery Hightower is," Tom announced. As they neared the building they'd seen glowing in the night, they discovered it was really a series of small wooden cottages with wood-shingled roofs connected by a broad open porch. The place was situated in a wide meadow and looked almost as though it were surrounded by a carefully tended lawn.

"Look," Ben pointed, "I see some people sitting on the porch." Indeed, under a vine-covered arbor, hanging with lavender flowers which as they got closer they could see were wisteria, there appeared to be three women in light pastel frock dresses and broad-brimmed sunhats, sitting at a white wicker table sipping from china teacups.

The road forked near the houses. To the left it went back behind to a barn and several sheds and what was perhaps a stable; to the right it curved around the front of the connecting porch and led up to where the ladies were having their mid-morning repast.

"Good morning," Tom shouted from the road, "we're looking for Professor Montgomery Hightower."

"C'mon up," called out a man whom neither of them could see. "There're steps over there."

Tom noticed behind him to his left a short flight of stairs led up to the raised porch. They had to detour back a few paces. The steps took them up so they approached the ladies in the sun hats from behind. Ben followed along obediently. He didn't have any idea what they were getting into. The whole show was Tom's now; he was the friend of Eli Hauptmann's.

From somewhere Tom heard a man's voice say, "Why, Dorothea, these two handsome young gentleman are coming to call on you."

"Of all times to have visitors," another voice answered.

Someone else guffawed.

As Tom approached, the three ladies stood up and turned to face him. Tom was just about to apologize if they'd arrived at a bad time when he found himself dumbstruck. The nearest lady, who was reaching out a white lace-gloved hand to him, appeared completely bald under the wide straw sunhat set back on her head and she had a full curly gray beard that reached down almost to the middle of her chest.

"I'm Monty Hightower," she said.

Automatically Tom took Hightower's hand in the ordinary male greeting. Hightower laughed embarrassedly. "You must excuse our, uh, costumes.

We weren't expecting visitors. People seldom show up here uninvited, you know. It's quite a long hike."

"Yes, sir," Tom muttered. "We know."

Another of the ladies spoke up. She was clean-shaven, about the same age as the first gentleman; she had a thin, almost delicate face, an aquiline nose and a long neck with pronounced Adam's apple. "I'm Alex McMahon. But you can call me Georgia," he smiled widely. "And this is Herbert Fadiman—he's Heloise this morning." He pointed to the somewhat younger and more roughly-hewn man beside him with a thick black mustache. "And lest you suspect our Professor Hightower of being more of an Abelard than I'm sure he'd want you to think, perhaps he should explain." The man laughed heartily at his joke. (Neither Ben nor Tom understood it.) "Dorothea, it's your turn. Explain."

The man who'd introduced himself as Monty Hightower, who was still shaking Tom's hand, replied hesitantly, "Well, you see, it was such a lovely morning, and being Midsummer's Day and all, we thought we'd just dress up. We all lived in England at one time, you know."

"Oh, I didn't know. And I hadn't realized it was Midsummer's Day," Tom answered as though somehow that explained it all.

"Oh yes, Summer solstice, June 24th," the man who'd called himself Georgia commented. "Funny thing. The Christian world celebrates the solstices on the wrong dates, you know. Christmas on the 25th instead of the 22nd and John the Baptist on the 24th instead of the 21st. Hmm! Calendar's off by three days."

"We've been traveling," Ben piped up. "You lose track of time that way too."

Hightower dropped Tom's hand and, in a nervous gesture, pulled the sunhat from his head. He gestured toward the chairs. "Please, please sit down. Perhaps you'd like tea or coffee... or maybe something stronger."

"Coffee would be great," Ben answered. Tom still seemed stunned. "We're just waking up."

"Well," said Alex McMahon, "you've walked a long way for just waking up. You've certainly earned a cup of coffee." He perched himself on the edge of his chair and poured a cup from a brilliantly-polished silver coffee pot. He handed the delicate fine-china cup to Ben. "And you?" he said to Tom.

"Please," Tom answered and then explained, "I'm a friend of Eli Hauptmann's in Chicago... "

"The Grand Duchess Maria Theresa," McMahon interrupted gleefully.

"You must forgive Alex," Hightower said. "She gets carried away sometimes."

"Oh, Monty, it's Midsummer's. We'd certainly look sillier dressed up like Bottom with mules' heads."

Though he didn't understand the Shakespearian reference any more than he had the Medieval historical one earlier, Ben laughed along with Alex. He'd somehow fallen into the playful humor of whatever was going on.

Tom was more serious. He was still trying to explain what they were doing here. "Sit down, sit down. Let me go get a couple more chairs." Hightower gestured again. "I'll take care of that," spoke up Herbert Fadiman for the first time. "You still had better come up with a good explanation." There was a jocular ring in his voice. As he walked into the house to get the chairs Tom noticed he had an odd gait, not a limp, but a sort of half lurch between steps.

"Well, I got it," Ben announced. "It's a summer morning tea-party."

"Right," Alex said, delighted that the young visitor seemed to understand that that was explanation enough. "If you can't dress up on Midsummer's Day, I always say, when *can* you dress up?"

Hightower looked down at the frilly white and yellow ruffled dress he was wearing. Then looked at Tom. Then looked at Alex. Then looked back at Tom, smiled, and said very matter-of-factly, "Now you were saying you know my friend Eli Hauptmann."

By late afternoon Tom and Ben had been shown to the little two-room cottage off the main house which Monty, now dressed much more like a gentleman farmer, told them was theirs "as long as you want to stay—and, of course, as long as you contribute to the community and fit in. But you'll find we're very easy-going."

"We'd certainly expect to earn our keep," Ben answered.

"Oh, there's lots of work to be done around here: from the barns and stables to the kitchen to the office. Either of you boys know how to work a printing press?"

"I was just working for a printer," Ben exclaimed. Then dropped his eyes, "Can't say I know anything about the press though. But I can learn."

"That's what we all said when the danged thing arrived. You can't imagine how much trouble it was carting that up the road."

"What are you printing?" Tom asked, always the sensible one.

"That's a good question. Well, now, we're hoping to start a small journal of ideas."

"Ideas?" Tom asked.

Monty smiled warmly. "If you know Eli, you must know some of the things he thinks about. I met him in England, through our friend Edward Carpenter. Edward has some very important things to say. I came back to America a few years ago, inspired by his example and eager to disperse some of his ideas. We're especially interested, you understand, in his notions of the intermediate sex. You do understand?" He said the last sentence hesitantly.

Tom cleared his throat. "Eli told me... "

Ben took a step closer to Tom and put his hand on his shoulder. Interrupting, he said, "I think we understand."

Monty smiled. "I thought so. But, you know, I was a little reluctant to ask. Well, now, I hope through this philosophical journal to reach out to others of our kind. I think they need to know they're not alone... and that they have special talents and sensibilities.

141

"You know," he went on in a rhetorical tone, "people's universes are affected by how they see themselves. Our people have seen themselves badly for centuries and sometimes participated in the badness, being sinners just as they were told they were. We believe it's critical we change how we see ourselves and how we participate in the world. Our effort around here is to create positive spiritual self-concepts and to educate our people about the really important role they have to play in the future of humankind.

"I am convinced," Monty announced dramatically, "that we are to be, not sinners, but saviors, that the earth has created us for a purpose that will become clearer in the future. Our task here at the Clear Light Colony is to educate our people to be receptive to the role the World Soul will have them play." He took a deep breath. "Do you know John Symonds or Heinrich Ulrichs?"

"Eli mentioned Ulrichs' name," Tom answered.

"They're also very interested in spiritual ideas. Edward's place in Derbyshire was always full of these Hindoo types talking about yoga and meditation and Brahmanism and all that. Very heady stuff. A bit pungent for my tastes, if you know what I mean... "

"No sir, I'm sorry I really don't know what you're talking about."

"Me neither," Ben agreed.

"Well, no matter. All very British, you know," he affected an exaggerated accent, "very exotic. Not quite for American tastes. But, on the other hand," he switched back to his normal professorial tone, "all that reminded me very much of our New England Transcendentalists and my dear friend Walt Whitman."

"I've heard of Walt Whitman," Tom answered.

"I'm sure you'll be hearing a lot more. But let's not overwhelm you your first day."

"It's very interesting, sir," Ben piped up. "I was in Catholic seminary. Was going to be a Jesuit."

"Well, well. You wouldn't have known it from looking at him this morning, but our friend Georgia," he smiled, "Alex McMahon is a Jesuit. Or, I suppose I should say, *was* a Jesuit. He was in the missions in India and went a little too native for his superiors. Went a little queer too," he added almost as an aside, "which is how I met him and how he ended up with us. But you two *must* talk. I'm sure you'll have wonderful things to share. Everyone here has wonderful things to share. But, come now, you must meet the rest of the colony."

The introductions to the other members of the Clear Light Colony went smoothly. There were a couple more men (none of whom were wearing frock dresses and sun hats) and four women (none of whom were wearing dresses or hats either). Altogether that made nine. Tom and Ben made eleven. They were surprised how easily they were welcomed.

"I consider myself a good judge of character," Monty explained as he was showing them around the grounds. "Perhaps I can have my head turned by a pretty face—like our young Ben, here—but not for long." He affected an obviously humorous scolding manner, "So, young man, you'd better mind your P's & Q's."

"Oh yes sir," Ben answered quite seriously.

"I certainly appreciate the difficulties you've had. I should say I'm sorry for you, but let me remind you that adversity builds character. It forces you to go inside yourself to find strength, to be your own person and not just do what other people tell you to. None of us is here because we experienced no adversity in our lives."

"Pardon?"

"Well, that sentence was a bit twisted. I meant to say that we're all here in the Clear Light Colony because we've experienced hardship and adversity and we've all decided that we would not let it grind us down. You know, the work of life must be to transform these difficulties—make gold out of dross or straw as in the old fairy tales. There's an important lesson here: learn to love hell and you'll discover you're in heaven. Ah, but I'm sermonizing at you again. You must go on with your stories."

The four of them (Herbert Fadiman had joined them along the way) were sitting in the grand—but practically unfurnished—living room of the main house where, Monty explained, he and Herbert lived and where were the communal kitchen, dining, living, and meditation rooms.

Ben's recounting his adventures on the road elicited a rambling discourse on the beauties of the wandering life that reminded Tom of Eli Hauptmann's apparently unrealistic but idyllic presentation of the life of the tramps and hobos. "Well, it's all changed now with the closing of the frontiers," Monty countered Tom's objection. "You must read this article by Frederick Jackson Turner that's just come out. It's precisely about that. There's just no room left for the wanderers and migrant laborers. Industrialization is putting an end to all that. Mark my words, the American experiment is being spoiled by the rise of big business trusts and holding companies. The dream is ending even as we speak. But go on, go on."

Ben was discovering a familiar pattern in Monty Hightower's personality: he was a brilliant man with wide-ranging ideas on almost every topic imaginable; and with every change of topic he would launch into a discourse that soon became what he himself called "sermonizing." But Ben recognized that there were so many things he could get from this man and this experience. He was moved with gratitude that he'd been brought here. Gratitude to the Blessed Mother. Gratitude to God. Gratitude to Tom (who was, in his life, obviously God's angel, he thought).

Ben continued recounting his story when he was interrupted again, this time by the entry of Margaret Travers. "Monty, I think you'd better come. There's a rider coming up the road. I can't tell but I think it's Sheriff Turnbull."

The Mayor, the Judge, and the City Council of Perspective, Colorado all turned out to be one man, the Sheriff. Oswald Turnbull was also the owner of the General Store and father to Henry Turnbull whom Tom and Ben had befriended yesterday.

"We got some trouble here, Professor," Turnbull said as he climbed down from his horse. "And it seems like these two young men you got here are the responsible parties."

Ben and Tom looked at each other, each with an expression of shock and dismay. Everything had looked so hopeful. Now suddenly...

"Come in, Ozzie. You mustn't start accusing without explaining first," Monty said cheerfully. Perhaps he knows how to deal with this fellow, Tom hoped.

"I ain't gonna let you sweet-talk me none, Professor," the Sheriff said. "But I'll be happy to explain." He stood his ground in the barn area behind the house with one hand holding to the reins of his horse. "Seems yesterday mornin' these two," he gestured with his chin toward Ben and Tom who were huddled behind Monty Hightower, "come into town rather mysteriously. Well, all the cash down at the train depot was missin' yesterday evenin' when Jake got ready to close up and go home. Jake remembered that as they were leavin' one of 'em had gone into the depot alone while the other one distracted him with silly talk. And this mornin' I find m' store's been broke into. The roast beef Henry made sandwiches for these guys with is stole. And the clothes pantry in back o' the church been ransacked."

"Why accuse us?" Tom asked. "We visited with the clerk, Henry; we paid for the sandwiches and gear we got."

"Well, who else'd done it. Havta be strangers. And you two the only strangers round these parts."

"Ozzie, I think the boy has a point. The very fact that they've been so public about their presence, the fact you know they're in town seems to suggest their innocence."

"Huh. Well, Monty, you got a point there. But what about the clothes and the money and my roast beef?"

"How much money was taken?"

"Only a couple of dollars, just what Jake keeps down there for makin' change. But it was his money. Jake's a po' old codger. He cain't afford to let some thieves have all his money."

"As a sign of my good faith in these boys, Sheriff, I'm willing to replace the money under the condition that you hunt out the real thief. Will you do that?"

"How 'bout my roast beef?"

"Ozzie, if I had a roast beef I'd be happy to give it to you." Exasperation was obvious in Hightower's tone. "But you know we don't eat beef or pork up here."

"Well, I guess, that's okay."

"These boys, by the way, showed up with barely more than the clothes on their backs. It doesn't look to me like they been through the Preacher's Poor Pantry."

"Well, I guess not. But look here, you boys, I don't like the looks o' you. You don't look to me like you done a day's work in your lives. I'm gonna be on the lookout for you. Hear?"

"Yessir," Ben answered. Tom said nothing.

Monty Hightower took a couple of bills from his wallet and handed them to Sheriff. "Tell Jake I said to take care of himself and watch out."

"I oughta be takin' those two into jail right now. But I'll give 'em another chance. But I'm only doin' this cause you're a good customer o' mine, Professor, not 'cause I believe their story."

"What story?" Tom said to Ben as the Sheriff turned and rode off. "He didn't even ask us what happened."

"Look, don't you two worry about this. There's a certain amount of tension in Perspective these days. And it has nothing to do with you."

"Who did steal that stuff?" Ben asked. "I mean, it sounds like it was somebody come up from the train depot." He turned to Tom and said ominously, "Josh?"

34

onty," Ben said, "I think maybe we know something about that money."

"Oh?"

"'Member I told you 'bout that guy that was chasin' us. What if he got off the train when he saw we'd escaped? That would've left him near the tracks, down by the depot. He could easily have sneaked in and got the money. That guy Jake is practically deaf."

"Well, that makes sense. I imagine the Sheriff will find him pretty soon."

"I want to go after him," Ben said. "I mean, me and Tom."

"Go after him?"

"Look, he's had me scared outta my wits for weeks now. It ain't right. And now I feel like I sic'd him on some poor unsuspecting town. It's my responsibility to do something about him."

"No, absolutely not. I forbid it," Monty held up his hand.

"Why?" Tom asked.

"Whatever you're thinking about doing. It isn't safe."

"I don't feel safe knowing he's anywhere near around here," Ben answered. "Look, we can go hunt for him round town and if we find him turn him in to the Sheriff."

"I'm not talking about your safety. I'm talking about the safety of the Colony."

"I don't understand. I don't think Josh is any threat to the rest of you."

"I don't mean your Josh either. I'm not as worried about him as I am about Colonel Dodson. Look, Ben and Tom, you're welcome here. I don't mean to sound anything less than happy you've come. You seem like nice boys and I think you're visiting us is exactly what we set this place up for. But I want you to stay on the property and stay away from town. There's too much going on as it is, without your complicating matters. Let the Sheriff find this guy. That's his job."

"I don't understand," Ben repeated.

"Will you explain what you meant about Colonel Dodson?" Tom asked calmly.

"This probably isn't any of your business. But I guess if you're going to live here any length of time it soon will be. Okay. I bought this land about five years ago from an old man named Jeremiah Hatfield. He'd been a prospector, then a farmer. He got the land just by staking a claim long before anybody owned land around here. He built most of the houses over a period of years, mainly I think just for something to do.

"Ten years ago this fellow Charles Dodson who'd been a Colonel in the Cavalry and fought in the Indian Wars decided he wanted to own this mountain. He had enough money to buy up most of it. All except for this place. Ol' Jeremiah took a dislike to him and wouldn't sell. Dodson and his men made numerous threats and apparently scared him enough that he moved off the land and went down to Denver to live, but didn't sell. He hated Dodson even more after that.

"I met Jeremiah when I was looking around for a place to build my retreat. I'd come back from England and hunted around the U.S. and decided I liked living in the mountains. So I came to Denver. One night in a saloon I got to talking to this old man who turned out to be Jeremiah Hatfield. I told him I was looking for land in the mountains. He told me he owned a wonderful place in a town named Perspective. Well, that really excited me. I mean everything just seemed so right.

"After I came up here and saw what he'd built I was even more impressed, though I must admit I was somewhat distressed that it was so far out of the way. But the train stopped at the bottom of the hill. So I went back to Jeremiah and asked him how much he wanted for it.

"He said, 'Pay my rent till I die. Won't be much longer.' Of course, it was a little more complicated than that. But the point was he had no family left. He'd been married once, but his wife had died and his two kids had disappeared long ago. He believed they'd been killed in the Civil War. He didn't have any need for money except to buy food and pay his rent. So he sold me the place for a very small down payment and an agreement to pay his room and board till he died."

"Sounds like a pretty good deal," Tom said.

"Yes, well, I think it was. Only Colonel Dodson didn't like it. He wanted this place. And he didn't like the idea of me buying it. He offered me money to sell it to him, but by that time I'd fallen in love with it. I hadn't realized he was such a no-good bastard."

Monty turned to Ben, "One reason I'm hesitant to attribute the theft to this guy who's been following you is that I wouldn't put it past Dodson to get one of his wranglers to steal the money and frame you two in order to turn the Sheriff against me. Let me tell you, it's been a long hard battle getting accepted in Perspective."

"So you're concerned Dodson will ruin your reputation or something to try to force you out?" Tom asked.

"It's more than that. A couple of months ago, Jeremiah Hatfield died. Somehow Dodson found out. Now he's filed suit against me to take the land."

"How?"

"It sounds crazy at first, but there's a hidden strategy. His case is that the deed for the property refers to this place as the 'Hatfield family farm.' And he's right it does. He claims that since we're not a family, this is not a 'family farm' and so the deed's invalid."

"That doesn't make sense. A family's just a bunch of people living together. But so what? You still own the place."

"Well, if the deed was invalid then the land still belongs to Hatfield's estate. But Jeremiah had no heirs and left no will. That means he died intestate, as the lawyers say, and his estate would revert to the State of Colorado."

"Then the Governor or somebody would just give it back to you. Right?"

"Dodson's got a friend who's head of the Government Land Office. I think they're probably partners in Dodson's deal. I don't see how he managed to buy up this whole mountain otherwise. If the land goes to the state, Dodson'll get it."

"But that's obviously unfair," Tom said. "No court or jury would uphold that kind of decision."

"You're right. But that's Dodson's hole card. The argument that we're not a real family is based on his discovery that we're urnings. He uses that silly term 'inverts' that makes us sound like we walk around with our feet above our heads. Frankly, I prefer the term 'shower,' but you know what I mean."

"Huh?" Ben was bewildered by all these confusing terms: "inverts," "showers." What kind of a word was "show-er"? he wondered. That's the way Monty pronounced it, like "one who shows."

"If Dodson goes to court and announces that the family farm has been given to a colony of inverts and sodomites, well… "

"I see," said Tom.

"That's blackmail," said Ben angrily.

"Yep," said Monty.

"How would he prove anything?" Ben rejoined.

"He wouldn't have to. All he'd have to do is create the suspicion. That would be enough. And that's part of why I don't want you two going back into town" he continued. "For the time being I'm trying to keep as quiet as possible. I've discouraged any of our regular visitors from coming out here this year. I've bought a lot of goods from Ozzie Turnbull and, God help me, I've made sizable contributions to Reverend Jackson at the Baptist Church in hopes of getting the town on our side.

"But the simple fact is we could lose Clear Light Colony just because of people's ignorance and prejudice and because of Charles Dodson's egomaniacal desire to own a mountain of his own."

"Dodson's suit sounded just as frivolous and unfair as that suit Georgie White has got against Elizabeth's dad," Ben remarked.

I just grinned. I figured they both could see perfectly well how I was crafting this plot.

35

he next day about mid-morning, Sheriff Turnbull came galloping up to the back of the house again.

"Somebody stole a baby pig from my yard back o' the store last night," he announced. "I searched all over town yesterday. There are no other strangers around here. When I took Jake the money you gave me he told me nobody has gotten off any trains and he ain't seen nobody come by on the road, 'ceptin' them two boys you got up here, Monty."

"I'm sure they didn't leave here last night. Besides, why would they steal food from you when I've invited them to eat at my table?"

"Because you don't serve beef or pork that's why. They want real food! No wonder they gotta steal."

"Ozzie, that is nonsense."

"I don't care what you say, Professor Hightower, I'm gonna take those boys in if this happens one more time, you hear? And, let me remind you, harboring criminals is a crime itself. This don't look no good for you neither."

"Look, Sheriff, let one of the boys tell you about this man they think has been following them. Maybe he's your thief."

Ben had been standing just inside the kitchen door, half out of sight. "Yeah," he spoke up, "let me tell you my story."

"Whadda I want with another story? Well, okay. What it is?"

Ben timidly stepped out into the light and described how they'd been chased by this big mountain man and had to jump off the train to escape him. He suggested that Josh could have come back along the tracks and have stolen the money from the depot and then come up to the town.

"I oughta put you under arrest for hoppin' the freight. Railroad police'd be happy to get holda you. You expect me to believe that story?"

"Maybe not, but it's true. And all you gotta do is look out for this guy Josh. He's real big and kinda simple-looking with a patch over his right eye. Pretty obvious."

"Well, if I see him I'll certainly ask him if he's been eatin' roast pig. And if he says no, I just might tell him what you be sayin' 'bout 'im."

After the Sheriff left, Ben started crying. "Why won't he believe me? It even sounded like he'd rather be on Josh's side than mine."

"There's a hard lesson, Ben, that you have got to learn. It's terribly unfair and terribly wrong and maybe someday somebody'll do something about it. But the fact is there's a wall of enmity between the breeders and the showers, I mean between the males and females and what Edward Carpenter calls the intermediates, us. (I guess, maybe it's not with the females so much as the males)," Hightower inserted parenthetically. "I don't think they even know what's going on. It seems like we're the ones aware of which side who's on, but they react to us almost automatically with hate and mistrust."

"You mean he knows I'm an urning?"

"Maybe. Maybe not. What he sees is that you're, well, pretty and delicate. You sure don't look like him. He may not understand what's going on. Actually, if he'd let himself get past the wall, he'd probably discover he liked you."

Monty was starting in on one of his sermons. "Maybe he's afraid of you because on some biological level he's attracted to you and that scares him. So he blames you for it. I don't know. It's all very perplexing."

"Isn't there anything we can do about it?"

"You can stay right here on the property."

"No, I mean, can't we do something to bring down this wall?"

"That's probably a question for the future long after we're dead. But maybe the first thing we have got to do is to learn to thrive in spite of—or even because of—the wall. I mean, people like us have been the great artists and mystics and philosophers all through history. Maybe what's helped them become great is that they had to become special; they couldn't just be like everybody else, because they weren't.

"Yesterday I remember I was saying people can grow through adversity. Maybe if there were no adversity our kind—the queer people that we are—wouldn't have any reason for being. Maybe it's the job of the showers in the scheme of things to transcend the world and thereby transform and save it."

"Show-ers?" Ben asked. Once again he felt bewildered.

"When I was a boy my daddy raised horses—real fine animals. He took the best ones to county fairs and horse shows all over the state. He didn't want the fillies getting pregnant when he was going to show them so he kept 'em in a special corral. They were the 'show stock.' My daddy always called 'em the 'showers.' They were for beauty. The rest of the herd he called the 'breeders.' 'Course the shower fillies got moved over to the breeder corral when they got older: the way animals contribute to the future is biologically. With people it's a little different: people can contribute spiritually too. But it's the same distinction: breeders and showers.

"There are people whose primary function is to breed; they are male and female, each representing half of the whole; they're important for the future; they're part of the Great Chain of Being and Great Round of Creation; they carry on the biological evolution this Mr. Darwin has got in so much trouble for telling us about. There are other people whose primary function is to show; they are special; they are both male and female simultaneously or something in the middle comprising both halves; they step outside the Round and break the Chain because it's only outside that people can be special; it's only outside that you can get a perspective. Those who do so carry on—or at least remind the rest about—the spiritual evolution of the race that is even more important for the future.

"And, mind you, the future is going to be very different. Thomas Malthus has calculated that unchecked breeding is going to become a terrible problem in the next century. The success of science and the invention of machines is going to change the way human beings understand truth and the way they understand the rules that govern behavior.

"Because our people have been outside the rules for so long, we are able to understand that the rules are changing. We can look at the rules from our perspective outside and see that modern consciousness is not shackled by old commandments. The rules for the future must be not based on claims to authority but on the reasoning of the mind and the urging of the heart. Whatever function same-sex love played in the ancient world—Greece and Rome and all that that Plato talked about—it's something different now. The needs of the world are changing, and because we've got a perspective on things, we're responsible for showing the way.

"What we are to show, I think, is the special virtues that come from blending maleness and femaleness: strength with gentleness, logic with feeling, resolve and diligence with nurturance and sensitivity. The polarity of the sexes has been the major source of conflict and turmoil in human history. War and greed and deceit are all generated by male posturing for female attention. Our lives show how masculine and feminine traits can be merged into a viable synthesis that transcends the conflict of opposites.

"We show what real success is. From our perspective, we can see that opulence and power and self-aggrandizement are illusions. From outside, we can see the real success is savoring life." Monty waxed eloquent. "Enjoy the beauty of the world, my son. Prefer the beauty to riches. Prefer experience and adventure to possessions and security. Prefer people to things. Strive to serve those around you and be grateful for their service to you.

"Live simply with the abundance life provides. There is more than enough of everything for everybody in the world if we all just take our share and watch out for others to make sure they get their share...

"Oh, I know I'm sermonizing again," Monty laughed, "and I know it sounds a little megalomaniacal but I believe that our claiming our rightful identity in the coming world shows the way for the human race to survive. We are the shining examples—like Jesus Christ—that resurrection comes from facing adversity and transcending it."

"Gee, Professor Hightower, that's very impressive," Ben answered.

"You can call me Monty," he smiled. "Or Dorothea, if you like."

"Say, do you really think Jesus Christ was, uh, shower and not breeder?"

Montgomery Hightower looked at Ben quizzically, with just a hint of mirth in his smile, "Well, wasn't he?"

36

hile Ben had stayed in the kitchen to help—and so was around when Sheriff Turnbull arrived—Tom had gone out to the stables with Margaret Travers. As Margaret was teaching him what chores needed doing, she got to telling him the story of her life. As it turned out, her story seemed to illustrate some of the same points Monty had made in his conversation with Ben.

"I been fond o' horses ever since I was little. My Pa owned a farm in Kentucky and had a few horses for draft animals. When I was nine or ten he bought me an over-the-hill racehorse named Nelly. She'd raced well as a filly but then lost her stride and weren't no good for racin'. And since she never foaled weren't no good for breedin' neither. I sweared it was 'cause she wanted nothin' to do with the stallions. So anyway Nelly got sold cheap to Pa. I started training her and—miraculously, Pa said—I got her back to racing quality. I was sure she just needed a woman's hand.

"Whether it was Nelly learnin' from me or me from Nelly, we taught each other the secrets of horse racing. I entered her in the county fair. And she won. We went to other fairs and won also. Then when I growed up and got to be a teenager, I wanted to race professionally. Pa tried to enter us in a semi-professional tournament, but we was turned down 'cause the judge said there weren't no proper jockey. It seemed to be a proper jockey, you had to be male," Margaret spat angrily. "So the next time we entered Nelly in a race, I cut my hair off and told 'em my name was Mike. They believed me and we won.

"To make sure the ruse worked, I took up chewin' tobacco and cursin' like a fiend. Just as I was about to move up to the big time, however, Nelly broke her leg and had to be shot. I did it myself.

"Well, I'd become a skilled jockey alright, but wit' no horse. So I turned myself full-time into Mike Travers and went out to get a job on the circuit. For several years, I was quite successful. Rode in the Kentucky Derby

151

twice, though I never won none of the really big races. Then one day I went and fell in love. And this time it wasn't wit' no damn horse," she joked. "But with Miss Isabel Hartshorne, debutante, coquette, and daughter of one of the richest horsemen in the whole state. At first I told myself the emotional attachment to Isabel was a natural consequence of me pretendin' to be a man. After all, part of the part was makin' crude remarks about all the women 'round the stables.

So I got me a job ridin' one of the Hartshorne horses. That gave me a chance to be around Isabel and, every so often, to actually talk with her. She was notoriously flirtatious, though I'd heard she never followed through. But she sure seemed to take a liking to this young Mike Travers and started spending more and more time at the track. 'Course I began to worry after a while, but figured nothing was ever going to happen. Isabel kept comin' round and sayin' how much she liked me, how she thought there was somethin' special 'bout me, something she said she ain't never seen in no man before.

"Well, one day I plumb lost my head, I guess, 'cause while I was helpin' her down off her horse, I just took her in my arms and planted a big kiss on her mouth. She giggled and squirmed, but she didn't pull away. That's when I got scared. I mean, I'd heard all the stories 'bout every other man who tried somethin' like this. She always slapped 'em silly. After I finally pulled away, she said, 'What's taken you so long, honey?' Well, she was so pretty and I was sure smitten. So I said, 'Look, here, Isabel, I think there's somethin' I gotta tell you.' 'I sure hope there is,' she replied and she gave me a little squeeze on the breast. 'How did you know?' I asked her. 'Who cares?' she said. 'You're my kind of people.'

"Well, I don't know how long she'd seen through my disguise. And I didn't exactly understand then why she preferred me as a girl. But I sure knowed I was in love." Margaret laughed and laughed as she told this story to Tom.

"Well, what happened?" he asked anxiously.

"We sneaked back to this shed behind the stables. We were sure nobody had seen us. And, well, we was just akissin' back there and pullin' the clothes off each other, when all of a sudden there's this helluva creakin' noise. And we looked up and one whole wall of the shed came crashin' down. And when the dust cleared, there was all the guys standin' around expectin' to see this prick-teasing Miss Isabel gettin' plugged in there. They were gonna get their revenge on her. I 'spect I was supposed to come outta there a hero. But that ain't what happened."

"What do you mean?"

"Well, boy, what they seen when the wall falls down was two girls in there lickin' pussy. And it wasn't long 'fore Mike Travers was blacklisted for good and Miss Isabel Hartshorne hauled off to an asylum."

"Oh, Margaret, I'm sorry."

"So was I. I tried to rescue her, nearly ended up in the asylum myself. After a while I gave up. Nearly killed me, but I'd learned myself an important lesson: that there were women who'd be more interested in me as a woman than a man. 'Course it took me a while to get used to dressin' like a girl and I didn't do it very often. Left Kentucky and came west. I discovered there were cowgirls just like there were cowboys. And I got me jobs on ranches. That's how I ended up in Colorado.

"One day I met this beautiful woman. She was the daughter of a country doctor and was helpin' out as his nurse. I'd broke my wrist ropin' a calf and got took in to the doc's." She grinned. "That nurse was Sophie. You know?"

"The tall lady you were with at breakfast," Tom answered.

"Well, Sophie had studied in Chicago and was a real sophisticated lady. But she cottoned to me that first day and, well, we been together ever since."

"How did you come to the Clear Light Colony?"

"Sophie's got a friend in Chicago, Miss Imogene Hedgeweather. You'll meet her. She'll be out here soon, I reckon. She's sort of a mystic type. Brilliant woman. Teaches history of religion or something like that at the University of Chicago. She's the one taught Sophie 'bout lovin' women. She was a friend of Monty Hightower's. He was movin' up here and needed somebody who know'd something 'bout horses. And, well, one thing led to another. And Sophie and me came up to live here.

"Tom," her voice suddenly dropped an octave and she sounded very serious, "this is a great place to live. It's pretty rough out there for people like us. I mean it ain't all jokes. Me and Isabel got beat up pretty bad when those guys realized what they was seein'. I understand why the Professor is worried about Colonel Dodson and I understand why he feels helpless... " her voice trailed off.

"I wish there was something we could do," Tom answered also feeling helpless.

"'Least we can all stick together," Margaret concluded. "Our kind of people gotta stick together."

37

om, we've got to do something about Josh."

"Do something? I thought Monty asked us definitely not to do anything."

"Yeah, but look, not only are you and I getting blamed for Josh's stealing food around town, now the Colony is. It's just gonna make the situation worse. Besides, now I'm getting scared Josh'll find me and... you know."

"You're safe as long as you stay out here and obey Monty's instructions."

"Today Monty told me that the most important thing people can do is to confront their adversities and transform them."

"What does that mean?"

"You know, be strong and learn from your difficulties."

"Yeah, but I mean in regard to your feeling that Josh is the one stealing food in town?"

"Oh, well, I think it means that I—or you and I, if you'll help, please—have to go find him."

"Then what?"

"We tell him to get out of town."

"Su-u-ure... "

"Well, then we beat him up."

"Oh, I see."

"I used to be so scared of him. But now I'm getting mad. I think there's a reason to be scared of him if we leave it to him to come to us. You know what I'm scared of... But if we go after him. Well, we take the offensive. I bet we can win."

"And if we lose?"

"Well, at least I won't have given into fear... "

"What if he kills you—or me?"

"If it comes to that, we kill him."

"Really?"

"Really!"

"Well, how are we going to get into town? It's a long walk."

"I was thinking: you spent the morning working in the stable with Margaret. Maybe you could, you know, borrow a horse?"

"No, Ben, absolutely not. It would just destroy our welcome here... Look, if you're feeling so heroic, why don't you ask Monty's permission. I mean, I'll go with you," Tom looked up at the ceiling of their little cottage, "—God help me for agreeing to this—if you'll get an okay from Monty."

"That could be hard."

"Not as hard as fighting Josh."

An hour later Ben was repeating his arguments to Monty. He explained why finding Josh would not only vindicate him and Tom, it would also ease tensions between Sheriff Turnbull and the Clear Light Colony. It would be a manly thing to do, maybe that would counter the suspicions Colonel Dodson might raise. "And, besides," he saved his best argument for last, "you said we have to confront our fears and transform them. I think this is the only way I can transform my fears and Josh's petty crimes."

Monty put up some objections, but finally agreed. He also let them take two horses on the condition that Margaret Travers go in with them. "It's not so much that I don't trust you as it is that the horses are indispensable."

Several hours after dark, the threesome rode into town. "How do you propose to find this guy?" Margaret repeated a question she'd already asked several times.

"We know he's been stealing food from the store. He might show up again tonight," Tom answered.

"That's a long shot though," Margaret objected. "'Specially if he stole a small pig last night. That's enough to live on for several days."

"You should see this guy," Tom rejoined.

"I have a plan," Ben announced. "It's a little risky. But, what the hell, I said I was going to confront my fears."

"A plan?" asked Margaret.

"Yeah. I think Josh wants *me* at least as much as any suckling pig. The only reason he's come this far pursuing us is his grudge against me for refusing sex... "

"...not to mention putting out his eye," Tom added.

"I think *I* need to be bait."

"What?"

"My plan is to walk down the middle of the road—from town here down toward the depot. He's probably somewhere camped out along there, isn't he?"

"Well, there are roads all through these mountains," Margaret observed.

"We may have to try them all," Ben answered, obviously resolute.

"How do you expect Josh to notice you?" Tom asked the sensible question.

"I'm going to call out his nickname for me. He'll know it's me."

"Nickname?" Margaret asked.

"Benjy Pretty-Butt," Ben replied and the sound of the words stung him even as he spoke them.

"Oh my," I said to Ben, "that must've been embarrassing. You did that right in the middle of town?"

"I didn't expect anybody to be in town. 'Course it turned out there were several people in the saloon who came out and hooted at me. But I think they thought I was teasing somebody else since I was calling out the name. But yes, Rick, it was horribly embarrassing. And I guess that's why I did it and why that was truly confronting my fear. Not only was I humiliated by the nickname itself, I was scared to death of what was going to happen if and when Josh heard me and went for the bait."

"And did he?"

"We walked down those roads for hours, trying sideroads that I supposed led down to people's houses. Finally just as we were about to give up, I heard Josh answer my call, 'Benjy Pretty-Butt'."

Just at that crucial moment, the phone rang. Elizabeth was calling to say that Georgie White's lawyers had agreed on a financial settlement, that included Dr. Steed's public apology and statement that so far as he actually knew Georgie was not a user of IV drugs.

"Dad doesn't like the last part. He says it's a lie. But this'll get the whole thing over with. I heard you favorably impressed the prospective buyer. Thanks, Rick. We're really gonna need the money. I hope you made him believe the place is worth every penny of the asking price."

I didn't say anything. I was feeling like this wonderful place was about to be pulled right out from under me. It occurred to me that I needed to confront my enemy. I doubted that walking through the streets of Boston calling out "Ricky Pretty-Butt" would have helped me or lured Georgie White out so I could confront him.

38

ut of the woods just ahead of where Ben was walking and Tom and Margaret were following a little ways behind on horseback, Josh appeared. "Hello-o-o there, young fella," he called out.

Ben wasn't sure if the salutation sounded friendly or angry. "Hello, Josh, I'm surprised to see you here. I thought you were on that train to California."

"But you got off the train. I been lookin' for ya. Where you been?"

"I don't think that's any of your business, Josh. I think you ought to just get back on the next train comes by and get out o' here."

"But I ain't finished with my friend Benjy," he said ominously. His voice had taken on an edge. "Seems ta me, we still got accounts to settle."

"How's that?" Ben asked.

"There's the matter of my right eye to start wit', Benjy. And then there's the matter of that pretty little butt o' yours. I told you back there in Chi that I wanted ya. I still do. And I'm gonna get you."

"No, Josh, you're not," Tom shouted from high on his horse.

Josh looked up surprised. Until then he hadn't realized Ben was not alone. "Hey, t'ain't fair," he shouted. "Here I am, po' Josh B'Gosh, all by his lonesome out here. And you done come along with—what's that?—two men on horses."

"I ain't no man," Margaret shouted, "but I'm strong as any."

"Well, I declare. A woman out here in the hills. Maybe you done brought me a present, Benjy. Maybe you brung her for me so's I wouldn't havta use your butt."

Margaret shouted something angry Ben couldn't understand.

"Josh, you shut up your talk like that. You ain't gonna git nobody out here. In fact, you're gonna git out o' town."

"Says you?" he laughed derisively.

"Look, Josh," Ben continued. "You ain't got no business here. I don't like your threats and I don't like your stealin' from the General Store. It's makin' problems where there don't need to be none."

Josh stepped up much closer to Ben, so he practically towered over him. Tom's horse reared and Tom used the occasion to make the horse's hooves pound out a warning to Josh.

"But I wants m' little Benjy," Josh replied, reaching out to stroke Ben on the cheek.

"I ain't a-scared you, Josh. When you tried to, to... "

"To jocker ya," Josh finished Ben's sentence.

"...back in that warehouse in Chicago, I didn't understand what was goin' on. Now I do. And now I'm even madder than I was then. But I ain't afraid anymore."

"'Twasn't nothin' to be afraid o' then," Josh answered, sounding almost like a child who'd been scolded. "I told you I wasn't gonna hurt ya none. I just wanted a lit'le lovin'. Ol' Josh got a right to that."

"But not from me," Ben answered. "I liked you alright, Josh. We had a good day together. But you had no right to expect me to let you... "

"So ya stuck your butt up in the air ta tease me and then ya blinded me."

"Josh, I didn't mean to hurt you. Look, I felt sorry for you. I didn't understand what was going on till it was too late. And then I asked you to stop what you were doin'. But you wouldn't."

"All I was doin' was pretendin' you was a woman. You knows youse the kind that likes t' git jockered. Wouldn't a-hurt ya none to let me take a little lovin'."

"Yes, it would have. And what you wanted wasn't love. Yeah, I guess I know what I like—but, Josh, look, me bein' who I am don't give you no right to abuse me."

"Well, la di da," Josh answered surly. "Now ya knows what ya like, do ya? One o' them back there? The guy, ain't it? Ya take his cock up yo' butt?"

With a burst of emotion that Ben would never have imagined he had in him—and would never have allowed himself if he'd premeditated it—Ben stepped forward and slapped Josh as hard as he could.

"Shut up, Josh, it ain't your business. We came down here to warn you to git outta town and stop stealin' or next time we find you, damn it, I'll put out your other eye." Ben was enraged. "And this time I'll mean to do it."

Josh kind of roared, obviously surprised that Ben had dared to strike him. Perhaps no one had ever dared challenge him before. Then he lunged forward grabbing at Ben.

Ben jumped out of the way and Josh stumbled, then grabbed at him again. This time he struck Ben with the backside of his hand. In an instant, Tom was off his horse and had jumped onto Josh's back, grabbing him round the neck with both arms. Josh rose up to his full height and tried to shake Tom off, but Tom clung tenaciously and then reached up with his hand and pulled on Josh's nose.

"Don't hurt him," Ben shouted.

"Hurt *him*?" Tom exclaimed. "What about me? Do something."

"What?" Ben called out a little helplessly as Josh thrashed back and forth trying to shake Tom off.

"Kick 'im in the nuts or somethin'."

"I'm gonna kill both you faggots," Josh bellowed.

Ben felt a sudden rush of strength. He pulled back his fist and then drove it hard into Josh's big belly. "Look, we've had enough o' you," he shouted angrily.

Still sitting on the back of her horse, Margaret let out a wild cat-call of encouragement. Tom squeezed hard on Josh's nose.

All of a sudden to everyone's surprised, Josh dropped to his knees and started crying. "Don't hurt Josh no more. Ple-e-ase."

"He's just a poor half-wit," Tom announced as he let go his stranglehold and stepped back.

"Ain't nobody ever dared punch me like that," Josh whimpered half to himself.

"'Course he's mighty big," Tom finished his sentence.

"And scary," Ben answered. He was surprised that he found himself feeling sorry for Josh. Standing up to his fears seemed to have dissipated them. He turned to Josh, "Look, I'm sorry I hurt you in Chicago. It was all a misunderstanding."

"All's I wanted was a little lovin'." Josh was blubbered, "No woman gonna love Josh…"

"That's not necessarily true, Josh. But you gotta learn to be polite. You can't force yourself on people like you tried with me. The ladies will be nice to you if you're nice to them."

"Ol' Josh'll try, Benjy."

"Okay, Josh," Ben answered warmly. "But not around here. Just git outta here. Hop the next freight that goes by."

"Okay," Josh answered sheepishly.

"And stay outta town and stay away from the General Store, ya hear?" Tom added to make sure the message was fully understood.

"Josh'll do what you say."

"And stay away from the Clear Light Colony," Margaret shouted.

Later as they were trotting back to the Colony with Ben riding with Tom, Margaret said she regretted her last comment. "I shouldn't've mentioned the name of the place."

"Yeah," Ben agreed, "he didn't know where we were before. Now he does. But I doubt it'd mean anything to him."

"I was surprised," Tom said. "I hadn't realized he was just a simple oaf. You'd got me thinkin' he was some kinda demon, Ben, with spies all over the place."

"Well, maybe I did exaggerate. I was scared. But the fact is regardless of how much of a simpleton he is, he's still strong as a bear and if he gets angry he can be dangerous."

"I don't doubt that," Margaret agreed. "You know, Ben, Monty Hightower would've been mighty proud of what you said back there. I mean about not being afraid of who you are and not letting yourself be abused on account of it."

"I was too," Tom said, turning his head to lightly kiss Ben who was riding behind him with his arms wrapped around his chest holding on.

"I hope that's the last we see of him," Ben said, shrugging off the compliment the other two had just paid him.

"Well, I thought you were going to have to kill him," I commented.

"It's amazing what a little bravery can do," Ben answered.

"That turned out to be pretty easy."

"That's what you think."

Later in the day, Hu Dorsey showed up unexpectedly at the front door.

"You never called," he said, "so I decided to come see you. And, you know, check out this place some more."

I invited him in though I was a little surprised and embarrassed. I hadn't intended to snub him exactly. Though frankly I'd been hoping he—and his offer to buy the place—would just go away. But now he hadn't gone away.

"Let me put a shirt on," I said as I showed him into the living room and gestured toward one of the chairs. I was wearing only my famous faded red gym shorts.

"Don't bother," he said. "You might just have to take it off."

Uh-oh.

I'd left a polo shirt hanging on a coathook in the entrance hall I noticed, and only had to take a couple of steps back to grab it. "Look, Hu, maybe we better reach an understanding," I said pulling on the shirt.

"Oh," he said. "I thought we had. I mean, I thought I was offering to invest enough money in this place that, well... "

"You thought what?" I said indignantly.

"I said I thought I was investing enough money... "

I simply laughed. "And here I thought you wanted me for my body."

"That too," he replied very matter-of-factly.

"Whoa, wait a minute. Let's start this all over again," I said.

"Is there a misunderstanding?"

"Well, yes, I think there is."

"I didn't think so. I mean, when I was out here the other day, I thought it was pretty clear you were interested."

A peculiar doubt struck me as he said that. "Do you mean your only interest in this place was me? Are you not serious about buying it?" I wondered what Elizabeth would say to me if I queered the deal—even though I kind of wanted to.

"Oh no. I'm gonna buy it. I knew that before I ever saw the place. When I was a kid and my mother and dad wanted to go out in the country, we'd always drive by here and Mom would tell me how she used to come up here and ride the horses. It belonged to friends of her family, you know."

"And me? Did you think I came with the furniture?"

"I didn't mean it to sound like that, Rick. I guess, my opening line wasn't very good."

"I'm kinda out of practice myself," I replied, all of a sudden feeling very nervous about this whole thing. Here was this guy I had the hots for only a couple of days ago and now he was ready to go at it, and I was going to have to explain...

"Maybe you just need a little coaching."

"Look, Hu, I need more than that. I, uh, well, it's not like I wouldn't like to. It's just I've sorta promised myself I wasn't going to."

"You take a vow of chastity or something?"

"Or something," I replied. "I came out here to be alone, you know. I needed to get my head straight on a few matters. One of them was, well, sex and love. I kinda think I've had too much of one and not enough of the other. And now I think it's too late."

"Too late?"

I wasn't sure how to say this. I didn't want to sound like a leper. But I didn't want to compromise the decision I'd made.

"I've just been learning how to calm down and be by myself. I don't want to get myself all worked up about something or somebody I can't have."

"Rick, you're talking a-mile-a-minute. And you're not making any sense. I didn't come out here to become your lover. I just... " His voice trailed off.

"Maybe that's the trouble. What I've been looking for all my life is a love I could be proud of. I never found it. Maybe 'cause I usually settled for sex. What I think I needed all those years was a lesson in courtship. But the irony is now that I know that, I'm in no position to take a lover. I don't think it'd be safe or fair to somebody else."

My heart was beating surprisingly hard. "Maybe we can be friends. I guess I'd be happy to, you know, share massages with you or something like that. But not yet. I don't want to risk falling in love and I don't want to do anything unsafe."

"Are you talking about you or me," he asked.

"Why, me," I said.

"Oh, is there something you need to tell me?" he asked warily.

"Yes, Hu, I guess there is."

"Then I guess there's something I need to tell you too..."

39

aybe Hu and I will really get to be friends," I said to Ben as he gently ribbed me about my adventure with the gentleman caller and prospective buyer.

He seemed quite encouraging. "You need friends, Rick."

"Then what am I doing out here in the middle of nowhere? I thought I was trying to get away from people."

"Maybe making friends and being out here isn't as much contradiction as you think. That's what we discovered at the Clear Light Colony."

After their nighttime adventure Tom and Ben slept late into the morning. They woke and came out to the kitchen in search of a cup of coffee just in time to join Alex McMahon in preparing lunch.

"We take turns cooking I trust you've noticed, and I've decided to prepare us a truly lavish salad and a most unusual baked treat the likes of which I suspect you've never seen before. It's called a quiche. French, you know. I studied in France," he tossed off as though everyone had done something in their lives in a foreign country. "Now there're several kinds of lettuce just beginning to come up in the garden. If you'll come with me, young man," he said to Ben, "I'll let your friend here grate the cheese."

As he followed the French chef toward the garden, Ben initiated the conversation Monty had urged him to have with McMahon. "Professor Hightower told me you'd been a Jesuit. Is that true?"

"Now, he told me the very same thing about you," McMahon answered. "It must be true about both of us."

"I guess so. I didn't last very long."

"Perhaps you'd like to explain."

"It's a long story. I guess I don't mind telling you. I told Professor Hightower... "

"Monty," McMahon interrupted correcting him.

"Okay. I told Monty what happened. It was pretty devastating. They threw me out, you know."

"Well, well, something else we share."

"Oh really?"

"I suspect there may be some similarities in our stories there as well."

After Ben told McMahon about his years at St. Athanasius' Seminary, McMahon responded with his own story.

"I'd been assigned to the Indian missions—in Asia, you know. I was supposed to be bringing the light of Christianity to the Hindoos. But frankly

I found them far more civilized than we. And after a while I think I began to appreciate their gods a lot more than my own. Perhaps I was having a battle with the old noonday devil... "

"What's that? Something in India?"

"Oh no, son. Doubt. Doubt is the noonday devil. Hits you in the middle of your life. After a while you don't see that your youthful idealism has accomplished anything. In my case, I saw I'd renounced an awful lot of things I really wanted. Oh, of course, the Order had given me a great deal. I don't mean to belittle that. I'd probably never have left Ohio if I hadn't entered the Church. But, well, once you've done those things, they don't seem all that exciting: Paris, Rome, Bombay... "

Just the names of the places McMahon mentioned thrilled Ben.

"...no, what I really needed was love. And the brotherly love of the Order just wasn't enough. I'd fought too long against 'particular friendships' all the while knowing that's what I really wanted. You remember about 'particular friendships'?"

Ben nodded remembering the euphemism for what he now understood to be the close bond—and physical affection—he felt with Tom Milam.

"The Hindoos didn't have the same notions about sex and marriage that we have. Nor did they seem to think it so unseemly that a man might fall in love with another man or a woman with a woman. Not that they encouraged such relationships exactly, but they simply seemed to understand that such things happen. After a while my own views had changed so much. I wasn't really a Christian anymore. I mean, I continued the mission and I said mass for them, but when one of the local priests suggested he would like to install an altar to the town's favorite god in my little chapel, well, I let him do it— Ganesha was the god's name, very peculiar god, I must say, with the head of an elephant. But the people all seemed so happy with Ganesha. Not like our Western God who seemed so stern.

"Well, that was the beginning of my downfall, I suppose," McMahon laughed as he bent over and inspected the plants growing in the garden. "Soon I fell in love with a native boy, a young man about your age, I should say. He was what they call Dravidian, one of the ancient hill tribes. The Dravidians have a most remarkable color, so dark they're practically blue. Well, my young man reminded me of another of their gods, Krishna—a sort of parallel of Jesus, it seemed to me. Krishna was an incarnation of their high God, Vishnu. Krishna was a shepherd and occasionally incarnated to save his people. Like Jesus. Christ/Krishna: same root word, you can hear how they sound alike?"

"Uh-huh," Ben acknowledged.

"Krishna wasn't quite so asexual as Jesus, however. He was a favorite of the village maidens. One of his 'saving acts,' it seems, was to multilocate himself so that on one night he was able to make love to all the maidens in the village at the very same time."

"In *your* village?" Ben asked incredulous.

"Oh no. This was all legend. But my point was that my young

houseboy reminded me so much of Krishna. Krishna is always portrayed as blue, you see. And, well, for all that I had believed in Christianity and devoted myself to priesthood, Jesus never made love to me. And Krishna did." McMahon sounded wistful and dreamy.

"The Hindoos and the Buddhists have this meditation tradition called Tantra that uses the energy generated in love-making to develop the soul. They see that sexual love can be a form of prayer—and not just a form of sin the way so many Christians think.

"Tantric practice uses breath-control to slow down sexual arousal and spread the energy all through the body—and the soul—and visualization and meditation to transform the human beloved into a manifestation of the Divine Beloved. My young Krishna was discipled to a Tantric *guru*—that's a teacher— in a nearby village. I never met the guru but my friend taught me many of the practices. He certainly helped me exorcize the noonday devil—as well as satisfy a lot of physical and emotional needs." Alex's voice trailed off.

He continued. "Then one day the Provincial showed up for Visitation. He came a day early for some reason and caught me with my young man. And then he discovered the statue of Ganesha in the chapel. And it was just too much for him. I think either one alone I could have gotten by with. But not both," the old man laughed.

"Let's see, I think this is enough for a salad, don't you," he held up his basket for Ben's inspection and then continued on with his story as he led them back toward the house. "Fortunately the Order paid my passage to Bombay where I met up with a British lord who happened to like Dravidian young men himself. He was a godsend, truly. Took quite a liking to me. He knew about this fellow Edward Carpenter and bought me a ticket back to England. At any rate, I lived in Derbyshire for a couple of years near Carpenter's farm and became a regular around there. That's how I met Monty Hightower."

"Wasn't there something you wanted me to do, sir?" Ben inquired as they reached the kitchen door.

"Oh, you did quite well. You listened to an old man's story."

Tom was waiting inside sipping on a second cup of coffee after finishing the job he'd been given. Together they helped Alex McMahon stoke the fire in the oven, then they washed the lettuce, while he prepared a pastry crust. Finally, after the quiche was baking, they set the table for lunch. Soon they were joined by the rest of the community.

"Well, my boys, Margaret tells me you were successful in hunting down this villain of yours," Monty Hightower said after the initial small talk while people were serving their plates.

"Yes sir," Ben answered. "But he wasn't much of a villain last night… "

"More of a pussycat," Tom interjected.

"No fisticuffs?" Monty asked.

"Hardly at all, sir," Ben answered. "I did threaten him with future violence if he didn't get out of town. But really I just told him I wasn't afraid of him and told him to stop harassing me."

"Ben was very brave," Margaret Travers spoke up.

"For all that I was—and still am—kinda scared of him, I really saw last night that he's just what Tom called a simpleton. He's big and strong and threatening. But he's also like a little boy that's easily intimidated. In a way I feel kinda silly having been so afraid of him."

"Well, I took one look at him and was afraid," Margaret commented. "He's big and strong—and maybe more of a bear than a pussycat. Potentially dangerous even if he didn't mean to be."

"Yeah, but all it took was standing up to him," Ben brushed off the suggestions of his bravery.

"Well, son, that's true about most everything we're afraid of. All it takes is a little courage. And courage often just means doing what you have to," Monty summarized the lesson to be learned. "I'm proud of you. Now, tell us, are you going to stay on a while here? Or do you have pressing business elsewhere?"

"No pressing business," Tom answered. "We've talked about this and, well, we would like to stay a while longer. But, Professor Hightower, sir, we want to earn our stay here… "

"No problem with that, as I told you. Everybody around here stays pretty busy and there's still more to do. And, well, once this awful business with Colonel Dodson is over with, we'll get back to inviting guests around. It gets very cheery—and very busy—then."

"Well now, if you're going to stay with us," Alex McMahon broke in, "then you must start joining us for the morning and afternoon sing." He clapped his hands merrily "I'm sure you'll love it."

"We slept late this morning," Ben answered, "but I think I woke up and heard a choir. I thought I was dreaming."

"Oh no, that was real," Monty answered. "We get together and sing and chant and maybe do a little dance, you know. Good for the spirit."

"Yes, Ben," Alex continued, "just like in seminary. Only without all those stuffy old rules." He laughed. "I've even taught them how to sing some songs to Ganesha and my dear Krishna."

"Who's that?" Tom asked.

Everybody laughed, while Ben whispered to Tom that he'd explain later. The whole group, it seemed to Ben, was marvelously easy going and relaxed, maybe a little frivolous, but apparently they could afford to be.

As the diners were finishing and a few people had gotten up and carried their dishes into the kitchen, Herbert Fadiman spoke up, "Monty, you mentioned Colonel Dodson. Any news?"

Hightower's face darkened. Through slightly clenched teeth he answered, "A note came yesterday saying he'd be coming around to discuss matters, as he put it, personally. I don't know what he thinks there is to discuss."

Ben noticed that a pall had settled on the room.

"You don't really think he has a case?" Margaret said.

"We've gone over this a hundred times, Margaret." There was an undertone of anger and exasperation in Monty's voice. "It doesn't seem to matter whether he has a case or not. If this thing goes to court, well, it could ruin us. No judge or jury is going to look very kindly at a community of showers."

"Yes, Monty, but remember to use my argument about being a religious establishment. This is probably how monasteries and convents got started in the first place," Alex said. "Monks and nuns aren't expected to be the breeder type."

"I agree, Alex. But I don't think that's the point."

"Yes, what can they prove?" asked Sophie, the tall, thin woman who'd been sitting next to Margaret. She was halfway through the kitchen door when she stopped and made her objection.

"I don't think they have to prove anything, Sophie. You know this whole matter may rest simply on innuendo. I'm not sure Dodson even has to make a specific accusation for the court to find against us. Besides, we may very well find the police up here peering into our bedrooms."

"I don't understand, sir," Ben asked timidly.

"Look, son, it may not matter at all whether Colonel Dodson has a real case against Jeremiah's will. All he has to do is make us seem undesirable. I don't think he even has to use words like sodomites to do that. In fact, just the suggestion is probably more damning than the actual accusation."

"That doesn't seem fair, sir. I thought the court would rule on the validity of the will."

Monty Hightower's voice was showing even more signs of annoyance and exasperation. "What difference would that make? He's out to ruin us and drive us out of here. What do you think the townspeople would say if they really knew who we were?"

"I think they'd think you were good people—and good customers," Tom answered.

"I wish you were right, boy," Monty said.

"Well, then," Tom blurted out, "they'd be wrong, damn them."

"There's a lesson here. Maybe it's the hardest one of all," Monty sighed. "I need to remind myself. Don't judge other people wrong.

"If there's one thing that being lovers of our own sex—and having such terrible things said about us—ought to teach us showers is to not blame others, not make them wrong, not even to have opinions about their lives. We see how false the opinions are they have about us. We ought to expect that the opinions—our own included—about all maligned groups are just as false. Indeed, we can see that the falsehoods about our lives propagated by 'righteous people' tend to bring about just what they condemn. Our special perspective allows us to see how such prophecies can be self-fulfilling.

"We certainly ought to recognize that, in general, judgments about others not only don't resolve the problems we're having with them—that cause us to have judgments about them in the first place—but, in fact, perpetuate and exacerbate those problems.

"We should long for truth. Our thirst for the world to see and respect the truth about our lives should parch us for the truth about all lives. It should be the hallmark of our personalities as showers that we tell the truth—"

"It's the very basis of our identity as showers," Alex interrupted. "We could only think of ourselves as showers, who share a kind of community, *because* we're open and tell the truth about ourselves."

"My God, I just realized something," Monty exclaimed, grabbing the back of his head with his right hand. "It's so obvious, but I just now got it. It's not what we do sexually that makes us showers, it's that we tell the truth about it. That's what we're supposed to show: telling the truth—even about what they say is the worst sin imaginable—not only transforms the sin but improves the karma of the whole world." Monty's face was practically glowing. The frustration and despondency of a few minutes ago had disappeared.

"Monty gets like this sometimes," Alex said with mock condescension, "That's why we love him." He reached out and touched Monty's hand. "*And* he's right, you know... "

Monty laughed heartily, standing up from the table as if to say the sermonizing was ended. "We may lose this battle to Dodson. Not respecting the truth of others' lives spoils the world for everybody. Dodson doesn't respect the truth of our lives. And because he doesn't, he can use it against us. Well, we may lose the battle but, in the long run, we win the war."

Under Sophie's direction, Tom and Ben washed the dishes and then set out in different directions to help with afternoon chores. Tom went off again with Margaret to the stables and Ben went to assist Alex in the garden.

Ben arrived to find Alex standing staring out into the vast distance which the Colony's location on the edge of the ridge gave them a vista on. He looked sad. "It'd be a shame to lose this place," he said to Ben as the boy approached. "I wonder where I'd go."

"How long has this threat been hanging over you all?" Ben asked, not sure what to say.

"We've known Dodson wanted the property from the time we arrived. Monty, Herb, and I were the original group. Dodson came over and offered to pay us double what we'd bought the place for. 'Course since Monty'd only agreed to pay Jeremiah's living expenses that wouldn't have amounted to much. We didn't tell Dodson that. I guess we could have gotten a pretty penny for this. But that isn't what we wanted. What we wanted was this," he made a sweeping gesture toward the expansive vista.

"It is a pretty view," Ben answered lamely.

"It's not just the view, Ben my boy. It... it's the soul. I mean, it's the openness of the soul, the perspective into the mind of God."

They both fell silent and looked out into the space of the open plain. A wind blew up from somewhere ruffling Ben's hair and whispering in his ear. The whisper seemed to speak of ancient memories, distant lands, long forgotten dreams. He looked at Alex McMahon's profile: the austerely worn face, the intense gaze, the slightly crazed look about his eyes, the laugh lines in his cheeks and brow that now had turned to worried furrows. He wondered at what this man had seen in his life. He wondered if he would ever see such things. Ben looked out into the open space and tried to see as far as England and France and even India. But, of course, those views were shrouded in distance. He listened to the wind and hoped perhaps he'd hear the parishioners of Father Alex's far-gone village singing songs to funny Ganesha. Then he laughed softly to himself at his own foolishness, and felt a pang of sadness for the gaunt old man. For a moment he envisioned Alex standing alongside a railroad track waiting to hop a freight.

And to his amazement, Ben realized that Alex would probably learn to do that with the same cheery devotion with which he'd planted and cultivated the lettuce in his garden.

Ben remembered what Alex had said earlier in the day about the noonday devil. Of course, he realized that he couldn't know what went on inside the man's mind, but he could certainly tell something from his demeanor, from the joy and cheerfulness that usually seemed to radiate from him, and from the deep feeling that surrounded him now. Ben was perhaps too young himself to understand the noonday devil or how its conquest could finally be resolved, but he was sure, as he stood next to Alex McMahon, that this man had successfully acquitted himself in the battle, even as Ben himself had the night before with a different kind of demon.

Alex turned away from the vista saying, "Come along now, Ben, we have cultivating to do. We must stop the weeds before they overrun us."

For the next couple of hours, Ben toiled cheerfully alongside Alex plucking weeds and loosening soil around the sprouting plants of the garden. Alex got to talking about his own experiences in religious life long before his fall from his Provincial's graces. Especially while studying in France, it seemed, he'd lived a very traditional and ancient style of religious life, rising at 3 a.m. to greet the morning with prayer and meditation, chanting the hours of the Holy Office five times a day, and going to sleep in the evening with the songs of Compline still on his tongue. "Oh, the singing was wonderful," he proclaimed. "It made up for the rest of the shit they put us through—oh, forgive me, young man. My indelicate words must burn your ears."

"I think I've heard the word before," Ben laughed, mocking innocence.

"It was my idea to institute a regular practice of singing and chanting here at Clear Light."

"Do you mean you chant office of choir?" Ben asked recalling his own experience of the ancient monastic liturgy.

"Oh no, no," Alex laughed. "No one but you and I could follow along," he poked Ben playfully in the ribs. "Certainly we sing some hymns, most of them Protestant," he said feigning orthodox Catholic horror at even the mention of such a possibility. "But most of what we do are old folk songs, some original compositions by Monty and by yours truly, whatever anyone wants to sing."

167

"Anything?"

"Well, we like it to be uplifting and happy. The point of our singing is to lift our spirits and set the tone for the day. We've been known to do some bawdy verse now and then, sailor songs, you know, but that really isn't our forte. And we don't often have sailors up here. More's the pity," he said half to himself and then grinned at what seemed to have been a delightfully lusty recollection.

"I remember how one of the nicest things about St. Athanasius' was the singing. I got pretty good at Gregorian Chant. It was sort of haunting, wasn't it?"

"If you mean that the music stays with you during the day, why yes. And I think that's the point of it. It's a great way to change what you're thinking. I mean, if you need to alter the content of your thoughts, say, to stop a particular recurring worry, you wouldn't have much luck just stopping it, but you could start singing something else, like an affirmation that you don't have to worry, and get the song singing itself inside your head. The melody and lyrics get into the mind and they wash away other concerns, and keep one's mind set on more eternal matters than day to day worries. In India I discovered the Hindoos are very enthusiastic about breathing. All their yoga exercises and meditation practice revolve around the breath. I think that's very significant. Do you recall that our word 'spirit' really means 'breath'?"

"I think I know that."

"I wonder if perhaps the Gregorian Chant originated in some sort of breathing meditation practice that has since been forgotten."

"Makes sense, I suppose."

"Ben, my boy, heed my words about this," Alex playfully shook his finger at Ben, "regardless of what you've been told about God, the Hindoos have discovered something we Catholics seem to have missed. God isn't out-there." He pointed up. "God is in-here." He pointed his finger to his heart. "The Hindoos say 'Brahman is Atman'."

"What's that?" Ben asked. He felt a chill as Alex spoke, as though some prophet of old had suddenly appeared before him and was revealing God's own truth.

"The Creative Spirit is your own Soul. God is found within."

"That's very beautiful," Ben answered, not altogether certain that he appreciated the significance of Alex's revelation.

"It means nothing really matters, son. I mean *everything* is God's experience of himself. You are a dream God is having. And that God is who you really are." Alex spun around on one foot almost like a ballet dancer, with his hand extended in a sweeping gesture. "Even if we lose this place and have to go beg for our supper, that'll be just another dream God'll be having."

"You mean we shouldn't even try to fight Colonel Dodson?"

"Oh no, I don't mean that at all. I suppose fighting Colonel Dodson's greed is also part of the dream. I mean that it's a great consolation to discover that the real you is secure in the universe. You know, I like living out here

168

because the peace and quiet allows me to remember that I really am a tiny sense organ of God experiencing his creation. Oh, it's all very wonderful." Alex's last sentence was choked with sentiment.

Ben didn't exactly understand. He wondered if perhaps one had to have fought that battle with the noonday devil to appreciate what the old former-priest was saying.

"But not former-priest," Ben said to me. "He was much more a priest than the Master of Students at the seminary who threw me out."

"I suppose you're right," I answered. "His message sounds a little like that Sixties stuff the Beatles were always singing about, you know, the Maharishi sniffing flowers and all that."

"Rick, you sound cynical."

"I just meant it sounds kind of old-hat."

"Is that because you've already integrated the message into your own soul?" Ben said snidely. "I didn't realize you were enlightened already."

"I didn't mean that."

"Alex McMahon pointed out what he called a 'great consolation.' It seems to me you, my friend, are in need of such consolation."

I thought for a moment of my doctor's dismal prognosis for me. I thought of the depression I'd sunk into back in Boston. I thought about my fears I'd have to leave this lovely place and go back to Boston again. And I thought about how I sometimes felt when I was out in the garden myself weeding or tending the flowers I'd planted; sometimes I forgot who I'd been all those years of my past and just was, here and now, in the present.

Ben interrupted my reverie. "Don't you think that's what Alex meant?"

40

 got two phone calls last night. The first was from Hu. He said he called to tell me that he sincerely hoped we could be friends. Apparently he was impressed—and flattered—by my demurral the other day.

"I'm not sure why, Rick, but somehow your rejecting my come-on really came across as loving. I'm not used to being turned down—whether that's because of my money or my looks I don't know—" I imagine it's both, I thought, but didn't say anything "—you seemed so honest. I guess it made me feel like you really respected me and cared about me." He sounded appropriately flustered. "I just wanted to say I like you and want to be your friend, at least till you go back to Boston."

"Okay," I said. "I appreciate your calling. I doubt I'm much better at this than you are so if you don't mind let's not talk about it anymore. Let's just be friends. Maybe we can get together for dinner this weekend," I suggested. "I've been wanting to get into town. Maybe Mexican food."

He said he knew a perfect place. He gave me the address and we set a time to meet. I reminded myself to be sure the station wagon would start. I hadn't been off the property in over three weeks—not since I filled up the back of the wagon with frozen dinners at the grocery store. What if the battery were dead? I wouldn't want to accidentally stand Hu up.

"Speaking of my going back to Boston," I changed the subject, "how are your plans coming on developing this place?" I was half-thinking that if Hu Dorsey really wanted to be friends, maybe he'd let me stay on in the house here, well, indefinitely.

"Originally I was planning to use the big house there for a clubhouse. That was when I was remembering my Mom's stories about the place. And that seems like the thing to do around here when you develop an area. It at least makes the buyers think they're going to be moving into an old-fashioned neighborhood with friends and all that." He laughed as though I would agree that in this day and age that was really just a scam. "But, you know, now that I've seen the place I'm not so sure. It's a neat old house and all that, but I really wanted to do something with the clubhouse a little more high-tech. I've been thinking I'd probably just tear it down... "

His words cut like the proverbial knife.

"I don't mean to rush you or anything, but, Rick, when are you planning on going back home?"

I was at a loss for words. "Oh, I don't know. Guess I'd better talk to Elizabeth. Have you signed the papers yet? I mean, when are you actually taking over?"

"That real estate man Lovejoy is supposed to be drawing up the contract. I know old man Steed is anxious to get his hands on the money. Legal expenses or something... "

"Or something," I agreed vaguely.

"Maybe we can celebrate the signing together. I'll come out next week and bring a bottle of champagne. You like Mumm's? We can christen the place."

I hadn't realized the time was so short. All of a sudden I realized I'd been a fool not to pay more attention to the future.

After I said good-bye to Hu I made myself a cup of tea and went to sit at a table on the patio to think about what I was going to do with the rest of my life. I remembered Marla and Elizabeth and me sitting on a patio, not unlike this one, though it overlooked the Caribbean. We'd talked in vague terms about the future. Just as I was remembering the smell of the salt air, the phone rang again. For a moment I hoped it was going to be Hu calling back to say he'd decided not to destroy the house and that I could stay. But it wasn't. It was Elizabeth. "I was just thinking about you," I said.

"Daddy's lawyer said the real estate agent is drawing up the papers. This guy Dorsey's gonna pay cash in full. Congratulations, Rick."

"Well, thanks. I can't claim much of the credit." I certainly didn't want to.

"The lawyer said Lovejoy told him that Dorsey 'liked' you... " She sounded almost like an old-time matchmaker.

"I think he'd have bought the place anyway. Apparently it used to be in the family or something. He's emotionally attached."

"Well, thank God for the money. I was afraid we'd never be able to sell that place. Daddy's practically crazy. All his blue blood patients have boycotted him. So he's only seeing the ones who don't pay. The papers are still keeping the story churned up, even though there's nothing new happening. Daddy stays up all night long. Says he can't sleep. He thinks he's flat broke."

"You both ought to come down here. Get away from it all. At least till it's over. This place would allow your dad a chance to rest. It's beautiful here right now."

"Been rainy and cold here," Elizabeth answered. "But we won't have that place much longer."

"All the more reason to come see it," I answered, hoping sort of desperately that if Dr. Steed and Elizabeth saw this ranch they were selling they'd change their minds. "'Lizabeth, do you remember when we were down in Key West a couple of winters ago, we talked about leveraging the contacts we'd made through the company with experts and famous authors to hold conferences and seminars. We all said we'd love to run a guesthouse in our old age... " I was obviously clutching at straws. "You know, this place would be ideal for something like that."

"That seems like a long time ago, Rick." Her voice sounded tired. "That was gonna take a lot of money. Back then I thought maybe one day we'd have it. I don't know anymore. Guess I'm gonna have to push my famous authors to write a few bestsellers," she tried to sound lighthearted. "Anyway, I've still got years to go before I'm ready for old age. I don't know about you, but... " Her thought seemed to be strangled in mid-sentence. There was a longish pause. "Anyway, Rick, maybe you can talk this Dorsey guy into... "

"He plans to tear down the house," I interrupted her. I realized that I had snapped at her. "Sorry," I said. I'm sure she took my outburst of anger to have been occasioned by her comment about old age. That was okay. As I thought about having to leave this place, I suddenly wished death would come for me quickly. I didn't want to have to do anything else.

I remembered Monty Hightower saying courage often just means doing what you have to, and I reminded myself to be courageous. Death wasn't going to be an easy out for me: the doctor had talked about years not months.

Tom had obediently followed Margaret Travers out to the stables. She said there was a lot of equipment—bridles, reins, saddles, etc.—that needed to be straightened up, cleaned, and oiled down. It was apparent to Tom she was preparing to vacate the place and wanted to leave the stables in order. Or perhaps she was planning on taking all that stuff with her.

She set him to soaping down and then oiling the saddles while she searched through cabinets and cubbyholes for more gear. "I been travelin' all my life," she said. "Guess I can pack up one more time."

"You really think you all are going to have to leave here?"

"Didn't you hear the Professor?" she snapped. "Sure I like the peace and quiet here, but I ain't one of them idealists like Monty or Alex. I mean, I been facin' reality all my life."

A little later Herb Fadiman came out to the stables and, at Margaret's instruction, currycombed the horses. To Tom, Herb's eyes looked blank, his face peculiarly empty. In spite of all the chatter in the stables Herb didn't say a word or seem to react to any of the humor. Margaret kept up her banter throughout the afternoon. She got Tom to recount stories of his life. He insisted they weren't as funny as hers, but by the end of the afternoon they were both laughing together uproariously. Herb seemed oblivious.

As they were going in to clean up, once out of earshot of the stable where Herb was still entranced in his combing the horses, Tom asked, "What's with Herb? I mean he seemed sort of distant."

"He has days like that. Sad story. Not so rare though."

"He's Monty's, uh, partner, isn't he?"

"Yeah, though I don't know how they handle that anymore. They were lovers years ago when Herb was just a young man. He was a student of Monty's. I don't know how long they were together then, but I think he ran off and joined the Navy. Monty had given up on him, I guess, long before he met Ed Carpenter and then went to England and lived at the farm there. But just before they moved out here, Herb showed up again. He was pretty sick and needed help. Monty took him in and got him to a doctor. Seems he had third stage syphilis. They treated him with all kinds of ghastly drugs, arsenic and god-knows what-all. Ain't really cured him yet. Tho' it seems like he's doin' better. But, you know, he has that funny way o' walkin' on account o' it and he's sometimes not so right in the head."

"That's terribly sad," Tom answered. Then asked quizzically, "What's syphilis?"

"Oh boy," Margaret responded. "I don't know what you been doin' with your thing down there," she sort of embarrassedly pointed toward his trousers, "but you sure better know what not to do. I think you should talk to Sophie. She's the nurse."

"I didn't realize sexually-transmitted diseases were a problem back then," I said to Tom as he started to describe to me the lesson Sophie Maxwell gave him before supper.

"Are you crazy, Rick? Of course, they were a problem. Much worse than now."

"Than *now?*" I challenged. "What about AIDS. There's no cure."

"There was no cure then for syphilis or gonorrhea or any of the other things sexually active people got. Penicillin's a relatively recent invention, you know."

"I guess I knew that. It's just, well, everything seems so much worse these days."

"That's just 'cause you had a brief respite during which most of these bugs could be killed with antibiotics. It's too bad, but, you know, now that new diseases have showed up that can't be cured, it just puts you back with the rest of the human race. And it's probably going to get worse."

"If there were all these diseases in the past," I asked, playing devil's advocate to some extent—I really wasn't all that ignorant of medical history—"how come we never heard about 'safe sex' till recently?"

"That's a very good question," Tom answered. "There certainly were condoms before, but the idea of 'safe sex' itself may be the single greatest contribution the gay liberation movement makes to human culture."

"Really?"

"Isn't that the point of the movement?" Tom asked.

"Safe sex?"

"No, silly, telling the truth!"

41

n the way in to my date for a Mexican dinner with Hu, I stopped at what turned out to be a sort of avant-garde religious bookstore. I was looking for more Joseph Campbell. I found the book version of the Bill Moyers interviews, then noticed a rack of tape cassettes. I was curious about the liturgical music Alex McMahon had talked about with Ben. I bought a couple of tapes of Gregorian Chant and one by some Jesuit seminarians.

The dinner with Hu was friendly. We didn't talk about "us" at all. Thank God. We barely talked about the future of the ranch or about my future.

I told him about the novel I was working on. He told me about a development project he was organizing downtown. We talked about coming out in college. We told each other our favorite jokes. We had a couple of Mexican beers over dinner and we told each other some more jokes.

At a lull in the laughter, Hu said he'd been meaning to tell me something. Uh-oh, I thought. He pulled a card out of his wallet. "This is the name of my doctor. He's the best in town. If anybody's going to know about strange diseases and new treatments, it's going to be him." He handed me the card.

"Thanks," I said honestly, then excused myself adding I had a long drive home. Hu seemed disappointed I didn't want to go out to the bars with him. We kind of half-hugged in the parking lot. As I drove off I realized Hu seemed lonely. I felt touched.

On the way home I listened on my Walkman to the tapes I'd bought. I was quite taken by the title song of the seminarians' recording, "Wood Hath Hope."

Late in the afternoon Alex McMahon told Ben he ought to go in and wash up. It was soon going to be time for the afternoon sing. Ben did as he was told and then showed up in the big room of the main house just as a bell began to clang.

"Right on time, my boy," Monty greeted him jovially, giving him a crudely printed songbook. He suggested he take a place on one of the cushions that were lined up in two rows down the middle of the room. "Alex usually leads us in a little meditation before we start to sing. He learned that sort of thing in India, you know—all very mystic," Monty held his hands up in the air beside his head and wiggled his fingers while he made a comic face and twittered a sound something like "ooo-goo boo-goo." "But, seriously," his tone changed, "it helps settle the mind… "

"I know about 'mental prayer' from seminary," Ben answered as he stood next to one of the cushions waiting to sit till the others arrived.

"Ah, yes, very similar. If Alex leads the meditation all you have to do is listen. If he doesn't, well, then you just sort of quiet your own mind."

"Yes sir," Ben replied. He felt a little nervous about what seemed to be the ritual nature of what he'd been expecting to be more of a sing-along than a liturgical service. In a moment the rest of the community filed in. Tom was trotting along obediently with Margaret. He took a cushion next to her, but exchanged a conspiratorial wink with Ben.

Alex had taken the cushion next to Ben. He'd sat down in a way that seemed to twist his legs preposterously. When he noticed Ben trying to imitate him, he amiably instructed him simply to sit tailor fashion. "There's no wrong way."

"Since we have a couple of newcomers with us today," Alex addressed the whole group, "I propose we keep the meditation short. I think I'll say a few words about focusing consciousness and then we'll get along with the singing."

He suggested they each breathe deeply, attending consciously to their breathing. He then repeated an idea Ben had heard him speak of earlier. "The breath is the life in us. And the life in us is the consciousness of God. As we breathe, slowly in and out, let us be conscious of our oneness with the divine consciousness. With each breath, let yourself think, 'Observe God.' Let yourself realize that God is present in all that you are experiencing right now, in all you have experienced so far today, and in all you will experience throughout the rest of the afternoon and evening."

Ben recalled a spiritual exercise he'd been taught at St. Athanasius' called "the practice of the presence of God." Previously he had imagined that had meant something like a schoolboy reminding himself that the teacher was in the room even when he couldn't see him and so he'd better behave. Today somehow the practice seemed peaceful, almost joyful, instead of threatening.

After a period of silence, Alex suggested they keep that same awareness now as they sang. He opened his book, announced a page number (apparently for Ben and Tom's benefit), and began to sing a church camp song Ben knew vaguely, "This little light o' mine, I'm gonna let it shine."

When that song finished someone else—Ben didn't have time to notice—announced another number and the group began to sing slowly and tenderly a song he remembered his mother singing to him when he was a child: "Believe me if all those endearing young charms… "

So, he thought, the songs don't have to be religious. He felt relieved at that. While the group sang the haunting, difficult melody, Ben noticed Monty Hightower's fine tenor rising above the others. He could hear a depth of feeling in those words that he had not particularly remembered in the song. And he heard a fervor in Monty's voice that made him realize that for all that it was "just a love song", it was truly a spiritual song as well. He glanced at Herb Fadiman, thinking that Monty's sentiments must rise from their relationship. And then he remembered the words Alex had just instilled in his mind: "Observe God."

As the second verse was moving toward its end, Ben looked over at Tom.

No, the heart that has truly loved never forgets,
But as truly loves on to the close
As the sunflower turns to her god when he sets
The same look which she turned when he rose!

He hoped his eyes could communicate the depth of his own affection at that moment.

Monty then began a strange chanting in a language Ben had never heard before: "Hare Krishna, Hare Krishna, Krishna Krishna… " He lost track of the words, then after a few more verses realized they were coming around again. There didn't seem to be very many words and after a while he caught on.

The chant kept going and going. After a while he recognized one of the words they were chanting as the name of that god Alex had told him about who made love to all the maidens in the village in the same night. He felt himself mesmerized. "Observe God," he thought.

Hmm! he was surprised at how erotic these songs were, while being at the same time spiritual and even what Monty had jokingly called mystic.

To his surprise the next song they did, started by Sophie, was a rousing "La Marseillaise."

Then again before he could see at whose initiation it was, the group began the mournful version of "When Johnny Comes Marching Home."

> With drums and guns and guns and drums a-roo, a-roo;
> With drums and guns and guns and drums a-roo, a-roo;
> With drums and guns and guns and drums the enemy nearly slew ya;
> Oh, Johnny, we hardly knew ya.

He could feel tears and sadness and he wondered if any of these men and women had lost loved ones to war. And he realized these songs sang not in glorification of war but in protest of violence and injustice and in compassion for its victims. "Observe God."

42

om found Alex McMahon's meditation a little tedious. He'd never been especially religious even though, of course, his mother had insisted he attend Sunday School when he was a child. He was therefore familiar with McMahon's first choice of songs—and was put off by it. The last thing he needed at this time in his life was to get evangelized. Then the haunting strains of that difficult Irish tenor melody began. His attention too was drawn by Monty Hightower's strong fine voice. Though he'd heard the song before, for the first time he began to notice the words. He watched Monty's face. In spite of the full beard that obscured so much of his countenance, his expression stirred Tom's own heart; his eyes were so alive. Tom noticed that Monty glanced over at Herb Fadiman and he felt his heart melt.

> Believe me, if all those endearing young charms,
>   Which I gaze on so fondly to-day,
> Were to change by to-morrow, and fleet in my arms,
>   Like fairy-gifts fading away,
> Thou wouldst still be adored, as this moment thou art,
>   Let thy loveliness fade as it will...

And though he'd just told himself he was not one for praying, he found himself praying that his love for Ben could endure such a hardship as he knew Monty's had for Herb. As the song was ending he glanced over and saw Ben smiling broadly at him and such a pang of love and affection burned in his chest.

He really didn't hear the rest of the songs, he realized as the last notes ended and the group stood up to leave. He remembered one of them had been some sort of foreign chant, but all he really remembered from the afternoon experience was his dreams for living his life with Ben, maybe here at Clear Light Colony or maybe—especially if the Colony was forced to move—somewhere else.

His emotions in the moment had got lost in the whirl of memories and dreams for the future. He thought, for the first time in a very long time, about the stories his mother had told him about her family's wealth and of her hope that one day his birthright might be recognized. He thought about the horse farm Jenny had told him about. As the rhythms of the music reverberated in the room around him, he dreamed that perhaps he could be the savior for the Colony, that he could go back to Texas and find that horse farm and somehow claim it as his legitimate inheritance as a long-lost heir. Alternately he thought he and Ben could continue their travels to California and the gold fields and strike it rich and go back and buy the horse farm whether the Milams wanted to accept him back into the family or not. Either way he could then take Margaret and Sophie and Monty and Herb and the others to a place where they would be secure and would not have to fear the threats of a man like Colonel Dodson, where he and Ben could be masters of the manor and live together happily, safe from the rigors of time.

As the community was filing out of the meditation room, Monty called to the two newcomers to join him on the front porch. "We've got about a half hour before dinner."

"I was very moved by that," Ben said after Monty asked him what he thought of their group ritual. "In spite of the fact that there was little overtly religious I thought it was at least as religious as any mass I've ever been to."

Monty smiled and turned to hear Tom's assessment. "Well, I'm not particularly religious, but I sure liked the singing. And you know, sir, I really like this place and what you're doing here. I'm grateful you've been so welcoming…"

"'Specially in view of the trouble with the Sheriff we seem to have caused you," Ben added.

"Nonsense, nonsense," Monty answered. "Turnbull doesn't know what to think about Dodson's attempt to run us out. Honestly, I don't know what the Sheriff knows, I mean, how much Dodson has said to him. But I'll tell you a secret that I think weighs on his mind. You met his son Henry, didn't you?"

"Sure, the first night we came through town," Tom answered for them both.

177

"And did you notice anything, uh, familiar about him?"

"What do you mean?" Ben asked.

Monty laughed softly. "I mean I think he's one of us showers. And I think Sheriff Turnbull knows that—and maybe isn't sure whether Henry knows it—and the Sheriff doesn't know how to think about Dodson's blackmail scheme... either because he's simply sympathetic with us or because he's afraid of getting pulled into it. That's what I think." Monty laughed again, more at himself apparently than at either Turnbull or Dodson.

Tom realized that for all the talk he'd heard from Eli Hauptmann and Monty about urnings and inverts and showers it hadn't actually occurred to him till now that people either were like this or they weren't. Before he'd always believed his same-sex feelings would go away either as he got older or as he learned to discipline himself more. Monty was saying that it had nothing to do with either of these. However different it might look like in different cultures or different societies or different situations, there were always two kinds of people: those attracted to the opposite sex and those attracted to the same sex. And they had basically different perspectives on the world as a result.

He might have been upset by this thought at one time, feeling he'd never be normal. But now he looked over at Ben who was chatting animatedly with Monty about the singing ritual and he felt immense relief that he no longer had to wait for things to change. He was who he was and Ben loved him that way. And that was all that mattered. How wonderful, he thought, to have other people like yourself around to support you in being who you really are! His thoughts were interrupted by Monty's saying almost exactly the same phrase.

"...who you are really is a part of this World Soul our friends in New England talk about," Monty was saying. "Our world is but the dream of God. Each of us really is God discovering what life looks like from each possible perspective. The point of meditation is to remind yourself of that identity and see that whatever happens is just another experience the World Soul is having."

Tom objected, "You mean you don't care whether Dodson takes away your property?"

"Well, of course, I care. I mean on the personal level, as Monty Hightower, I mind very much and certainly hope something happens to stop him, but on the impersonal level, as a single, tiny unit of the world, I can see it really doesn't matter very much. The world will go on. We'll go on... Hopefully somebody else will take up our work if we can't finish it.

"In the meantime, we've got to love what happens to us—that was what Jesus meant by the commandment to love God and love your neighbor. And we've got to love the world precisely because the world doesn't seem lovable—that's why it was a commandment. For when we love the world, we transform it so it, in fact, becomes lovable. Resisting only makes things worse. Loving them the way they are allows miracles to happen... "

The conversation was abruptly ended by the sighting of three riders galloping up the road toward the house. As they neared, Monty announced, "If my eyes haven't failed me that's Dodson and a couple of his henchmen. Guess he's coming around for the kill." He looked worried, in spite of his noble sentiments of a moment ago. "You boys stay here—or, I guess, better—why don't you go help in the kitchen. I'll take care of this."

As he strode toward the door, Alex McMahon was coming out, "Monty, I think you'd better come."

"I know," Monty answered solemnly.

As they'd been told, Tom and Ben went in and helped with the dinner preparation. Since Alex's lunch had been so fancy, dinner was simple: hot rolls and a vegetable stew that had been cooking all afternoon. While Ben helped with setting the table, Tom went to get more wood for the oven. Even though the kitchen was full of people, there was a nervous hush over the room.

When Dodson and his men had halted their horses abruptly in the back yard, causing a cloud of dust to billow up around them and shower Monty with dirt and gravel where he was standing waiting for them, the kindly old man invited them to join him in his study.

Since Tom had gone out for wood, he was able to get a good look at them. Colonel Dodson was a tall, stern-looking man with a face that had obviously once been quite handsome. He was dressed in a western-cut light brown suit with a wide brimmed white hat. In some ways he looked dashing and debonair. But there was a rigidness to the way he held his back and the way he moved that Tom found practically frightening. He didn't look natural at all. Pride, Tom explained that look to himself as Dodson dismounted and, with his two men behind him, followed Monty into the house by a side door.

A while later, Dodson came out of that door strutting. One of his men held his hat. "Thank you, Professor," he said snidely and then turned and looked around the place. "Well, well, well, guess I'm the new owner of the Clear Light Colony." He cleared his throat and spat on the ground almost at Monty's feet. Then he mounted his horse, reached down to his man and took his hat and put it on. While his henchmen mounted, Dodson carefully adjusted the tilt of the hat with both hands. Then he glanced down at Monty and said once again in a mean voice, "Thanks, Professor." He turned his horse around and the threesome rode off.

Monty walked back to the house. His shoulders were slumped; his face was grey; he looked a thousand years old.

"What happened?" everyone shouted chaotically as he opened the screen door and came into the kitchen.

"I'm sorry," he said, "what else could I do?"

"Monty, what happened?" Alex asked, raising his voice above the din.

"I agreed to settle. He can have the land, I told him, if he'll let us leave at our own pace. We've probably got till the end of the summer. At least that'll give us time to arrange to move somewhere. The important thing is the project the place."

"That'd give us time to get to California," Tom whispered to Ben.

Ben looked at him angrily, "You mean desert?"

"No, I mean, go find gold. Maybe we can buy a place for the colony to move to. Maybe in Texas."

"Do you really think so?" Ben asked, his eyes gleaming.

"Sure, why not?" Tom didn't say anything about his idea of finding the Milam's horse farm.

43

ell, did you two manage to save the day?" I asked, realizing that they might be starting in on the account of another whole adventure. And I wasn't sure I was going to have time to hear the end of the story. My own eviction day was coming soon.

"Well, yes and no," Ben answered. "Maybe Monty's acceptance and love saved the day. But for the next part of the story I'll have to report hearsay."

"You mean you weren't around for the trip to California?"

"No no, the next part happened that very night—in town. Sheriff Turnbull pieced together the story from Henry and a couple of other witnesses. And, I guess, I've embellished it a little."

"Let's hear it."

Just as the sun was setting, LuAnn McGuffy told her mother, whom she'd been visiting for the afternoon, that it was time she be getting home to fix supper for her husband Fred. It was nearly a mile uphill from the old farm house in which LuAnn Harriman grew up to the cabin where she'd been living the past two years since she'd gotten married to Fred McGuffy, an occasional prospector and an apprentice to Perspective's town blacksmith. LuAnn had been telling her mother how happy she still was with Fred. Though as she was walking home, carrying a heavy basket of preserves Mrs. Harriman had made up last year and which she insisted LuAnn take along as a present for Fred, she was realizing the magic had gone out of her marriage.

Fred had not wanted children yet. Working only as an apprentice blacksmith and not yet having found either gold or silver, he didn't think they could afford to have a baby. They'd virtually stopped making love nearly a year ago when Fred began to worry about money. LuAnn was just thinking how much she needed a little loving—and this line of thinking was only going to make her more upset and guilty about what was to happen next—when suddenly out of the bushes alongside the road came this giant of a man with a patch over one eye.

"Howdy," he said, just a little too loud.

It took LuAnn a moment to compose herself. "I don't reckon I seen you 'round here before. I'm Mrs. Fred McGuffy," she said.

"'M' name's Josh. Just passin' through. I noticed you comin' up the road and thought maybe a pretty lady like yourself might like a little companionship."

"Well, howdy, Josh. I'm just on my way home to fix my husband's supper. Guess you can walk a spell with me, if you like." LuAnn liked that the stranger called her pretty. Nobody had called her pretty in a long time. She might have been pretty except her nose was too big and life in the woods with no luxuries had already furrowed her brow and made her look a good ten years older than her actual twenty-three.

"Thanks, Ma'am," Josh answered and stepped into pace alongside her. "Wouldya like me ta carry your basket?"

"That'd be mighty nice o' you. Dang thing's heavy."

"Nothin' for Josh."

"You're sure a big man."

"You're sure a pretty lady." The repeat of the compliment both flattered LuAnn and alarmed her.

"You keep sayin' that," she said and blushed.

"You're sure a pretty lady," Josh repeated as though her demure response had actually been an instruction to repeat the compliment.

"Where you from?" she changed the subject.

"Everywhere, I guess. Been makin' my home back in these woods the past couple o' days."

"My husband sometimes goes out a' prospectin'. He lives in the woods. Never tried that myself."

"Wanna come see my camp?" Josh asked. "It's just back there a little ways."

"Don't guess I oughta be doin' that. Fred's probably at home waitin' for me." LuAnn intentionally added that last sentence even though she wasn't sure it was true.

"C'mon," Josh said. "Won't hurt ya none."

"Look, Mr. Josh, I gotta be gettin' home," LuAnn said a little more firmly.

"Hey, don't a pretty lady like you like Josh?"

"Sure, I like you. But, I mean, we just met. And I'm on my way home." Her voice was growing tense.

"C'mon back wit' me."

"No."

"Oh lady, my friend Benjy said the ladies'd be nice to me if I was nice to them. Ain't I been nice?"

"Sure, you've been nice, Josh. I'm just in a rush." They were still

181

walking side by side; LuAnn increased her pace.

Josh reached out and touched her arm lightly. She shied away.

"Don't, Josh."

"Benjy said ya would."

"Would what, Josh?" she asked annoyed at the way he was badgering her.

"Lemme jocker ya," he answered blithely.

"What?" LuAnn sounded horrified. She wasn't sure what that word meant. But she could guess. All of a sudden it occurred to her this was some kind of joke Fred was playing on her 'cause she'd been on his case about not making love to her.

She started to laugh. Then abruptly Josh closed his big hand around her upper arm. Curiously LuAnn had the presence of mind to say to Josh, "Give me my basket."

"Huh?" he asked.

"My basket, give me my basket."

He let go of her arm, then handed her the basket.

"Oh c'mon, pretty lady, lemme jocker ya."

"Josh, hear, you leave me alone what with your dirty talk."

Suddenly his face grew red. He grabbed at her again. She shied away and then swung the basket at him. It struck him in the abdomen and seemed to knock the air out of him momentarily.

"Hey, you coulda hurt Josh," he shouted. "Ain't no good to be nice. Gotta take what you want, Benjy boy," he said as though he were talking to somebody who wasn't there. And then he lunged at LuAnn, almost grabbing her by the shoulder.

"Git away from me," she screamed and swung around with the heavy basket again. This time the basket struck Josh lower and he recoiled in pain. "Git away from me."

LuAnn swung the basket one more time. This time it struck him on the thigh. LuAnn lost her grip and let the basket go just as Josh was lunging toward her again. He tripped over the basket and fell flat on his face in the road.

LuAnn let out a'running as fast as she could and hollerin' at the top of her voice. After getting a couple of hundred feet, she stopped and looked back. Josh was still lying in the road. Maybe he was crying. She couldn't tell. And didn't care. She just wanted to get home to Fred.

Later that night, Colonel Dodson and his two men, having returned from their visit to Monty Hightower's place, stopped in at the saloon in the Perspective General Store to have a drink and, maybe, to let Sheriff Turnbull in on their good news. But the Sheriff wasn't in, Henry told them. He took their order and set them up with a bottle of whiskey at the bar. The three of them were laughing about how timid ol' Hightower had been when they threatened him with exposing that den of corruption up there.

About that time, a big heavy-set man in a plaid shirt came lumbering through the door. He walked up to the end of the bar and asked for a beer.

"Hey, Mister, I don't recognize you. You from round these parts?"
Henry hollered down to him, without approaching the man.

"Just want a beer. That's all. No talk."

"Look, Mister, I gotta know if you can pay for a drink 'fore I serve ya."
Henry was especially suspicious because the man looked like a pirate. He had
a patch over one eye.

The man pulled out a couple of bills and held them up.

Henry looked at that money and then looked at the filthy way the
man was dressed. He whispered to Colonel Dodson who was standing practically
across the bar from him, "Maybe this is the guy those two fellas out at
Hightower's place was tellin' my pop about. How come he's got money?"

"Nah," Dodson answered. "Those two at Hightower's, they were the
ones robbed Jake and you. Him? He's probably a prospector or somethin'.
Maybe he's rich."

"I should serve him?" Henry asked timidly.

"'Course you should serve him. He's a man, ain't he?" Dodson and his
two sidekicks started laughing at a joke Henry didn't exactly understand—or,
if he did, didn't appreciate.

He walked down the length of the bar and set an open bottle of the
homebrew down in front of the stranger. "What's your name?"

"Josh B'Gosh," the man answered.

"Well, by gosh, too," Henry answered making meaningless small talk.
"Anything else."

The man shook his head, took a long swig out of the bottle, and then
leaned over and looked down at the surface of the old wooden bar paying no
attention to Henry.

"Well, you let me know if there's anything else." Henry took one of
the bills, then lay the change down in front of Josh. He thought the guy looked
pretty blue. Of course, in his career as a bartender, he'd certainly seen moody
drinkers before. He moved back over to where Dodson and his men were
laughing and cutting up.

Dodson poured himself another shot of whiskey, then raised his glass
and toasted himself, "To the new owner of the fuckin' Clear Light Colony!"
They all laughed as they downed the whiskey. "Hey, Henry, I don't see you
drinkin'," Dodson said. "C'mon, join us in a toast." Dodson poured whiskey
into a glass and pushed it toward Henry.

"No thanks, sir."

One of the henchmen said coldly, "Drink the toast, boy."

As Henry did as he was told, Dodson laughed. "Hey you, down there
at the end of the bar, want a drink? We're celebrating."

Josh turned his head a little and glared. His single good eye was
bloodshot. He raised his beer in a half-salute.

"Henry, pour that man a drink. We're celebrating vict'ry tonight,"
Dodson declared.

Henry poured a drink from the bottle in front of Colonel Dodson and then took it down to Josh. "C'mon, fella, join in the fun. The drink's on the Colonel."

Josh looked at the shot glass and then looked up at the three men at the other end of the bar. He raised the glass. One of Dodson's men shouted, "To the owner of the Clear Light Colony!" They all drank down the whiskey.

Josh got a funny look in his eye, "What you say?"

The man repeated his toast.

"Hey, hey, you got my friend Benjy up there, ain't you?"

"I don't know what you're talkin' 'bout, man," Dodson answered laughing. "Who's this Benjy?"

"Benjy lied ta me," Josh said. "He lied and po' Josh got hit in the nuts on account of it. I gotta find Benjy." More loudly, Josh shouted, "He done put out my eye."

"Po' Josh," one of Dodson's men mimicked.

Josh turned and went over to where the three were standing. "Take me up there to Benjy," he demanded.

"C'mon, man," Dodson said. "I don't know what you're talkin' about. And get away from me. You stink like a pig."

Josh glared at Dodson with his good eye. "I want Benjy. I'm gonna jocker 'im like I swore I would." He stepped closer to Dodson.

"Hey, man, didn't you hear the Colonel," one of the men said, "Step back."

Josh grabbed Colonel Dodson's lapel. "I want Benjy," he shouted again.

"Get away from me," Dodson commanded. "How dare you?"

One of the Colonel's men grabbed Josh's arm. Enraged Josh shoved the man and knocked him into a table set out in front of the bar. He turned back to Dodson and again shouted, "I want Benjy." He took Dodson by both shoulders and shook him, shook him hard, and then as the other of the Colonel's men pulled at Josh from behind, Josh hit Colonel Dodson with his fist.

There was a loud crack that, Henry said, could be heard throughout the room. Dodson's head swung back. Too far. Josh let go of him. His head swung around and then dropped forward as though it were a puppet's wooden head and its string had snapped. As Josh stepped back from the bar—and from Dodson's body—the Colonel slumped forward and then slowly, effortlessly, slid to the ground.

"Oh my God," screamed Henry.

44

Mine is the sunlight! Mine is the morning,
Born of the one light Eden saw play!
Praise with elation, Praise ev'ry morning,
God's re-creation of the new day!

The community had just sung "Morning Has Broken" when the gallop of hooves racing toward the house interrupted the silence. Monty looked around and then sad-faced said aloud, "More bad news?"

"Maybe it'll be good this time," Alex McMahon answered. "You want me to go see."

"I'd really appreciate that, Alex," Monty answered. Ben felt bad for the old man. He'd usually seemed so cheery, but since his confrontation with Colonel Dodson last night he'd seemed a ghost of himself.

When Ben asked if there weren't something they could do, Alex had urged him to just let Monty grieve a little. "After all," he said, "he's losing a lifelong dream. He deserves a little time to be depressed. He'll get over it. He's gotten over greater tragedies than this. His faith is strong."

While Alex went to see what the news might be this morning, Ben watched Monty's face. He thought he could see the turmoil going on inside his mind, his faith that from "God's point of view" nothing really mattered battling with the natural human emotions of disappointment, anger, and loss. After a moment, Monty looked around and noticed people were watching him. "Let's sing something," he said. He paged through his songbook then announced, "This one's a little too Christian, but how about 'It is Well with My Soul'?"

They began to sing the first verse:

When peace like a river attendeth my way
When sorrows like sea billows roll
Whatever my lot, thou hast taught me to say:
It is well, it is well with my soul.

Can one really believe that, Ben wondered, that no matter what happens it's okay? He thought about how humiliated he'd felt when the Master sent him home from St. Athanasius', how terrified he'd been when he leapt from the railroad trestle and later when Josh tried to jocker him in the warehouse in Chicago and then pursued him and Tom on the freight forcing them to jump from the train. Through all that could he have said "it is well with my soul"?

He gazed out the windows at the expansive view of the mountains and the open plain. He looked around at the others singing. He looked at Tom who was sitting next to him. Maybe all *was* well with his soul. Look how everything had turned out.

As the song was ending, Alex McMahon appeared at the door. With him was Sheriff Turnbull. "Everybody listen to this," Alex announced excitedly. Then he turned to the Sheriff, "How about repeating what you just told me."

Turnbull looked around the room at the anxious faces. "Don't know if I like this public speakin' none," he said.

"We're all friends," Monty said solemnly. "Whatever you have to say will be okay."

"Oh, Monty, just wait till you hear," Alex bubbled. Monty looked at him quizzically.

"Well, sir, I guess the most important thing to say is that y'all don't have to worry none 'bout Colonel Dodson no more. I mean I reckon his suit against your colony is kaput."

"How is that, Sheriff?" Monty asked, his tone beginning to change.

"Seems that fella you guys were tellin' us about," he looked over at Ben and Tom, "came into town last night and got into a fight with the Colonel and, well, killed him."

"Oh my God," Ben exclaimed.

Monty's eyes fell to the floor. "That's some news, Sheriff. I don't know whether to be happy or sad. C'mon, everybody," Monty turned his attention to the others, "let's go into the kitchen. Ozzie," he turned back to the Sheriff, "maybe you'd like a cup of coffee and you can explain this whole thing."

As the group stood up and started to move into the kitchen, Ben couldn't help but notice a wide smile growing on Monty Hightower's face.

"You mean that's it?" I objected. "The Clear Light Colony was saved because Josh accidentally killed your enemy?"

"Yup," Ben answered.

"But I can't use that kind of an ending in my novel. That's a *deus ex machina*, the worst kind of plot resolution. It's like having God come down and fix everything."

"That's what happened," Tom interjected, popping into reality next to Ben.

"Look, you guys, maybe we better come up with a different ending. I mean, there are rules about these things. If a writer sent me a manuscript with a plot that ended, well, magically, like this, I'd reject it."

Both of them looked downcast. They said nothing.

"I mean, the basic formula," I continued animatedly, "demands that the crisis has to resolve through the actions of the hero—or heroes—alone, not by coincidence or accident."

"Look, Rick," Tom answered, "this notion you've got about heroes may be fine for a Greek Mythology epic or a James Bond thriller or something, but it's unrealistic."

"Go on," I said, a little sternly, "I'm listening."

"How much control do you have over your own life? Do you think your fate has anything to do with your individual ability to solve the problems that confront you? What can you do about the cells in your nervous system that have gone haywire? What can you do about viruses that attack whole populations without anybody knowing anything about it? What can you, I mean as an individual *hero*," he said the word with a certain disdain, "do about nuclear war or the greenhouse effect or any of the things that are the real problems facing human beings today?"

"Well, I can certainly cast my vote the right way," I answered as though I was scoring a point.

"Right," Ben agreed. "You can participate with other people. You can contribute in a way that influences—even if only ever so slightly—how the mass of people are going to decide."

"It's that World Soul Monty Hightower was talking about," Tom added. "What counts isn't what you do as an individual, but what you do as a part of the larger mind of the world."

"Besides, Rick, I'm not so sure Josh's breaking the Colonel's neck was a *deus ex machina*. You know Josh only got so angry because I'd been courageous and stood up to him."

"Yeah," I agreed, "but your actions alone didn't resolve the crisis of the plot."

"Hey," Tom came to his defense. "Ben's actions set up the situation for resolution. Ben did something courageous. And it had consequences that were totally beyond what he expected. That's the lesson to learn."

"You live in a world of coincidences and accidents," Ben continued. "The difficulties that beset you come as coincidences and accidents, don't they? Why shouldn't the solutions? Don't fight 'em. Maybe they're the only way the World Soul can manage to communicate with you."

"Well, okay," I answered, feeling a bit browbeaten. "I still have some reservations about this plot. But we can talk about that later."

45

 spent the rest of the day thinking about alternate plot resolutions while I repainted one of the upstairs bedrooms. I liked the simplicity of the physical labor. I could bliss out and let my thoughts wander. I realized Hu was going to tear down the house, but I didn't want to let that threat undo the plans I'd already made for its renovation. After all, I came down here with a purpose. And I wasn't totally resigned to having to give that up, though I still didn't know what I could do about it.

I thought perhaps we could have Colonel Dodson come back out to the property and be killed there. But, still, it would have to be accidental. My heroes couldn't save the day by murdering the villain, not unless he were personally threatening them. And he didn't need to. He'd already won. I thought perhaps Monty Hightower could just stand up to him and say they didn't care about being exposed as homosexuals or inverts. That's how Ben—heroically, mind you—overcame Josh's threats. But that would be unrealistic. Monty's coming out wasn't going to impress the judge in some backwoods county courtroom. More likely it'd have gotten them all thrown in jail for crimes that the court dare not speak the name of.

Ben and Tom were probably right. The story they told was really the only one that made sense, even if it didn't fit the formula. Then it occurred to me that they told the story this way to teach me a lesson. That's why they said they were here, after all. Now, I asked myself, what is the metaphysical wisdom—deeper than Madison Avenue criteria for bestselling plots—that this story conveys?

I wondered what I'd learned from all my reading—and thinking and fretting and ruminating and communing with nature and even praying to some of those many gods ol' Joe Campbell talked about. What was the message?

Being a hero doesn't mean accomplishing great feats singlehandedly or winning by others' losses or changing situations to your liking, but being free enough from fear and desire—from ego and self-importance—to participate in life the way it is, I concluded. Stop resisting and start participating, I told myself. Be courageous. This is it. Take things the way they are. Follow your path. Things are liable to start happening your way—even by accident and coincidence—to help you along the path. And if not *your* way, then perhaps in the way that's really yours, the way that's in your best interests even when you don't know it. I think that's what Campbell was saying in those interviews with Bill Moyers under the rubric "Follow your bliss." Well, Campbell was the expert on heroes, I figured. If that sort of resolution of the hero cycle was good enough for him, it should be good enough for me.

Late in the afternoon I was cleaning my brush when the phone rang. It was Elizabeth.

"Oh, Rick, you won't believe what happened," she said and then she started crying.

"What is it?" I questioned.

She managed to calm herself and then answered with an hysterical sounding laugh, "Have I got some news for you—good and bad." She started to blubber again.

"How about the good news?" I asked. I hoped that would help her get hold of herself.

"Daddy's saved. I mean, Rick, the whole thing's over. That bastard Georgie White really got his," she said angrily. "But, Rick, Marla's dead too."

A shock went through me. "What happened?"

"Well, she was at work over in Cambridge and, I guess, heard the news on the radio... "

"What news?" I asked.

"About White," she answered impatiently. "And I guess she got excited and decided to come home early and, and wasn't watching." Through sobbing tears she finished her sentence. "Just as she was coming down the ramp off the bridge a semi-truck skidded into her lane, she didn't stop and the truck pushed the car off the ramp. She must've been thinking about Georgie White... Damn him!"

"Oh God."

"Rick, Daddy suggested we come down and spend some time there with you," her speech was fast and pressured. "I mean, I told him how much you liked it and how much it had helped you. And he said he needed to get away too and, well, now I don't have to stay here on account of Marla's job... " She started crying again.

After a moment a man's voice came on. "Rick, this is Robert Steed. I think I'd better handle this. Elizabeth's pretty upset."

"I understand, sir."

"Look, I imagine if you catch the evening news you can hear about what happened to George White. It's tragic. But, you know, for me—for us— I guess it's good news. I mean there'll be no more suit or lawyers' fees."

"Is there something I should do?" I asked helplessly, still confused.

"Well, I think we'll come down there to spend a while. Maybe we'll all be happier there. This is going to take some getting over. Do you think you can talk to this man Dorsey and see about delaying the transfer of the property?"

"Of course, I imagine he'll be cooperative. He's a nice guy. But, Doctor Steed... "

"Robert," he corrected me. "If we're going to be living together down there, you can't keep calling me Doctor. Besides, I think I'm through doctoring."

"Do you still plan to sell the land here?" I finished my question.

"I think we have to. I mean, honestly, son, I'm flat broke. Elizabeth's going to be in no shape to work for a while. Neither am I. I don't know how we'll manage if we don't get some of the money out of it. Though maybe your friend, Mr. Dorsey, will let us stay on for a while—at least till we can get our heads clear after all this."

"Doctor, uh, Robert, I have an idea. Let me talk to Dorsey about it. I'll get back to you. And," I added, "I'll watch the news."

Well, it was a hot story. Made the top of the national news. Let me summarize. Johnny Donatello, the alleged Mafia connection, and Georgie White were having lunch together in a private dining room at a plush hotel. Apparently a man whose teenage son had just died from doing crack followed Donatello, believing him to be ultimately responsible for his son's death, and burst in while he and White were having lunch. The distraught father started firing a pistol. He only wounded Donatello, but killed Georgie White—by accident. Donatello was so shaken up that when the hotel security arrived after

189

hearing the gunshots, he acknowledged that the two briefcases the men had were filled one with cash and the other with cocaine. Georgie White was buying a kilo from Donatello.

Not only did this turn of events end White's suit against Dr. Steed, it also proved Steed had been right that White was connected with organized crime and was probably a cocaine user himself.

"How did you guys do that?" I asked.

"Little ol' us?" Tom said mockingly. "What did we do?"

"I thought I was basing your story on my life." I said. "But you told me the plot resolution *before* it occurred. I thought you all were my imagination, you know, like myths the way Jung and Campbell talk about them, manifestations or something from my unconscious helping me sort through my stuff in order to cope—like seeing a therapist. But now I don't know... "

Tom and Ben smiled knowingly at each other.

"Maybe you really *are* ghosts," I went on. "Or maybe I created those events by writing about them? Have I got that kind of power?" I was full of questions. "Did you know this was going to happen? Do you get messages from the spirit world or can you read the Akashic records?"

"Are you still skeptical about coincidence?" Ben asked.

"So what do I do next?"

"Follow your path. I suggest you talk to Hu Dorsey as Dr. Steed asked you. And exercise a little courage to set up the situation to get what *you* need," Tom answered.

"Okay," I agreed. "Look, you guys seem to know things... "

"I told you we came to teach you some lessons you needed to know to cope with your predicament," Ben answered.

"Are there any more lessons?"

"I guess. We should add one more scene to finish the story. Then we'll tell you about the rest of our lives. There's more for you here, Rick," Ben continued. "But let's not go into as much detail. After all, this is getting long. Doesn't your formula for a first novel insist on a page limit?" He laughed uproariously.

46

 kerosene lamp by the bed cast an orangey radiance on the walls of the small cottage Tom and Ben had made their home—and onto the bare bodies of the two young men lying limbs entwined, basking in afterglow. Tom's skin shone dark golden in the dim light, Ben's looked creamy, especially against the clean white of the thick cotton sheets that had been casually thrown back to give them room to move about.

Their love for and appreciation of one another had grown in the time they'd been in Perspective. The joint vanquishing of the "demon" that had pursued them both drew them together and soothed whatever masculine fears they had that such closeness wasn't "manly." In fact, from being around Monty and his Whitmanesque talk about manliness, they'd come to develop a new sense of that word. They'd come to understand that manliness included not only being strong and assertive but also soft and receiving, psychologically sturdy but also emotionally vulnerable. It wasn't unmanly to be womanly. Man and woman weren't opposites, but complements. And by expanding the range of who each of them was, Tom and Ben could be both man and woman, complements for one another.

As they lay together, Ben was aware of how each area of his body touched or pressed against or slid along each complementary area of Tom's body. As they hugged, sometimes tight, sometimes loose, Ben squirmed or shifted just a little to change the points of contact between them. And with each change, the thrill of being with—and being in love with—Tom shot through him again. He could feel the solidity of Tom's chest, the roundness of his shoulders, the girth of his ribs. And when he shifted slightly he could feel the slight tickling of the dark hair that ran across Tom's breast. He could feel his own erect nipples just barely touching Tom's. And then when he pulled their chests together, he could feel the length of their bellies together. As he sidled back and forth, he could feel the ridges of muscle in Tom's abdomen and the softness of smooth skin where they touched just above the pubic bone.

In the weeks since they'd first recognized and responded to the sexuality of their feelings for one another, Ben had felt the touch of Tom many times. And yet each time, it seemed, the experience was almost new again—comforting in a different way, exciting for a different reason, burning with a different passion.

Today they'd been working hard around the farm and had thought themselves exhausted. They'd decided to bathe in the swimming hole behind the house where a rushing stream carried icy-cold water down the mountain, and then go off to bed early to get some rest. But the bracing water and then the touch of one another, once they were curled up in the white sheets of their bed, overcame their exhaustion.

In fact, they'd been playing at sex together for over an hour. They'd come once already, kissing and pressing themselves against each other, in an innocent, almost accidental surge of passions.

They'd been lying side by side, hugging and touching and occasionally whispering affections to one another, for a while now when Ben had become so acutely aware of each spot of touch and aware of how he could play that touch like a musical instrument creating ever new sensations and feelings. Because they'd ejaculated once, their penises were soft but still engorged and especially sensitive. As Ben held on to Tom, watching for the touch of these most sensitive spots, he began to relish the sexuality of their love. He realized how special it was that this man whom he really liked and cared about was open and available to him to play with and experiment with sexual adventures. And he felt himself growing hard again. He pulled away a moment so he could speak to Tom face-to-face. In doing so, he brought their groins together even tighter. The downward position of his slowly hardening penis was slightly painful. But he was amazed that the backward pressure also seemed to force his arousal out of the head and down into its base beneath the pubic bone, producing a yet new sensation.

"Tom," he whispered, "I was talking with Alex the other day about sex—you know, about what men do together."

"Uh-huh." Tom smiled and pecked Ben on the lips. He shifted and freed them both from their uncomfortably pressured positions, letting themselves lay long, side by side, between them.

"He told me about these meditations that some Hindoo gurus do in which they get themselves sexually aroused in order to generate spiritual energy. He said that according to these gurus this energy is God, like grace, I guess. They hold the arousal for hours at a time, sort of basking in the energy, Alex said, maybe never really letting go."

"Sounds neat. Sounds a little like what we've been doing… only I guess we let go, didn't we?"

Ben giggled. "Alex said sex is a lot more than just ejaculating semen for the purpose of reproduction. He said it's like letting down boundaries around the soul for the sake of generating spiritual energy. He said that's why it's real important you like and trust the person you're with, 'cause when their soul is open to yours what's in there can get into you… you know what I mean?"

"No," Tom laughed. "What's, uh, 'in there' to get into you?"

"According to Alex, the consequences of their past actions and intentions for future actions. I think he meant their luck; he called it their 'karmic patterns.' He said when you get into sexual consciousness with another person, their goodness or badness can rub off on you. It's like blending your life and, even, your destiny with theirs. If you do it to give good energy, you can contribute to the other person and generate more love and generosity in the world. But if you do it to get, you're liable to absorb the other person's bad thoughts and intentions and maybe even cause more bad intentions in the world."

"I like the idea of blending my destiny with you," Tom answered.

"And Alex said we can control the way this energy moves between us. You know, if we're both… " Ben was momentarily at a loss for words. This was all still very new to him and difficult to talk about. " …sucking on each other, well, you can see how there's this circle on energy coming in one place and going out the other. And it keeps going round and round and getting more and more intense."

"Yeah," Tom said, and he pressed himself against Ben's belly as if to

192

emphasize his agreement.

"Well, so Alex said one of the other things men can do with one another—that's real special and he said you gotta be very careful about doing it with somebody whose karma you don't mind getting mixed up with—is putting their, uh, cock inside each other... "

"Yeah," Tom acknowledged gently. He seemed to realize Ben was having a difficult time articulating what he was trying to say.

"You know about that?" Ben sounded both a little scared and a little relieved.

"Well, in principle, sure. It's kind of obvious, isn't it? I mean, cocks can go in openings and there are certain openings in other people's bodies."

"That's what I was so scared Josh was going to do to me. He called it jockering."

"I know."

"He tried it."

"Really?"

"Well, no, not really. I wouldn't let him. That's when I hit his eye with the knapsack. But he was trying to push himself inside me. And it hurt." Ben fell silent for a minute.

"Well, Alex said it doesn't really hurt," he continued, his voice a little softer, "not if you want to take the other person's spirit into you, then you can relax and open up."

"It ain't all spiritual," Tom laughed, a little mocking of Ben's religiosity.

"No, but Alex said when your cock's inside another person, it *really* generates this psychic energy. And... and, look, Tom, I was scared of Josh. I didn't want any of his destiny getting into me. But," Ben's eyes glowed as he smiled, "I love you and I do want *you* to."

"Blend my destiny with yours or, uh, jocker you?" Tom said the word extraspecially gentle.

"Both," Ben answered matter-of-factly, with clear determination in his voice. He could feel power surge into his groin as he said that, no longer afraid, aware that this was the right time and the right person and the right way to kindle this special spiritual, emotional energy that Alex McMahon had told him about. He kissed Tom and then let the kiss get stronger and more open and he squeezed himself as tight as he could against Tom's strong body, and grew more and more aroused.

Ben rolled them both over so he was on top. He raised up on his knees, leaned over the bed, and brought out a green glass bottle with a cork stopper. "Alex said to use olive oil," he whispered.

"You were planning this," Tom said knowingly.

"Sure," Ben said as he unstopped the bottle and poured out the oil into his hand. He quickly massaged Tom's penis with it and then just as quickly, letting out his breath with an audible sigh, sat down on Tom, taking him inside him all at once. He let out a squeak.

"Are you okay?" Tom asked. For all that he'd figured out what Ben had

193

been talking about, he was just as inexperienced.

"It hurt for just a second," Ben answered. "Hey, but it worked, just like Alex said."

That was the last of their conversation until after they'd both spent themselves, Tom inside Ben as he knelt behind him and took Ben's legs over his shoulders so they could look into each other's eyes—they tried several different positions (with varying degrees of success)—and Ben on his own belly at almost the same time. Tom held Ben's penis in his hand, stroking with the same rhythm with which he was thrusting, so that he could not tell if it were Ben in his hand or himself. It almost seemed to them that their bodies had become one. The shaft of pleasure and energy filled them both.

Tom remembered that demonstration of electricity at the traveling science show. The shaft that seemed to run between them now was like that rod that had developed the electrical charge. He looked at Ben almost expecting to see his hair stand on end, but saw instead a bright glow of affection and ecstasy in his eyes. This was the energy Alex had been telling Ben about, Tom knew. And he knew that same charge was glowing in his own eyes.

Ben could see the energy in Tom's face—in what was both a grimace and a smile. He felt it come surging up out of Tom. It ran up into his own body and then filled the space around them. He felt the boundaries of his soul dissolve and he himself was overwhelmed. They both seemed caught up in something beyond their individual selves. Their climaxes exploded together as they were engulfed in the psychic, karmic charge they had generated in the friction of their bodies and the mixing of their souls.

They didn't say anything more that night except a whispered "I love you," before they drifted off to sleep a little later. But the next morning, as they were walking over to the main house for morning meditation, Tom remarked, a little self-consciously, "Can we try changing places next time?"

Love had taught them both a lot. Their lives together were just beginning.

"Given the circumstances, we didn't have to use condoms, you know," Ben explained languidly.

"Now that we've tied up the plot, we need to get on with the lesson," Tom announced, breaking me out of the sexual reverie and pleasant torpor I'd lapsed into. "We've been waiting for you and it's time we let you in on the job we've got for you around here."

Time passed over Perspective like the flapping of a bird's wing. Day passed into night carrying Tom and Ben and the other members of the Clear Light Colony on their long leisurely flight into the reaches of their souls. The seasons changed peacefully. Clouds rolled over the mountains. Some days it rained. Some it snowed. Most of the days the sun shone brightly and the wind blew gently. And time was gone before they were aware of it.

For six years the two young men lived on at Clear Light. They had been welcomed just for being who they were that first Midsummer's morning when they arrived during the whimsical dress up tea-party. Soon they were welcomed and taken into the fold as the inadvertent saviors of the Colony.

Since neither came with a dowry, as it were, as did most of the other members of the community, Tom and Ben worked to earn their keep. After Herb Fadiman died a long and protracted death that threatened to drain the life out of the whole community—and probably would have had it not been for their faith and acceptance of things—Ben took over his job of managing the house.

Tom continued assisting Margaret with the horses and the farm. He got an unexpected assistant about the middle of their third year there. Joshua Anderson, it seems, was acquitted of the murder of Colonel Charles Dodson on grounds the death was accidental. He was, however, found guilty of the attempted rape of LuAnn McGuffy. The court, recognizing his mental deficiencies, sent him to the State Asylum where he was enrolled in a program for sex-offenders that a hundred years later sounds barbaric, but was then considered merciful. After being surgically castrated, Josh became quite docile. In recognition of a certain gratitude due him, Monty Hightower offered to take him on as an extra hand on the farm. And once he experienced love and comradely acceptance, he became quite kind and good-natured. Josh proved remarkably good with the horses.

Another newcomer to the Colony was the Indian squaw named Iena'wa, who also was called Hummingbird. As Henry had reported, Colonel Dodson had kept her for over ten years, virtually as a warprize, to do his cooking and household chores. After Dodson's sudden death and the consequent break up of his staff, Iena'wa sought refuge with Monty Hightower.

After several weeks at Clear Light, Hummingbird revealed that she was in fact a male. Once freed from the forced impersonation at Dodson's ranch, Iena'wa began to switch roles and identities freely—some days female, some days male. When Iena'wa appeared in male dress, he preferred to be called Flies Like Crow.

He brought a whole new spiritual and mystical tradition to the Colony. He told them of his tribal role as *winkte*, which he explained the French explorers called *berdache* meaning androgyne. He said that among his own people, the Lakota Sioux, such *winkte* were considered chosen by the gods to live outside the daily cycle of tribal life and to serve as contact with the invisible world of the spirits. Iena'wa taught them to see the gods and spirits that pervaded the natural world around them and instructed them that the spiritual quest should be to care for the earth and to live in harmony with all the other presences of nature—from the majestic mountains to the bubbling streams and tall trees to the animals of the forest and birds of the air to the great gods of the sun and moon that continually watch over the breast of the earth itself. He showed them that such consciousness of nature was a special function of those, like themselves, who do not breed offspring, but whose nurturing and protectiveness, for the very reason that these are not spent on individual families, are meant to be exercised toward all people and all nature.

About his own life, he was far less forthcoming. As often as Monty good-naturedly tried to get Iena'wa to report the details of his years as Dodson's kept-slave, the proud and honorable Indian refused to reveal any confidences. What went on between himself and his now-deceased master had nothing to do with his present life at Clear Light he always said. (Nonetheless, Monty appreciated the irony. He realized now that Dodson's psychological motivations must have been much more complicated than he'd previously imagined.)

Both Tom and Ben helped with the publication of the newsletter Monty had envisioned. The newsletter became a pulpit for Monty Hightower's intuition that, just as "showers" live outside the mainstream of breeder society, the spirituality tailored for them is one outside the mainstream of religions. "Because we don't fit in any one tradition," Monty proposed, "we can enjoy all the traditions. After all, Enlightenment is discovering the gods are all just clues that help focus human wonder. That's the spiritual goal of all religions. Our special perspective outside the traditions helps us see that that much faster."

Creating the Brotherhood and Sisterhood of Light as a network of spiritually-interested showers, Monty's efforts began to bring more and more visitors to the Colony. Especially during the summer, the place was often packed with guests who contributed to the community's upkeep. Some came simply for a restful vacation. Some came to meet others of their own kind and to let their hair down and feel free of the constraints of normal society. Still others came to join in the community's singing, meditation, and eclectic prayerlife.

Among those visitors frequently were Eli Hauptmann and Sophie's friend Imogen Hedgeweather. Tom always rejoiced when Eli arrived. He couldn't get over how much his life had changed since their chance meeting on the train. Imogen had become a devotee of the Ramakrishna Order after meeting Swami Vivekananda. She eagerly taught the mysteries of Vedanta to any and everyone interested.

During their time at the Clear Light Colony, both Tom and Ben learned the simple faith and spirituality that Monty Hightower personified. From loving one another and listening to Monty and reading his friends Walt Whitman and Edward Carpenter, they learned to heal the split between sexuality and spirituality the outside world took so seriously. Ben remarked that he learned to think a devout and fervent "O God" just as he was coming to orgasm, and to find in the experience not only physical pleasure and expression of affection for Tom, but also mystical union with the World Soul that, he said, must obviously delight in sexual activity, since in other contexts it uses it to recreate itself and, in "our context," inspires us with creative ideas and dreams that shape and beautify the world for those future generations. After six years, Tom and Ben decided their own creative inspiration was urging them to continue the journey they'd started when they accidentally came upon the Colony. Tom still talked about going back to Texas and finding that horse farm that his mother said should have been his inheritance. He no longer had any such expectation. But he hoped, if he could earn his fortune in California, he could go back and buy the land. And perhaps recreate something like the Clear Light Colony there.

It was the beginning of the Twentieth Century, an exciting time to be alive. They arrived in San Francisco on June 21, 1900 almost six years to the day from the time they found Perspective.

The Gold Rush had ended. Most of the dedicated prospectors had turned their sights to Alaska. But there were still gold nuggets to be found in the streams flowing out of the Sierras and Tom was still anxious to try his hand at panning for treasure. While Ben worked at a printer's shop in the City to make their living, Tom sought to make their fortune. After less than a year, he came back with enough gold to buy them a small house and to set Ben up in a business managing a housekeeping service for other gentleman couples like themselves. Ben hired young men whose interests did not turn to heavy labor or to marriage and family and helped them get their start in the city. Around themselves Tom and Ben built a circle of what Monty would have called non-breeding shower friends. Many of those friends joined them in occasional visits to Colorado and Ben branched out into running a small travel agency. They shared a dream of finding a place somewhere to build another branch of the Colony. Tom always said that should be in Texas.

Of course, for all that this description makes their lives sound amazingly progressive and idyllic, in reality they faced serious threats to their happiness and to their relationship. Especially because Tom continued to go prospecting in hopes of the big find that would allow them to return to Texas as wealthy and respectable gentlemen and because Ben had working for him a lot of attractive and available young men, their relationship was sometimes tried by their separation. Tom, for instance, had a brief affair with a sailor that threatened to take him beyond the boundaries set by their agreements for "a little outside recreation." And Ben once fell infatuated so hard, he had to dismiss one of his employees lest he lose control of his business and his life.

Having learned a lesson from their watching Herb Fadiman's unseemly death, they were both very careful to reserve certain extraspecial sexual activities to their time together and make sure that nothing they did recreationally could bring a marauder like syphilis into their lives.

They were careful too not to contaminate the emotions of their relationship. They loved one another and wanted the fullest life for each other. That sometimes entailed a careful balancing of their dependence and their need for freedom. In spite of the difficulties and trials, they persevered in their commitment. The biggest trauma of their lives in those days was the Great San Francisco Earthquake in 1906. Their house burned to the ground, destroying most of their possessions.

"How do you recover from a tragedy like that?" I interrupted the story, thinking that perhaps there was a lesson in the parallels to my own times.

"Faith," Ben answered.

"Perseverance," Tom added, "and perspective. I mean, managing to maintain a perspective. It was quite appropriate that Monty Hightower's place was in a town with that name."

"Out of disaster new things come," Ben said. "People learn lessons. They avoid making the same mistakes again. Sometimes, it just makes way for something new."

"How do you know it's going to be better?"

"You don't. It might not be. But it *can* be. The function of human life—at least on this plane of existence—seems to be to overcome problems. God doesn't seem to make the same judgments about problems human do. Whatever God is seems to relish the good *and* the bad. What God cares about is your willingness to experience life. That's how God experiences Godself. Isn't that what you've learned from reading Joseph Campbell? The message behind almost all the myths is that God chooses to joyfully participate in the sorrows of the world. So can you."

"That's also what we learned from the Clear Light Colony's spirituality," Tom chimed in. "You can love what doesn't seem lovable, find transformation in every change, see that good can come out of bad… "

My thoughts strayed for a second. I couldn't help thinking of Marla's car falling from the off-ramp.

"…when you're not making judgments or blaming somebody else for the problems, sometimes you can see the improvements the World Soul is urging."

"How do you know what's going to be an improvement?" I challenged.

"You don't, but improvements usually seem to always be in the direction of peace and harmony and greater awareness."

"Sometimes," Tom interrupted, "the changes aren't necessarily better, but they're still impressive and inspiring. Look how Chicago rose like a phoenix from the fire. That city we visited in 1894 was sure different from what would have been if there'd been no fire. And look how San Francisco was rebuilt—one of the most beautiful cities on earth."

"But how about the tragedies, the lives lost, families destroyed?"

"Yeah," Ben answered with an uplift in his voice as if to say, "Go on."

"How about disease?" I asked. "How about AIDS in my own times?"

"An interesting question," Ben replied. "What good comes out of AIDS?"

"Are you asking me?" I said.

"What do you think?"

"Well," I said, "I guess gay people have been recognized as a quote-

198

unquote real minority that exists because people are born gay, not because they give in to temptation."

"What else?"

"I don't know. You tell me."

"But we're you, Rick," Tom answered. "But, okay, look at the advances in medicine. Antibiotics were a great boon, it's true. They solved things like syphilis. But in a few decades from now most microorganisms are going to be resistant to them, and crowding and pollution are going to cause a whole new class of diseases to mutate into existence. By the end of your century, Rick, there are going to be terrible plagues caused by simple household bacteria that can't be killed with antibiotics. And nobody has been paying much attention. The medical and drug industries haven't had anything to profit by preparing to stop using antibiotics and finding ways to supplement the body's own defenses. But then—by sheer chance?—when the first of these plagues came along it was a disease of the immune system. It forced research into the field nobody had been paying attention to. Now when the other diseases appear, medicine will be ready for them."

"Like this thing I've got?" I interrupted, feeling they were proffering me hope I'd never imagined possible.

"You'll see," Ben answered. (I'd made an appointment with Hu Dorsey's doctor, by the way. Maybe he'd have a treatment.)

Ignoring my concern, Tom continued, "Ironically, that first plague was sexually transmitted. Thus not easily spread like, say, flu. But it's forced control of sexual activity and thus indirectly population control."

"But why gay men?" I objected. "We weren't responsible for over-populating the planet!"

"That's partly a fluke of history, I suppose," Ben answered, "though gay men are obviously the carriers of nature's messages about population control. But, you know, AIDS has certainly awakened gay men to a spiritual identity. Confronting death has a way of doing that."

"Yeah," I admitted, realizing Ben was describing exactly what had happened to me since the doctor gave me the Creutzfeldt-Jakob diagnosis.

"Maybe we're special. Maybe we're what Shirley MacLaine and friends would call a 'higher incarnation'." He laughed. "You know, the more enlightened souls come back to earth to take on the problems because they can handle them better, like Jesus taking on the sins of the world. Suffering seems to be the instrument, like a lathe for instance, that God uses to work the raw material of consciousness into a beautiful work of art. And the people who can do it are the artisans of the soul."

"That's pretty hokey," I said.

"Well, maybe so. But, look, if you were God and communicate through the events of history and you wanted to warn people to start studying immunology and to motivate them into practicing non-procreative sex, you might make your warning an immune disorder transmitted sexually. You'd want it to stay confined to a relatively small group and not get out of hand—

as it has in Africa, by the way, and threatens to in America because the public wasn't concerned about that first small group of God's messengers, misunderstood the message, and didn't start studying it soon enough.

"So, if you were God and knew such things, maybe you'd limit that small group to volunteers, I mean, you might ask your favorite friends to take on this special assignment."

"Now that's enough," I shouted. "You can't mean to say we volunteered for this."

"I was only suggesting a metaphor," Ben said, mocking defensiveness. "I think it's a better metaphor than the one the Fundamentalist ministers have been preaching."

Our conversation was interrupted at that point by the phone. Hu was returning the call I'd left at his answering service. I thought about the news Hu had confided in me the other day. Had he "volunteered" for his HIV status, I wondered. I felt sad for him. I also less much less alien from him than I had before. We had something in common.

"Hi, thanks for returning my call." I remembered Tom had urged me to be courageous as I started this conversation. I decided it was time I meddle a little. Maybe I could save the day, do some of that transforming Ben had been carrying on about.

"Hu, I've got an idea I'd like to talk to you about."

47

appy birthday," Elizabeth announced cheerily over the phone. I can't say I'd forgotten myself, but I had intended to put it out of mind. "How old are you?" she asked innocently.

"Forty-two," I admitted.

"That's not very old," she said. "Marla was only thirty-eight." Her voice sounded shaky.

"How're you doing?" I asked, trying to sound nonchalant.

"Better, I guess. Look, besides calling to remind you you're getting older," she struggled to laugh, "I wanted to let you know Daddy and I will be arriving this weekend. Can you meet the plane?"

"Sure," I agreed and took down the flight information and made plans to pick them up in the station wagon outside the baggage pick-up. I was looking forward to seeing them. I hadn't told them yet about my conversation with Hu. It was still uncertain. But things looked good.

Feeling generally better about how my life was going—even if it wasn't going long, it was going well—I sat down to write.

Along with thousands of other San Franciscans, Tom and Ben struggled to rebuild their lives. Tom was especially demoralized because this effort cost him all the money he'd saved. There just wasn't going to be any money left over to fulfill his mother's dreams for him.

Gradually they succeeded in putting the disaster behind them. Actually business in San Francisco was booming. Within a few years they had recovered and were doing better than before. Things got back to normal: with the normal joys and the normal problems.

In 1910 they learned that Monty Hightower had died at the age of seventy-five, a rich life. They missed the funeral, but did attend a memorial service in his honor in Denver a couple of weeks later. Over five hundred men and women showed up to honor him. "His death was a good one," said old Alex McMahon who preached the eulogy. He was one of only a few of the original community still left in Perspective. There was a flourishing community, but it was almost all new people now—Monty's legacy.

It was in the fall of 1918 that suddenly everything changed for Tom and Ben and for the rest of the world. Some soldiers on the East Coast, back from fighting the Kaiser, got sick one day. By the end of the next day most of the camp had developed the same symptoms: muscle and joint ache, respiratory difficulties, fever—the symptoms of influenza. But this proved to be no ordinary influenza. This was one of the three greatest plagues to hit the planet Earth in history. By the spring of 1919 when the disease disappeared as mysteriously as it had appeared, around the world over twenty-two million people had died in a matter of a few months.

Ben had worried about the news reports he'd been hearing. His mother had died in the influenza epidemic in 1889. He tried to avoid contact with the public, but that had been practically impossible. Tom came down with symptoms first. He got pretty sick, but then recovered after a week. About the time he was feeling well again, Ben came down with it.

"I put him to bed right away," Tom said. "Though I'd gotten over it, I was terribly worried. Already several of our friends had died. Maybe I was still a little delirious myself, I don't know. I just couldn't bear the thought of losing Ben. I thought if he failed to pull through maybe I'd kill myself.

"After a week, when I saw he wasn't getting any better I tried to get him into a hospital—especially because he'd stopped eating, not even the clear broth I was making him. But there wasn't room anywhere. Hospitals all over the city were already full of people with the influenza. I begged a doctor at one hospital to take Ben in. I literally got down on my knees and cried. He told me it wouldn't make any difference; there was nothing they could do to treat the virus. He said we were better off at home, away from reexposure from other sick people.

"I nursed Ben as best I could," Tom was crying as he recounted his story. "I wiped his body with alcohol to try to reduce the raging fever. I knelt by his bed and prayed. He was asleep or only barely conscious most of the time. The second night of that high fever I was afraid to let him sleep for fear he wouldn't wake up. I kept begging him not to leave me, not to die. I think I pounded on the bed, maybe even shook him by the shoulders. He hadn't eaten in days and had lost so much weight the bones in his shoulders felt like brittle sticks in my hands. I was afraid he'd break.

"But in spite of everything I did, he slipped into an unconsciousness from which I couldn't rouse him. I finally realized, I think, that he wasn't going to make it. I'd been hearing stories from everybody I knew about how their lovers or relatives had finally succumbed. You know, for a while I just couldn't believe that all those people were dead. I mean it just couldn't happen. Not like that. Not in matter of just a few weeks. But it was true.

"Then I was hoping Ben would at least come to long enough for me to tell him how much I'd loved him, to apologize for the pain I'd caused him, to remind him of all the good times we'd had. I stayed by his bed that last night and talked to him over and over about how we'd met and how we'd found the Clear Light Colony and how when he got better we were going to leave San Francisco and go to Texas to fulfill our dream and find the horse farm and create another Clear Light Colony there and how we were going to live to be old men together...

"By then, I knew it was all a fantasy—I mean that he was going to come with me. But at least I wanted him to wake up, to open his eyes and look at me so I'd know he'd heard me, so I'd know he didn't think I'd deserted him there at the last. But he never woke up.

"After three days that body I'd come to love so deeply just couldn't fight the fever anymore," Tom said. He sounded weary. "Ben was one of five hundred and fifty thousand people who died in the United States during that epidemic. He was only forty-two years old."

"Oh my God," I said.

"Happy birthday," Ben replied. "Getting your life in perspective?"

Ben looked tired. His eyes were dark, sunken into the sockets of his emaciated face. His hair, once such a beautiful reddish-gold, was thin and dry and dirty straw-colored. He reminded me, to my chagrin, of friends I'd left behind in Boston with AIDS.

He put his hand on Tom's and said gently, "You know I heard every word you said." He smiled and managed a weak laugh, "I followed you all this way, didn't I?"

Tom smiled warmly at Ben. I looked over and saw that Ben was beginning to resume his normal appearance. "We led wonderful lives," Ben said, half to Tom and half to me.

"Death is such a tragedy," I responded tritely. I could feel myself shivering—maybe in empathy for them, maybe in fear for myself.

"Oh, I don't know, Rick. Everybody dies at exactly the right time," Ben said with a little gallows humor, "I mean, always at the end of their life." I didn't laugh and he continued. "The tragedy isn't that individuals die. Everybody dies. That's intrinsic to being individual." I noticed now that in spite of his resuscitation a moment ago, he looked much older—and wiser.

"It is not mortality that is tragic, but our sense of priorities that lets some people die prematurely or grotesquely because other people think other things more important. We let Africans starve; we send money for bombs and guns to the Middle East and Central America; we kill babies; we let homosexuals and drug users get HIV because we don't want our own security threatened or our political and social opinions challenged. "

"Isn't it interesting," Tom added, "that this seems to be an issue of perspective. Monty Hightower taught that individuals are all various manifestations of the same one being—the World Soul, as he called it after Ralph Waldo Emerson and the New England Transcendentalists, or Brahman, as Imogen called it after Swami Vivekananda and the Vedantists, or Gaia, as the New Age science-mystics and those authors you used to work with, Rick, are calling it in your day..."

"Or just plain ol' God, as we all grew up calling it," Ben interrupted.

"If we all struggled to see that, we'd naturally feel more compassion, discovering that there is no one from whom we stand apart, no one who is truly not a brother or a sister, no one who is truly not ourself."

"Campbell says the most significant mythic event in the history of the human race was the manned landing on the moon," I said. "It gave human beings a perspective on the earth from outside. And that's symbolic of modern consciousness that is able to view itself with historical perspective... "

"From such a shift in perspective," Ben broke in, "we might realize that what matters isn't the fate of individuals anyway, but the evolution of the collective World Soul. That World Soul—or the natural ecology, if you will—is always striving to get things to improve. But people, operating from their limited viewpoints, make judgments about what's important to them and resist the gentle urgings. By that resistance they bring evil into being. This is what the myth of *karma* is about. If everyone just accepted things the way they are, then from that World Soul's greater perspective things would improve—on their own, just in the course of life itself."

"Then we ought to stop worrying about our own misfortunes, stop resisting, and figure out what we can do for the growth of compassion and evolution of the common Soul," I summarized, feeling a little like that nursery rhyme character who stuck his finger in the pie, pulled out a plum, and said "Oh, what a good boy am I."

Tom and Ben both grinned at me.

'd taken to playing my Walkman in the "big room" and singing along. I loved the echo. One of the songs I was playing for myself over and over again was "Wood Hath Hope" by those Jesuit seminarians.

It was sung a cappella, at first, by a quartet of innocent men's voices. It began as a jazzy chant, each word enunciated singly.

> Wood hath hope
> When it's cut it grows green again
> and its boughs sprout clean again.
> Wood hath hope.

The voices are joined by a folk guitar and the singing becomes melodic and wistfully joyful.

> Root and stock, altho' old and withered up,
> and all sunk in earth corrupt
> Will revive.
> Leaves return, water pure brings life to them
> and the tree lives young again.
> Wood hath hope.

Then the rhythm and melody change dramatically to a solemn dirge-like chant that cut right to the heart of what I'd been struggling with in the first months of this year.

> But for flesh waits death to strip the soul
> and breathe life out. Behold:
> All things end.
> Mortal lives, like a dried up riverbed.
> We sleep, lay down our heads
> To rise no more.

Then again the rhythm and melody change and, with a sudden surprise, become lifting and playful.

> But a strange thought: if a man could rise again,
> come home to a loving land,
> We would have hope.
> We would have hope,
> Like a tree we'd grow green again
> and our boughs sprout clean again.
> We would have hope.

Outside the windows of the big room the leafy trees in the ravine were a vibrant green. I liked the image of wood in the song. I thought of myself like a gnarled tree trunk that had been dead and then, with the transformation that had come over me these past weeks of spring, had begun to sprout new growth.

And this image made me feel a part of the earth: I knew trees—wood—grew right out of mother earth and remained a part of her; I began to feel myself—flesh—similarly an outgrowth of mother earth and a part of her beyond my individual existence. It was wonderfully comforting.

Maybe my ghostly imaginary friends were right: we human beings are all parts of a complex network of Life which makes itself known—if at all—through coincidence and luck. And the heroic effort is to pay attention to the connection to the network and let Life shape your life. They taught me that the essence of religion and spirituality is not the adherence to particular doctrines, but the creation of life stories about ourselves—or aspects of ourselves—in mythologically rich language. For thus we develop our spiritual self-concept, our sense of being connected to this network which comprises the World Soul.

I had created a myth to entertain and intrigue readers. I had devised a tale about the gay past, a myth about the message for humankind communicated through our gay lives, a myth about our place in the scheme of things, a myth about love. And in a curious way, the myth in turn created me. I stopped feeling cynical about love. I saw beyond myself. I found a reason to go on living in spite of the complexity of the modern world and the threat that that world was going to kill me.

In retreating to the country, confronting the reality of my mortality, and living the lives of my two mysterious characters, I connected to some deeper, spiritual reality, part of a collective gay history, in which as an individual I don't matter so much, but have a role nonetheless. I discovered it really doesn't matter when you live or who you are. Bad things happen to everybody. By relaxing and accepting life as it is—observing God—you can increase your tolerance of what's happening to you, even when it isn't what you want. By experiencing life through other people's eyes—being compassionate—you can get a perspective on your own experience so you don't take yourself too seriously, and you can find models of good behavior in their lives. By accepting reality, getting a perspective, and striving to behave well you can change your life so it makes the most of your situation whatever it is. Perhaps not so surprisingly, this often improves your luck so the bad things happen less often and the good things happen more.

Lost and grief-stricken after Ben's death, Tom sold all their belongings. It took him several months. He was despondent and moved slow. He wanted to wait till the spring before he left San Francisco anyway. He made a considerable sum on the sale, in spite of not bothering to be particularly shrewd in his dealings.

He was going to go back to Texas. He'd written relatives to find out what had happened to the Milams' horse farm. It was still in the family, he learned. The distant cousin who wrote back said he was willing to meet with him, but made no promises. The cousin certainly didn't recognize any familial claim. Nobody lived on the place, the man wrote; it was deteriorating badly and could use a caretaker. Perhaps Tom would be interested in the position. Perhaps he was.

First he went to Perspective. He was planning to spend a few months among friends in a familiar environment to recover emotionally. His wire that he was coming was unanswered. And nobody was at the train to meet him. He had to walk up that steep hill on his own. Just like the first time. He arrived at Clear Light to find that only Margaret Travers was living there. Everyone else, she told him, had died in the epidemic. Imogen Hedgeweather had been in Boston, one of the centers of the infection; she'd come out for a visit at Thanksgiving, unwittingly she'd brought the flu with her.

Tom stayed on with Margaret for a couple of weeks. In her old age she'd turned Roman Catholic. She had made friends with some nuns— "they're our kind of people," she told Tom—and she'd invited them to establish their novitiate on the property. Tom was welcome to stay, of course. But he had a dream to fulfill elsewhere.

He boarded the train in mid-June. Now that he was going home, his depression lifted. The long hours on the train were a wonderful meditation for him on his life, a time to remember the lessons he'd learned from Monty Hightower.

His train went first to St. Louis, then he transferred to the Southern Pacific line heading south to Dallas and San Antonio. As he passed through Dallas, he remembered Eli Hauptmann. He hadn't heard from him in a while. He wondered if he too had died. All part of the dream of the World Soul, he told himself and smiled.

Somewhere between Waco and San Antonio, Tom was drifting into a dream of his life at the Clear Light Colony, half-thinking about that first day they arrived for the Midsummer's Day tea-party and half-thinking of what kind of community he might manage to recreate in the hills north of San Antonio, and perhaps thinking also of his mother. As the train was starting over a shallow ravine, a support beam in the trestle snapped beneath it and the train slid off its track, carrying the cars crashing into one another into the sandy bed of the dry creek. It was very sudden. The last thing Tom remembered was sitting down at the table with Monty, Herb, and Alex in their wide-brimmed sunhats and frilly frock dresses. He marvelled to see that sitting with them, wearing an old-fashioned hoop skirt of emerald green silk was his mother Jenny.

206

49

 e were walking through the house, Elizabeth and I. "We can divide the bedrooms upstairs so we have more room for guests." I was animated explained my plan. "And we'll use the big room for lectures and conferences—and for singing and meditation," I added hesitantly.

Elizabeth didn't react. I figured I'd explain my ideas more at length later. I noticed that occasionally tears came to her eyes unexpectedly, I supposed when she was thinking of Marla. I must admit I too was tearing occasionally myself. It was partly for Marla and partly out of happiness. And partly out of missing Ben and Tom. After they completed their story, they thanked me for carrying on for them, wished me luck and then disappeared. Too bad. I had wanted to continue that conversation with them about plots and heroes.

I could still conjure up the fantasy of them making love. And, you know, I no longer felt cynical about love. Though I still felt a little bereft of the true love I'd never found and envious of those who had found it, I realized I no longer felt spiteful or bitter toward them. I think I really did wish that all young men—and young women too, of course—would find someone to love and to be loved by. I felt surprisingly calmer.

On the way from the airport, I broke my good news to Elizabeth and Doctor Steed, hoping they'd be as pleased with the plan as I. Apparently they were, because as soon as we arrived at the house, Robert called Hu Dorsey and told him he really liked the idea and suggested they go ahead and sign the papers as soon as possible.

"Hu doesn't like the house," I had explained. "He wants to tear it down. So I suggested to him that he could buy up all the land, except for the hundred acres or so around the house. I told him Elizabeth and I—" I purposely didn't mention Marla's name "—had been talking for years about running a guesthouse, maybe a sort of retreat center for other people who want to get away from the stresses of life in the big city. You know, these days a lot people are getting into spirituality, especially gay people. Maybe we can assist with that. And it would give us all something worthwhile to do. Right livelihood.

"Hu thought it was a good idea. He likes me, you know.

"There'll be enough money from the sale of the land to pay for any improvements we need to make. And the three of us can be the start of a little community out here. I bet pretty soon we'll have some more people living with us. And lots of paying guests coming to visit."

"Maybe we can have seminars on living healthy and overcoming stress," Elizabeth piped up, "and loss... "

"...and learning to love," I said. "It'll solve a lot of problems for all of us. Robert," I added respectfully, "you may have to become the wise old man of the place, you know."

A little to my surprise, he replied enthusiastically, "I'll grow a long gray beard."

I suppressed my curiosity about how he'd look in a straw sunhat.

50

u Dorsey came out that night. I happened to be out watering in the front garden, enjoying the light still glowing warmly in the western sky. I was admiring the Texas bluebonnets that had blossomed the night before in the meadow below the house, when Hu came driving up the road through that meadow. The wildflowers had transformed the rocky, scrubby field into a rolling blue sea of electric brilliance. Hu pulled up near where I was standing. He looked so pretty in the twilight. I felt a pang of affection for him. He hopped out of his sports car jauntily and came around. I reached out to shake his hand. Smiling, he opened his arms and took me in a warm hug. We held each other an extra long time. Finally he released the embrace, then gripped my shoulders lightly in his hands and looked me square in the eye. "I guess you'll be around for a while."

"Guess so," I said nonchalantly.

"Maybe we'll continue that lesson about courtship rituals," he said softly, then kissed me primly on the lips. The warmth of his touch felt good to me.

As we headed into the house, he stopped at the car and grabbed a paper sack and his briefcase. He'd brought a bottle of Mumm's Extra Dry and the contract, the new one that left Dr. Steed with the land around the house. Later I watched over his shoulder as he signed the contract and then passed it to Robert for his signature. Then I popped the cork and poured four glasses of champagne.

As we clinked our glasses together in a single toast, I commented to Hu, "I noticed your middle initial. An 'M'." My heart was beating nervously. "That doesn't stand for Milam by any chance, does it?"

"Then you know the Milam family originally built this place," he said.

"No, I didn't," I replied startled. I began to tremble so bad the champagne was sloshing out of my glass. I set it down on the table.

"How come you asked then?"

"Good guess, I suppose." I wasn't going to try to explain at that moment. "What *does* the 'M' stands for?"

"Millburn," he answered. "That was my mother's maiden name."

I sat down. My voice shaky, I asked one more question, "Did your grandfather work at a department store by any chance?"

"Oh, you've really been studying your Texas history," he said. "But that was my great-grandfather. He was a partner at Strinke & Millburn's. How did you know that?"

Feeling like I'd just crossed over into the Twilight Zone or something, I laughed. "Maybe I just picked it up from the walls of this old house."

I'm certainly not sure if I can claim that I brought about the resolution of this plot solely by my own efforts. But I had enough good sense and courage and enough of a meddling nature to turn the series of events in the direction I needed and wanted—or that Tom and Ben needed and wanted. As the hero of my own story, I managed to resolve the real problem I was facing. I mean that in saving the horse ranch and starting to recreate a contemporary version of the Clear Light Colony, I'd discovered a job for myself that might assist in the evolution of the World Soul.

I am still perplexed about what happened to me that springtime in Texas. But I know I learned that everybody's life is deeply rooted in Life as just what it is, Keats' "thing of beauty, a joy forever," an experiment by God at creating a universe, an opportunity to joyfully participate in the sorrows of the world. In making that discovery, I think for a brief moment two beautiful souls rose again, and Tom Milam and Ben Mayfield *and I* came home to a loving land. I found hope and my life grew green again and my boughs sprouted clean again.

I managed to get life in perspective.

The following words appear across the screen at the conclusion of the Audrey Hepburn/Mel Ferrer movie of *War and Peace* which I watched one night that spring:

> The most difficult thing—
> but an essential one—
> is to love life,
> to love it even while one suffers.
> Because life is all. Life is God.
> And to love life means to love God.
> Leo Tolstoy

And so Toby Johnson has finished his self-referential postmodern novel of innocence regained. In fact, however, this novel is not really self-referential, for Toby is hardly anything like Rick Carton. (Toby probably thinks of himself more as a younger Monty Hightower.)

Toby, whose full name is Edwin Clark Johnson, PhD, is a now partly-retired psychotherapist and longtime gay cultural activist. During the early 1970s, he worked at a conference center in Northern California and was a student and friend of the late Joseph Campbell. At the end of that decade, he collaborated on several writing and research projects with gay social commentator (and nicknamesake) Toby Marotta. Johnson is author of *The Myth of the Great Secret: A Search for Spiritual Meaning in the Face of Emptiness* (Morrow, '82), *In Search of God in the Sexual Underworld* (Morrow, '83), *Plague: A Novel About Healing* (Alyson, '87), and his bestselling *Secret Matter* (Lavender, 1990).

Toby and Kip Dollar, his lover since 1984, run Liberty Books, the quality lesbian and gay bookstore in Austin, TX. Toby is not suffering from AIDS or Creutzfeldt-Jakob's Syndrome, though like all human beings he faces possibly imminent and certainly eventual death. And so the lessons he decided to teach Rick Carton are lessons he wants to make sure he's learned himself.

The old Spanish mansion, by the way, really belongs to Toby's family. He and Kip have dreamed about making it over into a guesthouse/conference center, though there are strong reasons for preferring to locate such a project in the lush woods of the Pacific Northwest rather than the desiccated hills of Texas.

You'll all be welcome to visit.

The address of Liberty Books is
1014-B North Lamar Blvd.
Austin, TX 78703.

This book and its cover art were designed and composed by Tom Turbeville, a freelance graphic artist and Macintosh adept in Austin, TX. Tom, coincidentally, has property in western Massachusetts, not far from the home of the fictional Rick Carton. Tom thrives in the New England seasons. He dreams of developing *that* property into a guesthouse/conference center and art colony.

Secret Matter

When aliens arrived from space, Kevin Anderson had no idea the Visitors' real reason for coming to Earth would ever affect him. He was, after all, just a young architect fresh out of college working on the reconstruction of San Francisco after the Great 1996 Earthquake. But one bright summer afternoon at Land's End beach, Kevin met a Visitor. And his life was never the same again.

As Kevin uncovered layer after layer of the secrets of the Visitors' lives, the secret about his own life he'd been hiding even from himself became more obvious and more compelling. And he began to realize that his telling the truth about himself might help the Earth discover the truth about the Visitors—before it was too late.

Secret Matter is a delightful romantic comedy with an undercurrent of dramatic tension and suspense, the right touch of science fiction, and, as fans of Toby Johnson's will recognize, just the right measure of mystical wisdom to make this a novel you'll long remember—and feel a pang of fondness and pride for.

"Toby Johnson's fly blend of sweet romance, social commentary and entertaining science fiction gives new meaning to the concept of a 'genre' novel—the sort of easy-going read rarely found in gay fiction, and very welcome.

"Adding to the book's charm is its setting, a plausible post-quake San Francisco which seems, finally, in tune with nature."

Richard Labonte, A Different Light Bookstores

ISBN 0-938743-13-9 $10.00

Published by Lavender Press, *Secret Matter* is available in all lesbian and gay community bookstores.

P•L•A•G•U•E
A Novel About Healing

"Through a tightly constructed thriller framework, Toby Johnson has woven ideas of attitude and philosophy derived from such sources as Buddhist thought, holistic health, mythology, and Christian scripture. As incongruous as the various elements might sound, Johnson distills them into a cohesive whole.

"...While the melodramatic plot is absorbing, the growing closeness of the characters and the interrelation between their attitudes, feelings, and convictions—especially in making responsible decisions about life and death—are most compelling.

"...Without the cloying use of mysticism or conventional religion, Johnson demonstrates a curing philosophy of acceptance without defeat—an active serenity.

"...*Plague* is not alone in exploring spiritual resources in the face of AIDS, but it is certainly one of the most provocative and original works yet to do so."

Marvin Shaw, The Advocate

ISBN 1-55583-125-7 $7.95

Originally published by Alyson Publications, *Plague* is now available from Liberty Books, the lesbian and gay community bookstore in Austin, TX. Call 800 828 1279.

❏ **The Adventures of the Magnificent Kong and Brawny Mouse** by Lucina Kathmann. A humorous tale of a wonderful black woman and her courageous white lover who take an eventful journey to Mexico and change Acapulco and the reader for the happier. ISBN 0-938743-08-2 $8.95

❏ **The Cost of Love** by Alexis Rogers. A gay men's romance and adventure between two soldiers who meet in Vietnam and return to find themselves partners on the LA Police Force. A story as gritty as combat and as sweet as love itself. ISBN 0-938743-10-4 $8.95

❏ **The Holy Spirit Dance Club** by Joseph Puccia. Young Harold discovers a spiritual side of gay life he never dreamed existed in an exclusive New York disco. ISBN 0-938743-07-4 $9.95

❏ **I'm Looking for Mr. Right But I'll Settle for Mr. Right Away** by Gregory Flood. AIDS, True Love, the Perils of Safe Sex and other Spiritual Concerns of the Gay Male. A cult bestseller, just brought back into publication by Lavender Press. ISBN 0-938743-16-3 $8.95

❏ **The Rose-Bearer** by Lizabeth May. A lesbian romance in which opera star Suzette is pulled between her relationship and a determined temptress. ISBN 0-938743-05-8 $7.95

❏ **Secret Matter** by Toby Johnson. A romantic comedy in the science fiction idiom with an undercurrent of mystery and suspense, a delightful and unforgettable alien, and just the right measure of mystical wisdom to touch the heart. ISBN 0-938743-13-9 $10.00

❏ **Sweet Dark Places** by Lesléa Newman. A collection of lesbian poetry by a well-known writer, author of *A Letter to Harvey Milk* and *Secrets*. ISBN 0-938743-18-X $8.00

❏ **Things They Never Told You in Sunday School** by David Day. An immensely popular book written for gay Christians with relevant Bible texts examined in plain language. ISBN 0-938743-03-1 $7.95

❏ **We're Not Alone** by Rik Isensee. A coming out story by a psychologist who uses his expertise to produce a beautiful story of first love for both lesbians and gay men. ISBN 0-938743-09-0 $9.95

See previous page
for mail order information